GRACE

THE DIMARCO SERIES

JENNIFER HANKS

Hope you enjoy
this Crazy family!
♡ Hanks

GRACE
The Dimarco Series

Copyright © 2019 by Jennifer Hanks
ALL RIGHTS RESERVED

Published by Bravia Books, LLC
ISBN-13: 978-1-096072-29-4

Cover Art by CT Cover Design
Interior Formatting by Author E.M.S.

Published in the United States of America.

For my brother.
Thank you for always having a plan
and always making me your sidekick.

I will forever be your sidekick.

Acknowledgments

As always, I would like to thank my family, specifically my children who are incredibly supportive and patient when I'm facing deadlines and we're eating sandwiches for dinner…again. You are the reason I do all I do and the reason I can.

Thank you, Clarise at CT cover creations! This is our seventh cover together and it's always a pleasure to work with you. I continue to get compliments on every new cover and they're beautiful designs. We only have one more in this series, which I absolutely cannot believe! But there will be many more in the future, I'm sure.

Thank you, Judy Brown! You're support and friendship have meant the world to me, both during the editing process and all the times in between. You've become one of my biggest cheerleaders and I could never thank you enough!

Thank you, Jenny Simms for your proofreading services! We've only worked together twice now, but I feel we are really starting to find our groove and understand each other. Your professionalism is always top-notch and I value all of your advice!

Thank you, Amy, for another incredible job formatting my work! You've been an amazing friend to me as well as a support and I can never thank you enough!

Finally, I'd like to thank the readers! Without your unwavering support and enthusiasm, this family, this series, may never have gotten this far. We only have one more book in this series, but I promise we are far from done with the Dimarcos. They do have cousins, after all!

Chapter One

Grace

I hate police stations.

I hate everything about them; the sounds, the smells, and most definitely the feeling of hopelessness that lingers in the air. However, I promised my boss I would pick up his client who'd been taken in on an assault charge last night, and I'm a good employee, so here I am.

Looking around the sterile walls of the waiting room, I supposed, at one time, they were white but now bordered on gray with cold metal chairs pushed tight against the wall directly across from the front desk, one of which I was perched on. My eyes focused on the police officer manning the front desk chewing a piece of gum with a vengeance. And he wasn't just chewing it hard; he was chewing it loudly too, mouth open, making that sucking noise like too much saliva was trying to make its way out of his mouth. I wanted to suggest closing his mouth to alleviate the problem, but thought it might be wiser to just keep my mouth shut.

"Next." The bark from the gum chewer at the front desk made

me cringe. I was going to have to get close to that. I looked right, then left and assumed he meant me, seeing as I was the only one currently waiting. I hiked my purse onto my shoulder and walked to the desk.

"Hi." I smiled, meeting his eyes over the top of his black wire-framed glasses. He seemed unimpressed. Or mad. It was hard to tell, but from the lines around his mouth, indicating a permanent scowl, I assumed this was his expression most of the time. "I'm here to pick up Tyler Morgan."

His attention turned to his computer, and I watched him type a few things before he picked up the phone and made some type of call. Honestly, I had no idea what he was doing or who he was calling. I have two brothers who are cops, but I've personally never set foot in the station unless it was to meet one of them for lunch, and they always ushered me out quickly. Having seven older brothers, I was used to being bossed and pushed around, but over the years, I'd gotten very good at keeping to myself what I didn't want them to know.

My actual job, specifically.

"Have a seat," Officer Gummy muttered. "He'll be out."

Sighing, I went back to my seat and perched on the edge of the chair again. I am unapologetically a girly girl. I love all things girl, which I always thought was strange, having grown up with seven boys, but it's true. I'd tried at one time to be more of a tomboy just so some of my brothers would play with me, but it only took a few instances with bugs and a fall from a tree to figure out that it wasn't me. Mom absolutely loved my affinity for girl stuff, but my dad and brothers had no clue what to do with me, so they treated me like I was made of glass. That was okay sometimes, but there were times I wish they'd tried to understand me a little instead of tiptoeing around me. It's been better lately with most of my brothers having either girlfriends or wives and kids, but I still feel a little left out. They've always had an incredible bond with each other, all of them, and I'd just never fit into that.

2

As far as my job goes, I would never, ever tell them what I actually do. How could I tell my seven older brothers, all of whom are either in construction, law enforcement, or do some type of security work, and all stubborn alpha males, that I write romance novels inclined toward erotica? No way, never going to happen. Instead, I took law classes with the idea that maybe I'd like it and follow through, but I didn't. I hated it. Since I have some legal knowledge, though, I took this job when it came up as a way to pacify my family. I told them I was trying it out before I decided if I wanted to go on with law school. Yeah, I lied, but what choice did I really have?

I jolted out of the fog I'd been in thinking about my family when a shadow covered me. My eyes started at large feet in brown boots, up jeans-covered legs, and over thighs that had to be bigger than my waist. Each one of them. My eyes continued over a wide chest covered in a dark green T-shirt spanning a muscular frame and biceps. Ink swirled around his bicep, and for a moment, I imagined pushing his sleeve up farther so I could see the whole tattoo. I was already flushed by the time I made it to his face. And what a face it was. Strong jaw, covered in dark stubble, high cheekbones, and golden brown eyes the color of whiskey.

I stood slowly, watching his expression morph from one of annoyance to complete and utter disdain. I assumed that was for me. I realized his height was even greater after I stood. I've never considered myself short at five foot six, and I was used to giant men, with my brothers all topping out well over six foot, but this man might just make my brothers look small. I finally understood what people meant when they described someone as being built like a brick wall.

"Who are you?" His low, rough voice rippled over my skin.

I blinked a few times and then somehow got myself together enough to answer. "Hi." I stuck my hand out between us offering to shake his. "My name is Grace."

He stared at my hand, making no move to take it, his face hard with displeasure. I slowly dropped it back down. "Mr. Anderson sent me to pick you up."

"Why the fuck didn't he come himself?"

I smiled sweetly, trying to soften him up a little. It didn't work. "He had to be in court this morning."

"Are you an intern or something?" He narrowed his eyes.

"No, I'm not." I wasn't sure why my position was important to him.

He scoffed. "One of those legal errand boys he's got?"

I tilted my head. "You mean a paralegal?"

His eyebrows rose. "Is that what you are?"

I had no idea why we were having this conversation. I mean, if I had spent the night in jail, I'd just want to leave when my ride came, but this guy wanted my freaking resume. When he widened his stance, I knew we weren't leaving until he had my title, so I gave it to him.

"I'm Mr. Anderson's personal assistant."

He wrinkled his brow. "His what?"

"His personal assistant." I repeated.

"What the fuck is that?"

I sighed. "I take care of personal matters for him. Things he doesn't have time to do."

He narrowed his eyes. "So you're his errand girl."

"I'm not…" I stopped talking when he brushed by me, heading for the door. He pushed it open, and I was surprised when he stepped aside, gesturing me through in front of him.

"I'm parked right over there." I gestured toward the parking lot at the side of the building. He walked beside me, his long strides making me almost jog to keep up. And I was not a jogger. I hated jogging, running, any type of exercising actually. Honestly, I don't know if I'd run if someone was chasing me. I'd probably just taser their ass.

And yes, I do have a Taser courtesy of my older brothers.

I stopped beside my car and clicked the locks as he stood beside me.

"What the hell is that?" He pointed at my car.

"Umm…it's my car," I said, uncertain as to why he looked so put out. I love my car. I'd bought it myself, another thing my family didn't know about or I'd have to tell them how I had the money to pay for it, which would lead to talking about my writing, so again, just no. My parents bought me a car when I left for college from my cousin, Cole, who's a mechanic, and I'd kept it, but now that I bought my new baby, the only time I drive it is when I go home for a visit. "It's a VW bug." I beamed proudly, running my hand over the shiny yellow roof.

He put his hands on his hips and looked toward the ground. "I know what kind of car it is," he said through gritted teeth before raising his head to look down at me again. "There's no fucking way I'm going to fit in that car."

I scanned my eyes over his body, starting at his toes and working my way up and then looked at my car. I pursed my lips. He might be right. "What if we put the seat back the whole way?"

"You could put the back seat down so I was lying half in the trunk, and I still wouldn't fit." He scowled. "This shit is what I'm paying that fucker for."

I was getting mad. It didn't happen often, but it did happen, and when it did, I usually held on to it for a while. "It's not my fault or Mr. Anderson's that you're a giant."

He leaned down, one hand resting on my car, the other on his hip, his shirt straining against the muscles bulging in his biceps. I'd never liked the muscular type, having always preferred a man with more subtle looks since I'd started dating. I had always been surrounded by men who were physically fit and muscular and seemed to just sway toward the other side a bit. Lanky was probably the word I'd use.

"Anderson knows how tall I am because he's represented me in court before. Does he know what you drive?"

I chewed my lip, feeling embarrassed because Mr. Anderson does know what I drive, and he sometimes flakes out and forgets little things like how this giant was going to fit in my car.

"How tall are you?" I asked.

His face told me he was not impressed that I chose to answer his question with a question and not even an important one. "I'm six foot six. Is there a reason you needed that number?"

I shook my head. "Nope, just curious. I have seven brothers, and they're all over six foot, but they seem so much smaller to me now that I'm standing beside you."

He rolled his eyes up to the sky. "Good for you. Can you focus for one minute so I can figure out how the hell I'm getting home, out of these clothes, and into a shower?" His eyes met mine again. "Then I'm going to have a drink or twenty so I can forget about this conversation."

I furrowed my brow. "Do you really think that's a good idea? I mean, I saw your file, and you seem to get yourself into a lot of trouble when you drink. Plus, it's only"—I looked at my watch—"ten in the morning."

He looked incredulous, and for the first time since I started this conversation, I thought it might be best if I just shut my mouth and get him home. "Anyway…" I smiled, trying to appear cheery when truthfully, he could suck the joy out of a freaking carnival. "Why don't we try to see if we can make you fit?"

I walked around to the passenger side, opened the door, and bent down so I could get the seat pushed back the whole way. I stood, taking a step back, and stumbled right into his hard chest. And it was hard, like a rock, and huge. He was just so big everywhere. My writer's mind started to wonder if that meant he was big, well, down there too. I felt a blush work its way up my neck, so I moved away from him and gestured to the front seat. He growled but then lowered himself into the car and sat, his knees pretty close to his chin and his head rubbing the roof.

I made my voice sound perky. "See, you fit." I slammed the door and walked around the back so he wouldn't see me giggling. He looked ridiculous.

Chapter Two

Tyler

I didn't fucking fit. But in all fairness, I didn't fit in most cars. SUVs and trucks worked for the most part, but at six foot six, anything was a tight squeeze. I wasn't just tall either, I was big and broad. Interestingly, the qualities that made me feel like an outsider and freak most of my life were the same qualities that made me a good football player. No, not good, fucking great. I was the best damn center in the NFL before a hit ended it all for me.

Now I'm sitting in a yellow car with probably the most gorgeous woman I've ever laid eyes on, and I'm being a dick. She should be on billboards selling shit, considering every red-blooded male would buy anything she wanted to sell them. Her long dark brown hair is pulled up in one of those styles that girls do, and all I can think is I'd love to see it down. Preferably while she's naked since I know if what's under her clothes actually looks half as good as it seems, I'd probably never let her get dressed again.

"Where to?" Her happy voice filled the car.

I gave her my address, but then went back to staring out the window. I didn't bother trying to make conversation because I was shit at it and always had been. If it hadn't been for football, I would've been the kid always alone who never dated or even socialized. I was completely socially awkward. The good thing about high school and college is when you play football, it doesn't matter if you can talk to women. They'll fuck you just because you play the game. I don't play the game anymore, so my real world is closing in, which includes being alone with whiskey, my only friend. I've kept in touch with a few of the friends I'd made in college and the pros, but I've mostly avoided them. I don't have a thing to talk about if I don't play ball anymore. I didn't apply myself in college, so I didn't have a backup plan. I was going to play football until I retired. I was told that from the time I could hold a ball by my father, who played in the NFL, until one too many concussions forced his retirement.

"So…" I cringed when I heard her smooth voice. She was really going to try to make conversation. It was my worst fucking nightmare. "Why were you charged with assault?"

I frowned. Of all the things she could ask, she wants to talk about my assault charges? I stared out the windshield, knowing if I looked right at her, I wouldn't be able to talk to her, not sitting this closely anyway. Not to mention, I've learned if I'm rude to people, they stop trying to talk to me. "I hit someone."

"You really did it?" she asked, her voice higher than it had been.

"Yep." And I had. Most guys leave me alone because of my size, but there's always one who has to prove himself to the group of guys he's with or a girl he's trying to impress, and taking me down is a good way to do that. It never happens, and usually someone calls the cops and I get taken in for assault since I'm the only one left standing. I force myself to go out because I know if I don't, I could easily become a hermit. Besides, sometimes it's nice to just be in a room with people and not completely alone, even if I rarely speak to anyone while I'm out.

"So, what do you do, Mr. Morgan?" I guess she had no plans to give up on this conversation as easily as I'd hoped.

"Nothing," I admitted. And it wasn't a lie. Since my injury, I hadn't done anything. At first, I convinced myself my neck needed to heal, but it's been well over a year, and I still hadn't done anything.

That seemed to throw her off her game a little.

"Oh…" she muttered. "So what do you do for fun?"

I shook my head, still staring straight ahead of me. "Nothing."

I heard her GPS say the name of the lane I lived on and breathed a sigh of relief. I couldn't wait to get out of this damn car and away from this woman whose perfume alone was making me hard. She pulled up to the front of my house and threw her car in park.

"Wow," she exclaimed. Rolling her window down, she leaned her head out and looked at my house. "Your place is beautiful."

I grunted, but that was all I had left in me. I needed to get away from her because my only move when I felt nervous around someone was to be mean. I'd learned a long time ago that if you're mean, they'd just leave you alone. I really didn't want to be mean to her because she seemed nice, but I needed her to go.

I threw open my door and lifted myself out, groaning inwardly at the pain caused by a short ride in that small ass car. I'd planned to try to thank her for the ride at least, but when I heard her door slam, my temper rose.

"Do you have horses?" She pointed at the barn situated in the back corner, diagonal from the house.

"Yep." I stuffed my hands into my front pockets.

She came around to stand beside me at the front of her ridiculous car.

"I love horses," she said, her face full of excitement. "My dad used to take me riding when I was little, but then my idiot brothers wanted to come, and it kind of ended." She rolled her eyes. "They were too rowdy to be around the horses. Actually, they were jackasses a lot of the time."

The words sounded harsh, but she was smiling, and I could tell she was really close to them. I tried not to stare at her, but her short skirt and high heels muddled my brain. Not to mention her shirt, which looked like silk, was cut a little low. Not enough to see anything, but enough to make me want to see what was under it.

She must've gotten used to me already because she didn't seem to expect an answer. She just kept talking.

"Can I see your horses?"

See them? No fucking way, my mind screamed. "No."

Her eyebrows lifted almost to her hairline when her eyes widened. "No?"

I shook my head, staring past her at the wide front porch on my two-story house, wishing I could be inside right now to end the torment of her.

Grace.

Jesus, even her name is beautiful.

"Okay." She sounded disappointed, and for the first time in a long time, I wished I was capable of inviting her in, but that was impossible. That would mean spending more time with her, and I couldn't do that.

She put her hand out. "It was nice to meet you."

Don't shake her hand. Don't shake her hand, echoed through my mind, but I couldn't stop myself. The way she looked, the way she smelled, I knew I'd never be close to another woman who was like her, so I reached my hand out and wrapped it around her much smaller one. I shouldn't have fucking done it. I felt my cock harden to the point of pain and pulled away quickly, heading toward the house. I didn't even look back when she yelled goodbye, knowing if she noticed the bulge in my jeans, I'd have no fucking clue what to say.

I was such a fucking coward.

Chapter Three

Grace

"No, I swear. Charlie, if you were to look up the definition of dick in the urban dictionary, Tyler Morgan's picture would be there."

"I just can't believe he was that bad." My best friend from middle school and all through high school and college was so much like me we could've been sisters. We were and still are perpetual optimists, always seeing the best in everyone, but I replayed my conversation with Tyler over a hundred times, and I still couldn't see the good.

I plopped down on the couch in my small apartment, hugging a throw pillow against my stomach, and stretching my legs out lengthwise. "Trust me, he was."

"You know he played in the NFL, right?"

I thought back to my conversation with Mr. Anderson when he asked me to pick Tyler up, but nothing was coming to me. "I don't think I knew that. He seems young, though, so why doesn't he still play?" I shifted and pulled my legs up under me, finding a comfortable spot. "Was he kicked out for fighting?"

Charlie laughed. "Umm, no, that doesn't really happen. I think he played for Seattle maybe. I can't remember. Anyway, he got hurt. I do remember that." Charlie's a sports enthusiast to the point of blowing most men away with her knowledge of stats and games and players. And even though hockey was her favorite, she likes all sports and seems to know everyone who plays.

"Really?" I huffed. "He didn't seem hurt." I heard typing in the background and knew without a doubt she was looking him up because it would bother her if she couldn't remember. I knew that all too well having roomed with her all through college and having watched her on far too many occasions lie awake trying to remember something she'd forgotten.

"Here he is," she announced. "Tyler Morgan played four years in the NFL after a very successful college career." I listened as she paraphrased the article she was reading. "He was a center whose career ended early when his neck was broken during a play-off game." I heard her snap her fingers. "That's how I know him. It was almost two years ago, and they played it on repeat for months. It was an awful hit, Grace."

"Wow. Is that even possible? I mean, breaking your neck and still walking?"

"I don't know much about his particular injury, but that's what this article says." She hummed while she continued to read. "It also says he was forced into retirement, and he had been working toward playing again, but the doctor wouldn't release him."

I frowned. "Well, I feel bad now. Maybe he's still feeling a little lost."

"You know, I've met a few retired players, and some of them did seem lost without the game. It's kind of sad. Like they don't know what to do if they're not playing," she agreed.

"I asked him what he does, even just for fun, and he said nothing."

I heard her typing on her laptop again. "Wow, I just saw his picture. He's enormous."

"Yeah, I know. Imagine him in my car."

She laughed. "Oh my god, I can't." I waited for her to stop laughing but my mood lightened just listening to her. "Holy crap, he's six foot six and two-hundred-and-eighty pounds. Geez, you must have felt like a shrimp next to him."

"I actually did." I never felt like a shrimp by my brothers, not to mention I wasn't exactly small, but would describe myself as curvy. That was just an easy way to say I have big boobs and a big ass that no amount of exercise would change, so I stopped doing it. I hated it anyway.

"He's hot too."

"Yeah, that kind of gets overshadowed by his mood," I answered dryly.

"It says here he's never been linked to any one woman, always kept to himself, and turns down interviews." She paused. "Maybe he's shy."

I snorted. "I don't think he's shy. He was arrested for assault."

"I meant with women," she corrected.

"Oh," I laid down on the couch still holding the pillow against me. "I guess he could be. I don't know, Charlie. He just seemed moody."

"Well, just think, you'll probably never have to deal with him again. I know you don't like his type anyway. You know, the good-looking, muscular guys," she teased.

I rolled my eyes. "Ha-ha." I wrapped a piece of hair around my finger. "All right, change of subject. What are we doing tonight?"

We spent the few minutes making plans to go out. We're both still single, and we both like it that way. Charlie's a physical therapist who works long hours, and I'm always busy running errands for Mr. Anderson or writing, neither of which allow me great socializing opportunities, so we've decided that once a week we'd go out.

"You want to go over to Hanks; see if they have a band tonight?"

Hank's was the bar my brothers hang out in all the time, and my brother Cam's friend owned, so I knew why she wanted to go there.

"He won't be there. They've been working nonstop. Jake says they have more work than they can keep up with." Because of our ages, I'd always been the closest to my brothers Jake and Ben, spending a ton of time together growing up, but since Ben graduated from college and joined Jake in running our father's construction company, I hadn't seen them as much as I'd like to. When I'd first left for college, I couldn't wait to be on my own without my older brothers breathing down my neck and watching my every move, but now that I'd graduated, I was starting to miss them more, miss my family more. I'd even been thinking about moving closer to New Hope where I grew up and where my entire family still lived. I only lived an hour away now, but lately, that'd felt too far.

"I'm not going there to see Ben," Charlie snapped, but I'd known her long enough to know she was only snappy when she was embarrassed. "Besides, even if I was, he's not interested in me like that. He's pretty much said that out loud."

I frowned, thinking about my brother and his lack of love life. "Honestly, he hasn't been interested in anyone since Jackie, and that was in high school. I'm starting to really worry about him."

"I don't think there will ever be anyone special in his life if he can't let go of her, Grace. Last I heard, she had a baby. A boy, I think. As much as I've hoped over the years that your brother would notice me, I don't think I'm strong enough to be the woman who comes after Jackie. She was the one for him, you know?"

"He thought that," I disagreed, "but she wasn't. No one would do what she did to the person they loved, to their one person."

Ben had dated Jackie for more years than I could count, so many, in fact, that we all assumed they would get married someday. But when they were seniors in high school, she cheated on him, and it was over. Just like that. It seemed inconceivable to me at the time that a person could be in your life for so many years, could mean so much, and then one day, do something so despicable and so unforgiveable. I knew Ben could never forgive her for what she did.

I also knew he never really got over it.

"People do it every day, Grace," she said quietly. "They hurt each other, they lie, they cheat, and sometimes they do it while still professing their love, which was exactly what she did."

"I know you're right, but I just don't understand why people hurt each other that way."

"Grace, I think maybe you've lived in your books too long. I don't believe the men you think exist really exist. We read about them because it's not real in our own lives. The truth is, I kind of think the whole idea of love is made up. Maybe at one time it meant something, but now, I think it's just a word we casually throw around to get what we want."

I took a deep breath before releasing it slowly. "I don't want to live in a world where that's true."

"I'm sorry, sweetie, but I think you already do."

I knew a lot of Charlie's bitterness came from watching her parents' awful divorce when we were still in high school. She'd been the same dreamy-eyed teen I was then, loving the idea of love and reading all the romance books we could get our hands on. I didn't have one boy ask me out in school, not one romance until college because of my brothers warning them all away, so neither did Charlie since all the boys in our town knew my brothers were looking out for her too. Everyone knew my brothers were close and protective in our small hometown, so no one dared come near their baby sister or their baby sister's best friend. The boys smothering me was the reason I went away to college. I wanted to find my romance, to experience what most girls already had, to have what I'd been reading about since I was a teenager.

But hearing Charlie's words, that she didn't believe in love anymore, didn't believe it was out there, didn't believe it was lasting, made me question everything I'd always believed.

Made me question the stories I'd written, the stories I'd been so proud of, and allowed a little doubt to creep in. If what she said was true, then I'd been writing stories about things I believed in, things I'd always believed in, like love, and maybe it was all a lie.

Or just a fantasy.

Chapter Four

Tyler

Walking toward the waiting room just off the doors of the emergency department, I heard my name and cringed. I'd know that voice anywhere.

"Tyler?"

I watched her walking my way, her hips slowly swaying back and forth, and my stomach clenched. Her dark brown hair, so dark it's almost black, flowed down her back, and her blue eyes aimed straight at me.

She came to stand right in front of me. "What happened to your arm?"

"Broke my hand," I muttered, my eyes scanning a group of men who had lined themselves behind her to form a human wall. They all looked very similar, so I assumed they must be the family she'd mentioned during our one and only encounter. One that has played over and over again in my mind, torturing me, not allowing me to forget her no matter how hard I tried.

The men behind her were all fairly big, their expressions holding a combination of curiosity and derision while they appraised me. A smart man would have been intimidated.

I wasn't.

"How?" She threw her hands on her hips, angling her head to the side. "Were you fighting again?"

She sighed when I didn't answer, obviously frustrated with my silence. I wish I could explain that it's not her—I'm like this with everyone—but even that seemed too hard. Silent is what I am, I don't know how to be more than I am.

She shook her head and came to stand beside me. Her scent surrounded me, and her arm brushed against mine, causing goose bumps to run its length.

Her sweet voice broke the silence. "Guys, this is Tyler. Tyler, these are my brothers." She pointed at each one of her brothers and named them. "That's Ben, Cam, Jax, Chris, Brody, and Jake."

I nodded at them, but had no words. I never did.

I felt her eyes on me but stood stock-still, facing the row of large men in front of me. She was actually scarier to me than the line of men. Hell, that's all I knew from my time playing ball. A line of pissed-off men. That I could handle.

"Unfortunately, we're here because my other brother Luke was shot and is in surgery," she said, sadly.

I reacted unconsciously by turning my head to look at her. She looked and sounded so sad that my hands itched to grab her and pull her into my arms to comfort her, but I wasn't capable of that.

"I'm sorry to hear that. Hope he's okay," I said, hoping the sincerity was clear in my voice.

She breathed deeply and exhaled, her eyes never leaving mine. "I hope so, too."

"Aren't you Tyler Morgan?"

Caught in her stare, I startled when I heard my name and quickly averted my eyes. Watching a man walking my way, I knew immediately he recognized me. He put his hand out, which I knew I couldn't ignore, so I accepted his handshake. "Nice to meet you man. Name's Kyle." He introduced himself. "You're one hell of a center."

I muttered thanks, but he only continued. "It blows you got hurt. Would've loved to watch you play a few more years."

"You played for Seattle?" a man who rivaled my size, and was standing just off to the side of Kyle, spoke up.

I had no words, so I nodded.

"Saw that hit, man. You're fucking lucky to be alive." He threw out his hand, which I begrudgingly took, and he introduced himself. "Striker."

"Morgan?" One of Grace's brothers spoke up, but I had no clue which one he was. There were a lot to remember, and I'd been too distracted by how close Grace was standing to pay much attention. "Wait, are you the player who broke his neck?"

"I remember that," another said.

"Me too." Yet another brother spoke, and I started to appreciate it because if they were talking, I didn't have to. I only needed to stand and nod. "That had to be almost two years ago, right?"

"Yep."

"Wait." Grace turned her body again to face me. "You did actually break your neck? I mean I'd heard that but didn't believe something like that was even possible."

I looked down into her crystal-clear blue eyes and tried to think of something to say, anything so I wouldn't look like the ass I knew I seemed to be, but I had nothing.

"How the fuck do you heal from something like that?" Striker asked.

I forced my eyes from hers before I was totally lost in them. "Slowly."

"I'll bet." A brother shook his head. "Unbelievable, you lived through that and are still walking."

I looked back down at Grace and knew I'd had enough. I couldn't think of anything to say, and the more they all talked, the more questions they would have. "I have to go."

I glanced at the large group all staring at me, and muttered, "See ya." Wasting no time, I headed for the exit. I breathed a sigh of relief when I walked through the doors out to my SUV. Thankfully, the cast wasn't going to prohibit me from driving. There was no way I was climbing back into her car.

I slid into my vehicle, appreciating the soft leather seats and amount of space a vehicle like this allowed me. I rested my head against the headrest and sighed, happy to be hidden from the world. I'd had the windows tinted in my vehicle to feel isolated, at least to maintain the façade that I was happier alone.

I might not have been happier, but I was definitely better off.

Chapter Five

Grace

I frowned while watching Tyler walk away, wondering what I'd done to make him dislike me so much. It had only been a few weeks since I'd been responsible for taking him home. I never expected to see him in the hospital with a broken wrist.

"Something we said?" I turned to face the group of men still at my back and let my eyes slide to Kyle, the IT guy with Elite Securities, Jax and Brody's security company.

I sighed. "No, he's just really moody. Plus, I'm almost positive he doesn't like me at all."

Jax scowled, and said, "Impossible," at the very same time Ben said, "I could see that."

That earned Ben a chuckle from the group, but a punch to the arm from me. I wasn't surprised he said what he had because I could tell he was trying to lighten the mood a little. Plus, that was just how Ben, Jake, and I had always been with one another. When I'd gotten the call a few hours ago from my mom, I was a mess. Losing my brother Luke would be like losing a part of myself, and I knew my brothers felt the same.

"How do you know him?" I shifted my gaze from Ben, who was still grinning, toward Jake, who'd spoken, and my heart broke for my brother. Jake was taking the shooting on as entirely his fault. I understood why, considering the story my mom had told me on the phone about Jake's ex being there with a guy who was mouthing off. None of my brothers were good at walking away from a confrontation, but Jake was no doubt the worst one. I'd never known him to walk away from a fight, but I also knew he would if he had any indication that this would be the outcome.

I took a deep breath, bracing for the boys' reaction to what I was about to admit. "He's a client of Mr. Anderson's. I had to pick him up at the police station last week."

"Why the hell are you picking people up at the police station?" Brody asked, and I wasn't one bit surprised. I knew if they found out this was part of my duties sometimes, they'd all have something to say about it.

I rolled my eyes, hoping to downplay it. "It's something I do when Mr. Anderson's in court. I don't have to very often."

"What was he in for?" Jake asked.

"Assault." I said it dismissively, trying again to defuse the situation.

"Who the fuck did he assault?" Jax demanded.

"The better question would be is the other bastard still breathing?" Brody asked sarcastically.

I shrugged. "Of course, he is."

"Grace…" Jake started, but then his head jerked to look over my right shoulder, and his face turned ashen. I spun around and knew why when I saw my parents' expressions. The doctor had come out not too long before Tyler showed up to tell us Luke had pulled through surgery, but it was still touch and go and would be for a while. They'd been the first allowed to go back and see him.

I stepped forward. "How is he?"

Mom put her arm around my shoulders and waited for Dad to address the room. "He's okay. Has a long road ahead of him, but you all know Luke, and you know he'll pull through."

There were murmurs of agreement because that was true. Luke was strong, and I knew he wouldn't leave us if he was given the choice.

"Grace." I looked over my shoulder when I heard Charlie's voice and immediately moved from my mom toward her. She hugged me tightly, and when she pulled back, I saw tears in her eyes. "God, I'm so sorry. I was with patients and didn't have my phone. I just got your message and came right over. How is he?"

"The doctor came out a little while ago and said he's pulled through surgery, so now we just have to wait."

"What happened? Was he on duty?" she asked, but I shook my head. Luke's a detective with the police department, so it would make sense to assume he'd been on duty when he was shot. I was just about to tell her what I knew when her eyes shifted to something over my shoulder.

My head turned just as Ben stepped up beside me and started speaking. "It wasn't anyone's fault except that bitch Julie." He turned his head and frowned when he saw Jake sitting back in a chair, his head down, palms to his forehead, just as he'd been when I first arrived. His attention moved back to us, and he looked tormented. "Jake's blaming himself, but he didn't do anything wrong. He tried to walk away, but the prick Julie was with started saying shit about Braydon."

I closed my eyes briefly and breathed deeply. Jake wasn't going to back off if someone was talking about Bray. I knew that; we all knew that because none of us would either if it were our own child. Braydon was Jake's whole life and had been since he was born almost two years ago.

I opened my eyes again when I heard Charlie's voice. "How did Luke get shot?"

Ben rubbed his hand across the back of his neck. "I have no fucking clue. It all happened so fast. One minute, Jake and the prick were yelling at each other, and the next, a truck came out of fucking nowhere, and someone was shooting. Luke tried to protect

23

Jake and took the bullet." Ben let his concerned gaze once again find Jake. "He's not handling it well."

I laid my head on Ben's shoulder and grabbed Charlie's hand in mine. "We'll help Jake get through this."

Charlie smiled sadly. Ben moved to sit next to Jake, leaning in close, their heads together, talking in hushed tones. Some time later, Charlie and I found seats and sat down to wait.

And we waited.

It was a long night, waiting to see if he pulled through, and when he did, we all exhaled the breath I didn't think any one of us knew we'd been holding. I walked out that morning with Charlie to say good-bye at her car and agreed to call her with updates before I made my way to my car. Getting in, I pulled out my cell phone and called Mr. Anderson, explaining what had happened and that I would be in today but might need to leave if I got called back to the hospital. He agreed and told me to take my time coming in, which I appreciated.

I started the drive back into the city, not sure why I took the turns I did until I found myself moving slowly along the road in front of Tyler's house. I wondered for a moment if he was okay. My brother had an entire waiting room full of people for him, but Tyler had walked out of the hospital alone. And for some reason, the idea of him being hurt and alone had nagged at me through the night.

I continued to drive past, putting his beautiful farmhouse farther and farther behind me, knowing I would have no reason to see Tyler Morgan again.

And I didn't.

Until a year later when something happened that changed everything.

Chapter Six

Tyler

One Year Later

Leaning against the sterile white wall of the corridor in the hospital, I watched a doctor walk down the long hallway toward me, and my stomach dropped. I hadn't been able to take a deep breath since the call a few hours ago that my father and his wife were in a car accident. They'd gotten married years ago, and I'd only actually seen her a handful of times, one being when she, my father, and their two kids visited me after the game that ended my career. It wasn't that she wasn't a nice woman, but I didn't want a relationship with her.

She'd replaced my mom.

Dad met and married Tara after my mom fiercely battled cancer and lost. It was the same year I was offered a full scholarship to play ball in college. My mom and I were close, considering it was usually only the two of us while I was growing up. Dad was in the NFL and that was his whole life, even during the off-season. He was good to us, faithful to my mom as far as I knew, but we weren't close. Only when I played ball and succeeded did I feel any connection to him at all. He didn't even wait a year after Mom's death before he married Tara. He'd stood beside me at my mother's funeral and told me he didn't know how to be alone. He was social and loved being surrounded by people. I knew then that he wouldn't be alone long, but I didn't think he'd remarry as quickly as he did. He married Tara and bought a new house, one without memories of my mom everywhere he looked. And then he sold the only home I'd ever known, the only place I could still feel her when I visited.

So I stopped visiting.

Besides football, my dad and I never had much in common. I'd always been more like my mom. Preferring to take a back seat, I favored anonymity and the solitude it brought. She was the only person I felt comfortable being myself around. Being huge and socially awkward were an awful combination. I was the center of attention more often than not because of my stature. I was happy when it became apparent that I was good at football because it gave me a place to automatically fit in without doing much to earn it. I developed a reputation for being moody and quiet, but my skills on the field shone, so people just accepted that I was a bastard and left me alone for the most part. My reputation followed me throughout high school, college, and straight into the NFL.

My dad never understood why I didn't love the attention my football talents afforded me, as he had basked in the glory of the spotlight. I hated the spotlight, and over the years after Mom's death, I became more and more distant from my father.

Until I needed him. Until I had nowhere else to turn after my injury.

I'll never forget my father standing on one side of the hospital bed with the doctor on the other telling me he was sending me to a rehabilitation hospital, and it was likely I'd have full mobility again, but I'd never again play the sport I loved, the sport that gave me a place to fit, a place to belong.

It was in this same fucking hospital that I heard the words I felt ended my life. And here I was again, only this time standing on the other side, feeling the trepidation my dad must've felt standing beside my bed that awful day.

Anxiety I'd been feeling since I answered the phone not all that long ago heightened when a shadow crossed my feet. Lifting my head, I met the eyes of the doctor now standing in front of me, and I inhaled deeply, preparing to hear his words. After all, he was about to tell me if I'd lost the only other living parent I had.

"Mr. Morgan?" he asked.

I nodded but remained quiet. Standing in his white coat, his posture stiff, he should have seemed severe, but instead, his quiet demeanor was comforting.

He held out his hand to shake, and I accepted. "I'm Dr. Ryan." I nodded again, and it seemed enough encouragement for him to continue. "I'm sorry, Mr. Morgan. Your father's injuries were very extensive. We did everything we could, but unfortunately, the damage was too severe."

I blinked slowly. He was gone. My only family, all I had left in this world, had been ripped away. "And Tara?"

He shook his head. "Mrs. Morgan was killed at the site of the accident when she was ejected from the car." He put his hand on my forearm. "I understand they were in a sports car and hit by a rather large truck." He glanced at the papers in his hand. "An eighteen-wheeler, I believe I read." His eyes focused on mine again. "I'm very sorry for your loss."

I was still digesting the information when something occurred to me. "What about the kids?"

Dr. Ryan glanced at the papers in his hands. "I'm not aware of any children," he said. "They aren't mentioned as being involved in the accident."

I was relieved for that, at least. I really didn't know them at all, having only seen them a few times. Tara was a lot younger than my father when they married and wanted kids of her own, so they had them. Two of them. A boy and a girl. Fuck, I couldn't even remember their names. What the hell kind of person can't remember the names of his half-siblings? In my defense, they were young, and I hadn't been around for a lot of years. The past years I had been around, well, I had no excuse for that.

I thanked the doctor again before leaving and heading home where I crawled into bed and let the pain of loss surround me.

♡

"Hello?" My voice was husky with the sleep I was shaking off after being awakened by the ringing phone.

"Tyler Morgan?" A loud voice came across the line.

I took a deep breath, running my palm across my forehead and hoisted myself up, throwing my legs over the side of the bed. "Yeah?"

"Mr. Morgan, my name is Jeffrey Owens. I am, or rather was, your father's attorney."

I rubbed my eyes with the heel of my hand, trying to clear my mind after a shit night of sleep. "Okay."

"I've been informed that your father passed away last night. I'd like to offer my condolences and also say I was a close friend of your father's. He was a wonderful man and friend."

"Thanks," I grumbled.

"With that being said, there are some components of his will we need to discuss because of their rather urgent requirements."

"English, man," I spat, annoyed I was awake. But more so that I woke up and my father being dead hadn't been the nightmare I'd hoped it was.

I heard a light chuckle. "You sound just like your father, Mr. Morgan. Always quick to get to the point with no extra conversation."

"It's Tyler," I said, rubbing my chest where the ache settled at hearing Mr. Morgan. I'd only ever been Tyler my whole life to most people. Mr. Morgan only reminded me of my father. "Mr. Morgan is dead."

"Of course, Tyler." His voice was gentle and filled with sympathy. I stretched my legs out in front of me, my knees cracking and popping just as they have since high school. The years of players weighing well over two hundred pounds slamming into me had taken a toll on my body, but this morning, I reveled in the pain. At least, I felt something other than misery.

"So what did you need?" I asked gruffly.

"There are a few matters of the will that we need to sit down and discuss."

"I'll come to your office Monday. Just text me the address." I stood slowly, letting my body adjust to the new position before I made my way out of the room and down the stairs to the kitchen.

"This needs to be discussed today, Tyler. I've already spoken to Tara's family and they're waiting to hear from you concerning certain aspects of the will and the funeral arrangements," he said adamantly.

"Today? Why the fuck would you want to work on Saturday?" Heading straight to the Keurig, I dumped a coffee pod in and pushed start, already anticipating the first sip.

He chuckled again. "It's not a matter of wanting to but of necessity. Especially in this situation."

"Can't you just tell me now?" I asked.

"Your father was adamant if the time came that I needed to review this section of the will with you, I do it face to face, and out of respect for our friendship, I plan to keep my word."

I sighed as I obviously wasn't getting out of this. "Okay. Do you need my address?"

"No, I have your address. I'll be there within the next thirty minutes if that works for you."

It wasn't really a question, and it wasn't like I had anything else to do, so I grunted. "Yeah, sure."

"Would you like to have your attorney present?"

I took a huge gulp of the too hot coffee before answering. "Why?"

"I think it would be good to have someone there while we review some things. It's important for questions that you may not think of or consider at the time of discussion."

I rolled my eyes. Couldn't he just say it'd be good to have one there?

"Sure, whatever."

"I'll make those arrangements for you. I know Jason well."

I shrugged even though I was the only one who knew I had. "Sure."

"I'll see you soon, Tyler," he said. "Thank you for your time."

"Yeah, okay," I said, before pressing the end button. This was the last fucking thing I wanted to do this morning, but it didn't seem I had much choice.

Cup in hand, I made my way back up the stairs to the bathroom, my mind replaying thoughts of my father, the time since my mother died, and my anger at him for moving on and forgetting her. I took a few more sips of coffee before I set the cup down and made my way to the large shower I had put in right after I moved here. There was nothing I hated more than trying to squeeze my large frame into a standard shower, and I had the money to do something about it, so I did. That was one of the only things I changed about this house, though, and it showed. I knew it needed updating, new paint, new flooring, but I could never find it in myself to care. It was only me living here, and I didn't give a fuck what it looked like. I had no one to impress because I was alone.

And that wasn't going to change.

Turning on the shower, I stepped under the hot spray, then leaned my palms flat against the cold tile wall, and let the steamy water pour down over my head and back. I groaned when my muscles relaxed under the heated spray, flexing my back muscles that were arguably bigger now than when I'd played ball. I was determined after my injury to get healthy enough to return to the game I love, so I worked out, almost obsessively, but to no avail. The doctors wouldn't release me, and no teams wanted the medical risk I'd become. I lost my dream, my life, everything that mattered, but I hadn't lost my obsessive need to work out.

And last night, in a cruel twist of fate, I lost the only family I had left in this world. Pounding my fist against the hard, unforgiving tiles, I finally let the sadness overwhelm me and sank to the floor of the shower, lost in grief and acceptance of the loneliness washing over me.

Chapter Seven

Grace

"Why do you need me to come along again, Mr. Anderson?" I asked, pulling the seat belt across my shoulder and clicking it into place. I'd gotten a call from my boss not twenty minutes ago asking me to go with him to Tyler Morgan's home because of some pressing legal matter.

He pulled out of the parking lot attached to the new apartment building I'd moved into only six months ago and began the fifteen-minute drive from my apartment to Tyler's house. I'd finally accepted that I wanted to be closer to my family, especially after Luke was shot, and I found this apartment that cut down the one-hour drive I used to have to my parents' house to only thirty minutes. It was the best I could find to make the commute to work still doable for me and still be closer, so I felt like it was a good compromise. For now, anyway.

"His attorney is a friend of mine and requested my being there, but after talking about the situation, we decided he might need a"—he paused and rubbed his chin—"softer touch."

"Softer touch," I mumbled, before raising my voice to be heard by my boss. "What does that mean? What is the situation?"

"His father died last night in a car accident, and he lost his mother to cancer several years ago. The news his attorney plans to share with him may be overwhelming to him, but it can't wait, so I thought, well honestly, Grace, you're very good with people. Clients love you, and you've met Tyler, so I thought you might be more comforting than I would be."

Well. That felt nice. He wasn't a man to hand out compliments, so receiving one was quite an ego boost. Then I remembered who I might need to comfort and cringed. Our last encounter hadn't gone well, and I certainly didn't get any indication that he liked me very much. "I hope I can help, but honestly, I don't think Tyler likes me very much."

Mr. Anderson waved his hand dismissively at me. "Don't think that way, Grace. Tyler can be difficult and moody, but he's a good man, as was his father. I'm sure he likes you just fine."

I decided to keep any other thoughts to myself, but I wasn't an idiot. I knew when someone didn't like me, and all signs pointed that way with Tyler. He wasn't just moody and quiet; he was dismissive and a little mean. He couldn't wait to get away from me, and that much was obvious, so I had a bad feeling that Mr. Anderson's ideas of me being a comfort to Tyler weren't very accurate.

We drove in companionable silence until I recognized the area just outside New Hope, and my stomach rolled. It did somersaults when we pulled into Tyler's driveway and parked behind a very expensive looking Mercedes.

"Looks like Jeffrey's here already," Mr. Anderson announced.

I scrunched up my nose. "Jeffrey?"

"Mr. Morgan's attorney," he clarified.

"He goes by Jeffrey?" I asked, incredulous.

He turned his head in my direction after putting his equally expensive car into park and shut off the ignition. "That's his name, Grace."

I smiled softly before getting out of the car and following him to the front door. He went by his full name and not something shortened like Jeff? I hadn't known a lot of people who'd gone by their full name when it could be shortened, and the one's I had always seemed a little, well, uptight. But I refused to judge before meeting him. People were constantly surprising me, anyway.

I followed my boss through the front door of the beautiful two-story home I'd admired when I dropped Tyler off all those months ago. I peeked around Mr. Anderson's back, excited to see what the inside must look like since the outside was so amazing, and I frowned. It was sparse, at best. The door opened into a large living room, but I'd never seen so few pieces of furniture. A big recliner sat in the middle of the room facing a very large television hanging on the wall, and that was it.

That. Was. It.

I looked all around as if I was missing the furniture. Maybe it was elsewhere in the huge space, but I didn't see anything because it just wasn't there. How could that be? Where did his company sit? I had literally no space in my apartment and three times this amount of furniture. Still in awe, I didn't notice someone else had joined us until I heard my name.

"Grace," Mr. Anderson said and moved to the side until I was facing another man who was obviously an attorney. Even if I hadn't met Tyler, I'd know this was Jeffrey. I tried to hold in the giggle threatening to erupt. "This is Jeffrey Owens."

I smiled and stuck my hand out. When I felt Jeffrey's hand wrap around mine, I immediately wanted to ask what moisturizer he used since his skin felt softer than mine. He pulled my hand to his mouth and kissed the back of it, and I resisted the urge to wrinkle my nose, a bad habit of mine when something annoyed me.

"Grace," he said quietly. "A beautiful name for a very beautiful woman."

"Thank you," I said, pulling my hand free. I have to admit he wasn't a bad looking man. If I wasn't so turned off by the hand kiss, I might have enjoyed that compliment and the look of interest sparking in his eyes. I didn't mind the age difference even though, if I had to guess, I'd say it was pretty significant. He did have the lanky build I was usually attracted to, but I wasn't sure I could ever call him Jeffrey. It was just too formal, too stiff, and I was neither of those things.

At all.

He gave me one last long look before turning to speak with Mr. Anderson, and I took the moment to peek over his shoulder to see what was in the next room. Disappointed that I couldn't tell much other than it was a kitchen, I sighed, which earned me a wink from Jeffrey. A wink. Why was that sexy from some men and a turn-off from others?

My eyes flicked over the two men I was standing beside. Noticing the dress slacks and pressed polo shirts, I realized only the colors were different. Otherwise, it was as if they were wearing a uniform. It was Saturday morning. Who wore that on a Saturday morning? I looked down at my own clothes and cringed a little. I guess I could've tried a little harder to look professional, but in my defense, I was only given twenty minutes to get dressed. My jeans and sleeveless blouse were okay, but more like something I'd wear to lunch with a girlfriend than a business meeting.

I was ushered into the kitchen in the next moment where I sat on one of the four large wooden stools lining the long island counter. Looking around, I appreciated the light marble countertops and dark cabinets. It was stylish and simple, and judging from the living room, there was no way Tyler decorated the kitchen. If I had to guess, I would say it was exactly like this when he moved in, and he hadn't bothered to change anything.

Feeling heat against my arm, I glanced to see Jeffrey was standing close to my side, close enough that I could smell the spicy scent of his cologne. It was actually nice, and for a moment, I thought maybe I could forget my initial impression of him was a turn-off for me, but then Tyler walked into the room, and Jeffrey no longer existed.

Tyler's dark hair was still wet from a recent shower and haphazardly combed through. I scanned down his body from his wide chest covered in a simple black T-shirt to his jeans hanging low on his hips, dangerously low, in a way the woman in me appreciated. His feet were bare, which was unbelievably sexy on him, and for a moment, I wondered why I always gravitated toward lean, lanky men in trendy clothes and shoes when someone this virile wearing nothing special was making me feel warm.

It was obvious he hadn't seen me yet because as soon as he did, his eyes narrowed, and he whipped his head toward Mr. Anderson. I wish I knew what I'd done or said to cause this dislike he had for me. I'd never had anyone immediately dislike me like he did.

"What the hell is she doing here?" He was looking at Mr. Anderson but pointing at me.

Mr. Anderson looked back and forth between the two of us with his brow furrowed. I knew I would have to explain this to him on the way home, but I honestly had no idea what I would say.

"We're here as your representation and as your friend." He finally spoke up.

He glared at Mr. Anderson, ignoring me completely before shifting his gaze back to his own attorney. "What's this all about?"

"You may want to sit down, Tyler," Jeffrey directed.

Tyler shook his head. "I'm fine. Now tell me why you're all here, and why we're doing this shit on a Saturday morning."

Jeffrey still stood beside me so I turned my head to see his profile. He was either stalling or choosing his words carefully. Something told me it was the latter.

Jeffrey sighed. "There's no good way to say this, Tyler, so I'm just going to tell you your father's wishes bluntly."

Tyler nodded, but I saw his Adam's apple bob when he swallowed hard, the only indication this was anything more than annoying to him.

Jeffrey cleared his throat. "Your father came to me a few years ago with Tara, and they created a will in case they were both to die simultaneously. It's a rare thing, but in regard to money and children especially, it is encouraged because, well obviously we just never know what could happen."

My attention stayed solely on Tyler while he watched Jeffrey talk, and I saw the pain flicker through his eyes at the mention of his father. God, this had to be so hard for him.

"They decided then that, in the event of something happening to both of them, they wanted the children and their inheritances to be placed in your custody."

My eyes widened on their own before quickly flicking over to Mr. Anderson who stood stock-still, as we all did, waiting for Tyler's reaction.

Tyler gulped before his rough voice cracked the silence. "What?"

"You're now the legal guardian of your brother and sister, Tyler," Jeffrey said quietly.

Tyler put his palms flat against the counter, leaning deeply into it before pushing back and pacing the length of the island across from us.

"I can't be anyone's fucking guardian," he mumbled before snapping his head up and facing Jeffrey. He leaned into the counter again, but this time to get closer to where Jeffrey was standing. "What about Tara's family? Why aren't they taking them?"

Jeffrey sighed. "I understand you don't know Tara's family very well, but your father and Tara felt they wouldn't be an appropriate choice."

"And I would?" He shot back up to his full height, which was menacing mixed with his irate mood. "I don't know anything about kids. Fuck, I don't even know those two kids."

I felt my hackles rise. Why didn't he know his brother and sister? Was he not given the opportunity to know them?

He crossed his arms over his chest and shook his head. "I can't do it. I can't raise those two kids. What are my other options?"

Jeffrey inhaled deeply before he spoke. "Your father and Tara were very adamant that they live with you, and they were confident you would agree. They have no other options listed."

Tyler set his shoulders, the muscles in his large biceps flexing tightly against the stretched fabric of his shirt, and I recognized the stubborn stance immediately, having watched my own brothers do the same thing at different times in their lives.

Tyler flicked his eyes to Mr. Anderson. "How the hell do I get out of this?"

Mr. Anderson spoke, his expression full of sympathy. "Tyler, son…"

"I'm not your fucking son," Tyler growled. Yes, growled. "Tell me how to get out of this."

I felt my face heat with anger, and I knew I was going to say something to piss someone off, but how could he stand there and basically say he didn't want his brother and sister.

"Tyler," Jeffrey's voice interrupted my thoughts. "Tara's mother is an alcoholic. Tara has two sisters, one who's following in her mother's footsteps and another that seems bright and on a good path, but is only seventeen. You can't tell me you think that environment is better for them than living with you."

Tyler's voice was menacing when he answered. "I am not raising those two kids."

I pushed back from the counter when I saw Jeffrey shake his head in defeat and stood. I walked quickly around the counter and stood right in front of Tyler, his eyes trying to look anywhere but at me. I poked him in the chest. "What the hell's wrong with you?"

He uncrossed his arms and took a step back, but I followed, not one to be ignored. "Are you really that giant of an asshole to let some alcoholic and her kids raise your brother and sister? How can you be so insensitive? Can you even imagine what they're feeling right now? How confused they must be?" I got closer, so close I could feel the heat from his body. "How old are they?"

He shook his head, his eyes blinking slowly before finding mine.

"I don't know," he said softly. "I don't even remember their names."

If he'd been stubborn, or an ass, or yelled back at me holding firm to his decision, I might not have backed off, but the look on his face, so sad and forlorn, killed my anger faster than anything else could have.

I put my hand on his forearm, and his eyes snapped down, staring at my hand.

"Ask him," I said, softly. His eyes skimmed up my arm and over my chest until they were once again on mine. "They're your family, Tyler. They need you."

He didn't have to ask. Jeffrey jumped right in with the information, probably recognizing the moment as his chance to make this go his way. He reached into a folder lying on the counter and pulled two pictures out, placing them face up. "Your father gave me new pictures to put in this folder every year so they were always up to date." I glanced down to see two small faces smiling back at me. Jeffrey pointed at a picture of a little boy who could be Tyler's son, the similarities in their appearance being that similar. "This is Seth. He's seven years old and just started the second grade."

He shifted his finger to a picture of a little girl. She was quite possibly the cutest little girl I'd ever seen, and I have beautiful nieces. But this little girl—with her big smile, her left front tooth missing, her sparkling eyes, so full of life—was adorable. Her long brown hair in two French braids framed her face, and you could just see innocence and trust all over her. Tears filled my eyes, imagining the pain they must be feeling right now. If they even knew they'd lost both of their parents. "This is Sophie. She's five years old and just started kindergarten."

I looked over my shoulder at Tyler who stood close to my back, his eyes staring intently at the pictures, his face pale. Any anger I'd initially felt disappeared. I slid over and stepped back to stand beside him, placing my hand back on his forearm. He flinched, and

I sighed, feeling dejected that he didn't want my hand on his arm, so respecting his space, I began to pull my hand away. He laid his other hand over mine, effectively pinning it to his arm so I leaned in closer, hopefully conveying the support I felt he needed.

I looked up. My head only came to his shoulder, and I felt petite next to him, but at that moment, I recognized my small gesture was essentially holding him up.

Chapter Eight

Tyler

Seth and Sophie. Jesus, they were young. I pulled my hand away from Grace's soft skin and rubbed my forehead. I couldn't believe she was standing so close. Part of me wanted her to move away, but a bigger part of me, the part I was listening to, needed her close. Her hand on my arm felt like it was holding me together while I accepted the fact that I was now the sole guardian of my brother and sister.

I took a deep breath and lifted my gaze to my father's attorney. "What do I need to do?"

He shook his head, his brow furrowed. "I'm not sure what you're asking."

"I'll be their guardian," I said, my pulse racing with every word spoken until I felt Grace squeeze my arm, and I took a deep breath. I wasn't alone. I had been alone for a long time, since my mom died, but right now, at this moment, I wasn't alone. I wanted to savor it knowing that before long, she would walk out the front door and out of my life. I would not say anything to stop her. I would need her to go, but right now, I needed her so I could breathe.

Watching my father's attorney, Jeffrey, it was hard for me to believe he was a friend of my father's. He was younger than my father, but more than that, he seemed stiff and conservative and my father was anything but. He was outgoing and full of personality, so different than the man in front of me, but maybe my father had settled in the past few years. I hadn't seen him much, especially this past year, and that was my doing. He'd tried, constantly calling and stopping by, but my anger and bitterness made it impossible to be around me. I couldn't face the man who made a career out of his dream having the same dream for his son who ultimately failed him.

Hell, I failed myself.

"We'll have paperwork to complete, but we can do all of that after the funeral."

"Where are the kids now?" I asked, realizing I hadn't thought of that before.

"They're with the babysitter they usually stayed with when your father and Tara went out. I spoke with her, and she agreed to keep the kids until I had their permanent situation settled. She's a very nice woman who retired a few years ago from teaching and decided she missed kids, so she babysits occasionally."

I nodded, but he wasn't done. "There is something I foresee being a potential issue in the future."

"What's that?" I held back the groan when I felt Grace wrap her arm around my forearm, settling herself against my side.

Jeffrey's eyes narrowed, but he quickly made his expression passive and continued. "Your father left his three children equal parts of his monetary assets, but Seth's and Sophie's are in the hands of their guardian until they are twenty-one."

"Meaning?"

"Meaning that whoever has guardianship of the children also has control over their money and can potentially spend it. The will states that the money can also be accessed for any situation where there is a need, and it benefits the children." He pursed his lips.

"I'm concerned that Tara's mother may fight for guardianship for the sole purpose of the inheritance."

I felt my shoulders tense. "Can she do that?"

He huffed out a frustrated breath. "She can. And from what I know of her, I believe she just might do that. We have a solid will prepared by your father and Tara, but these things can be held up in the courts for months, sometimes years. I just want you to be prepared."

I lifted my arms to run my palms against the top of my head, realizing too late that moving my arm also moved Grace's, dislodging her hold on me. I felt the loss of her warmth immediately but knew it was for the best. I would've had to do it eventually.

"Tyler." My eyes snapped back to my attorney when he called my name. "For what it's worth, you've made the right decision, and you have two attorneys fighting in your corner. I have no doubt those kids belong with you. Your father had no doubt they belong with you. You'll need to remember that while we navigate this road."

Meaning I was in for a hell of a fight, and he knew me well. I either fought hard or retreated. There was no middle ground with me. Those times he was called to bail me out of jail, infrequent as they were, I'd fought and I'd done so without regret. The times when it mattered the most, though, I'd retreated. I should've spent the past year with my father instead of holed up in this house, pissed at the world for my loss and envious of anyone living their dream when mine had been stripped from me.

And now I'd never get that chance.

"I can go pick them up now and bring them to you if you're ready," Jeffrey said.

I nodded, knowing putting it off was selfish. "Do they know?"

"Yes," he said. "I spoke with them, along with Sarah, their babysitter. I wasn't sure how long it would take to settle all of this, and they needed to know because they'd been asking for their parents. I went to them before coming to see you this morning."

"How were they?" Grace asked, and I twisted my head to study her. She was so different than the women I'd known during my career, most of whom loved the fame of being tied to a professional football player. I knew without really knowing Grace that it wouldn't matter to her. Fame, fortune, all would be irrelevant to someone like her. My confidence with women was tied directly to the success in my career. Just another thing I'd lost.

Jeffrey's eyes softened when they looked at Grace, and I stiffened. Were they together? Was that why he seemed pissed when she leaned into me? And why the fuck did that piss me off?

"Confused, I'd say. That's why I'd like to get them here and settled as quickly as we can." He looked directly at me. "I have the name and number of a social worker for you who has dealt with these situations and has therapy options she'll discuss with you as well as programs that will help the kids grieve."

All this felt overwhelming, and I was relieved that Jeffrey had not only thought of that but also had a plan in place for the things I wouldn't have even considered.

"I'll go get them now and bring them to you."

I nodded and looked at my own attorney for direction. He smiled approvingly. "Would you like Grace and me to stay?"

I shook my head. "You don't have to."

"I'm staying," Grace announced, and I saw Anderson smirk before walking to the French doors in my kitchen to look out at the view.

"You don't need to." My voice was gruff.

She stepped in front of me, right in front of me, forcing me to look at her, and lowered her voice. "I know you don't really like me. I'm not sure why or what I did, but that doesn't matter. You need a friend right now, and whether we ever see each other again after I leave, today, I'm your friend. And a friend, a real friend would never leave someone when they're facing one of the biggest and most difficult moments of their life." She leaned in closer. Her sweet smell surrounded me, and for a moment, I imagined grabbing her and pulling her close. But then I remembered who I was and who I'd become and forced my thoughts back into the reality of the situation. "So I'm staying whether you want me to or not."

The sheer determination in her voice was only trumped by the look in her eyes. I had no words, so I nodded, earning me a grin before she backed away and wandered over to stand by Anderson. I excused myself and went to the barn under the guise of putting the horses out, but honestly, I needed a few minutes to myself. I took that time while I worked to think. I didn't have a job, but I didn't need one as I'd had the good sense to invest wisely while I played professionally. Not to mention, I wasn't a partier or ever felt the need to buy fancy cars or houses, knowing those things would only bring me more attention, and that was what I'd always shied away from. The most money I'd spent was on this place. I loved it the minute I saw it and paid the full asking price, knowing I wanted it. I felt at peace here.

I wasn't in the barn long before I heard car doors slam. I stood from where I'd been leaning in the doorway and moved slowly toward the back of my house, pausing for a moment to take a deep breath before walking through the door and pulling it shut behind me. Arriving back in the kitchen, I met Grace's eyes momentarily before following Anderson into my living room and coming face to face with my fate.

Two little figures stood just inside the entryway, looking around with wide eyes. Sophie's eyes darted to me as soon as she saw me enter the room, and I wouldn't have thought it possible, but they widened more. She left her brother's side and walked to me, her eyes never leaving my face.

The first words she spoke had the ability to break me. "You look like my daddy."

My eyes scanned over her long dark hair pulled back into a ponytail and her dark eyes realizing my family's genes must be strong considering both of these kids looked like me and my father. Having no words for her, I nodded.

"But you're bigger." She threw her arms up in the air and spread them wide. "Like a giant."

She was right. I was bigger than my father. He'd topped out around six feet, but I'd hit six feet in tenth grade and didn't stop growing until my first year in college.

I cleared my throat. "I am." Those were all the words I had at that moment. I hadn't seen this little girl, Sophie, I reminded myself, for a few years. I had no idea what to say to her.

"I'm Sophie. I'm five." She introduced herself and then pointed her finger back toward her brother who still stood quietly in the entryway. "And that's my brother Seth. He's seven." She said all this with pride clear in her voice. I had no idea why age was so important, but for some reason, I found myself grinning at her while she spoke.

I opened my mouth to speak, but she continued, undeterred by my silence. It struck me then that she was used to it when I glanced at Seth still standing back.

"He says"—she pointed at Jeffrey—"that you're our brother too. And that we're gonna live here with you now 'cuz we can't be with Mommy and Daddy anymore until we get to heaven."

I swallowed hard, her directness getting to me in a way I hadn't expected. Words failed me at that moment. I was still struggling with the loss, so my emotions were so raw, and this little tornado just blew into my life and forced me to face it all immediately.

I felt an arm brush against mine and looked over to see Grace kneeling in front of Sophie. Sophie's attention shifted to Grace when she spoke. "Hi, Sophie. My name is Grace."

Sophie's little head tilted to the side. "Are you my sister?"

"No, I'm a friend of your brother Tyler." Grace gestured back toward me.

"Your hair's pretty," Sophie said, and my eyes shifted from Grace back to Sophie.

"Thank you, Sophie. Your hair's pretty too."

Sophie's hand reached out and touched the end of Grace's long dark hair. "Can you make mine do that?"

Grace slanted her head to the side in confusion. "Do you mean make it wavy?" She nodded, and Grace smiled. "I can absolutely do that."

Grace glanced over Sophie's shoulder before giving her attention back to Sophie. "Do you think your brother would come over and talk to us?"

Sophie shrugged before announcing, "He's shy. But he's super funny."

Grace laughed softly. "I'll bet he is."

"Seth!" Sophie yelled as if he wasn't standing only a few feet from her and waved him over. "Seth, come meet Grace."

Seth walked cautiously toward us, his eyes never leaving his sister's until he reached our little circle, and Grace spoke quietly, causing his eyes to flick over to her. "Hi, Seth."

He smiled shyly and waved. I recognized the awkwardness he was feeling because I'd been in the situation where I'd felt that level of awkward more times than I could count.

Grace reached up and wrapped her hand around mine, tugging until I realized she wanted me to squat down beside her. I cringed when I heard my knees make the popping and cracking sounds that I was so accustomed to.

Sophie's eyes widened. "That's how Daddy sounds when he plays with us."

I felt a smile tug at my lips, knowing that was how most athletes sounded when they were older and their bodies had been well used.

"This is Tyler." Grace introduced me to my brother and sister standing in front of me, and the guilt that I had to be introduced to my own family overwhelmed me. I almost stood back up until I felt Grace's hand squeeze my own.

Chapter Nine

Grace

This might be the most awkward, frustrating, and heartbreaking interaction I'd ever been a part of. But at the same time, the most beautiful. Watching this little family come together was something I would've never imagined could be so powerful.

Watching from the corner of my eye, I saw Tyler grin at Sophie and sighed. I think I was already halfway in love with this little girl. She was going to be a force when she grew up. I silently fist-bumped all of womankind.

"Hi, Sophie." Tyler grinned and swung his head to the shy little boy standing just behind his sister's shoulder. "Hi, Seth."

"Is this your house?" Sophie asked.

I watched Tyler slowly turn his gaze from Seth who was staring at his feet, and I saw something lingering in his eyes. At that moment, I wished I knew him better to understand what that was. Something told me it was important.

He nodded at Sophie, and she stared at him expectantly. I elbowed Tyler in his ribs, causing him to grunt. "Use words." I whispered.

The glare I felt coming from him only made me smile. I refused to look at him until I felt him elbow me back, but nowhere near as hard. I was so surprised; my head snapped his way, and I would've sworn I saw mischief dancing in his expression. We held that stare until the tinkling sound of a little girl's giggle caused us both to look in Sophie's direction.

"You guys are funny." She giggled. She stepped back and elbowed Seth in the side, giggling even harder when he shot his little elbow into her side, a grin playing around his lips.

I laughed before turning my gaze back to Tyler. "You still didn't answer her."

He looked confused for a second until realization crossed his face. "Yes, this is my house."

Sophie's eyebrows lifted. "Where do we sleep?"

Concern flashed through his eyes, and I realized what he didn't have to say. He didn't have anything for them—beds, dressers, nothing. His eyes snapped up to Jeffrey before he stood and I followed suit.

Jeffrey, intuitively knowing what Tyler was thinking, spoke up. "All their things are still in your father's home. He left the home and most of its contents to you. Some are to be given to Tara's family, but everything belonging to the children is yours." He paused. "I think we'll save the discussions about the house and the other contents for another time. But you're free to pick up the kids' things as soon as you want to." He reached into his pocket and pulled out a keychain. "He left these for you. The house and garage key are on that."

Tyler reached out and took the keys, his fingers rubbing over the hard metal.

"Can we go get our stuff?" Sophie asked.

Tyler seemed to snap out of the fog he was in and looked back down at Sophie. "Uh…yeah. I just need to rent a truck or something."

I put my hand on Tyler's arm. I'd swear he clenched his jaw and groaned, but it was so fast that I knew I had to be mistaken so I moved on. I was sure we had to be past all the awkward moments we'd had before.

"I have a great idea," I announced. "I happen to know seven really strong guys, all with trucks and SUVs." I snapped my fingers. "Actually, I know more than that. We could have their stuff moved here in no time."

Watching Tyler's expression, I knew he was going to tell me no, but I decided I wasn't accepting that. He needed help, and I was helping. I lifted my finger and poked him in the chest. "Don't even think about saying no. You're getting our help."

"I don't need help," he grumbled.

"Oh yeah, who is going to help you carry the beds and mattresses?" I asked sarcastically. "Sophie?"

Sophie giggled. "I can't carry my bed." Her eyes got big and round. "It's a bed like princesses sleep in."

I knew what that meant, and from the frown on Tyler's face, he did too. It was huge and had to have a canopy of some kind.

I was going to win.

Tyler groaned, his head falling back, his eyes pointed at the ceiling.

I smiled triumphantly. "I'll call my family." I glanced around, looking for my purse. "I think I left my purse in the kitchen. My phone's in it. I'll be right back."

I was digging through the monstrosity I called a purse when I felt heat behind me.

"Grace, you do not need to call your family," Tyler muttered behind me.

"I don't mind." I kept digging. I knew I brought it. I really needed to clean this purse out. I said that all the time but never did it.

"They don't need to help me. They don't even know me."

I shrugged, shoving my hand down into the corner. "So. They've met you, and besides, even if they hadn't, they'd still do it."

I felt my phone and pulled it out, holding it up triumphantly. "Ah-ha! I found it."

"Why would they still do it?"

I put my purse back on the counter and turned to face Tyler. "Because I'm asking them to."

He furrowed his brow. "Does anyone ever tell you no?"

I stopped, thinking about that for a minute. They must've at one time, but I couldn't think of those times right now. "I'm not sure. I don't really ask for much."

He nodded but looked thoughtful, so I waited.

"Your brother who was shot…" My eyes widened in surprise when he continued, "He's okay now?"

"Yeah." I was shocked he remembered that, and even more shocked he thought to ask about it. "He actually healed well. He's back to work and he recently got engaged. My brother Jake did too." I smiled, remembering the best parts of the past year. "It's been a crazy year for my family."

He nodded again, but I knew he was done with the conversation, so I looked down at my phone and pulled up my contact list, trying to decide which brother to call who would make all the others help. I squealed silently when I thought of one better and pushed the number to dial my dad.

"Why are you doing this for me?" Tyler asked, his voice low.

I tilted my head in confusion, wondering if he was serious, but from the look on his face, I knew he was. "Because I'm your friend."

"Why?"

Determined to make him smile, I grinned. "I think it's your sparkling personality."

The grin I'd hoped for played around his lips just as my dad picked up the phone. "Hey, Dad." I paused and waited for him to yell out his hello to me in the booming voice I only knew my dad to have before I jumped right in. "I need your help with something."

He never hesitated, his voice making me miss home. "Whatever you need, baby girl."

I beamed. I could always count on my dad.

Chapter Ten

Tyler

"We're back," Grace sang out as she, Sophie, and Seth walked into the kitchen.

After she'd called her dad, he promised there would be trucks at my house in the next half hour and both attorneys had said their good-byes, Grace decided the kids needed to see the horses. I declined when she asked me to go with her, needing a few minutes to myself. She seemed to understand because, for once, she didn't push me to do what I was trying to avoid.

"Who wants a drink?" she called out while I watched Sophie climb up to sit on the one stool in front of the island.

"I do." Sophie's answer rang out clearly, but I'd only heard one voice. I looked around and saw Seth still hanging back by the door watching the room.

My eyes flashed to Grace who flicked her wrist in his direction, gesturing for me to go to Seth. I looked hesitantly at Seth and then back at Grace, who widened her eyes in a way that even I understood she was losing patience with me.

I lowered my head, putting my hands on my hips before taking a deep breath and making my way over to stand in front of Seth.

He didn't budge, his eyes stayed locked on the floor in front of him, and I knew instantly what he was feeling. He didn't fit. There wasn't a place for him, and he stood out because he thought he was odd. Suddenly, I was angry. Angry that I had to watch my little brother feel that way when it wasn't true, when he had Sophie, Grace, and me standing right in front of him.

I squatted down, my knees protesting when I was finally positioned. "Hey, kid."

He didn't answer, but his eyes cut up to look at me before moving back to his hands.

"Seth," I said and waited until his eyes finally made their way to mine, which seemed to take a long fucking time. "Did you see the horses?"

I saw his lips twitch and his eyes sparkle when he nodded his head quickly.

"Do you like horses?" I asked the question I already knew the answer to.

His gaze danced around the kitchen until it landed on his sister, who was chatting with Grace. I could hear her giggling behind me.

"Which one was your favorite?"

His eyes shot back to mine, and I held my breath, hoping he'd say something, anything. I knew I looked hard sometimes, mean even, but it was a shield I'd put up years ago and just part of who I was now. So I lowered it, smiled a small smile, and hoped he'd trust me if I didn't seem scary. I almost fell over when his small voice rang out.

"The brown one with the white feet."

I should've guessed that mare was his favorite. "She's my favorite too."

He grinned, and my heart thumped in my chest. It was like looking in a fucking mirror with this kid. I searched my mind for something else to ask him when it suddenly came to me. "Do you play any sports?"

"Baseball," he said quietly.

I'd never played baseball, but I watch it. I was football all the way from the first time I held the ball. "Do you like it?"

He shrugged, and I waited, knowing patience would probably pay off. "It's okay."

"What do you like?"

He glanced at his sister again, and I waited, watching him. My patience paid off again because his eyes came back to me and he leaned in close to whisper. "Football."

Why was he whispering it like it was a secret or something to be ashamed of? I couldn't ask him that, knowing he'd clam up, so I asked the obvious, at least the obvious to me. "Why don't you play football then?"

"Daddy says I'm not allowed cuz you got hurt so bad. He said you scared him."

I felt my body stiffen. My father loved football, so that didn't sound like him at all, but maybe over the past few years he'd become a different kind of father. I wouldn't know, since I'd spent my time feeling sorry for myself rather than helping myself or accepting my new family.

The doorbell rang, and my head jerked at the sound, interrupting my thoughts. I reached out instinctively and patted Seth's shoulder before I stood, turning around to see Grace already headed for the door with Sophie in her arms. I moved forward when she got to the door, coming up close behind her.

"Dad!" she yelled and moved into his arms, Sophie giggling when she was trapped in the hug.

I stepped back and moved to the side when eight men followed Grace's dad into the house, most either giving her a hug or teasingly shoving her around, making Sophie giggle even harder. She closed the door behind her and stepped back to stand beside me.

"Okay, everyone, this is Tyler. Some of you already met him at the hospital." She turned her attention to me. "I'll go through the line again in case you've forgotten their names."

I appreciated that because I didn't have a clue what any of their names were. She had been standing so close to me in the hospital that day, I couldn't see anything beyond her.

"Okay, that's Ben, Jake, Chris, Jax, Brody, Cam, and Luke, who you haven't met." She paused before continuing, looking at another man, but one who didn't look anything like her brothers. "I'm sorry, I don't know you."

Ben stepped forward. "Oh shit, that's right. You probably don't. Grace, this is our engineer, Chase."

Her hand shot out to shake his hand, smiling. His eyes were focused solely on Grace, and I felt my blood pressure rising. "Nice to meet you."

"You too, Grace."

She studied him a moment longer before turning back to me. "Oh, and my dad, Jack, of course. I think he was visiting Luke when we ran into you at the hospital."

I reached out, shaking all eight hands one after another until I was facing her dad. I put my hand out first. "Sir."

His eyes searched between mine while he shook my hand, but then moved from mine back to Grace when he dropped it.

"Who's this gorgeous girl?" His voice was loud, echoing through the near empty room.

Sophie pushed her thumb back into her chest. "I'm Sophie. I'm five."

"Are you going to help us move the furniture?" her brother Jake asked, his expression serious.

"No." She giggled. "I'm not big enough."

"Just ignore them." Grace pretended she was whispering but was, in fact, staring at the line of men in front of her. "Boys are weird."

Sophie giggled harder, and then her eyes shot past me toward the edge of the living room. "I have a brother too," she announced and pointed, encouraging the line of men to look where she was pointing. I could almost feel Seth shrink back into himself. "His name's Seth, and he's seven," she said excitedly.

"I'll bet he's awesome," Ben said.

Her eyes widened. "He is, and he's super funny."

It was obvious from their expressions that she was charming an entire group of grown ass men, and I completely understood because she'd already charmed me.

"You know Sophie," Jake said, a smug look on his face. "Grace has a pretty awesome brother too."

Sophie's attention went to Grace. "You do?"

Grace smiled. "I do." Then she leaned in close, pretending again to whisper to Sophie, and pointed at Jake. "But it's not that one."

That statement caused a lot of laughter and shoving between her brothers, Jake and Ben, both saying they were the one. I moved away, walking toward Seth only to feel someone step up beside me.

Chase glanced my way. "Thought it would be cool to introduce myself. That okay with you?"

I nodded, confused as to why he'd want to say hi to a seven-year-old kid, but maybe he needed a break from the Dimarcos. I knew I did.

I stopped walking to stand in front of Seth and frowned. His head was downturned, his fingers twisted together. I cleared my throat. "Seth."

His head shot up, his eyes on mine, but he didn't speak so I did, gesturing to the man beside me. "This is Chase."

He flicked his eyes toward Chase, a small polite smile on his face.

"Hey Seth, it's nice to meet you," Chase said, his voice quiet.

"Hi." His small voice wavered.

Chase squatted down, making himself eye-level with Seth. "I think you have the right idea to stay over here." Seth tilted his head in confusion. Chase gestured behind him at the Dimarco family who, from the sounds of things, were all talking at the same time. "They're kind of crazy."

Seth smiled shyly, bringing a grin to both Chase's face and my own.

"Grace is nice," he said, his voice soft.

"She's just covering up the crazy." He tapped his fist across Seth's shoulder jokingly, causing him to giggle.

"Hey fuc…"

"Jake!" Grace scolded, well aware what word he was about to yell.

"Shit, right. Hey Chase, what are you telling him about us?"

Chase made a funny face and leaned in conspiratorially. "See what I mean? Crazy."

Seth giggled harder, and I chuckled. He was right. They were crazy but in a good way. He stood, facing off with Jake. "Nothing, man."

Jake didn't look convinced, but he shrugged and joined the planning for moving the furniture. Sophie came running over and grabbed Seth's hand to drag him along behind her, and I was glad he had her. I would've loved that, someone to have by my side growing up, having my back, a built-in friend.

"My little sister is painfully shy," Chase shared, and my attention was immediately back on him. "I hate that for her." He gestured toward Seth. "It's funny, when you know someone who's that shy, it's fairly easy to see it in others."

He was right. I knew the minute I saw Seth standing by my front door that he was the same as me. I'd always assumed I'd gotten that from my mom, but it seemed maybe shyness ran on my dad's side of the family. "I'm not real social myself."

Chase grinned. "You don't say?"

I recognized the teasing, the good kind that I hadn't had since I lost my friends. Though lost wasn't the right word. I'd deserted them when their dreams continued and mine died because I couldn't face them anymore without overwhelming feelings of envy.

"You should bring him out to meet my sister. She's a horse trainer, but she also has summer camps and teaches kids how to ride. She's not shy with kids, but adults are a whole different story."

I nodded. "Maybe I will. Thanks."

He clapped his hand against the back of my shoulder. "I'm sorry for your loss, man. I can't imagine losing my father even though I'll have to face that someday."

I glanced at the Dimarcos but found it was easier talking to Chase one on one, so I turned back to face him. It occurred to me he'd probably guessed that, considering he grew up with a sister who most likely felt overwhelmed in crowds. "Your mom?"

Sadness flickered through his eyes. "My mom left us when we were young. Haven't heard from her since. Not one word." He took a deep breath, exhaling slowly. "Honestly, after she left, my sister fell more in to herself." He frowned. "She's the only girl."

"You have a big family?" I asked.

He considered that for a moment. "Well, I always thought we did, but then I met the Dimarcos." I chuckled along with him before he continued. "There are five of us altogether."

"That's still a big family." At least, I thought it was, considering up until today I only really had myself. I shoved my hands in my pockets when the silence lingered, feeling uncomfortable until I thought of something to say. "I appreciate you coming to help out."

He shrugged. "It's no problem. Ben and I were supposed to meet before the engagement party at Jake's house later this afternoon, but he called and said there was a change in plans. Honestly, man"—he chuckled—"any time spent with this family is entertaining, so it's no skin off my back."

"They didn't have to come if they were busy," I said.

He snorted. "Jack spoke. When Jack speaks, the boys jump, especially if it's for Grace." He lowered his voice. "To be honest, I was looking forward to finally meeting the infamous Grace because the way they talk about her you'd think she walks on water." He smiled. "After meeting her, I'm beginning to see why they feel that way."

I stiffened and looked away, feeling a surge of jealousy rip through me but quickly forcing it back down. Chase was a nice guy, a friend of their family, and obviously pretty damn successful. He was exactly the kind of man a woman like Grace would want and deserve.

Chase cleared his throat, causing me to look his way again. "No need to say a word, man, I completely understand. You can be assured Grace is not on my radar."

I frowned, wanting to tell him she wasn't on mine either or I wasn't on hers at least, but the words got stuck in my throat. I couldn't have been more relieved when I heard a voice call out.

"Hey, are we moving this damn furniture or what?" Jake called out. "We have a party to get back to."

We both turned and faced what, to me, felt like would be the longest day of my life before moving toward the group by the door.

Chapter Eleven

Grace

Leaning up against the wall, I watched the guys carry in the last of Seth's and Sophie's things. I'd gone along, riding with my dad, while Tyler, Sophie, and Seth rode in Tyler's SUV. I'd planned to ride with them, but one look from my dad and I knew I was riding with him.

We were barely out of Tyler's driveway before he voiced his concerns. "The boys tell me Tyler's been in some trouble."

I'd always had a hard time lying to my dad, never wanting him to be disappointed in me, but for some reason, this time, I wanted to defend Tyler more. I decided to choose my words carefully. "He has, but it was never anything he initiated. He was always defending himself."

"Luke said that assault charges were filed."

I took a deep breath before exhaling. "To be honest, Dad, I don't know the whole story, but Mr. Anderson said he's a good man who seems to find himself in bad situations, and I believe him."

Turning my head, I stared at my dad's profile and waited. I knew he wasn't done. "Gracie, I'm not gonna lie, darlin', I don't like this. Something doesn't sit right with me here, and knowing how big your heart is and how you never see the bad, well, that worries me."

"Dad." I sighed, again looking out the windshield. "I know he comes off hard, and trust me, when I first met him, I thought he was awful, but today, I saw something different."

"What do you mean?"

"I don't know how to explain it, but today, I think I saw glimpses of the real him."

Dad reached over and laid his hand on my knee, squeezing gently. "He just lost his father, Gracie. He's grieving, but it doesn't mean that's the man he is every day." My eyes flicked back to him, and I frowned when he continued. "Sounds to me like he has a temper, and what worries me is what sets him off."

"Dad," I chided. "You do know that I have seven brothers, all with tempers, all who have been in fights, all who have caused trouble their whole lives."

"Maybe so, darlin', but your brothers always know when enough is enough." His gaze flicked my way before looking forward again. "And that's not the point."

"Then what is, Dad? Do you think I can't take care of myself? That I don't make good decisions?"

He paused, which made me angry. I'd never given him reason to believe I couldn't take care of myself or make good decisions. Well, I hadn't for a long time anyway. I braced myself when he started speaking again. "You think with your heart, Gracie. You always have and that worries me."

"If any of the boys were in my position right now, would you be giving them this lecture?"

He lifted his hand from the steering wheel and ran it over the back of his neck. "I've talked to every one of your brothers at some point."

"Right, I know that, but that was to give them advice. Have you ever lectured them on their choices or questioned their decisions?"

I twisted my hands together in my lap. "You don't have to answer, Dad, because we both know you haven't. They've all made choices that weren't the best for them, but you just looked the other way and gave them time to figure it out on their own. Why don't you treat me the same way you treat them?"

He shook his head but still faced forward before dropping his hand from his neck to lay on his thigh. "Because they aren't my baby girl," he said quietly.

"Dad," I said just as quietly. "That's a double standard."

He huffed. "Probably is. But that doesn't change how I feel or how I worry."

I knew I wasn't making any headway in this conversation. My brothers and my dad always treated me like I was breakable, always stepped up to protect me, and I usually didn't mind. Most of the time, I appreciated them, and the times I knew they were wrong, I did what I thought was best, but I did it quietly.

I decided to try another tactic. "What happened to giving people the benefit of the doubt?" I reminded him of what he preached to us growing up. "What happened to sharing our family with those who need it?"

I saw his jaw clench and knew I'd struck a nerve. Dad never wanted to see people hurting or without family to rally around them when they needed the support, whether in good times or in bad. For as long as I could remember, my parents' home was open to everyone as long as they showed respect when they walked through their door.

"I still believe that, darlin'." His voice was low when he spoke. "I always will. But I need to know you're safe before I can even close my eyes at night."

I felt my eyes water and swallowed hard. Damn him. He always said things like that, things that were a direct link to my heart. I never wanted to be the reason he lost sleep, so I told him what I should've told him at the beginning of the conversation. "You don't have anything to worry about, anyway, Dad. There's nothing between Tyler and me." I tucked my hair behind my ear. "We're hardly even friends. I just felt bad for him today and wanted to help him out. I'll probably never see him again after we're done."

"I wouldn't be so sure about that, darlin'," he said quietly moments before we pulled into a driveway leading up to a beautiful house.

We didn't talk anymore about Tyler while Sophie and Seth led us to their bedrooms, and I watched as my brothers and Tyler began to disassemble their beds and load all their furniture into the trucks. I helped the kids pack their clothes and toys, watching them closely for any signs of sadness, but surprisingly, they both seemed okay.

I had a bad feeling that was going to change.

"Grace." I snapped out of my memory and smiled down at Sophie who was tugging on my hand. "Come see the room I picked."

"Okay." I followed Sophie down the long hallway, impressed with the layout of Tyler's home. It was large, having once been a farmhouse, but for a very wealthy family. It had five bedrooms, all with their own bathrooms. There was a door at the end of the hallway, but it was shut, and I could only assume it was the master bedroom. I couldn't help but wonder if it was as sparsely decorated as the rest of the home.

"This one!" Sophie called out when she pulled me into a room right in the middle of all the doors on the left side of the hallway. I smiled at Cam and Chris, who were assembling her princess bed, complete with the canopy I'd suspected. My gaze moved around the room, noting the plain white walls and gray carpet, but nothing made the room spectacular until I spotted the window seat on the far side. A little girl's dream or at least it had been mine when I was little. Charlie had one in her bedroom, and we'd spend hours there when we were younger, sitting in a mountain of pillows just talking.

I looked down at Sophie, who was grinning up at me. "I think you picked the perfect room."

She tugged on my hand until I started moving again, following her to the window seat. She raised her hand and pointed. "And look, a pool! I can sit here"—she jumped up onto the seat and faced the window—"and look at the pool."

I didn't know this house had a pool too. It had a cover on it, and from the shape the cover was in, I could tell it hadn't been off in a while. It was only late August, so we still had a month of nice weather coming our way. Maybe two if we were lucky.

I grinned at Sophie. "You'll have to talk your brother into taking that cover off."

Her little forehead wrinkled before I saw her eyes light up. "Tyler can do that. He's strong. Just like my daddy."

I smiled, but it didn't reach my eyes. I didn't think she'd fully digested the fact that her parents were gone. My heart already was breaking for her and her brother when their new reality would eventually set in.

"Grace." I turned to face Cam when he called out to me. I saw the bed was finished, and the dressers had been moved in as well. "I'm gonna head out. The party's starting soon, and I don't want to leave Syd to handle it on her own."

I nodded. I'd almost forgotten that Cam and his fiancée, Sydney, were having a combined party at Jake's house with Jake and his fiancée, Lanie, to celebrate their engagements.

"Okay." I walked toward both him and Chris. "Thanks, guys. I know this was the last thing you wanted to do today."

Chris lifted his chin in Sophie's direction. She was sitting with her face pressed to the window, looking at the vast land behind Tyler's house. I wondered what she was looking for. His voice brought my attention back to him.

"It's worth it to see her smile." He lowered his voice and stepped closer to me. "Do you think she understands what's happened?"

I closed my eyes briefly before meeting his concerned stare. "No, I don't. Or at least I don't think she understands it's permanent. Right now, this seems fun."

"I was thinking the same thing," he agreed. "Where's her brother?"

My eyebrows pulled down. I hadn't seen Seth in a little while, and from the small amount of time I'd known them, he was always with his sister.

"I don't know." Shifting my attention back to Sophie, I called out. "Sophie, where's Seth?"

She beamed and jumped down, ran right to me, and grabbed my hand.

"He's in his room. And guess what?" She bounced on her toes. "His room is right across from mine." She tugged on my hand. "Come see."

"I'll see you at the house, right?" Cam's eyebrows lifted, telling me it wasn't a question. He expected I'd show up to celebrate with him.

I leaned forward and kissed him on the cheek. "I'll be there."

I waved to my brothers while Sophie pulled me across the hall and into a room that was completely identical to hers. White, sterile walls, gray carpet, this room had no window seat but had a beautiful view of the other side of the house, including the barn and the horses. I was not surprised Seth liked the room where he could see the horses. He'd been mesmerized by them when I took him and Sophie to the barn this morning. It was the first smile I'd seen without his sister's prompting.

My eyes moved around the room until they landed on Chase squatting down beside Seth, talking to him, their voices low. Sophie spotted him at the same time as me and dropped my hand to run toward her brother.

"Seth!"

His little head lifted, and he grinned at Sophie. She didn't even give him a chance to speak before she was pulling him toward her room and talking loudly. "I'm going to ask Tyler to take the cover off the pool so we can swim. Grace said so."

I rolled my lips together; happy Tyler wasn't in the room to hear that. My head snapped to the right when I heard a voice from just behind my shoulder. "So that idea was yours, huh?"

I chuckled and turned to face Chase. "Maybe." I gestured toward the door where Sophie and Seth had just exited. "You're really good with him."

He put his hands on his hips. "My sister is shy, painfully shy actually, so I've had a lot of experience."

"Are you older than her?"

He nodded. "Yeah. I'm the second oldest in a family of four boys and a girl."

"Wow, a big family. We have that in common," I said, happy to meet another family big like mine. It wasn't too often I met families with lots of kids. Even Charlie only has her brother.

"Yeah, but not as big as yours." He smirked. "And not a lot like yours."

I slanted my head. "What do you mean?"

"Your family is different than most, you know. It's not all that common anymore for siblings to stay friends as adults and to spend as much time together as your family does."

"That's true," I agreed. "Aren't you close with your brothers or your sister?"

He contemplated that. "Close with my sister, yes. My two youngest brothers are in college, so I'm close to them but don't see them as much as I used to, and to be honest, I'm not sure they'll move back here after they graduate. They're only ten months apart in age and always together. My dad used to call them Irish twins."

I smiled but realized he missed one when I counted. "You missed a brother."

"Yeah, guess I did." He exhaled heavily. "My oldest brother. He's not always easy to get along with. Keeps to himself."

I laid my hand on his arm and squeezed gently. "I'm sorry to hear that."

He nodded, but his expression was haunted. My attention shifted when he spoke again.

"Hey, Tyler."

Chapter Twelve

Tyler

Closing the door behind Grace's twin brothers, I sighed. Some of her family was still here outside talking by their trucks, and honestly, I was ready for them to go. I needed some quiet, some time to myself, some time to clear my head. I appreciated their help, especially after we got to my dad's house, and I saw the number of things we'd need to move. The kids' stuff didn't even put a dent in what would eventually need cleaned out, but I wasn't ready to do that yet.

I didn't know if I ever would be.

I walked quietly up the stairs, hoping to get a few moments alone in my bedroom, but without even considering what I was doing I followed the sound of voices to the room a few doors away from the top of the stairs. I moved to stand in the open doorway and watched silently as Chase and Grace talked, but I didn't hear their words. I only saw how close they stood, how easily they spoke to each other and smiled. All my insecurities reared their ugly heads. I wanted to back out of the room and find a place to hide. I almost did, but then Chase noticed me and called out, causing them both to turn in my direction, the soft smile on Grace's face made my heart beat like I'd just ran the entire length of the football field.

I shoved my hands deep into the pockets of my jeans. "Hey."

"Everything moved in, man?" Chase asked.

I nodded, my eyes moving from Grace to him. "Yeah. The others are outside."

Chase put his hands on his hips. "Probably waitin' on me. I guess I better get going." He took a few steps but then looked back at Grace. "You coming to the party?"

She smiled. "I'll be there."

"There's a party?"

My head jerked to the side when Sophie blew past me, running straight to Grace. I watched Seth follow her into the room, but he hung back a little. Grace ran her hand over the ponytail swinging Sophie's long, dark hair side to side.

"There is," she beamed. "At my brother Jake's house."

"Should I wear a dress?"

Grace's head jerked back again, but she didn't lose the smile. It took me a moment to realize what Sophie was asking.

I stepped forward, ready to tell Sophie she wasn't going to the party, but before I could formulate how to do that, Grace spoke. "I think a dress would be too fancy. It's an outside party."

"Will you make my hair pretty?" Sophie bounced on her toes excitedly. "Like yours?"

Grace squatted down. "I think before we do anything, you need to ask Tyler if he's okay with coming to the party, and you need to ask Seth if he wants to."

My back tightened when I straightened and inhaled deeply. Go to a party with Grace's family? No fucking way could I handle that.

"Okay," Sophie said in a singsong voice.

She turned herself around and went straight to her brother. "Seth, will you come to the party too?"

He met her eyes and shrugged, but I saw the look on his face and recognized the hesitation immediately. She smiled wide and made her way to stand in front of me. Reaching up, she wrapped her little fingers around mine, pulling at my hand until I squatted down in front of her. Looking into her eyes, the same color as my own, the same as my father's, my stomach clenched.

"Can we go, Tyler?"

I shook my head but hesitated when her smile dropped. Running my hand down the side of my face, I forced myself to find the right words to explain why we couldn't. "I don't think it's a good idea, Sophie."

She angled her head, her little hand still wrapped around my fingers. "Why not?"

"Well," I flicked my gaze over her shoulder to see Grace patiently waiting standing beside Chase. Why the fuck did it piss me off that she was standing so close to him? "We don't know everyone there."

"Silly." Sophie giggled. "We'll know them when we get there."

I hesitated, but the idea of a family party and the expectation that I would socialize were paralyzing me. "We can't go."

Her face fell. "Oh." When she lowered her head a little and dropped my fingers, I felt something in my gut, something strange, uncommon to me, but I still recognized it. Guilt. Guilt that I was holding her back because I was too much of a fucking coward to step up.

Running my hand down my face again in aggravation, I reached out and laid my hand on her shoulder. "If you wanna go, we can for a little while."

Her eyes flew up to meet mine, and she squealed before throwing her arms around my neck and pushing her body in tight enough to mine that I swayed backward. "Yay!" she shouted before running over to Grace. I stood slowly and watched her bouncing up and down in front of Grace. "Grace, can we do my hair now?"

Grace smiled and nodded before looking at Chase. "Will you tell my dad I don't need a ride to the party?"

"Sure, Grace," Chase agreed.

She started toward the door, slowing when she got to me, and lifted her hand to lay against my shoulder for a moment before dropping it and leaving the room. I swallowed hard when my arm still tingled after she left.

Chase stepped forward and looked back and forth between me and Seth, who still stood off to the side, but his head was raised, eyes on us. "Wow, she's good, huh? Already has you wrapped around her little finger."

I huffed in defeat. "Yeah. Guess I'm going to have to get better at saying no."

He chuckled. "For some reason, I don't see that happening."

I grinned, feeling relaxed around Chase. He was right. She was going to be hard to tell no, but at some point, I'd need to figure out how to do that.

"Sophie's definitely got a handle on how to get what she wants."

He moved past me, slapping me on the shoulder, and then stopped briefly to stand beside me. "I wasn't only talking about Sophie, man."

He moved away, but he'd already planted the seed in my mind. Grace. He meant Grace. That was one female in my life I doubted I'd ever have the strength to tell no.

I looked over at Seth, standing quietly, his eyes locked on the door Chase had just exited. I turned my body to fully face him. "You doing okay, kid?"

His eyes flashed to mine briefly before flicking around the room. He nodded, and I remembered doing the same thing when people I was unfamiliar with spoke to me. Hell, I still did. I didn't want that for him. I wanted him to be better than me, do better than me, so I moved over to stand in front of him, and I squatted back down, knowing that with my height, I needed to if I had any hope of making eye contact with him.

"You wanna go to the party?"

He shrugged and lowered his head.

I reached out and laid my hand on his shoulder like my dad had done with me when I was small. His head jerked up, and I smiled softly knowing my dad, our dad, had done the same with him. "Do you want to go?"

When he lifted his shoulders, I was assuming to shrug again, Grace's words floated through my mind. "Use your words, Seth," I encouraged.

His eyes flicked back and forth between mine, but I was proud when he held my stare. His voice was quiet when he spoke. "Sophie wants to."

"But do you?"

He shifted, but I held tightly to his shoulder. "I like to go where Sophie goes."

I'd expected that answer. He used his sister like his safety net. I'd already seen that, and I'd only been with him a day. "Okay."

I stood and looked down. "I'm going to change. I'm sure Grace will let us know when Sophie's ready."

I waited, but he didn't respond, and I didn't push. He was going to have a difficult afternoon, and I didn't want to add to it. I wish I could make it easier for him. I wish I could make it easier for myself, but I'd learned a long time ago that wasn't possible.

And a couple of years ago, after I'd lost it all, I learned to stop wishing for the impossible.

Chapter Thirteen

Grace

Oh boy. I hadn't expected to be taking three more people with me to the party, but when Sophie smiled and bounced around, I found it impossible to say no to her. Obviously, Tyler did too, which was why I was buckled into the passenger seat of his enormous SUV with the kids in the back seat. Well, one of the back seats. This thing had three rows of seats. A quick glance out of the corner of my eye showed Tyler with his seat the whole way back, head close to touching the roof of the vehicle, and looking very uncomfortable. I'd imagine it was hard for him to put his giant frame into any vehicle.

Memories of him in my car brought a small grin to my face until something occurred to me. Twisting in my seat, I faced Tyler. "Hey, umm…at the party, could you please not mention riding in my car?"

He glanced my way, his confusion obvious before his eyes moved back to the road. "What?"

I threw my hand out. "Remember when I picked you up?" He nodded, so I continued. "Well, they don't know I have that car."

"Why would they care if you have a car?"

I sighed long and loud. "It's a lot to explain, but they know I have a car. They gave me one when I was leaving for college. It was older, my cousin who's a mechanic fixed it up for me, and I still have it, but the only place I drive it is to see my family."

"That doesn't make sense," he mumbled, and I totally agreed. It did sound ridiculous. I was in my twenties and hiding a car from my family, but he didn't understand what would happen if they knew. If I had to explain, well, everything.

"I know it doesn't." I ran my fingers through my hair, grabbed a few strands at the bottom and rolled them through my fingers. "But just don't say anything, okay?"

He glanced my way briefly again but nodded. I dropped my hair and turned to face the front window again. "I can get one of my brothers to take me home after the party, or my dad, so you don't have to worry."

"Won't they see your car?"

My head snapped his way because I thought he was being sarcastic, but when he glanced over, I saw only question in his expression.

"I live in an apartment complex and attached to it is a parking lot. It's pretty big. I park the car from my parents closest to my apartment and the other one farther into the lot."

"Aren't you going to a lot of trouble to hide a car?"

I huffed out a laugh. "Yep." I noticed where we were and pointed at a street on the right coming up. "Turn right here onto Clark Street." He made the turn, and the car became quiet once again.

I stared out the side window and spoke quietly not even sure he'd hear me, not even sure I wanted him to. "They wouldn't understand."

"Why not?" he replied, just as quietly.

I took a deep breath before exhaling. "I do something that earns me money, something I love, but something they wouldn't understand. At least my brothers wouldn't." I looked down at my hands and twisted them together in my lap. "I shouldn't be embarrassed about it, or embarrassed to tell them, but I am. So for now, it's a secret."

I saw Jake's house on the right and pointed. "Just pull alongside the road anywhere you can find a spot."

He found a spot down the street and pulled in before putting it in park and turning off the engine. I reached for my door handle but turned my head toward Tyler when I heard his voice. "Is it safe?"

This was the most he'd ever spoken to me without me constantly encouraging him, and I appreciated that. Maybe I was breaking down some of the giant walls he'd built around himself. "It's safe."

He jerked his chin up like he believed me, but he didn't look convinced. I pushed open my door and jumped out before I closed it, reaching for the door handle behind mine and swinging it open. I put on my best cheery face. "You guys ready to party?"

"Yeah!" Sophie yelled, and a small grin tugged at Seth's lips.

I helped them from the car, completely at ease after having done it many times with my own nieces and nephews. I hoped having a lot of kids around to play with would help Seth feel a little more comfortable being here.

Sophie reached up and grabbed my hand when I started walking up the sidewalk toward Jake's house. I noticed Seth and Tyler both stayed back a little, but at least they were both out of the car. Watching them together, I saw the similarities in their actions and their gestures, and it was becoming very obvious that Charlie was right, and Tyler is shy. It was still hard for me to believe, being that he played professional football and spent most of his time in stadiums filled with thousands of people, but I would admit there was a lot more to Tyler Morgan than I originally thought.

We rounded the corner of the house and headed toward the back, almost through the gate attached to the fence when my niece Lexi caught sight of me. I smiled when she dropped the toy in her hand and started running toward me, calling out her name for me. "Ti-Ti!"

I squatted down, catching her just as she slammed into me, forcing us back and causing me to land hard, on my butt. We giggled, and I kissed her on the cheek. "Hey, beautiful."

Her eyes widened. "Your wate." I rolled my lips together to keep from laughing when her face got serious. Sometimes she reminded me so much of her dad, my brother Brody.

"I am," I agreed. "But I brought you some new friends to play with."

I moved to stand and felt a hand grab my elbow, pulling me up off the ground. I turned my head quickly, meeting Tyler's eyes seconds before he dropped his hand and pulled back like he'd just realized what he'd done.

"Thanks," I whispered.

He nodded but didn't say anything. I directed my attention back to Lexi and smiled wide. "Lex, these are my friends." I pointed at Sophie. "That's Sophie." I moved my finger to Seth "Seth, and…" I got to Tyler whose eyes were focused on me and swallowed hard, taken aback by the intensity of his stare. "That's Tyler."

"Hi," Lexi said sweetly, then she looked at Sophie. "Wanna pay wif me and Mia?"

Sophie nodded excitedly and stepped forward to stand beside Lexi. I felt a rush of pride when Lexi looked at Seth whose face was pointed at the ground, and she moved to stand in front of him. She put her little hands on his cheeks, which was what she did when she wanted someone to pay attention to her, and waited for him to shift his gaze in her direction. She was shorter than him and much younger, but she'd always seemed older than her years to me. More intuitive. My mom had often called her an old soul, saying Lexi saw and felt things well beyond her years. This was a moment that I'd say she was absolutely right.

Her expression grew serious when his eyes met hers. "You pay too, Sef?"

He shrugged, and her expression changed like she was thinking of something.

"You pay wif Andy. Not Bway. He's cwazy." She rolled her eyes, and to my disbelief, Seth giggled. That seemed to make her happy, so she reached down and grabbed his hand, pulling him along beside her as she made her way across the yard with Sophie bouncing along on Lexi's other side.

I smiled at Tyler who just stared. He had yet to say anything since we got out of the car, but I wasn't surprised since it was obvious this wasn't something he'd wanted to do. I gestured over my shoulder. "That was Lexi. My brother Brody's daughter. She's, umm, well…determined, I guess is the right word."

"She reminds me a lot of her aunt," he said quietly, and I shivered when his arm brushed against mine. I didn't know what was going on with him, but the way he was watching me and the things he was saying were different than even just earlier today.

"Grace." I heard called out and felt a smile spread across my face. I turned just in time to see my brother Jax and his wife, Kasey, coming across the yard. "You made it," Kasey said when they got to me, and she threw her arms around my neck for a quick hug. She pulled back and smiled when I laid my palm on her pregnant belly. "Wow, you're really starting to show."

Her eyes lit up. "They say you show faster with the second pregnancy." She looked around quickly and smirked. "Where's your sidekick?"

I laughed. "Charlie's coming in a little while."

Kasey looked past me to smile at Tyler. "Hi, I'm Kasey, you must be Tyler."

He glanced down at me before clearing his throat. "Nice to mcct you."

She pointed beside her. "You know Jax."

His eyes flicked to Jax. "Yeah. Thanks again for your help today."

Jax gave him a chin tip, and I rolled my eyes at Kasey but startled when I heard Tyler's voice behind me. "Who's Charlie?"

JENNIFER HANKS

I looked back when I felt the heat of his stare and was surprised to see his eyes had taken on the coldness I recognized from before but hadn't seen much this afternoon.

Kasey's eyebrows rose. "You haven't met Charlie yet? I'm shocked." She turned her attention to Tyler. "I've known Grace since she was seventeen, and I don't think I've seen her very often without her best friend Charlie beside her."

"That's true." I nodded. "We used to spend all our time together, but now with her work and mine, it's getting harder."

Kasey snapped her fingers. "I'll bet you'll like Charlie, Tyler. She's a PT and a sports lover. You guys would have a lot in common." She motioned beside her again. "Jax said you played football."

"Charlie likes hockey," Jax said, his stare hard on Tyler, and I inwardly groaned.

Kasey waved him off. "She likes all sports, right, Grace?"

"Yeah. She does," I agreed.

"Well, come on, everyone's around the back on the deck." Kasey motioned, encouraging us to follow her and Jax. We rounded the deck, all eyes on us while greetings were being called out, and I turned to face Tyler whose face was stony, his jaw clenched tight.

I reached out and laid my hand on his arm. "You good?"

He swallowed hard, his eyes flicking around the yard before coming back to me. He nodded, but I wasn't convinced. I slid my hand down his arm and wrapped it around his, squeezing gently. "How about a drink?"

He looked at our hands joined before his eyes moved to my face again. "Sure," he answered quietly.

I tugged him to the deck, calling out to everyone we passed and stopping to give a few hugs along the way, but I held tightly to his hand, and he didn't shake me loose.

Actually, at one point, I'd swear he held it tighter.

Chapter Fourteen

Tyler

My heart was beating so damn fast, reminding me why this had been a bad idea. I followed along behind Grace, not willing to let go of her hand, feeling like if I did, I'd run for my vehicle. I hated these situations. I hated parties and social events. But more than anything, I hated that all eyes were on me. And those eyes were watching me like I was something that just crawled out from under a rock.

"Beer, man?" My eyes shifted to see Jake holding out a beer to me, looking at me expectantly.

I reached out and took it from his hand. "Thanks."

"Have a seat." He pointed at the chair next to where I was standing, and I reluctantly dropped Grace's hand. She looked back and frowned, but when I gestured to the chair, she nodded in understanding. I watched her look around until she saw a chair across the deck that was empty, and she started toward it.

I reached out my hand and touched her forearm to get her attention. When she looked back, I mumbled, "I'll get it."

Walking the short distance, I picked up the navy blue Adirondack chair and carried it in one hand back to where we'd been standing. She looked surprised that I'd done that, but I wasn't a complete dick. I did have some manners. Plus, I was being selfish. I wanted her to sit near me. I knew if she did, she'd carry the conversation. She seemed to understand in the short time she'd known me and from the few strange encounters we'd had that I didn't socialize well. Or at all.

I positioned the chair beside me and waited for her to sit before I did the same. Looking around the yard, I lifted the bottle to my lips and enjoyed the cool liquid running down my throat. I spotted Sophie sitting in a sandbox with Lexi and another little girl, her mouth moving, which didn't surprise me. She was my father. She could talk to anyone. I let my eyes wander again until they fell on Seth, and this time, I was surprised. He was at the bottom of the yard, his head bent close to another boy who looked about the same age as him, and I could see him talking. He held a baseball in his hand and the other little boy had on a glove.

"That's my son."

My head snapped up and met Luke's eyes. I leaned back in my chair and nodded. I didn't know Luke well, not any better than the others, but I did remember hearing he was a cop, and there wasn't a chance in hell a cop would like me. I guess he was tolerating me for Grace's sake.

"His name's Andy." He took a drink from his bottle before using it to point at a brunette across the yard, talking to the girl I'd met near the gate, Kasey. "That's his mom, my fiancée, Kate."

I cleared my throat. "Congratulations."

His eyes flicked down to mine. "Thanks." He took another drink from the bottle in his hand before letting it dangle from his fingertips. "You don't have to worry about Seth. Andy will bring him out of his shell."

I huffed before I could stop myself. Luke lifted his eyebrow, encouraging me to explain.

"It's not that easy."

Luke nodded slowly. "You know that from personal experience?"

80

I hesitated for only a second before I answered. "Sometimes what we want and what we're capable of are very far apart."

"Sounds to me like you're talking about more than just shyness."

"Hey." My head turned when Grace's sweet voice broke the lingering awkwardness. "What's all the serious talk? This is a party, you know."

"It's always a party for you," Luke teased, and Grace laughed before sliding the chair I'd gotten her a little closer.

She leaned over until her shoulder brushed mine, but her eyes remained on her brother. "I can't believe Kate's in the vicinity, and you're not all over her."

Luke dropped his head, shaking it, but he was smiling. One glance at Grace told me she was too.

"Hey, I made it." I tried to move over when Grace jumped out of her seat and leaned across me to hug a blond girl who'd just stepped onto the deck.

"Finally." Grace huffed and pulled back. "You know what these guys are like. I need my backup."

She laughed along with Grace, but then looked down, seeing that I was essentially trapped between them. Her eyes flicked to Grace before she pulled back and looked down at me again. "You must be Tyler."

Grace rolled her eyes, but did it smiling when I only nodded. "Tyler, this is my best friend Charlie."

"Hi, Charlie," I mumbled, disappointed I couldn't think of something clever to say.

"Sit." Grace pointed at her chair. "I'll grab you a glass of wine. Be right back."

"Hey, Charlie." Luke leaned in and gave her a quick hug before excusing himself to follow Grace into the house.

Charlie plopped down in the seat beside me and rolled her eyes. "Grace is so damn bossy." I snorted but couldn't stop the grin when Charlie continued. "Come on, tell me I'm wrong."

"Can't do that," I said, a grin still playing around my lips.

"I kind of love that about her," Charlie admitted, and I took the chance to look over, appreciating her love for her friend.

"I can see that."

She smiled and twisted in her seat, tucking a leg under her until she was fully facing me. "Because you're new around here, I'll give you some inside information." She leaned in a little closer and lowered her voice. "They're all crazy."

I chuckled and shifted my body so I was facing her more. "That's not inside information."

"Damn." She frowned. "Then I got nothin'."

I felt my body relax for the first time since I left my house. "I heard you've been friends for a long time."

Charlie pursed her lips, and her eyes looked over my shoulder, in thought, before coming back to me. "Eleven years, I think."

My eyebrows raised. That was a long time. A damn long time. I'd never had a friendship last a few years, let alone over a decade. "You're a physical therapist?"

"I am," she answered proudly.

"You love it," I stated plainly.

"I do. Well, I don't love where I work now. I'd rather be working for a team, but even as far as women have come, it's still pretty challenging to be hired to a team." She pointed at me. "Not impossible, though, so I'm not giving up yet."

When I only nodded, her smile dropped, and she put her hand on my arm. "Sucks you got hurt. I love watching football, so I can't even imagine what it felt like to play it."

Or to lose it was all I could think. I looked down, my eyes landing on her hand laying against my forearm, but I didn't feel an ounce of what I felt when Grace had done the same thing. I shrugged off the darkness I felt threatening to overwhelm me and met Charlie's stare. "I thought hockey was your favorite."

Her head jerked back. "Where'd you hear that?"

"Jax." I rubbed my hand over the scruff on my jaw, running her brothers' names through my mine. "Yeah, it was Jax who said it."

She moved her hand from my arm to lay on her thigh. "Well, he's not wrong, exactly. I love all sports, but hockey was my favorite when I was younger."

"It isn't anymore?"

Sadness flickered through her eyes, and I thought for a minute she wasn't going to answer. I even thought about telling her not to, but then she spoke. "My dad loved hockey. He took me to a game once when I was young."

When her eyes dropped, I reached out and laid my hand on her arm, hoping to offer her some comfort. "What happened to him?"

Her eyes met mine again, but all the happiness had disappeared. "Nothing tragic. My parents divorced when I was fifteen." She left out a huff. "One of those ugly divorces, you know the kind where everyone is consumed by the ugly and caught up in a tornado of hate and blame." I nodded, and she continued. "Well, that was us, and when everything finally settled, the only one left was me." She shook her head. "My dad was gone with a new girlfriend and even has another kid now. I lived with my mom, but she was gone too. She let me do whatever I wanted, didn't care where I was or who I was with. Thank god, I had Grace and this family or who knows where I'd have ended up. And my brother left for college and just never came home."

I opened my mouth to say something, but nothing came, and she waved her hand in the air, a fake smile tugging at her lips. "Sorry, I didn't mean to go on like that. It's all in the past. And anyway, who needs hockey? It's just grown ass men fighting, right?"

I grinned and decided to just go where she needed to go right now. I knew how she was feeling, better than anyone. I'd lost my parents too, not in the same way, but in all the ways that matter for us both. "I knew a guy in college who was on the hockey team."

"Yeah?" She smiled genuinely this time. "What was he like?"

I shrugged. "I guess okay. He had a mean right hook."

She laughed out loud. "Does that mean you lost?"

I huffed. "I don't lose."

She laughed harder, and watching her, I knew she'd be great working on a team with a bunch of guys. She was almost like one of the guys, funny and easy to talk to. She'd actually made the past few minutes the most bearable I'd had all day.

"Charles."

Her head snapped back, and she looked up, shielding her eyes from the sun. "Benji."

He looked around and then back down at us, his eyes settling on my hand still against her arm. His eyes flicked to mine before moving back to land on Charlie. "Where's Grace?"

Charlie frowned. "She went to get us drinks, but that was a while ago. She must be talking to someone."

"Yeah." He looked back at me and tipped his chin up. "Hey, man."

I pulled my hand from Charlie's arm and rested it on my leg. "Hey, Ben. Thanks for your help today."

He tipped his chin. His eyes once again flicking back and forth between me and Charlie before he finally spoke. "I'll go find Grace for you."

Charlie watched him go before she faced me again. "I don't want to keep talking about sad stuff, but I'm sorry for your loss."

I felt a wave of grief wash over me that I quickly buried. "Thanks."

She looked out past me into the yard and smiled. "I see your mini-me out there."

I followed her gaze and watched Seth throw the ball to Andy, a small smile on his face. My eyes quickly found Sophie when I heard her laugh from where she was still sitting in the sandbox. "Yeah, I guess he is."

She looked around a little more and frowned. "I'm sorry you seem to be getting the cold shoulder."

I was surprised she actually said what I'd already known. "It's okay. I don't like to socialize anyway."

She stretched her neck and looked around the yard before her eyes flicked back to me. "Where the hell is everyone?"

I didn't know what she was talking about. There were people everywhere. She stood, and I mirrored her movement. "Something seems off." She pointed at the large sliding door at the back of the deck. "I'm going to see where Grace is."

I didn't know what I was supposed to do, so I followed her. I wanted to know where Grace was too. It was time for me and the kids to go. I needed to. I'd liked talking to Charlie, but I knew the rest of her family wasn't exactly happy I'd come, and I needed to get home. I needed the peace my home brought me. I realized everything that had happened today had been good because it distracted me, but now that the adrenaline was wearing off, I was starting to feel the pain again, and I needed to feel that alone.

Charlie pulled open the door, and I followed her in. Closing it behind me, I quickly came to a stop when all eyes landed on me.

Chapter Fifteen

Grace

I was fuming. No that wasn't a strong enough word for what I was feeling facing off with my brothers. At least Dad and Mom weren't here. Just before we arrived, they'd left for the airport to pick up my mom's brother, who was flying in, not only for the party but also to stay with my parents for a week or so. He lives in Nevada, and about once a year, every year since he's retired, he and his wife fly in to spend some time with my family. My parents return that favor every year and fly out to visit with his family. When my mom told him about this party, they decided to come now and see all of us together, which didn't happen every visit.

When I heard the sliding door open, I jerked my head in that direction to see Charlie walk in followed by Tyler.

"What's going on?" Charlie asked.

"Nothing," I said before I let my eyes wander over my brothers. "At least nothing worth talking about."

Brody ran his hand around the back of his neck, but Jax was the one to speak up. "Grace, we're just concerned, but we can talk about it later."

Charlie moved to stand beside me, but Tyler stayed put just inside the doors. "I'm not talking about this later, Jax. What I do with my life is my concern. I do not interfere in your lives, and I expect the same respect."

"You don't have the shit to be concerned about that we do," Cam said, his jaw clenched tight.

I watched Tyler edge around the refrigerator until he came to stand closer to where Charlie and I stood, his eyes on my brothers. I pulled my attention from him and rolled my eyes at my brothers. "There's nothing to be concerned about." My eyes flicked over all of them standing across the room next to each other. This was my whole life. Them, all together, a team, a unit, brothers and then me, the youngest and the only girl. Thank god I'd found Charlie. She was always on my side. "You're just trying to bully me into doing what you want me to do or in this case, don't want me to do."

"What's going on, Grace?"

I felt Charlie's stare and turned my head to face her. "My brothers think I'm stupid for trusting who I trust."

"For Christ's sake, Grace, he was all over Charlie out on the deck when he's supposed to be here with you," Ben said, his fists clenched at his sides.

Charlie jerked back, and her eyes settled on Ben. "What? Who was all over me?"

Ben put his hands on his hips and leaned forward toward us. "You know exactly who the fuck I'm talking about, and you didn't seem to mind."

Charlie's face turned a bright shade of red, and she lowered her voice. "I would never do that to Grace, and you know it."

"She wouldn't." I pointed at Ben. "And you do know that, Ben. I expect this from the others, but not you and Jake." I shook my head and looked at Jake who hung back, just watching, not saying anything, but not defending me either. "How dare any of you judge me? This, right here," I pointed at the room at large, "is exactly why I keep stuff to myself."

"What stuff?" Chris stepped forward.

"None of your business." His jaw hardened. "And you know what else isn't your business?" I pointed at Tyler. "My relationships. How dare any of you judge someone you don't even know? This man just lost his father, found out he has two siblings to raise, and came to this party because his little sister wanted to come." I put my hands on my hips. "Do you think he really wants to be here? He has to know you're all being giant dicks to him because of some stupid assault charge that you know nothing about."

"Grace—"

Luke started, but I held up my hand. "Don't bother Luke. I'm sure you pulled whatever strings you have and looked into everything, but you know what, there are always two sides to the story, and you haven't even asked for his." I took a deep breath and exhaled slowly. "I don't answer to any of you. And I won't. I'll have whatever relationships I want in my life."

Jax put his hands on his hips. "Grace, don't be stubborn and do something stupid that you're going to regret or something we have to step in and fix for you."

My eyes widened, but I had no words. It turned out I didn't need any. Tyler moved to stand in front of me, touching my arm gently and moving me back a step until I stood right next to Charlie.

His eyes never left the line of men in front of him when he said in a low voice, "No."

Jax's head snapped back. "What the fuck do you mean, no?"

Tyler's voice stayed deep and low when he responded. "You're not talking to her like that." His head turned slightly, and I imagined he was looking at each of my brothers individually. "Any of you."

I felt warmth rush through me. No one ever defended me against my brothers, except my parents, but usually they chose to see both sides. It was why I never stood up to them, why I did what I did and kept it to myself because I knew there were some things in my life that I didn't want to argue about while standing alone.

"We're her fucking family, man. Her brothers," Cam said. "We're protecting her."

Tyler widened his stance and crossed his arms over his chest, making himself look impossibly bigger. I heard Charlie cough to disguise the chuckle that I was also feeling looking at my brothers' faces. They were stunned and pissed. Really pissed. I waited patiently, having no idea what to expect. No one and I mean no one had ever stood in front of my brothers like he'd take on every one of them in my defense.

Jax stepped forward, and I knew, I just knew they weren't going to back down. This wasn't Tyler's fight; he wasn't even my boyfriend. This was my fight, and I wasn't going to watch my brothers try to intimidate him. I moved to stand beside Tyler. His eyes flicked to mine, and he shook his head quickly.

I laid my hand on his arm and smiled softly before I faced my brothers. "Don't even think about it, Jax." His eyes settled on me. "Or any of you. This is my life, and I will do what I want, when I want."

"You're not doing this," Jax said, anger flashing in his eyes.

That was the wrong thing to say. I felt my face heat with anger and slid my gaze over each one of my brothers, stopping briefly on Jake who still hadn't said anything. He had something to say, I knew that, but he also saw me as an adult, Ben too usually. Although, today he seemed pissed, but by the way he was glaring at Charlie, it seemed he was angrier at her than me. I smirked before I turned to face Tyler. He looked down at me, confusion on his face when I reached up and put my hands on his chest.

"Lean down," I whispered.

He widened his eyes in confusion. "What?"

"Grace, if you're trying to prove you make good decisions, this isn't the way to do it." Brody's voice rang out, but I was done listening. More importantly, I was done talking. I'd always been more of an action girl anyway.

Frustrated, I curled my fingers until his shirt bunched in my hands and yanked him down, pressing my lips to his. I reached up and wrapped my hand around the back of his neck to hold him in place, but what started as a lesson for my brothers faded into the background when his arm snaked around my waist, and he lifted me off the ground so he could stand straight again. He slanted his head to the side, and he pulled my body in tighter against his, all the while his lips were hungry against mine. When he slipped his tongue inside my mouth, taking charge, holding me tight, my body lit up, my skin flushed, and I felt a tightness in my belly that I'd never experienced before, not ever, with anyone else. Moaning, I tightened my hold around his neck seconds before he dropped me to the ground and backed away.

We were both breathing hard when he ran his hand roughly along his face and took another step back. "Sorry, fuck, sorry Grace." He kept moving backward, unable or unwilling to make eye contact with me until he made it to the sliding glass doors.

"I gotta go," he mumbled and yanked the door open, moving quickly through it.

"Grace," Charlie said from where she stood right beside me. "Are you okay?"

I nodded, my eyes stuck on those damn sliding doors, but I was lying. "Yeah, I'm okay."

Shaking off the fog I was still in, I turned to face the room, but it was empty. I looked around in confusion until Charlie spoke. "They left."

"They did?" I was surprised. I'd been so angry with all of them. I wanted to shock them, but I never expected they would leave.

"Grace." I looked at my best friend. "They left when he picked you up. They were clearly uncomfortable watching their sister make out with someone." Her eyes shifted to the side before they met mine again. "And they were pissed, all except Jake who was grinning at his shoes when he followed the boys out."

My head jerked back, ignoring the Jake comment, focused entirely on what she'd said before that. "We weren't making out. I was trying to make a point."

Her eyebrows lifted. "Well, you definitely made a point. It was hot, like melt-our-Kindles kind of hot."

My eyes widened. "Oh, god." I put my hand to my forehead. "Damnit. Why did I do that?"

"I think the better question is, do you want to do it again?"

I met her eyes and couldn't lie again. "I never expected that with him."

She grinned. "Was it as good as it looked?"

"It was." I ran my fingers through the ends of my hair. "Like nothing I've ever experienced before." Her grin turned into a full-blown smile, but I wasn't feeling what she was. "But I think I made things worse now. With my brothers and with Tyler."

She threw her hand in the air. "Stop worrying about your brothers. They'll give you a hard time, get all bossy and intrusive, and then they'll get the hell over it."

She was right. I'd been down this road before with them, and that was exactly what they did. I was a little taken aback when she started speaking again. "I can tell you that any crazy teenage feelings I had for Ben died today in this very kitchen."

My shoulders dropped. "I'm sorry he said that to you. I don't know where that came from. He's usually so easygoing, you know that. And he thinks a lot of you, Charlie. He would never think you'd go after someone I was interested in."

"That's exactly what he thought, Grace." Sadness filled her voice, and I didn't blame her. Ben and Jake had been like brothers to her too for a very long time. She took a step forward and put her hand on my arm. "I would never do that. You know that, right? I would never hurt you that way."

"Of course, I know that," I said immediately. "And so does

Ben. He's just been different lately. I don't know, maybe you were right and it's this whole Jackie thing again. I'll talk to him."

"Don't bother. It won't do any good right now," Charlie said adamantly. "Besides, if he feels bad, then he can come to me with an apology. If he doesn't, then I'll know where we stand."

I hated that, but she was right. It wouldn't do me any good to talk to Ben right now when he was pissed at me, but when stuff with him calmed down, he'd know we were going to talk. He knew there was no way I would forget the shit he said.

My eyes settled back on Charlie, and I asked what was really bothering me. "What about Tyler?"

"I'm not sure, sweetie. He's a tough guy to read. I can't believe he stood in front of you like that and defended you to your brothers. I never thought he'd do that." I nodded my head in agreement because that had surprised me too. "But I did talk to him for a while outside, and once he loosens up, he's nice." She rolled her lips. "I do think he's shy."

"Me too." I sat down on the stool in front of the island and leaned my forehead against my open palms. "So, any progress I made on the friend front, I just blew."

Charlie laughed, and I looked up, curious as to what was so funny. "What's so funny?"

"You." She threw out her hand in my direction. "If you think you two were ever just going to be friends."

I sighed and looked out the sliding doors. I knew he'd left. He needed to. He probably needed to before I jumped him in my brother's kitchen.

"What are you gonna do now?"

I rolled my lips. "I'm not sure, but I can't just let it go. I have to talk to him."

She smiled. "I never doubted that."

Now if I only knew what to say to someone I wasn't even sure liked me, but kissed me like he was starving.

Chapter Sixteen

Tyler

My eyes slowly opened when I heard the sound of shuffling feet. I lay quietly trying to decide if I was hearing things or had been dreaming since the noise seemed to have stopped. When I saw a flash beside my bed, courtesy of the small nightlight Sophie demanded I put in the hall, I lifted my head and peered to the side.

"Sophie?" I pushed up to lean on my elbow and reached out to turn on the lamp sitting on my nightstand.

"I want Mommy."

Her lip quivered seconds before a large teardrop rolled down her cheek, followed immediately by another. I blinked slowly, looking toward the door where I saw another movement. Seth stood silently in the dark, his face pointed at the floor.

"Sophie…." I ran my hand down over my face. This was what I'd been afraid of. I didn't know how to handle this shit. Fuck, I couldn't deal with my own grief, let alone the grief of two little kids.

She sniffed and wiped a tear from her cheek with the back of her hand. It was then I saw she had her other arm wrapped around a small stuffed dog. "I miss Mommy and Daddy."

I felt my throat clog, and I swallowed hard. I knew how she felt. "I know," I said softly.

She sniffed again before putting her little hand on the mattress and lifting herself to her knees on the side of my bed. She crawled over my legs and looked back toward the door. "Come on, Seth."

I watched him walk around to the other side of the bed and crawl up the same way his sister had. "What are you doing?"

She crawled up to the pillows beside me. "Sleeping with you."

I laid there for a moment, while I felt the bed shift behind me and wondered what I was supposed to do. At a loss, I reached over and turned off the light before lying on my back and staring up at the ceiling. I heard Sophie sniff again from beside me and turned my head when she snuggled into my side, still clutching her dog. I lifted my head a little and saw Seth was lying close to Sophie, his hand held tightly in hers. Lying my head back down, I sighed again, feeling their grief and wishing I could take it away for them.

♡

I woke quickly when I felt a sharp stinging in my nose and my eyes began to water. "Son of a bitch." I cursed under my breath.

Looking down, I saw a small foot lying across my chin right before it moved, slamming into the corner of my jaw. I reached up and grabbed the foot gently, moving it from my face to the pillow beside me before I rubbed my hand across my forehead. I pushed up until my back was against the headboard and looked to my left. Sophie was still beside me but had somehow ended up with her head at the bottom of the bed while Seth lay beside her on his side, facing the other side of the room.

Swinging my legs out from under the covers, I sat on the side of the bed and bent my head to rest in my hands. Twisting my neck from side to side, I listened to the cracks before I stood and made my way to the bathroom attached to my bedroom. Turning on the water, I dropped my pajama pants, happy I'd thought to put them on last night. A lot of nights, I'd just crawl into bed naked, but after the kids were asleep, I'd finally made my way to my own room and thought I'd better wear something to bed just in case they woke up before I did this morning.

Stepping into the shower, I leaned my palms against the shower tiles and let the hot water wash over my back, easing the stiffness that was as much a part of me as the scars I carried from the sport I loved. Flashes of Grace chose that moment to go through my mind, and I groaned. I have no doubt she kissed me to piss her brothers off, but the minute her soft lips pushed against mine and her scent surrounded me, I lost my mind. I couldn't get her close enough. I wanted to feel her skin under my fingers, and I wanted to shove my hands in her silky dark hair. I wanted so much from her. Hell, I wanted everything from her until she moaned. It woke me up, brought me back to where we were, who our fucking audience was, and I dropped her back down, needing to step back and keep moving away to stop myself from pulling her against me again.

I nearly ran into the yard and told the kids it was time to go. I told them I wanted to stop at Dad's house to pick up a few more things, which we did because they seemed excited to do that and I knew it was the only way to get them to leave with me. Sophie wanted pictures from the walls, so that was what we took, while Seth decided he wanted Dad's old sports memorabilia from the man cave he'd made for himself. He had quite a collection from his time playing the sport he loved, but I told Seth to pick his favorites for now and we'd come back for the rest later. He did, and when I went in to his room to make sure he was okay before I went to bed, he had Dad's special things proudly displayed on his dresser. He was close to my dad, close to him in a way I never was, and now never would be.

I finished in the shower and turned off the water, then stepped out into the steamy bathroom and grabbed a towel. I dried off quickly and tied the towel around my waist before quietly opening the door. I was relieved to see both Sophie and Seth still asleep. They'd had a long night, but more than that, I needed a little time to myself. Time to drink my coffee and just sit in the quiet of the morning. Throwing on jeans and a T-shirt, I walked out of my bedroom and shut the door quietly behind me before making my way down the stairs and into the kitchen. It only took a few minutes until I was holding a hot cup of coffee and staring out the back window at the pastures.

Yesterday before we left for the party, I'd talked to my father's attorney one more time about the arrangements for the funeral. He said my father and Tara had arranged everything at the time they made their will, and the funeral would be Monday. Apparently, neither of them wanted anything big or extended over a few days so everything would be done at the church and then the graveside.

That was it, all wrapped up with a nice little bow. For them. But for us, it was only the beginning. I took a long drink from my cup, letting the quiet settle my mind in a way it hadn't been since I walked the lonely corridor of the hospital. Moving toward the door, I unlocked it and pushed it open, the early morning sun warm on my skin. I needed to let the horses out and clean the stalls, work that for me, right now, was mindless. Spending time in the barn always calmed me. I put my empty cup on the small wooden table I had sitting on the back deck before I headed down the few stairs and made my way to the barn.

It didn't take me long before I had my four horses out, horses that I adopted from the previous owner of this home when he became too old to live on his own. He'd decided to move in with his son and daughter-in-law closer to the city where he obviously couldn't have horses, but he'd specifically asked the real estate agent to find someone willing to keep the horses and care for them. I agreed immediately, loving the quiet and serenity of the area and learning quickly that I loved horses, something I'd never known about myself.

I'd just finished and made my way out of the barn, walking the short distance to the house when I heard a cry. I took off running for the house, only hitting one of the steps leading to the back deck before I burst through the kitchen door, stopping almost immediately when I saw Sophie standing in the kitchen, her face buried in the small dog still in her arms, her shoulders shaking with the force of her sobs.

"Sophie." Her head snapped up when she heard my voice, and she ran to me, her little arms wrapping around my waist, her face buried against my body. I loosened her arms and squatted down, which she allowed, but only until she could wrap her arms around my neck. I felt her tears hit the side of my neck and closed my eyes, letting my body absorb her sobs and waited patiently, until her cries finally quieted.

She pulled away slightly and wiped her cheeks with the back of her free hand, but she didn't move away. "I c-called your n-name. I c-couldn't…" She hiccupped, a lone tear running down her cheek. "F-find you."

I used my thumb to brush away her tear. "I'm sorry, Sophie. I was outside with the horses."

She breathed in short choppy breaths. "I th-thought you left me too."

I swallowed hard. "I'm not going anywhere, Sophie. I promise."

"Okay." She pushed her long, dark hair off her shoulder and sniffed again. "Can I have juice?"

"Yeah." I started to stand but realized she still had an arm around my neck, and she was not letting go, so I picked her up and carried her to the kitchen. Putting her on one of the stools in front of the island, I moved toward the refrigerator to get the juice. I grabbed a cup and poured her juice when something occurred to me. Sliding the cup to her, I watched as she picked it up and put it to her mouth. "Is Seth still sleeping?"

She took a long drink before putting the cup back down on the island and swiped the back of her hand across her mouth. "Yeah, he's really sleepy."

The chime of the doorbell caught us both by surprise, and we shared a look of confusion. Sophie recovered quicker than I did, and she jumped to the floor, heading toward the front door, almost there before I caught up with her.

I moved around to stand in front of her, and she stopped, looking up at me. "Sophie, you aren't allowed to open the door without me, okay? It's not safe."

She sulked but nodded. "Okay."

I rubbed my hand down over the stubble on my cheek and faced the door, taking a deep breath before I pulled it open, worried what was going to come at me from the other side. I stepped back when Grace's smile was the first thing I saw and bumped into Sophie. I reached down and wrapped my hand around her arm when she stumbled to keep her from falling.

She saw Grace and squealed. "Grace!"

Grace giggled and squatted down, readily accepting Sophie's hug. "Hey, Sophie girl."

"Did you come to play?" She looked behind Grace toward the driveway. "Did you bring Lexi and Mia?"

"No sweetie, I didn't, I'm sorry. Maybe next time." Grace stood and smiled at me, but it wasn't the smile I'd come to expect from her. I shifted uncomfortably when she was quiet, the heat from her stare consuming me, stopping me from making any kind of move.

"Can you come in and see me?" Sophie wrapped her hand around Grace's and tugged, but Grace didn't move. I realized she was waiting for me to agree.

I backed up and motioned for her to come in. "Yeah, come in."

She smiled softly at me when she passed, being pulled closely behind Sophie who was heading for the kitchen. When she reached out and let her hand graze my shoulder, I stood completely still, my body and mind not cooperating with one other. She moved well past me and still I stood, forcing my body to relax in the knowledge that she was once again in my space.

And once again, I'd have to pretend I could handle that.

Chapter Seventeen

Grace

He doesn't want me here. The thought continued to play through my mind, making me feel insecure, more insecure than I was only yesterday morning when I walked into this house with two attorneys, knowing Tyler did not want me here. And here I was again, only twenty-four hours later, but it felt a lot longer, considering all that had happened.

I followed Sophie into the kitchen, not looking back, not wanting to see the disappointment again on Tyler's face. I'd gone too far yesterday. I knew I had, but I hadn't been able to stop myself once I started, and I thought maybe he felt the same. Only by the look on his face today, I knew that wasn't the case. I owed him an apology and I came to do just that, but first, I'd have to find a reason to get him alone. This wasn't a conversation I wanted to have with a five-year-old standing between us.

"Seth's awake!" Sophie yelled from the stool she had sat herself on.

I turned in time to see Seth grin at Sophie and walk slowly toward the kitchen. Tyler walked in behind him, heading straight to the cabinet, and pulled a cup down. "Wanna drink, kid?"

I bent my head down to hide my own grin when Tyler spoke. Seth nodded and slid onto another stool right beside where Sophie was sitting. Sophie bounced around on her stool wiping her mouth with the back of her hand after she set her cup back down. "He likes orange juice."

Tyler smiled her way, then turned and pulled the orange juice from the refrigerator before filling the cup and sliding it toward Seth.

Sophie swung her legs, staring at Tyler. "Can we have pancakes?"

The surprise and then confusion on his face didn't shock me. I doubted he had any food in his house for kids. By the way he was built, I'd even venture to say he's an all-protein kind of guy. I stood quietly, waiting for his answer along with Sophie and Seth, who continued to drink their juice.

"I don't have pancakes," he admitted.

"What do you have?" She squirmed in her seat while she tucked her legs up under her butt on the stool.

"Umm…" He ran his hand over his cheek. "Not much, really."

"Cereal?" He shook his head, and she frowned.

He scratched the back of his neck, and mumbled, "Maybe we should go to the store or something."

"Okay!" Sophie beamed. "Can we go to breakfast at the Pancake House?" She motioned between her and Seth. "That's our favorite."

"Uhh…yeah sure." He looked them over. "Go get dressed, I guess."

They both jumped down, heading for the stairs when Sophie turned back around. "Grace, can you come for pancakes too?"

I looked down at her sweet face and melted, but I couldn't agree. Not yet anyway. "Well, I need to talk to Tyler for a minute, so how about I tell you when you come back down?"

She nodded excitedly before grabbing Seth's hand and running toward the stairs. I turned to face Tyler, but he already had his back to me, putting their cups in the sink. I closed my eyes and rubbed my hand across my forehead. Opening them, I saw he was once again turned toward me, but his eyes were moving around the room.

"Tyler," I started, his attention still anywhere but me. That wasn't going to work. "Can you look at me?"

His eyes flicked to mine slowly, and he crossed his arms over his chest. I sighed; this was going to be embarrassing. "Listen, I came to apologize." I moved around the island until I stood in front of him. "I shouldn't have embarrassed you like that yesterday." I threw my hand out to the side. "I was just so mad at my brothers, and I wanted to make a point that they have no say in my life, but I know that made you uncomfortable, and we're…" I gestured between us. "Well, that's not what we are." I grabbed the end of my ponytail and ran strands of my hair through my fingers. "I'm really sorry."

"I'm not mad," he mumbled.

I let out a sigh of relief. "Okay, wow, that's a relief." I took another step closer. "Thank you."

He nodded, but I watched his throat work as he swallowed hard. "Things good with your brothers now?" he asked, and my eyes widened in surprise. I wouldn't have expected him to ask.

"I don't know," I admitted. "I mean, it will be, but we haven't really talked. Charlie and I stayed at the party for a while, but we avoided them." I huffed out a sarcastic laugh. "Not very mature I know, but my brothers are so overprotective." I took a step closer to him and laid my hand on his arm. "Don't take anything they said personally, Tyler, they don't like most people in my life, well not of the male variety anyway."

"They're right."

My eyebrows shot up in surprise. "What do you mean?"

He took a step back and put his hands on his narrow jeans-clad hips, his expression blank and I let my hand drop to my side again. "If I had a sister, I wouldn't want her around a guy like me."

"It's none of their business who I spend my time with, Tyler." I narrowed my eyes. "And what do you mean, a guy like you?"

"Nothing." He grunted before his gaze shifted from mine across the room, staring hard at the stairs.

I sighed, wanting to hear what he had to say, but I knew the conversation was over. I followed his line of sight and jerked my thumb back over my shoulder toward the stairs. "How are they? Did they do okay after you left the party?"

He sighed. "I took them back to my dad's house to pick up more things, which they seemed to like, but then they were both quiet on the way home, so I'm not sure that was the best decision."

Sympathy for this little family swelled inside me. "It might just take some time. They're still processing this. You all are."

He ran his hand along his cheek and dropped his head, shaking it side to side. "I don't know what the fuck I'm doing with them."

I laid my hand along his arm, unable to stop myself from touching him when he looked so lost. "You'll learn. You just need time."

He huffed out a sarcastic laugh. "With Seth, I'm okay, but Sophie…" He ran his hand through his hair and that was when I noticed the exhaustion in his features. "I don't know. Like last night, I told her to go shower, but she told me I needed to go in with her and help her wash her hair. Then she wanted me to brush it and help her choose pajamas." His eyes met mine. "I don't know anything about little girls."

"You don't have to know everything, Ty. You'll learn as you go. I promise, you'll learn." I leaned my hip against the island. "Did they sleep okay?"

He swallowed again and shook his head. "No."

My stomach dropped, and I shuffled closer, once again closing the distance between us and laid my hand flat against his chest. "What happened?"

He ran his hand around the back of his neck, tension emanating from his body, but he didn't step away. "Sophie wanted Tara. I didn't know what the hell to say to her, so in the end, they both crawled into bed with me. I woke up this morning when Sophie kicked me in the nose hard enough that my eyes watered." I rolled my lips to contain the grin, but he wasn't fooled. I saw his lips tip up at the corners, a huff of real laughter escaping him. "She moves a lot in her sleep."

I smiled softly, sympathy and appreciation for him washing over me. "What are you going to do?"

"I don't know." He stepped back, my hand falling from his chest when he did. And I felt it like a loss. "Jeffrey said there's a grief counselor social services recommended, so I guess after the funeral tomorrow, I'll get the information from him and call to set something up."

"That's probably a good idea."

He nodded. "Yeah."

I waited, not surprised when he didn't say more, but something occurred to me. "What about school?"

He scowled. "Fuck. I didn't even think about school." He shoved his hand in his pocket and pulled out his phone, tapping on the screen before placing it against his ear.

"Grace!"

I turned when I heard Sophie's voice and smiled when I saw her running toward me with a hairbrush in her hand. "Hey, beautiful girl."

She beamed and stopped in front of me. "Can you braid my hair?"

"Absolutely. Jump up on the stool."

She moved to climb onto the stool, handing the hairbrush to me. "Do you like my dress?"

Looking at the light blue sundress with small daisies all over it, I grinned. "I love it."

She seemed pleased and settled back in her seat while I ran the brush through her long brown hair. With practiced ease, I started braiding her hair, having done it not only to myself but also to Charlie for years before she finally cut hers. She said she'd never learn how to do more than put it in a ponytail, so why not just cut it off.

I watched Tyler walk back into the house through the door off the kitchen as I was braiding, but his expression was blank. I waited as patiently as I could for maybe a minute before I had to ask. "What did he say?"

Tyler looked up from the phone he was still staring at in his palm, almost like he'd forgotten I was here or anyone was here for that matter. His eyes met mine briefly before softening when he looked down at Sophie sitting on the stool, holding very still while my fingers continued to work. "He said he'll call the school in the morning and explain, knowing they'll be excused at least for the week, but he said if the kids need more time, he's sure they'll accommodate us. I need to go there anyway and show my guardianship paperwork so they know I'm the contact person now. I guess I'll go Tuesday."

"I like school," Sophie announced, just as I heard footsteps behind me. Turning my head, I saw Seth standing just to the side wearing shorts and a T-shirt.

"Do you like school too Seth?" I asked quietly.

He shrugged, right before he said quietly, "It's okay."

"The bullies are mean to Seth on the bus. I told them to shut up, but they don't listen." Sophie turned her head, causing me to pause my fingers to take in her serious expression. "They're mean, mean boys."

"Bullies." Tyler's deep timbre caused goose bumps to break out across my arms. My eyes shifted to him, and I felt a shiver run through my body at the level of intensity in his eyes. "What do they do?"

"Nothing." Seth said quietly, his face once again pointed at the ground.

My eyes flicked from Seth back to Tyler whose expression was stern. "No more bus."

Sophie's eyes widened. "How will we get to school?"

He cleared his throat. "I'll take you."

Seth's head snapped up, his expression confused. "You will?" he asked quietly.

104

He nodded, his eyes focused entirely on Seth. I shifted so Sophie could still watch her brothers and quickly finished her braid, grabbing the small rubber band to wrap around the end.

"Do they bother you at school?" Tyler asked Seth.

"Sometimes," Seth replied, his voice barely above a whisper.

I moved around so I could see Sophie and the boys at the same time. She rolled her eyes. "All the time."

Seth shot a glare in Sophie's direction, but she crossed her arms over her chest, almost daring him to deny it.

Tyler cleared his throat. "I'll take care of it." He grabbed his keys from the counter and moved past Seth who was gawking at his back and Sophie who was smiling wide. I waited, wondering what he was going to do next when he swung open the front door and looked back at us. He gestured outside. "Are we going for pancakes?"

Sophie jumped down from the stool and took off running through the open door, Seth moving quickly behind her. I followed but stopped in the doorway to face Tyler with my back pressed against the doorjamb. Looking out toward the driveway, I saw the back door of Tyler's SUV close. I let my eyes drift back to Tyler, who stood completely still.

I gestured toward the driveway with my hand. "That was really sweet. What you just did for Seth, I mean. I'm sure just driving him to school will make a huge difference." I pushed away from the jamb and put my hand on his arm. "But Ty, you can't protect him all day at school from the bullies."

He leaned down so his face was close to mine, close enough that his scent surrounded me. I took a deep breath, unconsciously moving my body even closer, drawn to him in a way I'd never been drawn to anyone. When he spoke, a shiver once again ran through me. "They're my family, my only family, and I will always protect what's mine."

I gulped when he stood straight and stepped outside, motioning for me to step out in front of him. I did, lost in the realization that he sounded just like my brothers. Every single one of them would have said those exact words. I couldn't help but wonder what made Tyler change his mind about the kids and their place in his life over the past twenty-four hours, but I was happy he had.

I felt the door swing closed behind me and started down the sidewalk toward the driveway, still lost in the memory of the hardness in Tyler's eyes when he said those words. There were so many sides to him, so many versions I'd seen of him over the few times we'd been around each other that I felt a little lost.

I walked right past his SUV, in a daze, only stopping when I heard his low voice call out to me. "You coming?"

Turning around, I stopped and stared, hesitating before I threw my hands out to the sides. "What?"

He opened the passenger door and gestured inside. "To breakfast. You comin'?"

I exhaled heavily; my brow furrowed as I slowly made my way back to where he stood. Standing in the doorway, I faced him, but his expression, like always, was unreadable. "You're a complicated man, Tyler Morgan."

He didn't answer, and I wasn't surprised, so I climbed up into the seat and waited for him to close the door he was still holding open with his hand. When he didn't immediately, I looked over and felt my stomach tighten because Tyler was staring at me, a wide grin on his face, showing off a dimple in his left cheek I never even knew he had. A dimple. How was it possible that a small indent in his cheek made him look boyish and sweet, made him seem approachable, and for a moment, I wondered how I ever thought he looked hard. When he dropped his head and moved back, closing the door and making his way around the front of the vehicle to his own door, I held my breath because I felt something.

Something I'd never felt before.

And it sure as hell wasn't friendship.

Chapter Eighteen

Tyler

I pulled at the knot on my tie; the knot that felt like it was choking me, draining the life out of me slowly. Or maybe it was where I was sitting. I watched people walk up the center aisle of the church to stand or kneel in front of the two caskets, some crying softly, some carrying their sadness like a visible weight. The attorney, Jeffrey, told me there would be one hour open to the public for viewing before the service began, and he felt I should be there with the kids. They sat beside me, huddled together, Seth up against my side, watching a video on their tablet with the sound turned off. I couldn't make them sit and watch people crying at the casket, so I needed them to be distracted. Hell, I wish I was distracted.

When a woman walked up the aisle, followed by two girls, something felt strangely familiar about her, but I couldn't place her. I didn't know most of these people, although a few retired players who my dad spent a lot of time with had shown and stopped to shake my hand, patting Seth and Sophie on the head, obviously as unsure what to say to them as I was. Jeffrey was there, as well as my attorney, and I was grateful for them both. I knew Jeffrey had gone above and beyond the call of duty for an attorney in this situation, but I realized Saturday he was doing it out of respect and friendship for my father. I'd wondered a few times if my father had asked him to because he knew I'd be lost, especially in regard to Sophie and Seth.

I glanced at the pews across the large church to see they were full and realized almost the entire church was full. We sat in the first pew on the opposite side of the church, and I knew without turning around that the three pews behind us were empty. I think people left them empty assuming immediate family for my dad would sit there. They were right, and we did, but it was only the three of us. I'd been an only child to my mother and father, who were both only children in their families. My grandparents were long since deceased, and we'd never been close with them while I was growing up. Seth, Sophie, and I were all he had left in his family besides his friends, which filled the remainder of the pews behind us.

When the woman I'd watched walk toward the front of the church moments ago moved away from the casket, she turned to face me, and even without the scowl she sent my way, I would've recognized her as Tara's mother. They resembled each other strongly, as did one of the girls moving behind her. The other had more strawberry blond hair, green eyes, and was tiny. She couldn't be more than five feet and a couple of inches tall. Her eyes shifted to me and then landed on the kids. She looked nervous but slowed down as her mom and sister moved past, taking seats on the other side of the church.

She stood at the end of the pew, her hands twisting together, and spoke softly. "Tyler, right?"

I nodded and cleared my throat. "Right. And you are?"

Sophie's head jerked up and she called out. "Aunt Natalie!"

She stood and climbed over her brother and me, throwing herself at Natalie who caught her with a smile. "Hey, tootsie."

She giggled but held her tight, and I knew this must be the sister Jeffrey told me was close to Tara; the one who, if older, would have been a good choice to raise the kids. Sophie stood on the pew but leaned away from Natalie and looked directly at Seth. "Look Seth, it's Aunt Natalie."

Seth smiled shyly and held up his hand in a wave, which Natalie returned. "Hi, Seth."

"Aunt Natalie," Sophie said loudly, but lowered her voice when Natalie put her finger against her own lips, showing Sophie to talk a little quieter. "Can you come see me at Tyler's?"

Natalie smiled sadly. "I'm not sure, honey. Maybe we can talk about it later."

Sophie's smile dropped, her mouth opening to object, but I was already prepared to interrupt. "You can come anytime. I'll get your number from Jeffrey and text you the address."

Natalie beamed and swallowed hard. "Thank you, Tyler. I'll... um... I'll come alone."

I nodded, having the feeling she was used to that. I assumed her sister and mother hadn't been welcome at my dad's house either. She chatted with Sophie for another minute, then gave me and Seth another smile and a small wave before heading across the church to sit with her family.

"Grace," Sophie said in a loud whisper. Her little face swung toward me, her eyes wide. "Look, Tyler, Grace came."

I turned in my seat slightly, along with Seth who got up on his knees beside me, and put his hand on my shoulder, trying to see where Sophie pointed. I spotted Grace right away. It was as if my eyes knew exactly where they'd find her.

Grace lifted her hand in a small wave, but Sophie wasn't having that. "Tyler, can Grace come sit with us? Can everyone?"

My eyes hadn't left Grace until Sophie's voice broke through, and I thought about what she said. My head jerked her way. "What?"

"Can they sit with us?"

Still not understanding, I followed her finger when she pointed at the back of the large church and felt something wash over me, a feeling I couldn't identify. My eyes scanned over the entire Dimarco family lining the last few pews in the church on the side I was sitting with the kids. All the Dimarcos and spouses filled those pews, plus some other faces I recognized, like Chase, and some I didn't were sitting all together. My eyes finally landed on Jack Dimarco, who nodded his head, and that was all, but that was all I needed. I swallowed hard, completely in awe that a family who just met us would take time to be here today.

"Can they?" Sophie asked again.

"Yeah," I answered. I couldn't even remember her question, but before I could ask, she jumped down from the bench seat and made her way back the long aisle until she stood in front of Grace who was sitting near the end of the pew sandwiched between her brother Jake and Charlie. Sophie's arm flew out to the sides as if she was saying something was big, and Grace smiled. She turned her head and looked down the length of the pew and said something to her family who all looked at each other until an older woman, who had to be Grace's mom from resemblance alone, stood. Then they all stood and filed out of the pews they were sitting in while Sophie took Grace's hand in her own and walked beside her up the aisle toward Seth and me. Seth pushed himself closer into my side when he saw the line of people following his sister to the front of the church.

"Is this okay?" Grace asked softly when Sophie came to stand beside our pew.

I nodded but again had no words. I moved down so Sophie could sit beside me and Grace on her other side, Charlie stealing the end seat. I felt people moving in to the pews behind us and closed my eyes. I heard whispering, but I didn't open my eyes until Seth's weight shifted a little off me. Looking over, I saw Andy had sat down beside him, and they had their heads tucked close together, both now watching the silent video. My eyes flicked up to Luke, who gave me a chin lift that I returned before looking at his other side to see Kate tucked in close, Lanie, Bray on her lap, and

Jake on the other side of her, all names and faces I knew because Grace had told me, not because I'd really spoken to any of them. I didn't allow myself to look behind me because I already knew all those empty pews were full, and that strange feeling once again washed over me.

I felt a hand lay on my shoulder and squeeze, so I turned my head slightly, my eyes meeting Jack's for a moment and then his wife's. She offered me a small smile. Grace's smile. I was confused as to why they were all here, and as usual, the right words, the appropriate words, failed me. "Why are you here?"

I knew the words sounded bad. I heard them the same as everyone else, but I was surprised when Jack tilted his head for a moment as if he was considering something and squeezed my shoulder again. "We're here for you."

"You don't know me." I pointed out what was logical to me.

Jack leaned forward, his face serious, but his eyes were sad. "No one should have to go through hard times alone. And no one in our life ever will."

I slowly turned back around, looking to my left to see Sophie had repositioned herself to Grace's lap and was playing with the necklace that hung around her neck, laying on the top of her simple black dress. Simple probably on most, but not on Grace. Nothing was simple on or about Grace.

"Mr. Morgan?" My head snapped up to see the priest bending over slightly at the front of our pew. "Shall I begin?"

I swallowed hard and closed my eyes slowly. If he began, it was real. I wasn't ready for it to be real. I felt the air shift, and Grace's soft perfume envelop me when she moved. Her hand reached over and wrapped around mine, her body close, her leg brushing against my own, and I took a deep breath, exhaling slowly. Opening my eyes, I looked her way, and she squeezed my hand gently. I pulled my attention from her and looked again at the elderly priest. The priest who had married my dad and Tara. I remembered him. I remembered liking him.

I was suddenly relieved they'd chosen him, someone who'd known them when they were happy, known them when they were excited and hopeful, planning a family, and dreaming of their lives together. Lives that were stolen from them, from us.

I took another deep breath and nodded, my trademark nod when words failed me, which was more often than not. This time, however, I forced myself to speak for my father. "You can begin."

When he walked toward the front of the church and positioned himself between the two caskets, I finally accepted my dad was really gone.

And I hated myself.

Because I never once told him how much I'd loved him.

Chapter Nineteen

Grace

"How's the new book coming along?"

Fiddling with the corner of the napkin my margarita was sitting on, I glanced at Charlie but hadn't heard what she said, only that she spoke. "Hmm?"

She leaned forward. "I said, how's the new book coming along? What's going on with you tonight?"

I sighed. "I don't know." Picking up my drink, I relaxed my shoulders and rested my back against the soft padding on the pub stool.

She tilted her head to the side. "Is it your brothers?"

I shook my head. "No, I haven't talked to any of them since the funeral."

Her eyebrows raised almost to her hairline. "Really? Not even Jake?"

I took a sip from my glass and licked the salt from my lips before responding. "Nope. Don't get me wrong, I was grateful and proud of all of them for going to the funeral, especially proud that Jax and Brody were able to keep their opinions to themselves for the day, but I don't like how they treated me or Tyler so I've decided to lay low for a while. Stay out of everyone's way and give them a chance to settle down some."

"And are they?" She looked skeptical. "Settling, I mean."

"I talked to my mom yesterday, and she said the boys have all been working, but she anticipates seeing them on Sunday for dinner." I frowned. "She wants me there too."

"That doesn't sound fun." Her forehead wrinkled. "Which is sad because Sunday dinner at your parents' house is awesome."

I sat forward in my seat. "You should come with me."

She was shaking her head no before I finished the sentence. "Not this time, Grace."

"Because of Ben?"

"It's just time I separate a little," she admitted quietly.

I sat up straight and reached across the small pub table, laying my hand over hers. "Charlie, you're family. You know that. You can't just separate."

Her eyes moved to the table where they stayed for a long moment before she lifted them to meet mine. "I need a break. I need to kickstart my life, maybe start dating again. I don't know. I just need something to change."

I could understand that, but something told me there was a lot more going on with my friend that she wasn't ready to talk about yet. She would when she was ready, that was how it'd always been and I'd always accepted that about her. Sometimes, she'd just step away for a while, from me, from life, from everything. I hated it, always have, but I accepted it. She was my friend, my best friend, my sister, and I'd do anything for her, including let her hide for a while to sort out whatever needed sorting.

She glanced away, and something caught her eye, causing her to sit up straighter, and she did it smiling. I glanced behind me but didn't see anything. Confused, I looked back at Charlie. "What?"

She leaned in and lowered her voice. "There's a man at the bar who was looking back here."

I widened my eyes. "So?"

"He's exactly your type. Blond hair." She craned her neck a little and squinted her eyes. "I can't really tell his build, but he looks tall and lanky the way he's sitting." She wiggled her eyebrows, making me laugh. "You should go over there. He's been glancing over at you since we sat down."

"No."

She put her elbow on the table and leaned her chin on her open palm. "Why not?"

Her innocent expression wasn't fooling me. I narrowed my eyes. "Just say what you want to say."

She laughed and leaned her head to the side, her blond hair just skimming the top of her shoulder. "I just thought a cute guy might be exactly what you need to stop thinking about Tyler Morgan."

I rolled my eyes, but honestly, she wasn't wrong. I was thinking about him and had been since the funeral this past Monday. He looked so lost, the kids looked lost, and it was all I could do not to wrap my arms around him and hug him close. He needed a hug, still did, but I doubt he'd welcome it. Not from me, not from anyone.

After the funeral, we all went to the graveside, and I held my breath as both Sophie and Seth reached their little hands up to hold Tyler's while they watched the two caskets being lowered into the ground. After a prayer was said and the priest closed his prayer book, he nodded at Tyler, but Tyler wasn't looking at him. He was looking at the caskets. I'd slowly made my way to stand beside the little family as people started moving away, heading for their vehicles. Even though I had no idea what to say, I wanted to be there for them all the same. After a few minutes, he'd turned and the pain in his eyes almost brought me to my knees. I'd swallowed back the tears threatening again to fall and smiled softly down at Sophie who looked confused. I hadn't been surprised when my parents stepped forward, welcoming Tyler and the kids to their house, and even extending the offer if he'd like to invite people from the funeral, but he declined. He said he had to meet with the attorney to do paperwork or something. I didn't know if that was true or if he'd just wanted to be alone, but either way, he got what he wanted, and with Seth and Sophie in tow, he'd headed for his SUV. I'd watched him get in and sit for another moment, just staring forward, seemingly lost again in his own mind, which didn't seem the best place to be.

"Thinking about him again?"

Charlie's voice brought me out of my thoughts, and I met her all-knowing expression. I brought my palm to my forehead and rested against it. "What's wrong with me, Charlie? Why can't I stop thinking about him?"

"You like him."

I pulled my hand down and grabbed my drink once again, putting it to my lips for a sip. I met her eyes over the rim of my glass, knowing I didn't need to say the words for her to know she was right. We'd been friends long enough for her to read me well.

"Why haven't you gone over to see him?" Her eyebrows lifted in surprise. "I mean, it's Friday night, I figured you'd have been to his house three or four times by now trying to help out."

I laughed softly because she was right. Normally, I would've at least called to see if he needed help with anything, but I hadn't, and it was a little embarrassing to admit why. Blinking slowly, I took a deep breath and exhaled. "I don't know what I'm doing with him, Charlie. He has me off balance. I can't even tell if he likes me as just as a friend, let alone anything more."

"Grace," she said softly, "he may have you a little off balance, but you are the best judge of character I've ever met. You have the best instincts."

"But that's just it." I leaned forward. "This time, my instincts aren't working. I can't..." I lifted my shoulders in frustration. "I have no idea when I've been with him if he even wanted me around. He gives me nothing."

"That's not true," Charlie said.

"What do you mean?"

"The way he kissed you in Jake's kitchen, Grace." She smiled sadly. "If anyone ever kissed me like that, if anyone held on to me that tightly like I was the only thing he saw, the only thing he needed at that moment, well, I just think if I ever had that, I wouldn't let it go so easily."

"You can't let go of something you never actually had, Charlie," I said softly.

She sat quietly for a minute, but I watched her expression change from conflicted to acceptance. "You're right," she agreed, "but don't let go of the chance. Do it for yourself. Do it for all us girls who've never even had the chance."

"And if he rejects me?"

"Then you do what women have been doing for a long time. You pick yourself up, brush yourself off, and move on." She raised her glass. "Well, right after you tell everyone you know what a douche he is, of course."

I laughed and lifted my glass, clinking it with hers. "Of course."

We both took a drink, laughing together, which felt good, considering I hadn't felt much like laughing lately.

Charlie glanced over my shoulder and glared. "Crap."

"What?" I said, turning my head slightly to look over my shoulder in time to watch Ben walk to the bar and talk to the bartender, Logan, both of them laughing. Shaking my head, I moved to face Charlie again when the cute guy at the bar caught my attention and smiled. I returned it but then turned quickly toward Charlie, who was looking down at her hands wrapped around the bottom of her glass.

"I'm sorry," I said.

She looked up and smiled, but her eyes were sad. "You have nothing to apologize for."

"He's my brother." I rolled my eyes, hoping I could make her laugh and felt nothing but relief when she did. But her laughter was short-lived when Ben's voice interrupted us.

"Hey."

He set his beer down with a thud on our table, and we both glanced over, but I was the only one to speak. "What are you doing here, Ben?"

His eyes flicked over to Charlie, who was staring at her glass, before landing on me again. "Looking for you two."

"Why?" I leaned forward, putting my elbows on the table. "Did something happen?"

He ran his hand around the back of his neck and sighed. "No, nothing happened. Just wanted to talk to you. Figured I'd wait until you were drinking so you'd go easier on me."

Charlie glanced over at Ben, whose eyes were now settled on her, but she didn't say anything, and when he didn't either, I decided to help him along. "You owe Charlie an apology, you know."

"I know that." He answered me, but his eyes stayed on my friend. He took a deep breath, exhaling slowly, I assumed trying to work around his pride to apologize. My brothers were not known for their apologies, so if they gave you one, you knew it was sincere.

"I shouldn't have said what I did, Charlie. I know you'd never do shit like that to Grace." He ran his hand through his hair when she stayed quiet. "I was pissed and worried about both of you." He leaned down, placing his elbows to the table, putting his face closer to Charlie's. "You're like a sister to me, you know that. I can't stand to see you hurt or taken advantage of any more than I can Grace."

He grabbed her hand and held it in his. "I don't want you mad at me." He stood again and turned his face toward me. "Either of you."

I sighed and turned to Charlie. "What do you think? Should we actually let him off the hook?"

She pulled her hand from his and picked up her glass, her eyes now on me. "I don't know. His apology was pretty weak." She gestured with her glass in Ben's direction. "Almost sounded like something he got from a Hallmark card or something."

I laughed when Ben lunged for Charlie and threw his arms around her, making her squeal. I watched them tease each other, relief all over Ben's face and a smile that could light the room on Charlie's.

Taking a sip of my drink, I turned toward the bar when I felt the heat of someone's stare on me but saw no one. I chuckled to myself, knowing it was from one too many sleepless nights lately, wondering if Tyler felt anything for me but indifference.

I decided right then, margarita in hand, listening to my brother and best friend laughing across the small table, that I was done wondering.

Chapter Twenty

Tyler

"Yeah?" I scrubbed my hand down over my face and blinked, trying to wake up.

"Ty?"

I took a deep breath and exhaled, before pushing up to a sitting position, bracing my back against the headboard. Looking down at the bed, I saw both Seth and Sophie had again, crawled into bed with me at some point last night. I was grateful I had a king-sized bed. Otherwise, we wouldn't all fit with my size. "Yeah?"

"It's Dex. What the fuck, man? Why didn't you call me? I just found out about your dad."

I was surprised for a moment. Dex had played alongside me all through college. He was one of the best wide receivers I'd ever seen play the game, but when I was drafted to Seattle, he was heading to Miami. We'd talked over the years while I still played, often meeting up if we were near the other's hometown, but really hadn't over the last two. That was my fault. He'd tried, but I was always distant and a dick when he called. "Why would I call?"

"Jesus." He snorted. "Same old Ty. Why the hell wouldn't you think I'd want to know? I'd have been at the funeral if I had."

I had no words. Why would he come? I'd treated him like shit and ignored him for the past two years. "Umm...yeah, I didn't think about it."

"Yeah, well, I'm pissed, man. We've been friends a long damn time. You should've called."

I ran my hand across the back of my neck before I swung my legs over the side of the bed and stood. I knew I should say something, but I was stumped, so I waited, knowing he'd take the lead if I stayed silent.

"Anyway, doesn't matter. I'm getting my rental right now. I should be at your place in an hour or so."

My head snapped up. "What?"

"We're on a bye week, man, and I'm heading over to spend the weekend with you. I have to be back for practice Tuesday. I told Coach what was going on, and he gave me an extra day off, so get your moody ass in the shower and get dressed." I heard a door slam and an engine turn over before he continued. "Don't bother telling me not to come. I gave you enough time to get your shit sorted. I miss seeing your ugly face, so I'm coming."

I looked down and saw the call had been disconnected, but I still stood in place and stared at the now blank screen. Dex was coming to my house. He'd been here before, right after I moved in. I was still recuperating, pissed off at the world, and working out like a fiend trying to get a doctor to release me so I could play again. Seattle had already ended my contract and replaced me, but I was willing to be a free agent if I could have gotten well enough to be signed, but it never happened. He'd stayed two weeks and watched me wallow in my misery before he had to leave for training camp. He still called and texted, but not as much, and over the years, I became more and more distant.

I threw my phone down on the nightstand and headed for the shower, turning it on to hot and wondering how I was going to handle another person in my space. It had been a long week with Seth and Sophie, but thankfully, the grief counselor was able to see them on Wednesday and will see them together once a week for as long as they need her. I knew she was going to be a good fit when I met her. She's probably in her fifties and has a very soft way about her, including being tremendously soft-spoken. Seth took to her immediately, which made it easier to leave them while I sat in the waiting room, nervous as hell that they were going to come out worse than they went in, crying and upset, but they both came out smiling, showing me the pictures they had made. She told me she was happy to see them weekly and felt they should come together, but leaned in and whispered she felt for Seth's benefit that would be important. I loved that she understood his limitations. Maybe she could help him in ways I couldn't.

I moved from the shower and dressed quickly, glancing behind me one more time to see Seth and Sophie still sleeping. I would need to talk to the therapist about them sleeping in my bed and ask her what I should do. I always put them to bed at night in their own rooms, but I wake up every morning with two little people shoved up against me and taking up most of the bed.

Making my way downstairs, I made coffee and headed outside to put the horses out, hot coffee in my hand. The cool morning breeze felt good as I worked through my morning routine and headed back inside. I wanted Sophie to hear me moving around downstairs if she woke up. We hadn't had a repeat of the last time, but I can still hear her cry in my mind sometimes when I think about that morning. I'd never want to hear her cry in fear again.

I was barely back in my kitchen when I heard the doorbell and made my way to the front door, still shocked I'd be opening it to someone who should've written me off a long time ago.

I swung it open and couldn't stop the grin pulling at my lips when I was face to face with one of the only friends I'd had in college. He moved through the door and gave me a one-armed hug, slapping me hard on the back of my shoulder. "Hey, man."

I stepped back so he could move past me into the house where he dropped his bag and turned to face me. I closed the door and put my hands on my hips. "I can't believe you're here."

He smirked. "I almost didn't call and just showed up, but I figured you'd have a fucking panic attack or something."

I couldn't help but chuckle. Matt Dexter was the only person who didn't give a shit how moody I was or how much of an asshole; he teased me for it, and we moved on. "See you haven't changed either."

He laughed. "Why the fuck would I change? Look at me."

I actually laughed along with him, almost forgetting how he'd tried to come off cocky, and he did to some, but I knew him, really knew him, and he was kind of a nerd. It was why we hit it off right away. We both felt a little like misfits.

"That's a really bad word."

I snickered when I heard Sophie's voice and turned to see her standing just inside the living room, staring at us. When I glanced back at Dex, I saw the confusion on his face and knew I needed to explain. I gestured for Sophie to come over, which she did and stood beside me.

"Sophie, this is my friend Dex."

She wrinkled her nose. "That's a funny name."

Dex chuckled. "Dex is my nickname. You can call me Matt if you want."

She beamed, so I looked at Dex and explained. "Sophie's my little sister. She and our brother, Seth, are living with me now. I'm their guardian."

Understanding moved across his face, and he jerked up his chin at me. Breaking the silence, Sophie spoke up. "Did you come for breakfast?"

"Yep." Dex smiled down at her again. "And I'm staying the whole weekend."

Her face lit up, and she clapped her hands together. "Yay! I love sleepovers. I'll go tell Seth. He'll be excited too."

"I see she didn't get your genes, huh?" I heard him tease and turned from where I was watching Sophie bound back up the stairs.

Grinning, I shook my head. "No, she didn't. But Seth did."

Dex reached out and put his hand on my shoulder, squeezing. "Fuck, sorry, man. This has to be a huge fucking adjustment for you."

"Yeah, it has been." I shook off the sadness threatening to overwhelm me and motioned toward the kitchen. "Want some coffee?"

"Absolutely."

He followed me to the kitchen where I dumped another coffee pod in the machine and slid a mug under. Grabbing the milk from the refrigerator, I set it down in front of him before turning back and grabbing the now ready cup of coffee.

"I have some news."

I lifted my head at the seriousness of his tone. "What news?"

He added milk to his coffee, and I waited for him to look back up, surprised when I saw his serious expression. "I'm retiring."

I leaned my hip against the counter, facing him. "You're only twenty-nine."

"Actually, I'll be thirty next month."

"Why would you retire now?" I shook my head, confused.

"Because I'm done." He ran his hand around the back of his neck and continued. "I'm tired of the constant pain, tired of the hits that feel a hell of a lot harder than they used to, tired of feeling like I'm fifty years old because my knees and shoulders hurt so damn bad." His took a drink, and I waited for him to continue, which he eventually did. "I told you in college this was a short-term plan for me, man."

I nodded because he had, and even then, I remember wondering why he would only want this career short-term, but I'd never asked. "That why you're here?"

He scowled. "I'm here because my friend just buried his father, and he was the only family he had left." He contemplated that. "Well, at least that's what I thought."

I thought of Seth and Sophie and realized I'd probably never

124

even told him about them. Back in college, I did all I could to pretend my dad hadn't moved on and started a new family. Hell, up until a week ago, I did that as an adult.

"I wanted to come tell you in person, anyway." He raised his wide shoulders. "I figured you wouldn't understand why I'd voluntarily walk away from the game."

"I don't," I admitted. "I'd do anything to play again."

"You were going to die playing that game, Ty, and you almost did. I watched that and realized I didn't love the sport enough to give it my body and my life. I want to do other things. I still love tech shit, still always messing around with gaming. I want a chance to do it and do it while I can still walk and feed myself."

I grinned at his exaggeration, which was only slight. We knew of retired players who were so crippled that getting out of bed was a hardship for them. "What's your plan?"

He sat back and crossed his arms over his chest. "I'll finish this season. Doubt the team will make it to the play-offs; we just don't have the talent this year. It's a young team minus a few of us, and the kid taking my place is good, really good. Better than I ever fucking was, Ty."

"I don't believe that. You're an amazing receiver."

"I was Ty, but I'm losing my edge. I just don't feel the same rush anymore, so it's time to go. I told Coach. He didn't like it, but he was cool with it. My contract's up this year anyway."

"Then what?"

He smirked. "Well, then I thought I might move here and spend some time with my friend, trying to figure out my next move."

My jaw dropped a little. "You're moving to North Carolina?"

"Don't have much family, Ty, you know that. Only went to college because I got the football scholarship, which I was thankful for, but no reason to go back there. Thought this might be a good next step."

I thought about it for a minute and made a decision. "Wanna stay here while you figure shit out?"

He laughed. "Like college again, really? Don't you already have enough people living here?"

"It's a big fucking house. Plenty of room."

He looked around the large kitchen and into the living room, then his eyes wandered to the stairs. "You sure?"

"Yeah."

"Then, yeah, man, I'd love that. Except I'm guessing in this place we won't have the revolving door of girls."

I laughed. "Nah, I already scared most of them off anyway."

He threw his head back laughing and I realized it had been too damn long since I let myself laugh, let myself enjoy time with anyone.

Let myself have a friend.

Chapter Twenty-one

Grace

Sitting in Tyler's driveway, I took a deep breath and exhaled slowly. I hadn't heard from him, and I'd given him my number after the funeral, telling him if he needed anything that he could always call me.

He hadn't.

And now I was sitting in his driveway, and I was so nervous, I couldn't even manage to pull myself out of the car. I was overwhelmed with insecurity, which I hated because as much as I appeared confident, and in some ways I was, relationships with men had always been difficult for me. A lot of it had to do with my brothers while I was growing up, and I think that lack of experience in high school caused me to question myself with men and my understanding of their behaviors. I just couldn't read them. And I absolutely couldn't read Tyler. I wasn't even sure he wanted my friendship, let alone anything more, but for some reason, I couldn't stay away from him. He wasn't my type, he wasn't even someone I could imagine dating or having a relationship with, but I couldn't forget how it felt to have his big hands on me, wrapped in my hair, let alone his lips on mine. Running my hand through my hair, I took another deep breath, and wondered why there was another SUV parked in the driveway right beside Tyler's, but this one was silver, not black like Tyler's. Did he have company?

Honestly, none of that mattered when I obviously had feelings for him. I was only stalling, and it was time to go in his house and really feel this out. I was either going to be a part of his life in some way or I wasn't, but I needed to know, so if I wasn't, I could just move on. Pushing the car door open, I stepped out and ran my hands over my hair, smoothing it down, wondering not for the first time why I spent so much time doing it this morning. I was glad I'd only put on jeans and a T-shirt, so at least I didn't look like I tried so hard even though this was the third outfit I'd put on before leaving my apartment.

I slammed my car door and made my way quickly up the driveway to the door, not giving myself time to change my mind again. Knocking, I waited, hearing voices on the other side getting closer and closer until the door was pulled open and a small body hit my legs.

"Grace!"

My eyes immediately flicked down, and I ran my hand over Sophie's smooth brown hair. "Hey, beautiful."

She grabbed my hand and moved forward, pulling me along with her. Looking to my left, I saw Tyler standing beside the still open door and smiled. "Hey, Tyler."

He stared at me a moment, long enough to make my nerves kick back up before he nodded and closed the door behind me. "Hey, Grace."

I dropped my eyes. He didn't look happy to see me. Actually, he almost seemed annoyed. I glanced down at Sophie again, determined to spend a little time with her, and then go. It'd been stupid to come.

She tugged on my hand again, bouncing on her toes. "Guess what?" she said excitedly. "Tyler's friend came to see us, and we're going to the Pancake House. I'll go get Seth; he's outside playing with the horses."

I watched her skip away before my head snapped up, and I looked across the room, seeing a really good-looking guy. Honestly, who was I kidding, he was ridiculously hot, and he was smiling at me. He started toward me, and I returned his smile. "Hi, I'm Matt Dexter." He gestured with his head toward Tyler. "Friend of this guy."

He got to me and held out his hand. I slid mine into his cool, firm grip. "Hi Matt, I'm Grace."

He dropped my hand when Tyler came to stand beside me, not close, but near enough that my pulse picked up. Damn him. "You can call me Dex, all my friends do." He gestured toward Ty. "So, Grace, how do you know my boy?"

I lifted my hand and tucked a piece of hair behind my ear. "Umm…" I had no idea how to explain the way we met without telling him that Tyler had been arrested. I didn't know if he wanted him to know that.

"She works for my attorney." Tyler's deep voice broke the uncomfortable silence. "Picked me up at the jail."

I turned my head to look at him but saw his eyes were locked on his friend who was chuckling. "That shit still happening to you, man?"

I saw a grin spread across Tyler's face, and my eyes moved quickly between the two men. "What do you mean?"

Dex's eyes glanced between the two of us, a wide smile on his face. "Back in college, on the rare occasions Ty would go out with us to celebrate a win or something, there was always a guy who would think he was tough enough to take him on. It was like Ty had a fucking target on his back or something."

"What would happen?" I let my gaze flick back and forth between them again, enjoying the smile gracing Tyler's face. He actually looked happy.

Dex crossed his arms over his chest and leaned back, still smiling.

"Ty would kick his ass, his friends' asses, and then we'd leave."

Tyler looked over at me, a small smile on his face, that damn dimple winking in his cheek. "He's exaggerating."

He grinned. "Not by much, man."

"You helped with the friends," Tyler said.

He rocked back on his heels. "Ahh, the good ole days."

Tyler chuckled, and I looked over in disbelief, seeing a side of him that I'd had yet to see. I smiled and watched his eyes drop to my lips before the grin disappeared from his own. Aaand…we were back to disliking me again.

"Grace." My eyes moved away from Tyler's and landed on Sophie and Seth coming toward me. "Are you coming with us?" She bounced on her toes. "Can I ride with you?"

I giggled, unable to stop it, because she was just so entertaining. I looked over at her brother. "Hi, Seth."

His cheeks turned pink, but his eyes stayed on mine. "Hi, Grace."

"Can you, can you, can you?" Sophie chanted.

"Umm…" I looked from her sweet little face up to Tyler, but I couldn't read his expression at all, so I let my eyes move away from him to Sophie. "I don't think—"

"Of course Grace can come, Sophie." Dex answered for everyone.

I smiled hesitantly. "Thanks Dex, but I'll just let you guys go and catch up."

"You should come, Grace."

I swallowed hard and looked up at Tyler when he spoke. "Are you sure?" When he nodded, I looked back down at Sophie and smiled. "I guess I'm coming too."

"You should invite Charlie." My head snapped up to look at Tyler who had spoken again.

I jerked back in surprise. "What?"

"Charlie," he repeated. "You should see if she wants to meet us there."

I was so taken off guard that I only nodded and reached into my purse, typing out a quick text explaining we were all going to the Pancake House if she wanted to meet us. She replied immediately that she did and would meet us there in fifteen minutes. I repeated her message out loud and felt everyone moving around me, I assumed getting their stuff to leave, but my eyes were locked on my phone. Did he have feelings for Charlie? I mean, she said nothing happened between them at the party, and I believe that, but did he feel something for her?

"Ready?" He pulled the door open, and I lifted my head, planting a small smile on my face. I moved past him, and he stepped out behind me, turning to lock the door. "You riding with us?"

I shook my head. I couldn't do that because I needed a few minutes to myself. "No, I have some things to do after, so I'll just drive myself."

I looked forward and made my way to my car only to feel him come up behind me. Pulling open my door, I turned when he said my name. "Did you need something?"

"What?" I answered, still feeling out of sorts.

"You came over this morning," he reminded me. "Did you need something?"

Did I need something? I think I got my answer without even having the conversation. "No, just wanted to say hi to Sophie and Seth."

Something moved across his face, and I waited, thinking he might say something, anything, but he took a few steps back. "Okay, well, we'll see you there."

I slid into my seat and shut the door, starting up my baby. Throwing it into reverse, I wished I'd just stayed in bed this morning.

Chapter Twenty-two

Tyler

"So, Grace, huh?"

I looked over the top of my bottle and glared. "Don't go there, man."

"She's wow." He whistled low. "I mean, you'd be an idiot to let her get away."

I lifted the bottle to my lips and looked over at my friend while I took a drink. Setting it back on the table, I leaned forward. "You shouldn't have asked her to babysit tonight."

He shrugged. "Why not? She pretty much offered."

She had. At breakfast. "I should've said no."

Breakfast had been torture, just like it had been last Sunday when I sat at a table with her and the kids. At least I could count on Sophie to keep the conversation going. Seth and I were lousy at that and usually Grace was good at it, but today even she was a little quieter. It seemed like she was upset when I asked her to invite Charlie, but I wasn't sure. All I knew was her face dropped, and I didn't like it. I almost told her to forget it, but then I remembered Dex was with us, and selfishly, I wanted Charlie there. He'd always had a thing for blonds, and she was so outgoing, I thought maybe they would hit it off and he'd get his eyes off Grace. It was a selfish, prick move, especially to a friend who would drop everything and come because my dad died, but the thought of Grace with him made my skin feel like it was on fire.

Not ten minutes into breakfast and Dex said we should go out for a beer tonight. I gestured to the kids, appreciating I had them as my reason for hiding, but he only pointed out I could get a babysitter. When Grace offered, I should've shut it down, but Sophie got excited and Seth actually smiled, so when Dex thanked Grace, I didn't argue.

"What's the story with the friend? Charlie?" He motioned for the waitress and held up his bottle before showing her two fingers. She nodded and moved to the bar.

I grinned. "Interested?"

He considered that. "I might be. She's funny as hell."

"She's smart."

He smirked. "I like them smart. Hate trying to have a conversation with someone who only wants to talk about her hair and last damn shopping trip."

"She might be smarter than you."

He snorted. "Don't get crazy, man."

I chuckled. He did like smart women because he was so damn smart. Anything else probably bored the shit out of him. I looked up when the waitress dropped two more beers on the small pub table we were currently sitting around and watched her shoot a flirty grin in Dex's direction.

He winked and watched her walk away before bringing his attention back to me. "What is this place?"

I looked around. "I have no idea, never been here before."

"But Charlie and Grace think it will keep you out of trouble?"

I shrugged. "I guess. They said they know the owner, and he runs a clean place with great security."

He gestured toward the door, and I turned to watch a group of people coming in. "Looks like things are picking up."

"Great." I grunted, listening to him chuckle. Turning back to face him, I brought up what had been on my mind since this morning. "You're really done, huh?"

He took a long drink from his bottle. "I am." He inhaled deeply and looked over my shoulder before his gaze landed on me again. "I know you miss it."

"Every fucking day," I admitted.

"Maybe you just need to find something else to do that you love as much."

I snorted. "Like what? I don't have your brains, man. All I had was football; it was the only damn thing I was ever good at."

"That's because it's the only thing you ever did." I cocked my head to the side and waited for him to continue. "You never even tried anything else or let yourself be interested in anything else. Your focus was always just football, like nothing else even existed. Now's the time to find out what else you like." He leaned forward, one hand on the glass bottle, and tapped it against the table. "You may not love it, Ty, but you may find out there's more to life than that game."

"Guess I really don't have a choice, do I?"

He barked out a laugh. "No, you really fucking don't."

"Tyler?"

My head snapped to the left when I heard a familiar voice, and I barely contained the groan. Barely, but I did, out of respect for Grace. "Hey, Ben." I looked behind him to see Jake walking up. "Jake."

"Hey, man," Jake said, lifting a bottle to his lips and taking a drink. "I'm surprised to see you here."

I gestured with my hand toward Dex. "My buddy's in town. Thought we'd get a beer."

Ben extended his hand, which Dex took right away to shake. "I'm Ben; this is my brother Jake."

Dex smiled, then dropped Ben's hand to shake Jake's. "Hey, guys. How do you know Ty?"

"He's, uh"—Jake paused before continuing—"a friend of our sister."

"They're Grace's brothers," I explained.

I saw Dex grin and nod. "I met Grace this morning."

Ben's head whipped in my direction. "This morning?"

Fuck. Dex was such a troublemaker. I shot him a dirty look, but he only smirked. I knew I needed to offer an explanation, not because these two deserve it, but to save Grace any more trouble with her family. I glanced back at Jake and Ben. "Grace stopped this morning to see Sophie and Seth."

Jake tapped the bottom of the bottle against the table and smiled. "Sounds like Grace."

"Then she went to breakfast with us." Dex leaned forward, his elbows on the table. "And she brought her seriously hot friend."

I saw Ben straighten and look directly at Dex. "Who?"

"Charlie."

Something flashed in Ben's eyes, and if I knew him better, I'd have guessed it was anger, but he seemed to get ahold of it quickly. "Charlie's a good girl."

Dex agreed. "Yeah, she is." He gestured to the other two stools around the table. "You guys want to sit?"

Jake glanced at Ben before he pulled the chair out, sat down, and leaned back, arms crossed over his chest, looking completely relaxed. Ben followed.

"You guys went to college together?" Jake asked.

"Yeah," Dex answered. "Played ball together."

"You still play?" Ben asked.

Dex nodded. "I play for Miami, but this is my last year. I'm retiring."

"Aren't you young to retire?"

I snorted, but immediately regretted it since all attention came my way. Dex frowned. "Ty doesn't think I should retire."

My head snapped in his direction. "I never said that."

Dex faced Ben and Jake again. "Football takes a toll, man, and

135

at almost thirty, I'm just tired of every damn thing hurting. Wanna get out before I'm forced out by another injury."

"Makes sense," Jake said. "You have plans after?"

Dex slapped his hand against my shoulder. "Moving here."

Jake's eyebrows shot up. "Really? Why?"

"Wanna hang out with Ty. Catch up. We haven't had time since college, plus I need a change of pace. I'm so damn tired of the heat in Florida."

"When will you move?"

"Probably right after the season, maybe after the first of the year."

"No family?" Ben inquired.

He shrugged. "I have family, but we're not that close. I've always been closer to Ty than my own family."

My head jerked in his direction. I was surprised at that, but he continued, shocking the hell out of me.

"I could never count on the little bit of family I had. Got into college on a full scholarship, met Ty, and finally had someone I could count on." He grinned again. "Not to mention, it was so fucking fun hanging with this guy. Every damn time we went out, he was approached and harassed by dicks. He always tried to walk away, but they never let him. I think most just wanted to see if they could take him down. They couldn't." He leaned forward, his elbows resting on the table and laughed. "One time, one of them was trying to impress his girl, started mouthing off to Ty. The dude was like five and half feet tall."

I snickered, remembering that guy. He was a dick. Dex slapped my arm.

"Remember him, man?"

I nodded, and he laughed harder. "Anyway, Ty warned him no less than ten times to just move on, but the douche wouldn't, kept at him, so Ty stood and fucking dwarfed this guy." He shook his head. "You'd think the dumbass would've seen his size and backed off, but he didn't. Christ, he only came to his waist."

I took a chance and looked over at Ben and Jake, who were laughing along with Dex, and exhaled a breath I hadn't realized I was holding. Without knowing it, Dex was defending me to these two, explaining my side, something none of them asked for before they judged me, and something I wouldn't have offered.

"So, Ty turns and starts moving toward the door. I got up and followed as did some other guys from the team, all waiting to see what would happen next but wanting to watch his back for him because he'd had ours more times than we could count. It was all good, and we were almost to the door, but then the little douche punched him in the lower back." He spun his bottle around on the table. "What he didn't know was Ty had a lower back injury in the last game and suffered through hours of therapy. So, Ty turns around, and we braced, waiting for the signal, but it never came. Ty grabbed the asshole's shirt and picked him up off the ground with only one arm, swung his other arm out and slammed him in the face." Dex sat back and made a face of distaste. "Fuck, the blood flew off the guy's face, landed on Ty, landed on us. He broke the fucker's nose. I never saw so much blood."

I looked over at Ben and Jake surprised to see they were still laughing, with their eyes on Dex, and I grinned down at the bottle in my hand before putting it to my lips and taking a long, cold drink.

"Then we're all ready, you know, braced for whatever was coming our way, and Ty just drops the douche to the ground, straight to his back, and I swear we all fucking flinched when his head hit the floor, and then he walked the fuck out."

"What happened after?" Ben asked.

Dex shrugged his shoulders. "Nothing. Stupid shit didn't even have anyone with him except his girl, so we just walked out."

"Then Coach showed up," I grumbled.

"Oh shit, that's right." Dex motioned back and forth between he and I. "Ty and I shared an apartment with two other players, and the next morning Coach shows up and asks for the story. We all told him because Ty never really spoke then either." He rolled his eyes and snickered, "And he says to Ty that he's not allowed in the bars anymore. Ty was so fucking relieved when he said that because he hated when we dragged him out with us, so Coach basically let him off the hook for socializing."

Ben settled farther back in his seat. "That what happened the night you were charged?"

He didn't need to be more specific. I knew the night he was talking about. "Basically."

"But no trouble since?" Jake asked.

"Haven't been out."

Jake sat up and leaned his elbows on the table, bringing all his attention to me. "That was over a year ago."

I shrugged. "Yeah."

"You just don't go out at all?"

"I only went out to avoid being completely alone, but it's not like I miss it."

"That's just sad, man," Dex said, earning a punch to the shoulder from me. I laughed along with him, forgetting until tonight how much I missed hanging with him.

I looked at my phone and noticed the time. "We should probably get going, man."

Dex frowned at his phone. "Ty, it's only eleven. I'm sure Grace is fine."

"What about Grace?" Jake asked.

"She's babysitting for Ty—" Dex explained.

"She offered," I cut in quickly, not wanting any misunderstandings.

"Sounds like Grace," Ben confirmed.

I looked around and spotted the sign for the restroom. "I'll be back, and then we can go."

I heard Dex and Grace's brothers start talking again as I walked away and headed toward the bathroom. Finishing up, I washed my hands and walked out, heading back to the table when I saw our waitress. Stopping in front of her, I leaned in close due to the music getting louder. "Can we get our bill?"

"Sure." She smiled sweetly. "Just give me a minute."

I nodded and moved the rest of the way, almost to the table when a hand landed on my chest. I closed my eyes briefly before opening them and glancing down at a man who was probably around six feet tall, his eyes angry.

"Excuse me," I said, attempting to move around him, but stopping when he moved with me.

"Saw you hitting on my girl."

"Wasn't hitting on anybody, man. Just need my bill, so I can leave."

"Damn right, you're going to leave, and I better never see you in here again," he threatened, getting close enough to shove against my chest with his hand.

I rolled my eyes and looked over his head, but Dex wasn't paying attention. "Dex, man, it's time to go," I called out.

His eyes shot up, and he scowled when he saw what was going on. I gestured to him that we needed to leave, and he jerked up his chin before standing up.

The guy in front of me dropped his hand, and I looked over to see six men at his back. I dropped my head and ran my hand along the back of my neck. Son of a bitch.

"You scared?" He reached up and shoved me again, but I didn't move. One of the guys cracked his knuckles, annoying me even further, and luckily, Dex made his way to stand beside me.

"What's going on guys?"

"This douche thought it was okay to hit on my girl."

Dex snorted. "Yeah, right."

The guy took a step to the side, getting in Dex's face. "You calling me a liar?"

"Abso-fucking-lutely," Dex spat out, and I groaned.

"Dex," I warned.

"Yeah, Dex," the douche said snidely, "Better listen to your pussy friend before I kick your ass."

Dex laughed, but I'd had enough. "Let's go."

I took a step back in an attempt to move around him and came face to face with two guys from his group. I turned to say something to Dex just in time to see the first guy pull his fist back and swing at him. Dex's head snapped back from the hit across his cheek, but he only grinned. "Oh, it's on, motherfucker."

I never even had time to react before a fist slammed into the side of my face.

I turned my body to face the two men standing before me and scowled. "That was a mistake."

Chapter Twenty-three

Grace

Flicking through the channels on the television, I sighed when there was nothing interesting on. I needed something to do to keep me awake, since it was now going on midnight and still no Tyler or Dex. I didn't know what came over me during breakfast when I offered to babysit, except that Tyler was smiling, actually smiling like he was happy, and that was all because his friend Dex was sitting across from him. Dex was funny, I'd give him that, and in a lot of ways, he reminded me of my brother Jake. I thought more than a few times, if they ever met, they'd get along very well and probably stir up a lot of trouble together.

Breakfast had been fun with Charlie and Dex keeping it light. I thought for a moment or two that I saw a spark of attraction between them, but as we finished up, they didn't make plans or exchange numbers, so maybe I was only seeing what I wished for. I loved Charlie; she was my sister, my best friend, and I'd never once been jealous of her...until today. Tyler talked to her and smiled at her. The most I got was an occasional grin that usually ended before I had any time to enjoy it. I was starting to wonder if I'd ever know what I did to cause such a rift. Why couldn't he be as friendly and easy with me as he was with Charlie? I knew she had no interest in him, but it was still a hit to my confidence that I couldn't seem to stop thinking about him and why he specifically asked for her to come to breakfast.

I sat up quickly when I saw headlights turn from the street into the driveway and not for the first time, wondered what my place was, so I stayed seated. It took a minute until I heard the key in the lock and both Tyler and Dex came through the door, one laughing and one looking very pissed off.

Then I stood.

Because they both looked terrible.

"What the hell happened to you two?"

Dex closed the door behind them and made his way over to me. I scanned his face, taking in the bruise under his eye already turning dark shades of purple before I looked down his body. The skin on his knuckles was torn, littered with dried blood, and I could already see bruises on his hands and arms.

He smiled when he stood directly in front of me. "Just like old times, sweetheart. Felt good, I have to admit." He moved past me and threw a look back at Tyler. "I'm heading to the shower, man. See ya in the morning. Night, Grace."

I glanced at him when I heard my name and sent a small wave his way before turning to face Tyler again. "What happened?"

He sighed loudly and dropped his head. "Some assholes started a fight."

I slowly crossed the small amount of space until I stood right in front of him. His one eye was already swollen, the colors dark purple and red, his bottom lip was cut open on the side, dried blood staining it and part of his cheek. Then I looked down at his hands and saw bruises already forming on his knuckles, the skin torn just as Dex's had been. He shifted to the side and started toward the kitchen when I noticed he was walking as if he was holding his side.

"Did you hurt your side?"

"Took a hit to the ribs, that's all."

I followed him, watching as he got a glass of water and a bottle of ibuprofen. Dumping a bunch in his big hand, he lifted them to his mouth and swallowed them down. I moved around him and grabbed the first-aid kit I'd seen in the cupboard last weekend when I was looking for a cup for Sophie. I gently reached for his hand, wrapping only his fingers in mine and pulled him to the chair at the small round table.

I positioned him in front of the chair and pointed. "Sit."

He sat but looked at me curiously. "What are you doing?"

I laid the kit on the table and opened it up. "You're a mess. Have you even looked in the mirror? And I watched you take the pills using your left hand so that tells me your right side is hurting, and you probably won't be able to clean these cuts very well, considering you're right handed."

I pulled out the peroxide first and a few cleaning pads and laid them on the table. Tyler was so tall that I was able to stand in front of him and his face was just shy of being level with my face. I poured some peroxide on the pad and looked at his face closely. Up close, he looked even worse. Laying my left hand against his cheek gently, I tilted his head a little to the side and wiped carefully along his eyebrow that had been split open. He didn't make a sound, but I felt his body tense and knew it had to sting.

"You wanna tell me what happened?" I asked quietly, getting a new pad and putting more peroxide on it, working my way along his cheek.

"No," he grumbled, but it sounded more like a pout.

"No?" I asked.

He huffed. "They started it."

I rolled my lips together to hide the smile while I once again switched out my dirty pad for a clean one and continued down his cheek. "What did they do?"

He was quiet a moment, and I assumed he wasn't going to

answer, so when he started speaking, I was surprised. "One of them thought I was hitting on his girlfriend who I found out by the end wasn't actually his girlfriend. It was a fucking mess."

I ignored the pang of jealousy at the thought of him flirting with another woman and gently turned his head so I could inspect the other side of his face, which seemed like it fared better. "Did you win?"

He scoffed. "Hell yes, we won."

"Police?" I inquired, hoping no one called the police.

He shook his head slowly. "No."

"Good," I said, reaching for the ointment and opening the small tube. I liberally added it along his cuts, knowing they were going to bruise and hurt in the morning, but at least they wouldn't get infected.

"Where did you learn to do this?" His low voice rumbled through the quiet night.

This time, I let the small smile form. "My brothers were giant pains in the ass when we were young. Always getting into shit, fighting with their friends, with each other. My mom and I had a system for cleaning them up before she sent them back outside." I smiled softly at the memory of standing beside my mom while she patiently cleaned the boys' cuts, usually not asking questions unless she found out the boys were fighting with each other. I'd been too young to help with my older brothers, but I cleaned up Jake and Ben more times than I could count.

His eyes flicked up to mine, and my stomach jumped. His face was so close to mine, battered and in pain, and all I thought was if he'd let me, I'd kiss every one of the cuts, every one of the bruises until he stopped hurting. When he dropped his eyes, I reached down for his hand. Lifting it gently, I started the whole process over, letting silence fill the room while I wiped away the blood and added the ointment, cringing when I saw what bad shape his knuckles were in.

I reached to my side and put the ointment back in the case

along with everything else. That was the best I could do, and truthfully all he needed, except time which would heal all. I felt his large hand gently slide along my hip, and I turned my head abruptly, surprised he was touching me on his own. His face was lowered, his eyes on his hand, his thumb running circles along my hip while his fingers flexed. My breath was shaky when I breathed in, but I lifted my hand and laid it along his cheek. He leaned his face into my hand and lifted his other hand to lay on my opposite hip. Frustration coursed through me. I couldn't take it anymore. I needed to know what we were doing, so I could understand what I was feeling, what I wanted.

"Ty," I whispered, and his fingers tightened on my hips.

"It's been a long time since anyone did that for me," he said softly.

I waited, silently willing him to look at me, but he continued to stare at his hands, his grip tight on my hips. "Did what?"

He swallowed hard, and I watched his throat in fascination. "Took care of me."

I reached out and put my other hand on his cheek until I could tilt his head back. When his brown eyes, infused with streaks of gold, locked on me, I shivered. I knew he felt it when his eyes flared, and his hands tightened almost painfully on my hips. Throwing caution to the wind, I lowered my head and skimmed my lips over his gently, being mindful of his cuts. He shifted, and I thought for a moment that he was going to push me away, but he didn't. He pulled me closer, adjusting my legs on the outside of his thighs and lowered me until I straddled him, his hardness pressing against me. I whimpered while peppering soft kisses on his lips, my hands now laying on his shoulders, shoulders that were so big and so strong, they felt like they were made of stone.

One of his hands left my hip and ran up my back until it tangled in my hair and he groaned, long and loud. When his palm slid around my head, he pushed my mouth against his tightly.

I pulled back gently, speaking softly. "I don't want to hurt you."

"Not letting me kiss you the way I've been dreaming about is hurting me," he growled, and my breath stuttered.

"Ty." I sighed, dropping my lips back against his and letting him control the kiss. It was slow and deep, and when he pushed his tongue inside to rub along the side of mine, I felt it all the way to my toes. Pushing my body tight against his, he dropped his hand from my hip to my ass and squeezed, causing me to wiggle closer.

I rubbed my hot center shamelessly against the hard ridge below me, gasping when he shifted me a little and found the spot where I needed him the most. I pulled my mouth from his and laid my forehead against his when my body started escalating, my stomach clenching, the beginnings of an orgasm taking hold.

"You gonna come for me?" he growled, his hand flexing against my ass.

I nodded, trying to catch my breath as my body reached for what it was craving.

He buried his face against my neck, moving slowly up to my ear where he whispered, "Are you wet for me?"

I threw my head back and moaned. "God, yes."

He buried his face against my neck. "Fuck, Grace, you feel so good."

I was almost there; I just needed a little more. Grabbing his hand, I pulled it up between us and laid it over my breast. He squeezed his hand; his fingers found my nipple and gave it a little tug before he ran his hand down over my stomach and up under my shirt. His rough fingers slid over my soft skin, lighting my body on fire when he plunged his big hand under my bra, and he laid it over my breast. He ran the tip of his finger around the outside of my nipple, teasing me, making me rock harder against him.

"Please, Ty," I chanted.

When he closed his thumb and finger around my nipple and squeezed, my thighs clenched tightly, my clit pulsing harder and harder until I thought I would lose my mind if he didn't do something. Sensing it somehow, he brought his other hand from my hair and ran it down over my chest and stomach, his other finger and thumb moving to my other breast. He ran his fingers between our bodies, until it lay against the apex of my thighs, and I squirmed to get closer. He fluttered his fingers against me softly, but I didn't need soft. I needed more. He flexed his fingers, pulling them away from me and squeezed my thigh, whispering against the flushed skin of my neck. "What do you need, baby?"

"More." My breath hitched.

He ran his finger along the seam of my jeans, and I pushed down hard on his hand, a whimper escaping my lips. He ran two fingers up until he reached my clit; how he knew where the exact spot was, I had no idea, and I didn't care. I just needed the pressure from his fingers. I pressed my lips to his neck and rocked against his rock-hard cock. God, he felt huge under me, and if he would've opened his jeans and slammed inside me, I know I wouldn't have stopped him. I was that far gone.

"Right there, baby?" His low voice sounded against my ear.

I nodded my head vigorously, ready to beg, needing him to end this torture. I'd never been this turned on, and we hadn't even removed our clothes. He pressed his fingers hard against my clit and rubbed in slow circles. I rocked against him harder, pulling my face from his neck and letting my head drop back, panting, feeling my orgasm bearing down. I just needed a little more, but I had no idea what that was. Tyler shoved his face against my neck, his teeth scraping the sensitive skin before I felt him suck my skin into his mouth. The harder he sucked, the harder I rocked, moaning when I felt a hot sensation through my belly and thighs. I'd never felt anything like that. Not with anyone.

He sucked hard one last time before his lips moved up to my ear. "Fuck, Grace. I wish my cock was buried in your pussy right now. I'd fuck you hard and fast." He increased the speed of his fingers and added more pressure. "I'm going to come in my fucking jeans just watching you. Christ, I've never seen anything in my life as beautiful as you right before you come."

His words, his fingers, his hot breath on my ear, and his hard cock pressed tight against me caused the orgasm bearing down to finally take hold.

And I blew apart.

My hips moved fast, seeking more friction while his palm squeezed me tightly. I felt his groan against my mouth as he absorbed the scream forced from my body, leaving me shaking, my body jerking against his, my mind deliciously blank.

I have no idea how long it took for me to come back from the best and hardest orgasm of my life, but when I did, I was laying against his chest with his hand once again, buried in my hair and his warm breath against my ear.

"I love your hair."

His quiet voice sounded loud in the silence of his kitchen, and I sighed against his chest, my body still ringing in the aftermath of that orgasm.

"Thank you," I whispered, snuggling in closer, my eyes heavy, my body relaxing into the comfort of sleep in the warm cocoon of his body.

He was silent for another moment before he spoke. His warm breath fluttered along my forehead when he leaned down close and said gently, "Do you want me to drive you home?"

His words forced themselves into my hazy mind slowly, repeating themselves over and over again. Home? He was kicking me out after that? I had no idea what to say or how to answer. I hadn't planned on staying, but he was obviously ready for me to go. I felt him softening below me, so either he came when I did or he was losing interest and losing it quickly.

A big part of me was thinking it could only be the second option, considering he was ready for me to leave. Breathing deeply, I exhaled and pulled my body from his, careful not to meet his eyes as I maneuvered my body and untangled us. Standing up, I smoothed out my hair with my hands and rubbed my hands along my hips. Finding some strength even in the face of rejection, I pasted a small smile on my face and looked up. He stood close, his hands jammed in his pockets, his face flushed, his eyes locked on mine. I couldn't read him. That alone drove me crazy. I could always read people, and I was good at it, but I had no idea what was going on in that head of his.

"I'm okay to drive."

He took a step closer. "I don't want you driving if you're tired."

I shook my head. "I'm not."

I turned from him and found my purse on the island where I'd dropped it earlier, then slung it over my shoulder and headed for the door.

I felt him catch up to me and pull the door open so I could walk through, which I did, intent on walking the whole way to my car without turning back, not looking behind me until I reached my car and saw him standing in the open door, his hands still jammed in his pockets. I was barely in my car before he closed the door, and I dropped my head, laying it against the steering wheel, trying desperately to convince myself that I didn't want to cry, that I was only emotional because of that fantastic orgasm, but losing. Trying to shake off the feeling while blinking back tears, I shoved the key into the ignition, started it up, and threw it into reverse.

I cursed myself while I drove home. Thankfully, it wasn't far—only about fifteen minutes—but really all I wanted was my pajamas and my bed, where I could pull the covers over my head and try to forget the mistake I just made. I wasn't even paying attention to my surroundings while I drove, which my brothers had preached to me about hundreds of times, but I was tired and lost in my own thoughts. I pulled into my parking spot, grabbed my purse, and got out, locking the car before making my way to the building. I startled when I saw a vehicle parked in front of the building but immediately settled when I saw who was sitting in the driver's seat.

I slowed down and raised my eyebrows in surprise, but all that earned me was a small smile and a wave. I returned the smile and walked more confidently into my building, feeling something warm wrap around me. Getting into the elevator, I leaned against the back wall and wrapped my arms around myself, my smile lingering.

It wasn't much. It probably wouldn't be considered romantic to most. But to me it said more than words could from a man whose actions spoke for him.

Tyler had followed me home.

Chapter Twenty-four

Grace

"Hey, Mom!" I called out when I opened the door. Hearing no response, I made my way past the living room and headed toward the kitchen. "Dad?"

"In the dining room." His loud voice carried through the house, and I giggled quietly. After throwing my purse down in the kitchen, I made my way to the back of the house, following the sound of voices, but they were strangely quiet. Quiet was not something this house ever was.

"Did you start without me?" I teased just as I crossed the threshold into the dining room and stopped. Looking around the table, my eyes widened, and I stared.

Jake and Ben were sitting at the table, right across from Ty and Dex, and they all looked the same, faces beat to hell, knuckles torn up and big-ass grins on their faces. Dex wiggled his eyebrows at me, laughter dancing in his eyes, and I smiled back, his happiness contagious. My eyes skimmed over Lanie sitting on the other side of Jake, but she only widened her eyes and lifted her shoulders when my gaze locked with hers.

"Gracie." I dropped Lanie's stare and faced my dad when he called my name. "We were just about to start, but the boys wanted to tell us a story first."

I took a few steps closer to the table, resting my hands along the back of an empty dining room chair, my eyes scanning over Jake and Ben, and I cringed. "What happened to you guys?"

Ben leaned back in his chair and smirked. "We hung out with Ty and Dex last night at Hanks." His face and Jake's looked just as bad as Tyler's and Dex's. If I didn't already know they'd won, I'd wonder. Their faces all looked beat to hell.

I tore my gaze from my brothers and looked at Dex and Tyler. "How are you two here?"

Dex gestured toward Jake and Ben. "Your brothers invited us last night. Thought it might help explain why they look like they do if we all did it together. They also promised us a homecooked meal, and I haven't had one of those in a long time, so…" He trailed off and his eyebrows furrowed in confusion. "Didn't Ty tell you last night?"

Tyler's eyes met mine after he scowled at Dex, but I shook my head. "No, he must've forgotten."

His gaze burned into mine when his low voice rumbled. "I had other things on my mind, that's all."

He held my stare long enough that I swallowed hard and felt a flush working its way up my neck, remembering what he had on his mind last night. I opened my mouth to say something, but I just didn't know what that was going to be, so I snapped it shut when I remembered we had an audience.

"Grace."

I startled out of my Tyler fog when a female voice called out, and I couldn't have been more thankful. I leaned back until I could see into the living room, surprised when I saw Charlie. It wasn't often she made it to Sunday dinner at my parents' house, not anymore anyway. When we we're teenagers, she was here every Sunday, right by my side, being teased by my dad and brothers and soaking up every minute of it. Her parents' divorce had been hard on her, and she'd clung to my family for normalcy. Well, as much normalcy as my family could offer. Smiling, I waved her back. "What made you come today?"

"Your dad texted me."

Jerking my head back to the table in front of me, I looked at my dad who only shrugged. "Haven't seen Charlie in a little while, so it was time to make that right."

Charlie moved into the dining room and smiled at my mom and dad. I knew they missed her. They'd practically raised her from the age of fifteen, and for them, that meant something. More than something actually.

I threw my hands on my hips and searched the faces at the table. However, this time it was me avoiding looking at Tyler rather than him avoiding me. "Okay, what's going on?"

Charlie came around to stand on my other side, putting her directly in front of the table, and it was obvious to everyone she'd finally taken a look around the room. "Oh, my goodness what happened to you guys?" Her eyes widened while she looked at each man individually. "Jesus, did you fight with each other or a whole freakin' team of guys?"

I stopped, having never considered that. Tyler never really said who he'd gotten into a fight with. "Wait, did you guys get into a fight with each other?"

Jake leaned back and looked at me out of the corner of his eye. "Fuck no, we didn't fight each other. You really think I'd take on that giant son of a bitch." He gestured toward Ty by nodding his head in his direction.

"Language, Jacob," Mom reprimanded.

I glanced around the room, finally noticing a lot of little people were missing. "Where are all the kids?"

"Playing upstairs," Mom said. "We assumed this wasn't a story for little ears."

Dad pointed at the empty seats next to Dex. "Okay, come sit down. The boys were about to start telling us their story."

Charlie and I looked at one another before rounding the table and sitting beside Dex and Tyler, with Charlie next to Dex and me on her other side, facing Ben, Jake, and Lanie.

Dad's raised his eyebrows, eyes flicking between the boys. "All right, what happened?"

"Did you guys already start?"

A voice yelled from the living room, and I cursed silently, leaning my head back. I knew that voice. We all knew that voice. This was going to go to shit quickly.

I wasn't surprised when Luke and Kate rounded the corner with Andy hot on their heels. Luke stopped immediately in the doorway and put his hands on his hips as he took in the group around the table.

"Hey, guys," I said, looking directly at Andy when he popped out around Luke's leg. "Hey, Andy."

"Hi, Aunt Grace." His brow furrowed as his face scanned over the table until his stare landed on Tyler. "Hey, you're here." His voice sounded excited when he pointed at Ty. "Is Seth here too?"

Tyler grinned. "Yeah, kid, he's upstairs."

"Cool." He leaned his head back to look up at Kate and Luke. "Can I go play?"

Kate ran her hand over his hair while Luke's eyes continued to bore into my brothers. "Yeah, Andy, go ahead."

She moved around Luke and reached down, grabbed his hand in hers and pulled him to sit beside Ben, her taking the seat on the other side of Luke. She tried to hide her grin when she looked across the table at Charlie and I sitting with Dex and Tyler.

Luke sat back in his chair and crossed his arms over his chest. "I'm assuming none of you ended up at the station, or I would've known about this."

"No," Ben started, shaking his head when we heard another voice call out from the living room.

"Back here," Dad called out.

I wasn't surprised to see my brother Cam and his best friend Pike turn the corner, but I was a little surprised his twin Chris wasn't with them. They were always together. Luckily, their girlfriends Lucy and Sydney get along really well or that could be very awkward. They looked around the room slowly, gazes wandering over the boys, and Pike dipped his head with a smirk on his face.

"Where are the girls?" Anna asked.

"Syd's volunteering at the shelter today. They're short staffed." Cam offered an explanation before he grabbed the seat next to me.

"Where are Chris and Lucy?" I asked.

Cam smirked. "They're at Landon's new apartment. Lucy wanted to help him get his things organized."

I smiled knowingly, able to read between the lines. "So, in other words, Lucy wanted to check out where her brother is living now."

Cam laughed. "Exactly."

I shifted my attention to Pike. He rarely left his girlfriend, Bella, or his little sister Savannah at home when he came to my parents. Pike loves our family, having never had one of his own, so he rarely misses dinner.

"Bella's with Savannah who has a cold. I told her I wouldn't be long, but I needed to stop by to clear up any, well… misunderstandings." Pike folded his large frame onto the dining room chair.

It was starting to make sense now since Pike is in charge of security at Hanks. "Were you working last night?"

He nodded. "I was."

Dad leaned forward, elbows to the table, fingers steepled under his chin. "Anyone want to fill us in?"

Jake sat forward. "Long story short, Ben and I met up at Hank's last night to grab a beer and ended up hanging with Ty and Dex."

"You're Dex." Luke's eyes landed on Dex, but it wasn't a question, more of a statement.

Dex grinned and leaned back in his chair. "I am."

"Oh, sorry, guys," I said, realizing nobody but Jake and Ben had officially met Dex. I gestured toward my brothers but kept my eyes on Dex. "Dex, that's my brother Luke, my brother Cam, and unofficial brother, Pike." I glanced down at Pike, who grinned softly and threw me a wink. I knew, as well as everyone else how much the title of unofficial brother meant to Pike. Gesturing behind me toward Dex, I let my gaze roll over my brothers. "This is Matt Dexter, a friend of Ty's."

"I'm assuming this happened at Hanks." Dad dropped his fingers and gestured for someone to continue.

Jake smirked across the table at Dex, and I groaned. I knew if they met, they'd hit it off. Rubbing my palm across my forehead, I felt Charlie drop her hand to my leg and squeeze before shooting a smile my way.

"Yep," Dex began with a grin. "Ty left the table to go to the bathroom, but on the way back was stopped by some pu—" He glanced in Mom's direction before continuing, "Some person."

Charlie giggled beside me, and I saw Dex shoot her a flirty smile and a wink. I leaned in closer to her, and whispered, "Did you just giggle?"

She blushed and dropped her head. Yeah, she was busted. Charlie didn't giggle. Maybe there was something going on between her and Dex.

"Dude started mouthing off, Ty tried to walk away a few times, even motioned for Dex to leave, but the jackass wouldn't quit." Ben sat up straight and leaned forward. "Ended up he had six assholes with him, all looking for a fight. One took a cheap shot at Dex, another at Ty, and it was game on."

I leaned forward and faced my brothers. "How did you two get involved?"

"We jumped the fuck in, Grace." Jake defended their actions. "Not going to let it be two against seven." He looked at Tyler with something similar to respect in his eyes, which shocked me. I guess they bonded last night over bloodshed. "The best part was when one of the bastards hit Ty in the face when Ty wasn't even looking."

Jake laughed when Dex snorted, cutting in and finishing the story for Jake. "And Ty looks at him and says…" Dex lowered his voice, trying to make it as deep as Tyler's. "That was a mistake."

I chanced a glance at Tyler and breathed deeply when I saw the grin on his face, the dimple standing proudly in his cheek. Looking among the four guys, watching them either laughing outright or grinning at each other, I felt myself relax some, glad that at least two of my brothers had moved on from the last encounter.

"This where you come in?"

Hearing my dad's voice, I looked his way and followed his line of sight to Pike.

"In a way. I heard the commotion, but I was in the back. One of my guys was covering the door and the other was already escorting someone out, so by the time I made it, the fight was finishing up."

"You four took care of all seven?" Dad's eyes scanned the boys who were all grinning at each other, Ty included.

"Yes, sir," Tyler answered reluctantly, his grin dropping when Dex jammed his elbow into his side, forcing him to speak.

Dad sat back in his seat. "Good."

"Dad." Luke frowned before he looked at Pike. "They gonna press charges?"

"Nah, I made sure they understood it was all on video that the boys were only defending themselves, and that he and his crew are no longer welcome at Hanks."

Luke eventually nodded after sending some fierce glares in Tyler's and Dex's direction, but he also sent them toward Jake and Ben, so I felt at least some of his hostility toward Tyler was subsiding. "Looks like they got in some good shots."

"We were fending off seven of them." Dex smiled. "You should've seen them, man."

"He's not kidding," Pike said with something close to pride in his voice.

Luke faced Pike. "Why are you okay with this? You run a tight ship there."

"I do," Pike agreed, "but that douche has been in before, and he bothers Melanie every damn time. Never knew it until last night when she told me." He ran his hand around the back of his neck, his eyes locking on Luke's. "He's lucky these guys got to him first. Joe was escorting someone out when it was happening, which was good because when I saw the look on his face while Mel was telling her story, I knew he would've killed the bastard for the shit he's been saying to her."

"Like what?" Luke asked.

He scanned the table before facing Luke again. "Should probably have her tell you. He's also tried getting her alone, gets in her space a lot."

"Why didn't she tell you before?"

"She's quiet, man, doesn't say much, doesn't like to make waves. She's been like that since Henry hired her, but she's a damn good waitress. I'm hoping this will get her to speak up if there's a next time."

"Bring her in to talk to me," Luke encouraged.

"I'll try to convince her," Pike agreed. "But it won't be easy."

"Tyler." We all turned when we heard the sound of Sophie's little girl voice. She stopped and her face lit up when she spotted me first. "Grace!" She squealed, bouncing on her toes beside my chair. "When did you get here?"

I ran my hand over her ponytail and smiled. "A little bit ago, but I heard you were playing."

Her expression filled with distaste. "It's all boys up there." She rolled her eyes. "Boys are so boring."

"They are," I agreed. "Are you going to eat with us?"

"Yep," she sang out.

I patted the seat next to me. "Would you like to sit beside me?"

She nodded enthusiastically and looked down the table. "Tyler, I'm going to sit with Grace, okay?"

He chuckled. "Yeah, Sophie, it's okay."

She climbed into her seat and got up on her knees. "Can you take me home, so I don't have to ride with all the boys?"

I heard my dad chuckle from down the table, but I kept my focus on Sophie. "Sure, I can do that."

"Yay!" She clapped her hands together. "I can't wait to ride in your yellow car."

I closed my eyes, knowing Sophie just sold me out without knowing it. I was not ready to turn my head to face my family.

Crap.

Chapter Twenty-five

Tyler

Fuck. I watched as Grace's relaxed posture stiffened, and she kept her head turned to face Sophie. I knew she was avoiding her family, probably hoping they hadn't picked up on what Sophie said.

"Yellow?"

I blinked slowly when I heard her dad's voice. She turned her head to look at her dad, but her eyes found mine first, and I gave her a small nod, hoping she felt my support, knowing there wasn't much more I could do to help her. Not knowing if she'd even want my support after last night. I didn't know what the hell I'd been thinking, but when she was standing so close, cleaning my cuts, I think I lost my mind. I had to touch her, couldn't stop my hands from reaching for her no matter how hard I'd tried. Her skin was just as soft as I remembered from when I had her tight against me in her brother's kitchen, her scent just as intoxicating. When she started rocking against me, my only thought was I needed to get her off, needed to watch her come. Fuck, it was a beautiful sight. And I wasn't ashamed to admit that I came in my pants just from her grinding down on me while she orgasmed.

But it was what I did after that I was kicking my own ass about.

I hadn't meant it to sound the way it did. I'd wanted her to stay, wanted to lay with her pressed tight against me all night, but I knew she couldn't. How could I have her in my bed knowing Seth and Sophie would end up there eventually? How would I explain that to them? They'd been through enough, and Sophie was already attached to Grace. I couldn't let her get that close, allow her to get her hopes up that something between Grace and I could be permanent, and then watch Grace walk away. I didn't want her to lose another person she loved, so I said the dumbest fucking thing I could have.

And I wanted to take the words back the minute they left my mouth.

But I couldn't. So I'd followed her to the door, trying to find the words, any words, so she would know how fucking amazing I thought she was. I'd needed her to know that if I was any other person or this was any other time, I'd pull her back into the house and spend the night wrapped around her.

Those words never came. But then again, for me they never did.

As soon as she got in her car, pretending I hadn't hurt her feelings, I texted Dex to keep an eye on the kids while I followed her home. I didn't want her driving home alone, tired and most likely confused and distracted by my behavior. He agreed before I was even out the door. I trailed her the whole way to her apartment and parked in front of her building, wanting her to see me, hoping she'd come over and talk to me, needing to make it right between us.

She hadn't.

But she did smile.

I wasn't sure if she would forgive me or ever want to see me again after that, but now she sat staring at me, her eyes filled with uncertainty. I wanted to save her from this conversation, but she needed to have it. I nodded again and smiled softly when she took a deep breath.

She bit down on the corner of her lip before shifting her attention from me to her parents. "Yeah, I got a new car."

"Why?" Anna asked. "Did something happen to your car?"

She shook her head. "No. I just wanted to get one by myself."

"Can we assume you're not planning on going back to college?"

She swallowed hard, glancing quickly at Charlie before facing her parents again. "No. Not right now, anyway. I like what I'm doing, and I make decent money, so I think I'm just going to keep doing it for now."

I saw Charlie reach over and lay her hand over Grace's, her eyes staying locked on Jack and Anna. I shifted my attention back to them, not surprised when Jack sat forward and placed his elbows to the table, eyes on Grace. "If you like what you're doing, that's all that matters, Gracie." He smiled and her shoulders relaxed. "Now, what kind of car did you get?"

"You should have asked one of us, Grace. We would've come with you." Luke spoke up.

Her eyes shifted down to her brother. "I know you would've, but I wanted to do it myself."

"Why?" Luke looked genuinely confused.

She bit down on her lip, considering her words. "Because I wanted it to be something I knew I did on my own."

"But—"

"It's done, Luke." Jack interrupted, and I looked down to hide the grin when the voices at the table quieted. It was obvious when Jack spoke, everyone listened. "Now, Gracie, what kind of car did you get?"

"It's yellow." Sophie sang out from beside Grace.

"I got that darlin'." He grinned at Sophie.

"It's a VW bug."

"A yellow VW bug. Really, Grace?" Jake snorted out a laugh from across the table. "Does it have peace symbols and love stickers all over it too?"

Grace shot an annoyed look in Jake's direction, but she couldn't hold it and before too long, they were both laughing, the rest of us not too far behind them.

"It's a great little car." Grace defended her choice after the laughter died down. She shifted her eyes to me. "Tell them, Tyler, you've seen it."

I snorted. "It's little, all right."

When Grace's eyes lit with amusement, I knew we were both remembering me jamming my giant self into that car.

Dex's head snapped back and forth between us, his eyes finally landing on me. "What's so funny?" When I didn't respond, he turned his head to face Grace. "Wait a minute." He leaned forward, elbows on the table. "Don't tell my Ty's been in that matchbox car."

"It's not a matchbox car." Sophie giggled. "That's what Seth has."

Dex grinned at Sophie before he continued. "Was he?"

Grace sighed but couldn't contain the grin. "Yes, he rode in my car."

"Oh, my god," Jake said through a fit of laughter. "You're telling me that you crammed your ass into a VW bug?"

"Why the hell would you do that?" Ben spoke up.

I shrugged. "She was my ride."

"Did you fit?" Ben asked.

My eyes flicked toward Grace, who was laughing now, unable to hold it in any longer, and I couldn't blame her, I knew I'd looked ridiculous that day. I nodded, my lips tipped up in a smile. "I rested my chin on my knees the whole way home."

Ben, Jake, and Dex laughed harder, and even Luke grinned, which shocked me.

"What's so funny?"

All heads turned to face the doorway where Jax and Kasey stood with Mia at their side.

"Mia!" Sophie yelled and jumped up to drag Mia back to where Sophie was seated beside Grace. The two girls were giggling when they sat down, their heads together, and I heard whispering.

"We were just listening to a story about Ty riding in a VW bug."

Jax's eyes slid over to where I sat and scanned me briefly. "Was it a convertible?"

Fits of laughter broke out again while Jax and Kasey found their seats. The table was filling up, and I knew from the party last weekend that there was still a lot of family not here. Where did they put everyone when they all showed up?

"It's Grace's new car," Jake said, and I watched closely while Jax and Luke shared a look.

"That's our cue to leave." Pike and Cam stood, saying their good-byes, promising to come next Sunday. I wondered what this was like, every Sunday, people coming and going, stories being shared. I never had this, never even knew it existed until today, and I quickly silenced the part of me screaming to experience more of it.

"You got a VW bug?" Kasey's voice broke me out of my thoughts.

Grace nodded happily. "Yep."

"What color?" Kasey smiled wide, her attention solely on Grace until Sophie's voice rang out.

"It's yellow."

Kasey sighed. "I've always wanted one of those cars and always thought I'd pick yellow or white." Jax snorted and rolled his eyes. Kasey shot him a glare before she shoved her elbow into his side. He smirked and rubbed his side like it had hurt. "I can't wait to see it, Grace."

"I'm hungwy."

Everyone's heads, once again, turned to face the doorway where Bray, Andy, and Seth now stood.

"You're always hungry," Jake teased Bray, who giggled and ran around the table, climbing onto the seat beside Lanie.

"Boys, find a seat," Jack said to Andy and Seth. Seth's eyes scanned the faces at the table until they landed on me, and I nodded. He walked over to sit beside Mia with Andy sitting right beside him. When everyone was seated, Jack's loud voice filled the room. "Let's eat."

"Please tell me you won," Jax grumbled, his eyes flicking around the table. I sat quietly while Dex was introduced and the story was told again, a little abbreviated this time since the kids were now in the room, but the same story, nonetheless.

I watched Grace talk to her family, a wide smile on her face and wondered, not for the first time, how the hell someone like her ever ended up in my life.

Chapter Twenty-six

Grace

I breathed a sigh of relief when everyone began passing food, the conversation about my new car officially over. For now, at least. It had gone well, better than I'd hoped, and I didn't even have to mention my writing. If I had my way, that secret would die with me.

"How has the school year started, Kasey?"

Kasey shifted her attention down the table toward my mom before she answered. "Pretty good. I have a decent class this year."

"You're a teacher?"

She shifted to face Dex who had spoken. "Yeah, I teach fourth grade."

"I bet you're everyone's favorite teacher." Dex grinned and threw her a wink.

"Watch it," Jax warned from beside her, but Jake and Ben laughed.

"That's what I always say," Jake said.

Jake and Dex thinking the same way did not surprise me in the least. Kasey only shook her head and smiled, used to the teasing in our family.

"We go to school tomorrow," Sophie announced, twisting her body so she could see her brother. "Right, Tyler?"

"Right, Sophie."

Kasey looked confused for a moment, but then realization dawned on her face. "They missed last week."

Tyler nodded, not needing to say more because everyone was well aware why the kids missed the last week of school.

"I like school," Sophie said loudly, but then frowned. "But Seth doesn't."

"You don't like school, Seth?" Kasey faced him, but his eyes were locked on the plate in front of him. "Why not?"

"Because of the bullies," Sophie said before shoving a forkful of mashed potatoes in her mouth.

"Bullies?" Dad's head jerked back.

"Sophie," Tyler said but to no avail; she was already moving on.

Sophie swallowed. "They're mean boys, but Tyler said he's going to drive us to school so the bullies on the bus won't be mean to Seth anymore."

"What do they do?" Luke sat forward, his elbows now resting on the table.

"They say mean things and shove him. I tell them to knock it off, but they push me away."

"Somebody pushed you?" Tyler's low growl came from down the table, and all eyes turned to watch him, but his attention was focused solely on Sophie.

She nodded and shoved another fork of mashed potatoes in her mouth. "Yeah, but now they won't anymore cuz we won't have to ride the bus."

"Who are these boys, darlin'?" Dad asked, and I rubbed my hand across my forehead. My family was wading in, and Tyler had no idea what that meant for him.

Sophie shrugged. "I dunno. I just call them mean boys."

"Your friends ever help you, Seth?" Jake asked, concern marring his features too.

"Seth doesn't have friends." Sophie looked up at Jake. "He has me."

Jake grinned, and I heard a few chuckles around the table, but when I looked at Seth, his cheeks were bright red, and I knew he was embarrassed. I reached up and ran my hand along Sophie's shoulder. "Sophie, maybe you should let Seth answer some questions."

"He won't," she said matter-of-factly.

"You should come to my school." Andy spoke up. "We only had one bully last year, and the principal made him stop."

Seth's eyes flicked to Andy, and he smiled before dropping his head again.

"Tyler." Kasey faced Tyler, whose head lifted from where he was watching Seth to look at her. "Where do you live?"

"142 Elm," he answered.

She faced Luke. "If I'm thinking of the right area, isn't that right on the edge of the district?"

Luke pulled his phone out of his pocket and started typing out a text. "Hang on, I'll have Marty check. He's covering the desk today, but I think you're right."

"What does that mean?" I asked.

"If it's where I'm thinking, the kids would technically be required to go to New Hope Elementary now that they live with Tyler."

"Change schools?" Tyler asked, and Seth's head shot up, his eyes searching Tyler's face.

"Yeah." Luke nodded. "Although, the school would probably make accommodations for this year under the circumstances, if that's where the kids wanted to be and felt comfortable."

When Luke's phone beeped with an incoming text, the table quieted. He read it before facing Tyler again. "They're right inside the boundary line for the school district."

"So New Hope is their new school." Tyler confirmed.

"Yes, but like I said, I'm sure the school would accommodate you this year if that's what you want."

Tyler's eyes met mine before moving toward Seth and Sophie. "Do you want to stay in your school or move to New Hope?"

"I don't know anyone at New Hope." Sophie pouted.

"Well"—Kasey smiled at her—"you know me, and I could personally introduce you to your teacher."

"Would I get to see you?"

"I'll make sure you get to see me," Kasey promised.

Sophie looked thoughtful for a moment before she agreed. "Okay."

"Seth?" Tyler faced him and shook his head at Sophie when she looked Tyler's way and opened her mouth to speak.

Seth only shrugged.

"Seth," Andy said excitedly, "you could be in my class. Right, Aunt Kasey?"

"Maybe," Kasey answered but looked toward Tyler and nodded, telling me without words that she would do everything in her power to make sure that happened.

Seth's eyes lifted and studied Kasey for a moment before a small smile graced his face. He swallowed hard and glanced back and forth between Tyler and Kasey. I think we were all holding our breath, waiting to see if he'd say the words I knew he wanted to say. I was so proud of him when he finally did. "I'd like to go to New Hope."

"Well, that's settled then." Dad smiled. "Seth and Sophie are moving to New Hope Elementary." His face grew serious, and his attention landed on Luke. "What are we doing about the bullies?"

Luke ran his hand along the back of his neck. He had to have been expecting Dad to bring it up, and there was no way he was letting that go. "I'll have a talk with the principal and the bus drivers."

Dad only nodded, but I knew he was happy Luke was going to do something about it. It didn't matter that Seth wouldn't be on the receiving end of the bullies anymore; someone else would and that wasn't acceptable to Dad especially, but to any of us really.

"If that doesn't work"—Jake smirked—"Dex and I will have a chat with them."

Jax snorted, causing Luke to grin, his eyes flicking back and forth between Dex and Jake before landing on Dex. "I have a bad feeling about you two." I heard chuckles around the room. "When are you leaving?"

Dex laughed. "Tomorrow, man." He sent a grin Tyler's way. "But I'm coming back."

Jax groaned. "You are?"

Dex laughed harder. "I'm retiring after this season, and Ty's letting me stay with him until I figure out what the hell I'm doing next." His eyes shifted from Jax to Charlie. "I can't wait to get back."

If I didn't know my brother so well, if I hadn't grown up close to him, and if I hadn't been there through one of the worst times in his life, I probably would've missed it. But I had, so when the need to look at Ben pulled at me, I did, and the tension coming from him was palpable. No one else seemed to notice, conversations resumed, and I could hear Kasey telling Tyler what he would need to do to get the kids settled into their new school, but all the time my eyes stayed locked on my brother. His head was down, his eyes on the table in front of him, while his hand flexed around the glass of water sitting near the plate, and when his eyes finally lifted, I saw the one thing in them I'd hoped I'd never see again, hoped he'd never feel again.

Sadness.

The kind of sadness that comes from somewhere deep, somewhere you protect to keep from feeling the pain of hurt, of acceptance, of loss.

The kind of all-consuming sadness that can change you.

I knew, in that moment, that my brother was feeling that sadness.

What I didn't understand was why he was accepting it. Why wasn't he doing what he so obviously wanted and needed to do?

Why he was letting himself be hurt? But I knew I'd eventually see the fallout.

All I could hope was that Ben would eventually come to know that the one thing he was fighting, the one thing he was keeping himself from, could bring him all the happiness he'd been craving.

As if a light bulb turned on, I faced Tyler and watched him grin at Dex, who was talking about their football days in college, as I realized my brother and I weren't all that different.

Almost like he could feel the heat of my stare, Tyler lifted his head and met my eyes. I smiled softly, a new sense of excitement filling me, and watched Tyler tilt his head, obviously confused, but he wouldn't be. Not for long, anyway. Because I had made a decision.

It was time to go after my own happiness.

Chapter Twenty-seven

Grace

"Wanna tell me what's going on?"

I picked at a piece of lint clinging to my black yoga pants while listening to Charlie chuckle in my ear. I'd been waiting for her to ask, and to be honest, I was surprised it had taken her this long.

I grabbed my cup of coffee from the table and took a sip, considering my words. Finally, with a sigh, I answered. "I like him."

"I know that, Grace, but did something happen that you haven't told me? Because I got the feeling at your parents' house on Sunday with all the staring at each other you two did, that maybe something had happened."

I snorted. "What about you and Dex? What was up with that giggle? I even saw you blush."

She cleared her throat, but when she started speaking, I could hear the smile in her voice. "He's nice. I like talking to him. He's really smart when you get past all the flirty stuff."

I sank down deeper into my couch cushion and pulled my leg up onto the couch with my foot flat so I could rest my coffee mug on my knee. "Did he get your number?"

"Yeah," she admitted, almost shyly. "He called me too when he landed, and we talked."

As happy as I was for her, I thought back to my brother and felt a weight settle in my stomach. "I hate to bring him up, but what about Ben?"

"What about him?"

"Well"—I hesitated—"you've liked him for so long, but now it seems like you're just done."

"I am done, Grace," she said quietly. "I know you've always secretly pulled for us to get together, but it's never going to happen, and I'm so tired of being alone. Alone and waiting for someone who may or may not ever see me as more than a friend or worse"—she groaned—"a sister. I deserve more, don't I?"

"Yeah, of course you do," I said quickly. "And I want more for you, but I saw something in him when you and Dex were together, and it looked very much like sadness."

"Your brother always looks sad around couples, Grace. He has for years, and I don't think that's going to change unless he lets go of Jackie, which he obviously hasn't done yet. I've told you before that I don't want to be the woman who follows her. I don't ever want to be someone's second choice or consolation prize." She paused and her voice softened. "I want to be the first person he thinks of when he wakes up. I want to be the one he calls with exciting news, the one who consoles him through hard times, and the one he wants and needs. I want that from someone."

"And you think that person is Dex?"

"I don't know. Maybe, maybe not. But I know it's not Ben."

She sounded confident, but I knew her better, and I knew Charlie's heart wasn't going to let go of Ben just because her mind knew she should. "Let me ask you this, Charlie, who do you think of when you wake up, Ben or Dex?"

"I think of coffee," she joked. "You know that."

I laughed, knowing the conversation was over, at least for now. I also knew if my brother didn't get his head out of his ass, he was going to lose any chance he might have with her. Maybe Ben and I needed to spend some time together, so I could tell him what a dumbass he was being. I was thinking of a way to get him out, just the two of us, when Charlie's voice interrupted my thoughts.

"Back to you, Grace, not more stalling. What happened?" she said, her voice stern.

I sighed. "We made out."

"What?" I heard the surprise in Charlie's voice.

"Believe me, I'm just as surprised as you are." I admitted.

"When?"

I took a quick sip of coffee before I answered. "Saturday night."

"Go on."

"They came home beat up, and when Dex went upstairs, Tyler sort of talked to me about the fight. Anyway, I cleaned him up the way I used to with my mom when the boys got into scrapes, and one thing led to another."

"Who initiated?"

"He did. Actually, it was the hottest make-out session of my life," I admitted.

"But…?" She trailed off.

"Afterward, he pretty much kicked me out."

She hesitated a minute, and I wondered if she took a drink or was thinking. I could tell by the condemnation in her voice that she'd been thinking. "He kicked you out?"

"Well, he did it nicely. But yeah, he definitely wanted me to leave." I paused, remembering how I felt when I saw him parked in front of my building. "He followed me home, though, to make sure I got there safely I guess."

"Hmm…"

"What does that mean?" I asked, suspiciously. "That hmm, what are you thinking?"

She hesitated only a moment before answering. "I was just thinking that was pretty sweet and wondering what happened that he needed you to leave."

"Yeah, me too. As a matter of fact, I've been trying to figure it out all week."

"So what have you figured out?"

"He either doesn't like me or—"

"He definitely likes you. We can all see that," Charlie interrupted.

"Well, then the only other thing I can come up with is he got nervous, after, well you know."

My doorbell ringing made me jump in surprise since my apartment had been so quiet this morning. "Hang on, Charlie, someone's at my door."

I heard her say okay and set my coffee mug down on the floor by the couch before I moved toward the door. Peeking through the peephole, I saw a flower deliveryman on the other side. Swinging open the door, I smiled.

He returned the smile. "Grace Dimarco?" When I nodded, he continued, "These are for you." I thanked him and took the huge bunch of red roses and closed the door.

"You got flowers?"

"Yeah," I answered Charlie and made my way across the small apartment to my kitchen where I laid them on the counter, looking for a card.

"Who are they from?"

"I don't know," I said, turning the flowers over, but still not seeing any card. "There's no card."

She whistled. "I can only think of one guy who would send you flowers and be too shy to write a card."

"Yeah, me too," I said, unable to keep the happiness out of my voice. "There are at least two dozen roses here Charlie."

She whistled. "Well, what are you waiting for? Go thank him."

I looked at the numbers on my microwave and frowned. "It's ten in the morning on a Saturday."

"So?"

"I didn't want to bother him today," I admitted with a sigh. "I've stayed away all week, but I texted him on Tuesday because the kids started at New Hope, and I wanted to see how they did. He was short with me, and I got the impression he needed some time to himself."

"Have you talked to him since Tuesday?"

"No, I didn't want to bother him. His dad just died, Charlie, only a couple of weeks ago, and as much as I want something with him, I realized after Sunday that I need to give him some time to adjust to everything that's changed in his life."

"Maybe that's why he sent you flowers. As his way of calling you this time," Charlie suggested.

I considered that. "Maybe you're right."

"Of course, I'm right."

We both laughed and said our good-byes with the promise of going out later tonight. We usually try to go out together on Friday nights, but Charlie worked late last night, and I was tired from running errands for Mr. Anderson all week, plus I hadn't been sleeping well. Too many nights I'd lied awake wondering how to navigate things with Tyler, never having a good answer by morning, and every day trying to talk myself out of stopping by.

I was even starting to annoy myself with my indecision. After dinner on Sunday, I'd been so sure of what I wanted and what I thought he wanted. I followed him home, taking Sophie to their house in my car just as promised and even went inside, but something had changed during that short drive, and I felt a wall between us that hadn't been there at my parents' table. I decided to leave, and when he didn't argue or try to stop me, I told Seth, Sophie, and Dex good-bye and headed for the door. I paused when I felt his heat behind me, hoping he was following me outside so we could talk, but he only opened the door for me and stopped at the threshold. At that moment, I decided to walk away and give him some time.

That was almost a week ago.

Making a quick decision, I grabbed my coffee mug from the floor and put it in the sink before I headed to the bathroom to take a shower. I was his friend, and if for no other reason than that, it made sense for me to check in on everyone.

I think.

Chapter Twenty-eight

Grace

"He wasn't home."

I settled back in the booth and watched Charlie for a reaction, but she only shrugged. "Did you call him?"

I lifted a glass of wine to my lips. "Yep."

"Did he call you back?"

I took a long drink before I set my glass back down. "Nope."

She narrowed her eyes. There was the reaction I was waiting for. "He didn't call you back?"

I rolled my lips together and shook my head. "Nope."

"Huh," she said and rested her back against the soft leather of the booth across from me, crossing her arms over her chest. "That doesn't make sense."

I sat forward and rested my elbows on the table. "Am I just making this something in my mind that isn't really there?"

She rolled her eyes, making me grin. "Come on, you know better than that. I see it, your family sees it. It's why your brothers are so pissed off. We all can't be wrong." She picked up her glass and took a sip. "When you two are near each other, the rest of us can actually feel the sexual tension."

I rolled my eyes and relaxed against the seat again. "That's not true."

"Grace," she said, her voice implying I was an idiot.

I laughed and dropped my head, reaching out to play with the edge of the napkin my drink was sitting on. Lifting my head, I met her eyes. "Then if everyone's right, what's going on?"

She made a sound of frustration. "I don't know." Her eyes lit, and she sat up. "Maybe he wants you to chase him. Maybe that's like his kink or something."

I wrinkled my nose and tried to hide the laughter I was holding in. "Did you really just say kink?"

We were both laughing when the waitress came to our table with a glass of wine and set it down in front of me. "That man at the bar"—she gestured behind her—"sent this over."

My eyebrows pulled down, but I sat up further and looked over my shoulder to where the waitress was pointing. I lifted my hand in a wave to the man sitting at the bar and gave him a small smile before turning back to Charlie. She had her lips rolled together hiding a smile. It wasn't the first time we'd had drinks sent over, but it hadn't happened in a while, so I was a little thrown off.

"He would also like to buy you a drink," the waitress said, her eyes now on Charlie, "but wanted me to ask what you'd like since you've had two different drinks."

Charlie sat up straight and looked down at her drink before lifting her eyes to the waitress again. "That's nice, but tell him I'm fine."

"Sure," she said, and we both watched her walk away.

"He's cute," Charlie said, her eyes looking over my shoulder.

"Yeah, he is cute," I agreed.

"And your type."

I lifted the new glass of wine and put it to my lips. "Not anymore."

I took long drink, enjoying the fruity flavor while Charlie laughed.

I put my drink down when something occurred to me. "How did he know you had two different drinks?"

She considered that for a moment. "He probably asked the bartender what we were drinking."

I realized that actually made sense, and I hadn't thought of it. I looked around the club, noticing a lot of twentysomethings and realized I wish we'd gone to Hanks tonight. At some point, the club scene had lost its appeal for me, and I knew Charlie preferred Hanks, having never been much of clubbing kind of girl.

"Are you going to talk to him?"

Charlie's voice interrupted my thoughts, bringing my attention back to her. "If he ever calls me back."

Her eyebrows lifted, and she chuckled. "I meant the guy at the bar."

I put my palm against my forehead, embarrassed I assumed she meant Tyler, but I'd honestly already forgotten about the guy at the bar.

"Boy, you have it bad," she teased, and I glanced over where my phone was lying on the table beside me when it beeped.

Tyler: Sorry I didn't call you back.

I grabbed my phone, and with wide eyes, I looked back at Charlie. "It's Tyler."

She gestured for me to keep talking. "What did he say?"

I glanced down at my phone, re-reading the text before my eyes found her again. "That he's sorry he didn't call me back." I took a long drink of my wine. "What do I do?"

She frowned. "What do you mean? Answer him." She leaned forward and put her elbows on the table. "Just be you, Grace. Do what you always do."

I exhaled nervously and tucked my hair behind my ear before I texted him back.

Me: Were you busy with the kids?

I showed Charlie my phone and widened my eyes. "Why did I text that?"

She laughed and sat back. "I'm texting Dex because I told him I would tonight. You talk to Ty and be yourself, Grace. That's the girl he likes."

"He just throws me off balance." I admitted.

She arched her eyebrow. "That's not always a bad thing."

I smiled and glanced down when my phone beeped again.

Tyler: We went to the gravesite.

My stomach clenched, and I swallowed hard. That had to be so difficult for them.

Me: How did it go?

I saw the bubbles pop up and settled further into my seat.

Tyler: It was hard.

My eyes filled with tears, unable to imagine what they were going through.

Me: I'm sorry.

Then I quickly texted again.

Me: Are you okay?

Tyler: Yeah. Kids are good. They just went to bed.

I tapped my fingernail against my lip and smiled.

Me: Whose bed?

In my mind, I saw him grin and hoped it was true.

Tyler: Theirs.

Tyler: For now.

I giggled when his second text came through and startled when the bubbles popped up again so I held off on texting him back.

Tyler: What are you doing?

I squealed a little that he was keeping the conversation going and looked up to see Charlie grinning at me.

Me: Out with Charlie. It's our weekly tradition, so we can catch up.

Tyler: Talking every day isn't doing it for you?

I laughed when he sent a smirking emoji because I never pictured him as an emoji sending guy. I'd imagine it wasn't something he did often, but I loved that he was teasing me.

Me: Hang on, I'm trying to wrap my head around you making a joke.

I hit send and then immediately regretted it. Damn texts. Why couldn't you take them back after you sent them? They should have a thirty second policy to retract a text after you realized it sounded completely stupid.

Tyler: Thank you.

I frowned. What was he thanking me for?

Me: For what?

Tyler: Making me laugh.

I actually felt tears in my eyes and choked them back. This man, god, he gets to me in a way no one ever has before. I wished, not for the first time tonight, that I was with him. I decided this was it, and I was going for broke.

Me: Want me to stop by?

I waited for his reply, my stomach a ball of nerves anticipating his answer. Of course, it took longer for him to respond, longer than it had before, giving me time to convince myself he was trying to find a nice way to turn me down.

Tyler: Yes, but it's probably not a good idea.

Me: Why not?

I had to ask. I had to know what he meant. I'd been assuming his distance had been because of the kids and all the changes, but maybe there was something else, something I'd been overlooking. Or worse, he only wanted to be friends, and I was pushing for more.

Tyler: Because I could become addicted to you.

My eyes widened at the honesty in his statement, and I was excited we were finally making progress, but it faded when the bubbles appeared again.

Tyler: I already am.

My heart started beating faster, and I reached forward to grab my glass, taking a much-needed and longer drink this time. I glanced over at Charlie, but her fingers were moving quickly on her phone and a smile lit her face. She wouldn't mind if we left; it was obvious she wanted to talk to Dex tonight. Our girls' night out had quickly become a girls' night out plus men, but I knew neither of us cared.

Me: I'm coming over. Just have to call an Uber.

Tyler: See you soon.

He wanted me there. I squealed a little and looked up at Charlie who was smiling back at me.

"Are we leaving?" she asked.

"Do you mind?"

"Hell no." She grabbed her purse, while I pulled up the Uber app. "This place is a little pretentious for me."

I looked around the club again and frowned. "Yeah, me too."

"Next time, Hanks."

"Definitely," I agreed, grabbing my purse. "Let's go."

The Uber was waiting outside already, and we climbed in, giving Charlie's address first since her apartment was closer, and Ty's house was a little farther out. I gave her a hug before she climbed out of the back seat and then promised to call her as soon as I could tomorrow. Settling back in the seat, I laid my head back when I felt a little dizzy, probably too much wine or maybe just the excitement of where I was heading. When the dizziness persisted, I opened my eyes and lifted my hand to my forehead, taking a deep breath when a feeling of nausea choked me. I shook my head, hoping to shake it off, but a wave of black floated across my eyes, and when my head felt too heavy to hold up anymore, I let it drop back against the seat.

My last memory was someone calling out, "Miss."

Chapter Twenty-nine

Tyler

I was pacing in the kitchen where I'd been on and off throughout the night when I heard a soft moan. I took a drink from my coffee mug before I set it down and made my way over to the couch. Grace's eyes fluttered, and I took deep breath, exhaling slowly, my body finally starting to calm. Because she was lying on her side, I sat in the curve of her hip and reached out, pressing my palm against her neck, relieved when her pulse was still strong and steady.

Her eyes fluttered again before they opened, and she winced in the light of the morning before slamming them closed again.

"Grace," I said quietly. "You need to wake up and drink some water."

She moaned, moving her hand to lay over her stomach, and I felt sympathy overtaking my worry. I'd been there, we all had when we'd drank too much, but seeing her sick was overwhelming me. I didn't have to consider what that meant because I already knew.

"Grace," I repeated, just as quietly.

She opened her eyes slowly and blinked a few times, her head flopping to the side, settling her attention on me.

"What happened?" she whispered. "Why do I feel so sick?"

I laid my hand on her forehead. "Do you remember anything?"

She moved her head on the pillow and groaned. "The last thing I remember was being in the Uber."

I sighed and stood, then walked to the kitchen and grabbed her a bottle of water from the refrigerator. I made my way back to the couch and resumed my seat, seeing she hadn't moved an inch.

"You need to sit up a little and drink."

I pushed my arm under her shoulders and pulled her up, but she moaned again and laid her head against my arm. I ran my hand over her hair and laid my head against the top of hers. "Baby, you need to drink. You threw up a lot last night."

"Oh god." She groaned. "I threw up? In front of you?"

I grinned. Having lived with four guys through college, I'd seen a hell of a lot worse, but I liked teasing her. "Yeah. It was pretty fucking gross, considering it started outside in the grass."

"Oh my god, stop talking."

I chuckled and twisted the cap off the bottle that I'd set on my lap. "Drink."

This time, she lifted her head, took the bottle from me, and drank some. She licked her lips, waited only a few seconds, and then put the bottle to her lips again, drinking until I pulled it away. "You may want to take it slow."

She laid her head down against my shoulder and snuggled close. "Why can't I remember?"

"You had too much to drink," I surmised.

"That can't be right," she said, her voice quiet. "I only had three glasses of wine, and I never even finished the one that guy sent over."

My body stiffened, jealousy rearing its ugly head that some douche was sending my girl drinks. Shit, where did that thought come from? I shook my head to clear those thoughts away and focused on what she was saying. "How much do you normally drink?"

"Not much, but three glasses of wine shouldn't have even made me tipsy. I usually drink a glass every night. It's in my refrigerator at home right now."

My mind started turning, remembering the times in college when some assholes would drug women, sometimes in the bars, but more at the parties, to make them pliant. I gently pulled her from my shoulder and laid her back down.

"What's wrong?" she asked, her voice still too fucking quiet.

"I think you were drugged."

"Drugged? You mean like roofied?"

I moved to the kitchen again and grabbed her purse, digging through the monstrosity until I found her phone. Making my way back over to the couch, I sat down beside her again. "That's exactly what I mean." I hit the button and her phone lit up. "What's your code?"

"My birthday. March 6th."

"You used your fucking birthday, Grace?" I lectured while I tapped in her code. "That's the first damn thing people try when they grab your phone."

I went to her favorites and found Luke's name, hit call, and held the phone to my ear. It was Sunday morning at eight am, but I knew he'd answer. After all, Grace was calling, and from what I'd seen, when Grace called, the boys answered.

"Grace."

I swallowed hard, knowing how this shit would eventually go, especially considering he sounded like I woke him up. "No Luke, it's Ty."

"Ty," he said sharply and I heard sounds like he was moving around. "Why the fuck do you have my sister's phone?"

"I'm calling you for her."

"Why is she even with you?"

"You really want to do this, man?" I asked angrily. "You wanna fight with me while your sister, who I'm pretty fucking sure was roofied last night, is sick on my couch?"

"What?"

"Yeah." I heard the fear in his voice, but I didn't fucking care. I was tired of taking their shit, and I was done paying the price for everything I'd ever done. "And I thought I'd call her brother, who's a fucking cop so he could come over and help, but if you can't stand that she's with me, then I'll just call the station myself."

"No, man, I'm on my way right now," he said roughly. "Thanks for calling me, Ty."

He hung up, and I threw her phone on the coffee table next to the water bottle. She was sleeping again so I watched her for a few minutes before I headed back to the kitchen and made myself a fresh cup of coffee to drink while I waited. I was happy I'd let the kids stay up late last night to watch a movie, putting them to bed around eleven because at least now they were sleeping in. It wasn't long after I'd put them to bed that I'd finally given in and texted Grace.

Earlier in the day, I'd seen she'd called my phone after we'd gotten back into my SUV at the gravesite where we were visiting our dad and their mom. I even visited my mom while we were there, something I did every Mother's Day and something that never got any easier. I was going to call Grace back then, but I couldn't. I was too raw, and I knew I'd say things I wasn't ready to say and she sure as hell wasn't ready to hear. I waited until I wasn't feeling so vulnerable, which took a large chunk of the day, but then it was movie time with Seth and Sophie, so I sat and watched it with them. As the movie played on, though, the need to talk to Grace had grown stronger and stronger.

I didn't know what I expected to happen while texting her, but it hadn't been her coming over. I wouldn't even let myself go there, knowing I'd only be disappointed when she couldn't stay, but when she said she was, I didn't have the strength to argue. I needed to see her. I'd just confessed I was addicted to her, and that wasn't an exaggeration. She'd inserted herself into my life in a way that I never wanted to lose, didn't even want to consider the option that I wouldn't see her or talk to her.

I saw an SUV through the front window seconds before it turned into my driveway, so I made my way to the door, pausing only to check on Grace before I continued. I swung it open before Luke ever had the chance to knock.

"Hey, Ty," he said, the disdain for me out of his voice, at least for now, so I moved aside and let him in.

His eyes went straight to the couch, and he ran his hand through his hair. I knew what he was seeing, she looked so pale and small lying on the couch and not at all like the ball of energy usually bouncing around. "Jesus." Shaking his head, he turned to face me. "Why do you think she was roofied?"

I shoved my hands into the front pockets of my jeans. "I didn't last night when she showed up in an Uber. Just figured she drank too much. But this morning, she woke up and told me she only drank three glasses of wine, including one sent over by some douche at the bar."

I didn't even bother hiding my jealousy when I told him that and ignored the small grin on his face while I continued. "She said she didn't finish the glass he'd sent."

"Thank god for that," Luke said. "We're going to need to wake her up so I can ask some questions." I nodded and followed him to the couch. "Was Charlie with her?"

"Yeah," I answered.

"Call her," he directed while he sat on the coffee table and leaned over toward Grace. "Ask her to come over."

I grabbed Grace's phone and unlocked it before shoving it in Luke's direction. "Charlie's number is in her favorites."

I raised my eyebrow expectantly and continued holding the phone out to him when he stared at me. I was making a statement, and he fucking knew it. He held my stare until I saw movement out of the corner of my eye and swung my attention toward the couch.

Luke did the same, and I think we were both surprised to see Grace had just sat up.

"Jesus, why don't one of you just pee on me to make your point." She grabbed the bottle of water and stood, standing still for a minute, and I reached out, wrapping my hand around her elbow. She nodded when she was steady. "I'm going to shower. We can talk when Charlie gets here, okay?"

Her voice was quiet, but her sassiness was back, which gave me a huge amount of relief, and from the look on Luke's face, he felt the same.

"Take your time, Grace," Luke said.

She patted him on the chest and moved toward me. "Do you have a toothbrush I can use and maybe a T-shirt or something I can put on since I smell like vomit?"

I wrapped my arm around her back, laying my palm on her waist. "Yeah, I'll get it for you."

I heard Luke talking to Charlie behind me while I walked her up the stairs and into my room. She smiled softly at the two little figures sleeping soundly in my bed but kept moving until she got to the bathroom. I turned on the shower for her so it would get hot and grabbed an extra toothbrush out of the cabinet before facing her again. "I'll put a T-shirt on the counter."

She moved close and laid her forehead against my chest. "Thanks, Ty."

I kissed the top of her head and ran my hand through her silky hair. "You never have to thank me, Grace."

She pulled back and looked longingly toward the shower. "Go on, get a shower. I'll be downstairs with your brother."

She sighed. "Just don't kill each other okay?"

"I can't make any promises," I teased.

Her lips tipped up in a smile before she winced and put her hand to her forehead. "Maybe some ibuprofen too."

I felt the anger I'd been keeping in check at the thought of someone putting something in her drink swell inside me. "Whoever did this will not get away with it, Grace, I promise you that."

She laid her hand against my chest. "Ty, I'd rather have you than vindication, so don't get into any trouble okay?"

I let her words settle over me before I started toward the door. "You have me, Grace. For as long as you want me."

Chapter Thirty

Grace

I let the hot water run over me for a few extra minutes even after I finished washing my hair and myself. The scent of Ty's shampoo and body wash all around me made me think of listening downstairs both while he was on the phone with Luke and to their conversation once Luke arrived. When they were ready to argue over who was going to wake me up, I'd had it and forced myself to sit up. The comment I made about peeing on me would have made me laugh on any other day, but today, I could only laugh on the inside. My head hurt too bad to really laugh, though the shower was helping, and I was guessing if I drank some more water, I'd start to feel better. I didn't even want to think about how much I'd vomited or where, but I knew I had to be a little dehydrated after that.

Turning off the water, I stepped out and grabbed a towel before quickly drying off. I picked up a T-shirt Ty had laid on the counter and slipped it on, happy it went to mid-thigh before sliding my panties on underneath. I didn't want to put them back on either, but they were all I had, and I couldn't be walking around his house without, so I was stuck. I ran a comb I found through my hair before quickly braiding it off to the side and brushed my teeth. Checking myself over in the mirror, I decided I looked better than I had but still kind of gray, so I gathered my clothes and piled them on the counter before tiptoeing out of the bathroom and through the bedroom. I pulled the door closed behind me when I saw the kids were still sleeping, smiling a little at the sight of them snuggled in Ty's enormous bed.

"I don't know when it could have happened."

I recognized Charlie's voice when I rounded the corner into the kitchen. She jumped off the stool when she saw me and threw her arms around my neck. "Oh my god, Grace, what the hell? Ty and Luke think you were drugged somehow."

I pulled back from the comfort of her embrace. "That's what I hear."

"But you were fine in the Uber. We were talking and laughing, do you remember that?"

I smiled softly at Ty when he handed me some ibuprofen and another bottle of water. "Thanks." He nodded, and I turned back to Charlie. "I remember that and you getting out of the Uber, but then everything after that is gone."

I took the pills and a long drink from the water bottle before sitting on a stool. Charlie sat beside me, and we faced Luke and Ty on the other side of the counter. I knew Luke was ready to start firing questions my way, so I met his stare and gestured for him to start. "Go ahead, start asking."

He grinned, but his eyes told a different story, one where he was still worried and a little angry. "You sure you're ready?"

"Yeah." I finished the bottle and barely sat it down before another one appeared in front of me. I smiled again at Ty who gave me a chin lift, but didn't speak. He wasn't hiding his anger quite as well as Luke.

"Charlie told us you were at a club in the city called City Lights." I nodded, and he continued, one hundred percent in police-mode now. It was kind of surreal to see him in action. I knew what he did, but I'd never actually seen him do it. "You had two glasses of wine and then a third was sent to the table."

"That's right," I answered.

"Who brought it?" he asked.

"The waitress."

"What did she say?"

I took a deep breath and exhaled slowly. "Umm, she said something like, there's a man at the bar that wants to buy you a drink and set it on the table."

"Anything else?"

"She asked me what I was drinking," Charlie said. "I don't know if that's important, but she said he wasn't sure what to send over for me because I'd had two different mixed drinks."

"Did you let him buy you a drink?"

Charlie shook her head. "No. There was vodka in both so two was my limit."

Luke eyebrows shot up in surprise. "You get drunk fast on vodka?"

I snorted, earning me an elbow to the ribs, but I answered for her anyway. "No, she gets mean and wants to beat up anyone who even looks at her."

Luke chuckled. "Interesting. I'd almost like to see that."

She gave Luke her best glare, but he wasn't put off at all. He'd been on the receiving end of my glare too many times to be intimidated by hers. "Isn't Grace the one on trial here?"

Luke actually laughed that time and turned his attention back to me. I just finished another long drink of water and could feel the headache starting to lessen. It wasn't gone, but at least now I didn't feel like my head was going to explode. "Okay, Grace, so you drank the glass of wine?"

"Well, not all of it." I rubbed my hand along my forehead. "I was texting Ty and sipping it when Charlie and I decided to leave. We grabbed an Uber and dropped her first and then I came here."

"So you didn't finish it?"

I shook my head. "No."

Charlie laid her hand on my arm. "I'm glad you didn't, Grace. Could you imagine what would've happened to you if you had?"

"How could someone drug my wine if the bartender poured it and the waitress delivered it?" I asked the obvious question, at least obvious to me.

"It happens more than you think, especially if the place was busy."

"It was really busy, actually," Charlie answered.

"Did you know the man who sent it over?" Luke continued.

I thought back, trying to remember if I'd seen him before, but when I couldn't, I turned to Charlie for help. "I didn't recognize him, did you?"

She furrowed her brow in thought. "He looked kind of familiar to me, but he also looked like every twentysomething in a pretentious club, so maybe that's all it was."

"Can you describe him?" Luke asked.

I thought back before I answered, but my description was going to be vague. "He was blond. I don't know what color his eyes were, but they looked light so probably not brown. I would describe his build as lanky, I guess, from what I could see anyway."

"He was exactly the type of guy Grace always dates, if that helps," Charlie stated, earning herself a glare from me.

Luke frowned. "That doesn't really help me since Grace never introduces us to the guys she dates."

"Christ, I wonder why," Ty mumbled sarcastically.

"Anything else?" Luke asked, ignoring Ty's comment and looking back and forth between me and Charlie.

"I don't think so," I answered.

He nodded. "Okay."

"So now what?" Charlie asked.

Luke crossed his arms over his chest. "I'll go to the club, have them pull the security tapes if they have any, and see if I can get a picture of the guy actually putting something in your drink. The only trouble I see is the camera angle will have to show him not only doing it, but also the waitress immediately delivering it to you and you drinking it. I'll also talk to the waitress and bartenders and any security in the building. Hopefully, someone will have something useful to share."

"Do you need anything else from me?" I asked.

He shook his head and dropped his arms. "No, Ty already gave me the details of how you were once you got here. You didn't go to the hospital, so we don't know exactly what was put in your drink. You could go now, but with the amount of vomiting you did, I doubt there's anything left in your system."

"How was she?" Charlie asked, and I leaned into her when I heard the worry in her voice.

Ty took a deep breath and exhaled heavily, pushing the water bottle toward me, reminding me to drink, which I did while he talked. "The Uber driver actually came to the door and said he'd brought her home, but she was passed out in the back seat. I went out and pulled her from the back seat but stopped about halfway up the driveway because she started to throw up." I cringed, but he continued. "After that, I got her inside, where she threw up on and off for about an hour before finally passing out on the couch." He rubbed his hand along his forehead and looked directly at me. "I wish I'd considered you could've been drugged because I would've taken you to the hospital. I never even thought of it."

"Ty." I reached across the counter and laid my hand over his. "There's no way you could've known. Plus, you took great care of me. Look, I'm awake, clean, and somewhat hydrated."

I squeezed his hand, watching him until he nodded and his lips tipped up at the corners. It wasn't much, but I'd take it.

"Okay," Luke said, making his way around the counter. "I'm taking off. Keep your cell on you, Grace, in case I need to get a hold of you with questions." He put his hand on the back of my neck and squeezed before kissing me on the cheek. I looked up at him when he started to talk. "You staying here?"

"She is." Ty answered for me.

My eyebrows lifted at his definitive answer, but I just turned my attention back toward Luke and smiled. "Guess I'm staying here."

"I think that's a good idea," he said. "Just in case you start to feel worse."

"Glad I have your permission," I answered sarcastically, giggling when he wrapped his arms around me and squeezed tightly.

He pulled away and took a few steps backward. "I don't really have a choice. Ty already peed on you."

My eyes widened, and I laughed out loud when he hollered good-bye to everyone and left.

"Ewww, what does that even mean?" Charlie wrinkled her nose. "Because I'm really hoping right now that you didn't actually pee on her." Her head turned sharply from Ty to me. "Oh wait, is that his kink?"

"What?" Ty asked, his face adorably confused.

I laughed even harder, holding on to the side of my head when the headache reminded me it was still there—better, but still there. "Ouch." I leaned against my hand. "No, that's not his kink. And stop saying that."

Charlie threw her hands in the air, but she was laughing too when she spoke. "Then why would he pee on you?"

"He didn't pee on me," I explained. "I was listening to Ty and Luke argue, and I said why doesn't one of you just pee on me. You know, to mark their territory."

"Ohhh." She nodded. "That makes more sense."

We both turned our heads toward Ty who was across the counter, his eyes flicking back and forth between us and wearing a huge grin on his face.

"Tyler, you have a dimple," Charlie announced and I giggled. "I never noticed it before." She wiggled her eyebrows. "Very manly."

He snickered and dropped his head, shaking it side to side, only looking up when I called his name. "Can I have some coffee?"

His eyes softened. "You can have anything you want, baby."

When he turned his back to us to make the coffee, Charlie elbowed me and sighed deeply with her hand over her heart.

I smiled dreamily, knowing the smile was going to stay with me all day.

Chapter Thirty-one

Grace

Pushing through the door to the building, I made my way over to the far wall holding the mailboxes for the residents. I slid my key into the lock and pulled out the few envelopes inside before closing the small door and locking it again. I began leafing through the mail and made my way up the stairs to my second-floor apartment. Once inside, I threw the mail onto the counter and headed for my bedroom, needing to get out of my heels and skirt. Leaning one hand on the wall, I lifted my left foot and then right, sliding off my three-inch nude pumps. I tossed them into the closet and reached for the zipper on my skirt, pulling it down and slinging my skirt over the chair in the corner of the room, my blouse following closely behind. I quickly pulled on my black leggings and black tank top and threw on my favorite light blue long-sleeved tee over it, which was so big it had a habit of sliding off my shoulder. I didn't care, I just wanted to be comfortable.

I sighed at the feel of my comfy clothes and made my way back out to the kitchen, grabbing a bottle of wine from the refrigerator and pulling a glass down from the cabinet. I poured enough to make me forget what a crappy day I'd had and sat on one of the two stools against the island. Kicking my legs up onto the other stool, I leaned back and enjoyed the first long sip of my favorite Moscato.

Four hours of sitting in the courtroom with Mr. Anderson today definitely solidified my decision not to go to law school. I don't usually spend time in the courtroom, however, he told me that was where he needed me today, so that was where I was. But oh my god, I was so bored I couldn't even concentrate. Between his cases, we would meet and go over some of the tasks he had for me. Things he needed me to do for him since this was going to be his only free time before he leaves for vacation tomorrow. I wished about twenty minutes in that I'd suggested he just call me at home and go over his list.

After a few more much-needed sips of wine, I felt my body relax, and I picked up my mail. Leafing through, I saw all bills until my eyes landed on one white envelope with my name and address typed out but no return address and no postage stamp. That was odd. Putting down my glass, I skimmed the envelope through my fingers, but curiosity got the better of me, and I slid my finger under the sealed flap. It lifted easily, and when I glanced in, I saw a neatly folded piece of white paper.

Sliding it out, I unfolded the letter and noticed it was very neatly typed, almost with a professional look. Before even reading it, I looked at the bottom for a signature, but there wasn't one, which was confusing. Going back to the beginning, I started reading.

My Grace,

I've been thinking about you. Knowing now what you like, what turns you on, what you need from a man has been helpful. I'm so glad you described it in detail for me. I just want you to know I've been paying attention to the details you provided.

I've been waiting a long time for you, but I'm a patient man, so I'll continue to wait. Soon, the time will be right.

Your love.

P.S. The red roses on the table in your living room are as beautiful as you are.

My fingers trembled when I read the short letter for a second and then a third time. I didn't understand. Who was this person, and what was he talking about? I read it a fourth time, and my back snapped straight. How could he know where I have the flowers sitting? My instincts were humming when I carefully looked around my room. Was he watching me? My eyes flicked around the room, looking for anything that might look like a camera or something. The memory of my brother Brody's wife, Gia, being watched and stalked by a man who was infatuated with her flashed through my mind. I remembered hearing that Brody had one of his employees, a tech genius named Kyle, do a sweep of her apartment, and he found all the recording devices. Maybe I should call Brody.

I moved quickly out of my seat, but almost as suddenly, I sat back down. I didn't have much to tell them, except that I got flowers and now a letter. I'd actually forgotten about the flowers since that very same night I'd been roofied. I came home Sunday night after agreeing to let Luke meet me here and check out my place. Everything looked good, so he left but told me to lock up and call him if anything seemed off or I felt uncomfortable. Luke had visited the club, but they didn't have any security tapes, so all he could do was talk with the staff. I talked to him Monday night, and he'd interviewed everyone, but even the waitress couldn't remember what the guy looked like because it had been so busy that night. I knew for Luke it wasn't over, but for me, I just needed to move on. Although I wouldn't be going to the clubs anytime soon.

And surprisingly, that didn't bother me. I knew I wouldn't miss it.

I grabbed the letter again and read it, slowly this time, dissecting his words. Was he someone I'd met? How would he know what turned me on? The only man I'd been somewhat intimate with lately was Ty, and he wasn't stalking me. All he'd have to do was crook his finger my way, and I'd go running. I smiled at the thought, but it wasn't that far off. We'd texted this week and even had one really long conversation on Wednesday, but I hadn't been back to his house. I'd invited him and the kids to my place tomorrow for dinner, and I was excited when he agreed. It would be the first time I'd have him in my space. We couldn't do anything, but I think we both knew without even having the conversation that we needed to slow down a little. Not only for our sakes, but for Seth and Sophie.

Looking around my apartment, I decided to go talk to Ty in person. I needed to ask him about the flowers, but more than that, I hadn't seen his face since Sunday, and I missed him. Not to mention the fact that I didn't want to be in my apartment at that moment. Grabbing my keys off the counter and my purse, I moved quickly back outside to my car, all tiredness forgotten. I was already pretty certain Ty hadn't sent the flowers, because at some point, I think he would've mentioned it, but I hadn't really asked. We'd both been very distracted by what happened Saturday night, but in either case, I needed to know because if he didn't send them, then I had a bad feeling the man who wrote the note had, and he was letting me know he saw that I'd kept them.

And had them sitting on the small table in my living room on display.

Pulling into the driveway, I parked next to a small, gray car before getting out and making my way to the front door. I rang the bell and waited, smiling when Sophie's little voice got louder and louder, telling me she was coming for the door.

"Grace!" she squealed when the door swung open, and she slammed into my legs.

I leaned down and hugged her to me, rubbing my hand along her back. "How are you, beautiful girl?"

She threw her head back, her expression filled with happiness. "Where were you? I missed you."

I ran my hand over her dark hair and smiled. "I was working, but I couldn't wait to come see you tonight."

"Yay!" she shouted and threw her arms in the air before spinning around and facing a young woman standing not far behind her. She grabbed my hand and dragged me forward after I quickly shut the door behind me. "Grace, this is Aunt Natalie."

I held out my hand, which she shook, a smile also gracing her face. "Hi, Natalie."

"Hi, Grace," she said sweetly.

My head snapped up when I heard the door in the kitchen close, and my stomach clenched. Tyler had barely turned the corner into the living room before Sophie flew across the room and grabbed his hand, pulling him toward me. "Look Tyler, Grace came."

His eyes landed on mine and held for an uncomfortable amount of time, but I couldn't look away, and it seemed he couldn't either until another voice spoke. "Hi, Grace."

I looked around Tyler's wide shoulder and noticed Seth standing close to Tyler, Sophie now beside him. Shocked Seth initiated the hello, I paused, but only for a moment before I responded. "Hi Seth."

"Will you eat with us? We get to have pizza," Sophie said excitedly.

I nodded. "You got it."

"I'm going to get my ponytail holder so you can braid my hair," Sophie yelled as she flew from the room, grabbing Seth's hand on the way and making him laugh.

"She's been talking about you since I got here."

I turned when I heard the soft voice. Natalie shifted back and forth on her feet.

"She's pretty amazing." I answered.

"She is." She glanced at the stairs. "I've missed her, both of them, actually."

Confused, I looked over at Tyler who was watching me. "Natalie is Tara's sister."

Realization dawned on me when I looked more closely at Natalie. I'd seen her at the funeral and graveside but only briefly because a tall, older blond woman was dragging her around. If I wasn't wrong, she'd also had blond hair the last time I saw her, but now it was a dark brown. I reached my hand out and laid it on her arm. "I'm so sorry for your loss." I ran my fingers over my own hair laying across my shoulder. "I'm sorry I didn't recognize you from that day."

She smiled sadly. "It's okay." She reached up and tugged on her long brown locks. "I dyed my hair." Her eyes misted, but she took a deep breath and continued. "I needed to stop seeing my sister every time I looked in the mirror, you know."

I moved closer and wrapped my arms around her, pulling her close, holding her tighter when she sniffed. "I can't even imagine losing someone I love so much."

"She was the only normal one in our family." She wiped the moisture from her cheeks with her fingertips. "Now she's gone. And I'm stuck."

She pulled back, but I kept my hands on her shoulders and tilted my head in confusion. "What do you mean stuck?"

She ran her hand over her forehead and took a deep breath, exhaling slowly. "I was supposed to move in with them after I turned eighteen."

"When do you turn eighteen?" I inquired.

"Three days ago."

I let my eyes travel over the sadness in her features. "What did you do for your birthday?"

She waved her hand dismissively. "Nothing. My mom never celebrated our birthdays." She looked over my shoulder, almost dreamily. "Tara always did something. She would've really celebrated this birthday because we were both excited that I was going to move in with them. We were both looking forward to it."

"Found one!"

I slowly shifted my attention from Natalie toward the stairs where Sophie bounded down, holding up a red ponytail holder, Seth hot on her heels. I smiled softly at Natalie again before heading toward Sophie who was already in the kitchen and planting herself on the stool.

"Can I watch?" Natalie asked. "I've never learned how to French braid."

"Sure," I said, before gesturing toward Seth. "Maybe you can do Seth's while I do Sophie's," I suggested, smiling huge when Seth laughed.

I'd only just begun when the doorbell rang again, and I heard Tyler's voice, the smell of sauce and cheese drifting toward the kitchen. I finished braiding Sophie's hair, answering Natalie's questions while I went along. I tried to stop my eyes from drifting toward Tyler while he got out plates and napkins, but I failed. Miserably.

The only thing that made me feel better was that he seemed to be failing too.

We ate, listening to Sophie talk about school, and surprisingly, Seth even spoke some. It was obvious he was thrilled to be in Andy's class, something I knew Kasey had a lot to do with, but he also seemed more content with the school itself. It was definitely better than when he talked about his old school. I asked questions and so did Natalie who obviously enjoyed being with the kids. You could see her love for them shining in her eyes while she listened to them chatter.

"Aunt Natalie!" Sophie called out and jumped down from her stool. "Can you play with me?"

"Sure," she answered. "But let's clean up our plates first."

I waved her off. "I'll help Tyler with these. Go play."

"Thanks, Grace." She smiled sincerely and followed both Sophie and Seth to the stairs. I waited until I couldn't hear their voices anymore to turn back and face Tyler, but he was already out of his seat putting dishes in the sink. I pushed off my stool and took my plate over to the sink and saw his back stiffen the closer I got.

I moved forward until we stood side by side. "How are you?"

"Good," he blurted, abruptly.

I laid my hand on his forearm until he shifted and looked at me. "Is something wrong?"

He leaned down on his elbows, which put his face closer to mine. "I'm having a really hard time not touching you Grace."

Warmth enveloped me at his admission, and I shifted closer, forcing him to stand so I could push my body between him and the sink. "You shouldn't deny yourself. People say that isn't healthy."

His lips tipped up at the corners. "Who says that?"

I rolled my lips together and stood on my tiptoes. "Does it really matter?"

He angled his head down until his lips touched mine. I barely heard his groan over mine before he lifted me and set my butt on the counter beside the sink, pushing himself between my legs. He kissed me hungrily like he was starving, and I held on, wanting everything he was willing to give me. I wrapped my arms around his neck and pulled his body as close to mine as I could get him. He shoved his hand into my hair and positioned my head to deepen the kiss. Our mouths bit at each other while our tongues dueled, but it wasn't enough for either of us, and we pulled apart, breathing heavily.

I laid my palms against the sides of his neck when he lowered his forehead to mine. "I missed you this week."

His lips curved into a smile. "You don't know what that does to me."

"Tell me," I whispered.

He groaned and kissed me softly one more time before pulling back and lifting me off the counter. "I can't, Grace. I don't know how to say it, and I can't show you." He pointed at the stairs right around the corner where the kids had just gone. He was right. This wasn't a great time.

I leaned my hip against the counter. "Then at least tell me how you're doing with the kids and everything."

His eyes flicked between mine for a long moment before he finally answered. "Better."

I smiled softly. "Good." I gestured to the stairs. "The kids seem good."

"They're doing better too. They like their therapist and seem to be settling in at school, Seth especially."

I leaned forward and tugged on his shirt with my fingers. "Did you hear him say hi to me first?"

"Yeah. He's been talking more, initiating more conversations with me, especially about Andy."

"He found his best friend," I pointed out.

He reached forward and ran his fingers through the tips of my hair. It was as if we couldn't stand this close without touching each other in some small way. "He needs that."

"Are they still sleeping with you?" I asked quietly.

He exhaled heavily and dropped his hand. "Most nights."

I nodded, but then we both grew quiet, and I knew why. At some point, we were going to have to find a way to be alone and figure things out, like what we wanted from each other. We'd never really had the opportunity to have that normal relationship when the beginning was all about talking, getting to know each other, all the good stuff. We just kind of fell into this with each other, and there are too many unanswered questions. For me at least.

Shaking it off, I asked the question I didn't want to ask in front of the kids. "Did you send me flowers?"

His head jerked back. "Flowers? No."

I rolled my lips together. "I didn't think so."

"Who the fuck is sending you flowers?"

"I don't know. There was no card." I hesitated before continuing because I knew bringing up Saturday night would put that hard look back on his face. "I got them last Saturday morning and then Saturday night happened, and I completely forgot about them." I rubbed my palms together. "Until today."

"What happened today?" He put his hands on his hips, his expression a mix of concern and anger.

I swallowed hard. "I got a letter in the mail. Well, less of a letter, more like a note, but in either case, it was kind of creepy."

His eyebrows pulled down. "Creepy how?"

"It was what it said that was creepy." I tried to shake off the feeling of dread beginning to take hold. "I guess I have a secret admirer."

"Or a stalker." He spoke the exact thoughts I'd been having.

"Maybe. Hopefully, it was a one-time thing."

He scowled, his expression clearly telling me he didn't agree. I patted him on the chest to reassure him before walking to the counter where I'd laid my purse and keys and picked them both up. I suddenly felt bad for laying all this shit on him. He already had enough to worry about, and I'd just brought more to his door.

"I'm sure it's nothing to worry about." I gestured behind me with my thumb in the direction of his door. "I'm pretty tired, so I think I'm gonna go."

I backed up a few steps toward the door only stopping when he spoke. "Grace."

I smiled what I hoped was a reassuring smile. "Yeah?"

He took a few steps forward. "You should stay."

God, I wanted that, but I couldn't. I wouldn't want to leave, not tonight, not when I was feeling vulnerable, and a sleepover was out of the question, so I needed to go.

While I still had the strength.

I leaned forward and pushed up on my toes, kissing him softly on the lips. "I'll see you guys tomorrow for dinner, okay?" When he nodded, I gestured in the direction of the stairs. "Will you tell the kids I said good-bye?"

I waited for his trademark nod, then I spun on my heel, heading out the door and straight to my car.

I was on a mission.

I needed to go home and figure out who was trying to get my attention by scaring the hell out of me.

Chapter Thirty-two

Tyler

Flexing my hand against the steering wheel, I pulled into the parking lot attached to Grace's apartment building, put the SUV in park, and sat still. I shouldn't go in there, but I was worried, especially because she seemed concerned even though she'd tried to play it off as nothing. I did not like seeing the worry in her eyes.

And I fucking hated that someone was sending her shit to scare her.

She'd barely left before I jogged up the stairs and into Sophie's room where the three of them were snuggled together on Sophie's bed watching some Disney movie.

I lifted my chin in Natalie's direction when she looked up. "Can you stay with the kids for a while?"

She nodded, a smile spreading across her face. "Yeah, no problem."

"Thanks," I mumbled. "I'll be back as soon as I can."

"Take your time," she said. "I don't have any plans tonight, and I'm not exactly excited to go home."

I'd felt that same tightening in my gut that I've felt over the last week when I've spoken to Natalie on the phone. I knew her home wasn't safe, had even heard her mother's nasty words in the background when I'd been on the phone with her, but she insisted all was well. She'd called a lot since the funeral, but today was the first day she was able to come over, and I was glad she wasn't in a hurry to leave.

I'd thanked her, told the kids I'd be back soon, but they didn't seem to care, only snuggling in tighter against Natalie with their eyes on the movie. I stared for a minute, suddenly happy they'd had her in their lives and still did, something permanent, something they hadn't lost. I decided to ask her to visit them more often, hoping she'd agree.

Grabbing my keys, I moved from my vehicle and to the front door of her building, pulling the front door open, pissed that there was no security in the building. Anyone could walk right in. I'd seen a call box on the outside beside the door, but it obviously wasn't hooked up, meaning anyone could walk in just like I had. I looked across the small lobby to the mailboxes, which not only have the apartment number but also the tenants' last name on them. I shook my head, becoming more pissed as I made my way up the stairs to the second-floor apartments. She was only two doors down from the elevator, and I paused in front of her door to take a deep breath, trying to control the anger simmering in my body.

I barely knocked before she pulled open the door, wearing that same damn outfit she'd worn to my house, which shouldn't be sexy, but on her was fucking incredible. Although to me, every time I'd seen her, she'd looked incredible. Hell, I held her hair while she vomited and then cleaned her up, and even that hadn't turned me off.

She smiled hesitantly when I just stood there. "Tyler?"

"Can I come in?" I asked abruptly.

"Umm…" She hesitated this time, even looking beyond my shoulder before she answered. "Sure. Where are the kids?"

She backed up when I moved forward, and I followed her into

the apartment, closing the door behind me. "They're at home with Natalie."

"Oh, okay," she mumbled, and I took a minute to look around her apartment. It was small, but it was definitely Grace's, with color everywhere. I looked from her red couch to the turquoise pans stacked on her stove. My eyes continued their perusal, appreciating how homey her place was and thinking how cold my house still seemed even with all the kids' things in it. The anger I'd left at the door reared its ugly head when my eyes landed on the vase of flowers sitting on the side table in the living room.

"Ty, is everything okay?"

I gestured in the direction I was looking. "Those the flowers?"

"Yeah," she answered.

I finally broke my stare with the vase and looked at Grace. "Where's the letter?"

"On the counter, why?"

I moved past her and grabbed the open letter off the counter. Reading it quickly, I felt my body tensing with each word. When I finished reading it for the second time, I threw it down, put my hands on my hips, and faced Grace. "Do your brothers know about that?"

She sighed heavily. "No, not yet."

"Let's go."

Her eyes widened when I grabbed the letter from the counter and walked past her straight back to the door I'd just come through. "What? Go where?"

"To see your brothers."

I turned toward her when I got to the door, just in time to see her throw her hands on her hips. "No," she said calmly, but I saw the fire in her eyes. "And you can give me the letter back right now, Tyler."

I widened my stance and crossed my arms over my chest. "I'm taking you to talk to them."

"I'm not going with you."

"Why the hell not?" I yelled.

"Why not?" She threw her hands in the air in frustration. "Really?" She put her hands back on her hips and moved a few steps closer to me. "I already have seven brothers, Ty, I don't need another one to boss me around." She moved past me where I stood beside the door and grabbed the door handle, pulling it open. "So you can go."

I put my hand on the door and slammed it shut, ignoring the pissed-off expression on her face. "I'm not going without you." I leaned in, putting my face closer to hers. "And apparently you do need someone to step in if you haven't already taken this shit to them." He waved the paper in the air. "You have a fucking stalker, Grace, and you're walking around calm as can be acting like nothing could happen to you."

"We don't know that I have a stalker, Ty."

"Jesus, Grace, someone sent you flowers with no note, a letter with no signature that's fucking creepy, and do I need to remind you that you were roofied less than a week ago."

"No, you don't need to remind me, seeing as it happened"— she patted her chest—"to me. I was there, remember?"

"Yeah, I remember, Grace. I also remember sitting up practically the whole damn night because I was worried about you."

She sighed. "Ty."

"No." I shoved my hand through my hair. "Don't Ty me, like you think I'm overreacting." I held up the letter. "This shit is real, Grace. Someone is trying to get to you, and I have a bad feeling it's only going to get worse if we let this go."

"I don't want to overreact and involve my brothers," she admitted. "You don't understand what they're like. Trust me, once I open the door for them to move in and take care of this, they will never let me out of their sight."

"Good."

"No," She raised her voice. "That's not good. I don't want that."

"Do you want to get attacked, or even worse, raped?" She jerked back, and I knew I finally had her attention. "The flowers, the drug, this fucking letter, Grace, this guy is not doing this for nothing. He wants to fuck you." I took a step closer to her. "That's why women get roofied, for Christ's sake." I held up the letter again. "And from the sounds of this creepy-ass letter, he's crazy enough to not stop until he gets what he wants."

"You don't know that," she said, but she was wavering. I could tell by the tone of her voice that she wasn't so sure anymore that I wasn't right.

"I don't know?" I said, dropping my voice. "Are you fucking serious?" I moved even closer until the toes of my shoes pressed against her bare feet and leaned down. "I've only had one real taste, and I'm obsessed with you. Wondering what you're doing, who the fuck you're talking to, who's putting his hands on you. One. Fucking. Taste. And I'm hooked. It's been pretty fucking difficult to stop myself from wanting you, so how the hell would someone who's unstable stop himself?"

She was breathing heavily, the rise and fall of her chest evidence of that, but it seemed the anger she'd been holding in so tightly was subsiding. Her eyes met mine, and she pushed herself forward, closing the small amount of space left between us and pressing her body to mine. I couldn't stop the groan when I felt the long lines of her body tight against my own, and I couldn't stop myself from reaching for her and wrapping my arms around her back. She lifted her face and skimmed her lips along my jaw, and a small whimper escaped her when I lifted her while pressing my lips against hers and demanding entrance. She wrapped her long legs around my waist and pressed tight against my cock, making me groan again. Fuck, I was hard already, and she barely touched me.

"You think about me?" she whispered against my lips.

"You know I do."

She pulled back, putting a whisper of space between our lips, but my eyes stayed focused on her mouth. "I don't know that, Ty."

Tightening my arms around her, I squeezed her tighter against me. "When you're near me…"

I trailed off, my words lost, but she wouldn't allow that. She pushed me. She demanded more of me than I ever had of myself, and I was starting to crave that, crave her in a way that couldn't be healthy for either of us. "Tell me."

I pressed my lips against hers, but she pulled back and tucked her face against my shoulder, her lips skimming up my neck until they reached my ear. "Tell me, Ty. Tell me what you want."

I turned our bodies and slammed her back against the wall by the door, pressing her tighter against my hard cock and angling her just right so I could thrust against her. She moaned and her dropped her head back, leaving her neck wide open. I skimmed my teeth along the silky skin of her neck, right up to her ear while I thrusted. "I want to fuck you, Grace." The shiver that ran through her body when I whispered in her ear spurred me on. "I want to thrust deep inside you, so deep that you'll still feel me the next day." I ran my tongue along her ear. "Every time you move, I want you to remember how it felt to have me inside you."

"Ty." She panted, putting her palms against my cheeks and pressing my lips against hers. This time, I didn't hold back. I needed her, and fuck, I wanted her. Our kiss was fast and wet, our tongues dueling while our hands pulled at clothes. I kicked off my shoes, moved us from the wall, and back the short hallway to her bedroom. She wiggled down my body, and I groaned while I watched her pull her top over her head. She quickly removed her tank top, leaving her in only a bra and those tight damn pants.

"Fuck, you're beautiful," I said.

She moved closer to me and ran her hands under my shirt, forcing it up until she couldn't reach anymore. I grabbed the hem and ripped it over my head, my lips finding hers again as soon as I threw my shirt across the room. I shoved my hands down the back of her pants and under her panties to palm her bare cheeks, pushing her pants down when she moaned against my mouth. She kicked off her pants and reached for the button on my jeans without her lips ever falling from my own. When her small hand dipped inside and wrapped around my cock, I lost the little bit of control I was holding on to. I picked her up and threw her on the bed before I tore my jeans down my legs and followed. I came down over her and found her lips once again, shoving her bra up so I could feel her breasts against my hands. I dropped my head, sucking her nipple into my mouth, noticing the harder I sucked, the harder she pulled my hair, and I fucking loved that, so I sucked harder. I moved between her breasts, the whole time listening to her moans getting louder and making me impossibly harder.

I ran my hand down over her belly and slid my middle finger through her slit, dropping my head to her chest when I felt her wetness trickle across my finger.

"Ty." She panted.

I lifted my head and laid my lips against hers. "Yeah."

"I need…"

I licked the seam of her lips and slipped my tongue inside when she opened her mouth, then pushed my finger into her pussy slowly. Her hips shot up, and I kissed her leisurely, keeping the same speed as my finger.

She pulled her lips away from mine. "Faster."

I slid my finger out and pushed in two together, but I kept my pace slow while I ran my tongue along her throat. She pushed her hips up, trying to get me to go faster, but I loved hearing her sounds, loved feeling her body against mine, and I was too damn selfish to let it end quickly. She arched her back and moaned long and loud when I pressed my thumb softly against her clit and rolled it gently.

She slid her hands down my back and around my sides, her moans increasing, tremors moving through her while I felt her body climbing. When her hand dipped lower, I wasn't prepared for it. I was too invested in her, but she wrapped her hand around my cock, and my own body jerked. She caught me off guard enough that she could move, and before I knew it, she had me on my back, and she was holding my heavy cock in her hand. She positioned me at her opening and pushed me inside, letting her head fall back as she slid my long length inside her.

I grabbed her hips when she settled on my lap and leaned over, pressing her lips to mine. "God, you're big everywhere, aren't you?"

I would've grinned if I didn't feel like I was going to explode. She was tight, tighter than any woman I'd ever been with, and I wondered if I was even going to need her to move for me to come.

She sat back up and lifted her hips up, sliding slowly back down, finding her pace. I gritted my teeth together and squeezed her hips harder, knowing I was leaving bruises on her skin, but I couldn't stop.

I slid my hands up her body and placed them on either side of her face, tugging her down and smashing my lips against hers before I pulled back and looked into her eyes. "If you're going to be on top, Grace, you better fuck me hard."

Her pussy tightened even more, telling me my Grace liked it a little harder, a little rougher, maybe even a little more forbidden. I knew I was right when she sat up, lifted her body, and slammed down. I groaned and grabbed her hips, helping her take my cock faster and harder each time. I thrust my hips up when she was slowing down and then reached between us, found her clit, and flicked it relentlessly while she rode me. Fuck, she looked beautiful. I ran my hand up her side and squeezed her breast with my hand, her size spilling out over my palm.

I wrapped my thumb and finger around her nipple. "Come for me, Grace. I need to see it again. It's all I fucking think about." I flicked my finger faster against her clit and felt her pussy tighten just before she called out my name and blew apart.

I grabbed both of her hips and thrust hard, harder than I probably should have, but I was out of control with her, and seconds after she came, I came with a roar.

It took minutes for our bodies to relax, but eventually, our breathing evened out, and she slid off me, cuddling into my side. I felt the wetness follow her and cursed myself. Fuck, I hadn't even thought about protection, and I know she hadn't either. It didn't matter; we'd deal with whatever happened and we'd do it together because now that I'd had her, I'd do whatever it took to keep her.

"We forgot protection."

Her soft voice sounded from beside me, and I exhaled a deep breath. "Yeah."

"I'm on the pill," she said. "And I'm clean. I've only been with two other guys, and it's been a while."

"I do not want to know that shit, Grace."

I felt her tense before she lifted herself and propped her chin on my chest so she could see my face. "What shit?"

"I don't want to know how many men you've been with while I'm lying next to you."

"I was only telling you that so you'd know I'm clean."

I rolled her over onto her back because she sounded hurt, and I didn't want that. I'd never want that. I propped myself up on my elbow beside her and ran my hand down her body slowly until my palm cupped her. "You letting me in here, Grace, is like a dream come true. And we do need to talk about protection and all that shit so the next time we get carried away, we know the deal, but not while I just had my one and only dream come true, baby." I kissed her softly. "Okay?"

She smiled softly. "So you're saying pick my time and place better next time?"

I grinned and dropped my head, shaking it. "Yeah, baby, I'm saying there's a time and a place, and this isn't it."

She giggled, and I dropped back down beside her, but I let my hand lay against her, liking the feeling of her heat on my palm. She turned her head on the pillow, locked her eyes to mine and lifted her finger to run the tip along my bottom lip. "You're the dream I never knew I had, Ty." Her eyes looked watery, but I stayed silent, holding my breath in anticipation of what she might say. "And now I understand. I never knew enough, never lived enough to dream up someone like you. But I'm glad I didn't." She rolled to her side, dislodging my hand so I slid it up her thigh to rest against her hip. She snuggled in tight against my chest, her eyes never leaving mine. "Because the surprise of you was better than I could have ever dreamed."

I felt a pull in my chest at her words and laid my lips against hers, kissing her slowly before I settled back against the pillow, hoping she could see in my eyes and feel in my kiss the words that just wouldn't come to me. When she nodded and smiled, wrapping her arms tight around my waist, I knew she heard my words too.

"Ty, I know I can trust you, but I still have to ask if you've been tested," she said, almost shyly.

I ran my fingers down the long strands of her hair. "I haven't been with anyone since I got hurt."

Her head snapped up. "Wasn't that over two years ago?" I jerked my chin up in acknowledgment. "Why not?"

My eyes flicked back and forth between hers. "I'm not good with women, talking to them and all that shit. Football spoke for me in the past, so I didn't have to do much more than say hi, and they took it from there. I think some of them even got off on it." My eyes lifted from hers to watch her hair float through my fingers. "Without football in my life, I just didn't bother."

She traced her thumb across my bottom lip, bringing my attention back to her. "You're better than you think you are." She lifted up to rub her lips across mine. "You got me."

I felt my lips tip up in the corners. "That was all you, baby. You weren't giving up on me, and I figured that out pretty fast. What I couldn't figure out was why."

"I saw you, *the real you*," she stressed. "A few times, when you let the mask slip, I knew that man was someone I wanted to know. We all wear masks sometimes, Ty, but when we find the person we can take that mask off for, we've found a person worth knowing."

She laid her head back down on my chest, and I felt her finger tracing the tattoo on my chest, right above my heart, with her fingertip. I waited for the pain to wash over me, like it always does, but it never happened. Instead, all I felt was calm. "This is beautiful."

I swallowed hard. "It's for my mom."

"Tell me about her," she whispered and tightened her arm around my stomach.

I lifted my hand and ran my fingers through her silky brown locks while I shared a part of myself with her that I'd never shared with anyone. "She was quiet but funny, so damn funny when it was just me and her. She hated crowds, but I did too, so we'd do things like go hiking or have movie night at home. She always found a way to make everything fun." I smiled, remembering her laughing during movies. "She loved looking at the stars, but she could never pick out the constellations. She even bought a book and still couldn't find the damn things." I chuckled, and Grace propped her head on my chest. "When I got the tattoo, I just told them to do some constellations in swirls of color because that's what I imagine when I think of her."

"I wish I could've met her," she whispered.

"Fuck, Grace"—I sighed—"she would've loved you."

She reached up and kissed me softly before dropping back down and laying her head on my chest again. I'm not sure how long we laid there, enjoying the solitude we could never have at my house right now before the worry for her started to settle back into my bones. I pressed a kiss against the top of her head. "You know what we have to do."

She was quiet for a moment before she spoke. "Round two?"

Her hopeful voice made me laugh, and when she looked up, wiggling her eyebrows, I laughed even harder. I'd never been with anyone who could make me laugh the way she can and does. "It's time to call your brothers, baby."

She frowned. "Are you sure I can't distract you with sex?"

I rolled and then lifted myself off the bed, taking her with me because she could definitely distract me with sex if she wanted to, and while lying together naked, it wouldn't take very much effort.

I picked her shirt up off the floor and handed it to her, pressing a kiss to her lips before I grabbed my jeans and headed to the bathroom, calling out behind me. "Call your brothers, Grace."

Chapter Thirty-three

Grace

I did not want to do this, and as the clock ticked closer and closer to the time I knew they'd arrive, the more I didn't want to do this. Tyler wasn't hearing no, though, that was obvious, and what I didn't want to admit to him or myself was that I was afraid. The note was creepy, he wasn't wrong, but I'd been wanting to handle it on my own. The problem was, I had no idea how to do that.

After I dressed and procrastinated a little, I called Brody and explained a note had been addressed and delivered to me that seemed suspicious. I barely had the words spoken before he told me to sit tight, and he would be right over. I knew he wasn't coming alone. I just had no idea how many were coming with him.

"You okay?"

I looked up from the couch where I sat, running my fingers through the ends of my hair and tried to smile reassuringly. "Yeah, I'm fine."

"You ready to tell me why you don't want your brothers to

know about this?" He held up the letter he once again gripped tightly in his hand.

I dropped my hands to my lap and sighed. "They'll blow it out of proportion. You know that."

He nodded but didn't look convinced. "This have anything to do with why you didn't want them to know about your car?"

"They won't understand. At least, I don't think they will, but I'm starting to think I don't care if they do."

He pushed off the wall where he'd been leaning by the door and made his way to the couch, sitting down beside me. "You trust me?"

I thought about his question and realized I did trust him. It had been almost an unconscious decision because I didn't remember ever feeling like I couldn't, especially after he defended me in my brother's kitchen.

I grabbed his hand and held it mine. "I trust you, Ty."

He leaned in, putting his body impossibly closer to mine. "Then talk to me. Tell me what the hell you're trying so hard to keep a secret."

I wanted to tell him. For the first time, I really wanted to tell someone, but an abrupt knock on the door stopped me. He dropped his head, but I leaned in and put my hands on either side of his face to lift it so I could see his eyes.

Leaning in, I pressed a hard kiss to his mouth before pulling back. "I'll tell you. I promise."

He nodded and stood after I walked by his legs heading for the door. I felt him behind me, becoming my own personal wall of strength when I swung open the door.

Brody and Jax came through the door, their eyes soft when they looked at me, but hardening when they landed on the man at my back. I closed the door and spun to face them, throwing my hands on my hips. "Before we start, I expect you both to be nice to Tyler. He's here as my…" I trailed off, not sure what to call him since I knew we were definitely beyond friends now, but we hadn't called our relationship anything. When Tyler dropped his head and grinned, I waved my hand in the air. "Well, he's my something." I poked them both in the chest, one at a time. "Be nice."

Jax was the first to nod, which actually surprised me. They were both hardasses, but Jax was usually the worse. "Tell us what's going on."

I pointed behind me at the flowers still sitting on the table. "Last Saturday, those flowers were delivered with no card, so I didn't know who they came from. I thought..." I trailed off again, but my head jerked toward Tyler when I heard his voice.

"She thought they were from me."

Jax's eyes flicked back and forth between us. "But they weren't."

I shook my head. "No, but I didn't know that until today when I finally asked him."

"Why did you wait so long?" Brody asked, and I could tell he was genuinely surprised.

I looked over at Tyler whose eyes were as wide as mine. He gestured with his chin toward my brothers, encouraging me to continue. I turned my head to face them again. "Didn't Luke tell you what happened Saturday night?"

"No. What happened Saturday night?" Jax asked suspiciously.

"I can't believe he didn't tell you," I mumbled, shaking my head.

"Grace," Brody snapped.

"She was drugged at a club in the city," Ty announced, and my brothers' eyes both flashed.

"You were drugged?" Jax asked in a low voice while Brody pulled out his phone and started texting.

I cleared my throat, happy I wasn't Luke at that moment. It only took a minute to update Jax and Brody on the events of Saturday night, including Ty's role in everything, which only seemed to increase the tension.

Jax looked back at Brody. "What'd he say?"

223

"No leads, no security cameras, and no one saw shit." Jax swore and ran his hand over the back of his neck, the universal sign in my family among the men that they were frustrated.

"I thought you said you got a letter," Brody said.

Tyler held out the letter he still gripped tightly in his hand and the memory of him dropping it when he wrapped his arms around me flashed through my mind. The thought of his strong body lifting me like I weighed nothing and pressing me against the wall made me flush, so I quickly shook my head to clear it. I didn't need to give my brothers any more ammunition against Ty. "She got this today."

Jax took the letter, and I watched as both he and Brody reading it, their jaws clenching harder with each word read. By the end, I wasn't sure how they hadn't cracked a couple of teeth. Without speaking to each other, Brody pulled out his phone again and tapped a few things before holding the phone to his ear. I listened to him talking to whom I assumed was Kyle, giving him the information and my address.

He ended the call and slipped his phone back into his pocket before looking my way. "Kyle's on his way, and he'll check for bugs. He has a tracker that I guarantee will find any if they're here and then hopefully can trace them back to something, a phone, a computer, something."

"So you think my house is bugged?"

Brody put his hands on his hips. "I'm not sure, but we're not taking any chances." I nodded, and he continued. "Explain the letter to me."

He gestured toward the letter Jax still held, but I didn't understand. "What do you mean?"

"What does this person mean, 'I know what you like now, what turns you on?'" Brody put his hands on his hips. "Can you think of anyone who would know those things about you? Anyone you've turned down?"

I shook my head. "No, not anyone."

Brody's eyes shifted toward Tyler. "You a patient man?"

I felt, actually felt the tension roll off Tyler when he straightened and faced off with my brother. I stepped between them, already sensing where this was going, and put my back against Tyler's chest. I knew neither of them would do anything with me standing between them. "Stop it, you guys. Tyler had nothing to do with this."

It was as if I hadn't even spoken when Ty growled behind me. "Are you seriously asking me that shit?"

Jax narrowed his eyes. "Seems kind of coincidental to me that she was safe until you came into her life."

"Jax!" I snapped.

"Do you really think I'd be here right now and would've encouraged her to call you two if I had anything to do with this shit?" Tyler pointed out.

"I won't pretend I know how someone who's unstable thinks."

Tyler inched forward and pressed tight against my back, putting him closer to Jax. "What the fuck is your problem with me? Is it me? Or would it be any man she was seeing?"

"Our problem" Brody's voice was tight. "is how fast you've become such a big part of her life."

I raised my hands and put a palm on each of my brother's chests. "I've known Tyler for over a year, you guys." I didn't bother to tell them that we hadn't had contact all that time.

Jax glanced down at me. "Then why haven't we?"

My eyes widened. "Because of this. This is exactly what you guys do with men in my life who aren't you."

Jax's eyes softened. "We want you to be safe, Grace, that's all."

"I am safe," I stressed.

"If you're so safe, then why are we here?" Brody raised an eyebrow.

"This is a rare occasion," I defended.

"Exactly. Your safety has only been a concern since this guy came into your life." Brody gestured toward Ty.

"That's fucking ridiculous." Ty snarled behind me.

"You have a record, man, so that means you're not safe, not safe enough for our sister." Jax motioned between him and Brody. "And now, we're standing here because she got flowers, was drugged and received a letter with all kinds of sexual implications, and you're, not surprisingly, in her home. A home you apparently have access to." Jax leaned in a little further. "Tell me, are we even going to find anything, or were you just hoping this fucking letter would have Grace running right to you?"

"What the fuck does that mean?"

"It means"—Brody lowered his voice—"that maybe you aren't so patient."

Tyler wrapped his arm around my waist and yanked me back into his body, holding me tightly. "I don't need to be patient."

My eyes widened when Tyler's words finally connected with my brothers, and their faces hardened even further. I dropped my hands and rolled my lips together, trying to think of a way to defuse this situation when I heard Tyler's voice again.

"As a matter of fact—"

I spun around so fast it made me dizzy, and I slapped my hand over his mouth. "Stop talking, Ty." His stare stayed hard on my brothers until I reached my other hand up to wrap around his neck and pulled until he looked down at me. My eyes widened. "Just stop talking."

I let my hand fall from his mouth when his eyes slowly roamed over my face before finally settling on mine again, and I saw the corners of his full lips tilt up. That was when it occurred to me. He was fucking with them. What was wrong with him? He was egging on my two retired military, special forces brothers and enjoying it. He was also proving he wasn't going to take their shit anymore, the same he'd done with Luke last Saturday. I widened my eyes further when it was obvious he knew I'd figured it out but couldn't contain my smile when his grin started to grow. I dropped my hands and wrapped them around his waist, planting my face against his wide chest, laughing quietly.

The loud knock on the door broke through the awkward silence in the room. I felt my brothers move, so I stood on my tiptoes and pressed my lips against Ty's, sighing when his arms tightened. I dropped back down, knowing how quickly I would get lost in him, and I couldn't. We had an audience and questions I really needed answers to.

Kyle moved swiftly through the door but stopped right inside and looked among us before a wide smile broke out on his face. "Looks like I came just in time for the show."

I shook my head, but did it while returning Kyle's smile. "No show. The tantrums have been averted." I raised my eyebrows. "For now, at least."

Kyle laughed and looked over my head at Tyler. "Hey, man, good to see you again."

Tyler tipped his chin. "Thanks for coming, Kyle."

He shifted his attention back toward Brody. "Where can I set up my shit?"

Brody led him past us to my kitchen where he and Kyle began to set up shop. I turned, still in Ty's arms, and snuggled close, taking a deep breath. I didn't think I'd ever felt before what I felt when he was holding on to me. Safe, comfortable, happy—just to name a few. My eyes landed on Jax, who was watching us closely, and I stepped out of my comfort for a minute to talk to my brother. The oldest, the one who would have the most trouble trusting anyone, the one who would lay down his life for all of us.

I stepped right up to him when Ty eventually dropped his arms. "Jax." His eyes dropped down to mine, and I continued. "I'm happy. Right now, I'm so happy I could do a girly dance in the middle of all this crazy stuff that's been happening." I relaxed a little when he grinned. "Please be happy for me, support me, and trust me." I laid my hand on his forearm. "I need you to trust me."

His eyes flicked back and forth between mine, and I saw him nod his head slightly. He wasn't a hundred percent on board, but he'd nodded, and I was taking anything I could get. I leaned up and kissed him on the cheek. "Thank you."

I shifted back in front of Tyler and sighed contentedly when he wrapped his strong arms around my waist and pulled me back to lean into him. When he bent his head down and brushed his lips over my shoulder, I dropped my head to the side, giving him more room. We stayed just like that and watched Brody and Kyle make their way through my tiny apartment. Jax stood in front of an open laptop, his forehead creased from his scowl.

I held my breath, and Tyler's arms tightened when they all met at my counter and looked at the screen together. Brody shook his head.

"What?" I asked, unable to take the quiet any longer.

"You're all clear," Kyle said.

I looked at them. "What does that mean?"

"That means no bugs," Kyle explained. "There's not a recording device to be found inside your apartment."

Relief washed over me, but they didn't seem to feel the same. "Why don't you look relieved?"

Brody took a deep breath and exhaled heavily. "Because that's not exactly good news."

"I'm confused. Isn't that the news we wanted?"

"Not necessarily." Kyle explained. "If there were recordings here, I would most likely be able to trace them and that could lead us to who sent the letter, but with no recording devices…"

He trailed off with a shrug of his shoulders, but I could see the frustration in his expression. In all of their expressions. "So that means…?"

"That means," Jax answered for the group, "we have no fucking leads, which means we have to wait for his next move."

"And Luke had no leads." Brody slammed his fist on the counter. "Fuck. We got nothing."

I didn't like the sound of that, and from the anaconda-like wrap Ty's arms had around me, I had a feeling he didn't either.

"You're staying with me," Ty growled at the same time Jax said the same words.

Their eyes locked, and I knew any truce we'd come to only minutes before was over. I dropped my head in defeat. This was going to be a long night.

Chapter Thirty-four

Tyler

Why the fuck was I hanging a happy birthday sign in my house, and why did I agree to this? Did I agree to this? I remembered a conversation this morning while drinking coffee on my back deck with Grace about Natalie's birthday. I remembered her saying it was sad no one even acknowledged it, especially because it was a big year and Tara had planned to celebrate it with her. I remembered Grace getting excited about an idea she had, but at that moment, she had shoved her chair closer to mine and leaned over to talk to me, and I was fucking lost. Lost in her voice, lost in her scent, lost in her eyes, hell, she could've told me she was moving in permanently, and I would've agreed. I just wanted her to stay close, and I'd agree to anything to keep that smile on her face.

And why didn't the idea of her moving in permanently send me into a silent nightmare? Her close every day, every night? The idea of that, of living with someone, would've scared me only a few months ago, but now the idea has only made me feel, well, calm actually. She's made me feel a calmness I haven't felt in a while, she's made me feel accepted, and I wasn't sure I've felt that since before my mom died.

"That looks great!" Grace clapped, and I dropped my hands, stepping back to look at the glittery sign announcing her birthday.

I turned, facing Grace, and noticed all the work that had been going on behind me while I was hanging a sign, lost in my thoughts. It was amazing to me what could be accomplished in such a short amount of time when it involved Grace and Charlie. They took the idea and ran with it. Before I realized what I'd agreed to, she had her phone to her ear and was running up the stairs.

I'd won last night, but I also think it was obvious I wasn't giving in. Grace agreed to come home with me for the night and stay today while Brody and Kyle installed an alarm at her apartment. It was the only compromise her and her brothers could come to since they wanted her to move in with one of them for a while, and she wanted to stay home. For once, I became the voice of reason in a situation and asked for option three, which Brody suggested. The alarm was the winner, and nobody said a word when I repeated my earlier mantra that she was coming home with me. She'd driven her car, and I followed, trying to think of a way she could sleep in my bed with me, but I couldn't come up with one, so once we were at my house, I suggested the guest room Dex had just vacated the past week. She agreed and grabbed my shirt, pulling me down so she could kiss me softly. Then she said good night and walked right upstairs. I stayed downstairs, needing some time to myself so I wouldn't go up and carry her to my bed for the night. After a couple of beers, I was tired enough to crawl into my own bed, but not before I tortured myself by peeking in the spare room to see her. It took all my willpower to walk away, but when I woke up with Sophie's feet once again in my face, I was glad I'd had that willpower.

"What do you think?" She gestured behind her.

My eyes scoured the balloons and streamers decorating the room, making it happy and bright. "It looks great."

She chewed on the corner of her lip. "I don't think I forgot anything. The kids got her presents with Charlie and me this morning," She began ticking things off on her fingers. "I have pizza coming, but I also have my mom making this amazing dip she always makes, and the girls all want to contribute so we'll have a ton of food. Bella's mom is a fabulous baker and is making cupcakes because they are pretty quick and easy for her."

"Wait." I held up my hand. "The girls? Your mom? Who all is coming to this party?"

She smiled. "Everyone."

"But she doesn't even know your family," I pointed out.

"She will after tonight. Plus, she doesn't really have any family left that she would want here, although Sophie said she has a friend she used to bring to Tara's when she visited and asked her to bring that friend. Her name's Erica."

"You're sure Sophie didn't blow it?"

"I'm sure." I nodded. "After you texted and asked her to babysit, I had Sophie call her and ask her to bring a friend. Sophie actually made up the story that they needed four players for the game she and Seth picked out and they only had three, so they needed Erica to come." Grace leaned in closer. "She begged pretty hard, and from the little I've seen with Natalie, she doesn't tell Sophie no."

"I'm not sure anyone tells Sophie no," I grumbled.

"You will," she said confidently. "When you need to say no, you will."

"I don't tell you no."

She grabbed my shirt with her hands and pulled me down until her lips brushed my ear. I groaned at the contact and wrapped my arms around her waist. "You don't want to tell me no."

Without thought, I turned my head and crushed my lips to hers. She opened her mouth immediately, and I didn't hesitate to deepen the kiss. I lifted her, so I didn't have to bend and I could press her tighter into me, and our kiss turned hungry, our bodies shifting restlessly against each other.

"Ewww."

I jerked back when I heard the familiar voice and watched as Grace rolled her lips together before dropping her forehead against my shoulder and laughing quietly. I turned to face the person attached to that voice.

"That's gross." Sophie wrinkled her nose, and I didn't even try to stop the grin.

"It's not gross," I said.

"What if your breath smells bad?" Her expression was pure distaste, and I grinned wider, allowing Grace to slide her body down mine until her feet hit the floor. I didn't groan when her body slid against mine, but fuck, I wanted to.

"My breath doesn't smell bad," I answered.

Her eyebrows pulled together. "How do you know?"

Grace giggled, but when I looked her way, she was watching Charlie, who was laughing silently behind Sophie, Seth standing close to her, but his expression seemed thoughtful and his attention was on Grace.

I flicked my attention back to Sophie. "I just know."

"Can you smell it? 'Cause sometimes in the morning when I'm in your bed, you talk to me, and it smells bad."

I rubbed my hand along my forehead. "That's different. That's morning breath. Everyone has that until they brush their teeth."

She tipped her head back. "But sometimes after you brush your teeth, it smells like coffee."

This conversation wasn't going to end, and I could've kissed Grace again when she finally stepped in. "I like the way his breath smells, Sophie. That's why I don't mind kissing him. And someday, when you're much older, you'll want to kiss a boy too."

"Ewww." She made a gagging sound, causing Seth to laugh really hard. "I'm never doing that. Boys are soooo gross." I snorted out a laugh when she rolled her eyes while saying so in such an exaggerated way.

"Okay." Charlie clapped her hands together. "It's five o'clock, and Natalie's supposed to come at seven, which means people will be showing up soon. What else needs done?"

Grace contemplated that for a minute before answering. "We have food coming and drinks, decorations are up—"

"They look so pretty," Sophie interrupted.

"Thank you." Grace curtseyed, making Sophie laugh.

"Can I keep the balloons in my room after the party?" she asked.

"Of course, you can," Grace answered but then gestured toward me. "Unless Ty wants them in his."

Seth giggled, and this time, he was the one to answer. It was quiet, but it was completely unprompted, and I heard the happy sigh go through the adults in the room. "I don't think Ty's a balloon guy."

I snorted. "You got that right, little brother."

Seth beamed at the nickname, and I took note of that. He was coming out of his shell more and more, and I had a lot of people to thank for that, a lot of changes made to help him along, including the change of school and the addition of a whole lot of people in his life.

"I need to put on my party dress!" Sophie faced Grace. "Do you think Lexi and Mia will wear party dresses too?"

Grace pulled her phone out of her pocket and knelt. "Let's call them and find out."

I listened to them talk to both Lexi's mom, Gia, and Mia's mom, Kasey, but my eyes were on Charlie, who was smiling at her phone while she texted. I took a step closer, and she looked up, a blush spreading along her cheeks.

"Dex?" I guessed.

"How'd you know?"

"I talked to him yesterday, and he said you've been texting." I paused before finally deciding to tell her what I'd told him. "I told him to be sure about this and not jerk you around. You're too nice for that. In the world we lived in for a long time, nice girls weren't the norm. Girls wanted the same thing we did, fast and easy."

She arched an eyebrow. "Who says I don't want that?"

My eyes widened. "It would shock the hell out of me if you do."

She shook her head. "I don't. But I also don't want serious. For now, I just want to have a little fun, and Dex is fun."

"He is that," I agreed, my eyes finding Grace still holding the phone out, the sound on speaker, with both Seth and Sophie surrounding her.

"He's also ridiculously smart," she said and an involuntary smile formed on my lips. "Also true."

"And great in bed."

I nodded, but then jerked back and focused my attention on Charlie, shocked until I saw the devious expression on her face. She laughed out loud. "I knew you weren't listening to me."

"I was," I defended myself. "Until…"

"Until Grace." She sighed, moving to stand a little closer. "I think a lot of things in your life didn't start until Grace came along."

I ran my hand along the side of my face. "I'm starting to think that's true."

"It's the last half of your story."

"What?"

She gestured toward Grace. "Ask Grace. I think that will start a conversation you need to have." She leaned in and lowered her voice. "Just a piece of advice, Ty, because I like you, and I like Grace with you. I think you're good for each other, but there's a big part of her life she hasn't shared, with you or anyone, and it's something she holds close to her heart." She pulled back but kept her voice low. "She wants her love story, believes in it, and she won't settle for anything less."

I nodded because I could've guessed that about her, but I had a feeling Charlie was trying to tell me something without breaking Grace's confidence. "She shouldn't settle for less."

Charlie smiled, but it wasn't her usual smile, and it never reached her eyes. "No, she shouldn't."

"Neither should you, Charlie."

She looked at Grace, and I saw what I knew Charlie was seeing. Grace was vibrant and beautiful, and not one to give up easily on anything, including people. Charlie dropped her head and sighed, her words quiet, but I still heard them. "We don't all get the fairy tale, Ty." She looked up at me and smiled softy. "The trick is learning early if you're a fairy-tale girl or not. It eliminates a lot of heartache along the way."

She patted my arm and walked back over to Grace, laughing when she reached her, but I didn't know at what because I was lost in thought. There was so much I still didn't know about Grace, but I knew I wouldn't have to wait much longer to find out. She wanted to share her secret; I knew it, and Charlie knew it.

I was just hoping it was something I could handle.

Chapter Thirty-five

Grace

"Surprise!"

I clapped my hands when Natalie pushed through the doorway and stopped, eyes wide, completely and utterly stunned. She just stood for a moment until Sophie ran over and yelled surprise again. A girl stood to her side, also stunned, but she recovered quicker than Natalie, and the longer she stood still, the quieter the room became.

And then she started to cry.

My eyes shot to Tyler, who had the same look of on his face that I knew I had on mine. He was standing on the other side of Seth, who still stood between us quietly. Did we do the wrong thing? Maybe we shouldn't have had this party. My mom started to move toward the door, motioning for me to go with her. We got to Natalie while she still cried with Erica's arms wrapped around her in a tight hug.

I put my hand on her back and leaned in close. "I'm so sorry, Natalie. We thought this would be fun, but we shouldn't have done it."

Natalie pulled back, sniffling, her eyes red and swollen, still full of tears, and bent down to pick up Sophie who was standing in front of her legs. "It just took me by surprise. No one has ever thrown me a party before."

"Do you love it?" Sophie asked excitedly.

"I really, really love it." She sniffed; her expression still full of wonder.

When my dad moved across the room to stand by me, my mom and I grinned at each other. "Hi, darlin', I'm Gracie's dad. You can call me Jack." She nodded, but he wasn't finished. "Have you met everyone?"

She wiped a lone tear from beneath her eye and shook her head. "No, but I saw most of you at the funeral. I can't believe how big your family is."

Dad chuckled. "That's what keeps it interesting."

"Tyler's lucky to have you." She smiled, but it almost looked sad. "Seth and Sophie too."

"You have us too, whether you want us or not." He winked, and her shoulders sagged, like some kind of weight had been lifted right off them. I heard my family chuckling, knowing this was Dad, and we expected nothing less from him.

He took over then, just like we knew he would, and I bent my head to hide the smile when he reached out and stole Sophie from Natalie, before putting his arm around Natalie's shoulders and guiding her across the room. I could hear Sophie giggling while he carried her along as he made introductions for both Natalie and Erica.

My mom rolled her eyes at me, but I knew she loved this part of him. His heart never seemed too full to take on another lost soul and you could easily see just how lost Natalie was. Something told me her anchor had been Tara, and with her gone, she was drifting.

"Grace, can you give me a hand?"

I nodded at my mom and followed her into the kitchen. She

pointed at a stool and I sat, waiting while she poured two glasses of wine, sliding one my way before lifting hers and taking a sip. Out of the corner of my eye, I saw Ty talking to Chase and smiled. Those two have really hit it off, and I love that for him, but I wish he had that with my brothers too.

"They'll come around."

I gave my attention back to my mom. "Who?"

She gestured toward the room at large with her glass. "Your brothers."

I frowned, not at all surprised she knew my thoughts, but that she was so positive when I was feeling anything but positive. "I'm not so sure."

"I am," she said confidently. "Your Tyler's making strides with your brothers. They're starting to respect him, I can tell."

I got stuck on something she'd said. "I'm not sure he's my Tyler, mom."

She took another sip of her wine, which I mirrored. "Brody and Jax stopped at the house this morning."

I rolled my eyes. "Were they telling on me?"

Mom chuckled. "No, but they did tell us about the letter you got and are upset that no one told them you were drugged last Saturday night."

"I know they're mad about that, but they're going to have to get over it."

"They're not mad at you; they're mad at Luke, but they'll work that out. And from what I could tell by the conversation this morning, they seemed to respect that Tyler was there with you and helped you guys come to a compromise." She shook her head. "I think the man deserves a medal if he could make any of you compromise; you're all so damn stubborn."

That was true, so there was no use trying to deny it. "He's calm. I think I need that in my life."

"I think you do too, Grace. He's also grounded, and I think you and he balance each other well in that way."

"Are you saying I'm flighty?"

She set her glass down and leaned her hip against the island. "I'm saying you've always lived your life as a dreamer, and there's nothing wrong with that. It's just nice to know you have someone in your life who can keep your feet on the ground while you dream."

I smiled down at my glass. She was right. I'd always been a dreamer, and I wasn't ashamed of that, but I was very different from everyone else in my family. "So, you like Ty?"

She looked over at him before her smiling eyes met mine again. "I do. And I also like that he's giving your brothers a run for their money. They need that." I laughed along with her. "And you need to know someone is always on your side." She gestured toward Dad. "Your dad was like that with my brothers, you know?"

"Really?"

She waved her hand in the air. "Oh yeah, don't let him tell you anything different, but your uncles hated your dad when I first started dating him."

"Why?"

She sighed. "For a lot of reasons. I was their sister, and they felt I needed them to fend off any man." She rolled her eyes, and I laughed again. "But your dad was, well, your dad. You know how he is, Grace, and when he loves, he loves with everything he is, and he decided right from the start that he loved me. He drove your uncles crazy because they couldn't scare him off."

"How long did it take them to get over it?"

"It took a little while, but they all came around. They just needed to see that he was going to stand by me."

"Why are you telling me this now?"

"Because when I see you with him, honey, when I see you look at him, I see in your eyes what I always saw in my own."

"What do you see?"

"Peace." She grabbed my hand and squeezed. "You've always been looking for your other half, the one you would love forever,

240

the one to build a family with, a life with. I know that because I've never seen in your eyes with anyone else what I see when you're with him." She kept my hand in her own and squeezed again, looking across the room at my dad. "I knew when I met him that I would follow your dad anywhere, Grace, and that I'd met the one man I was supposed to love for the rest of my life."

I drifted some, lost in my own thoughts until she dropped my hand and picked up her wine glass. "Now I think it's time to tell them about your books."

I'd just taken a drink when she spoke and choked on wine, my eyes watering when it burned my throat. Mom turned from me and calmly grabbed a glass, filling it with water and handing it to me. I took a long drink, still coughing while she waited patiently until it settled, and I set my glass down. I peeked over my shoulder to see everyone still talking and laughing, no one even looking at us, but I still felt like all eyes were on me. "How?" I stumbled over my thoughts. "Just, how?"

She lifted her eyebrows. "You lent me your Kindle when we went to visit your uncle George, remember, because mine had gotten wet and wasn't working properly. You had a lot of good books on there, but I was drawn to one collection in particular written by Grace Monroe."

"I didn't think you'd ever think it was me," I confessed.

"Grace, you chose my mother's maiden name as your last name, and I know you. I know what you like to read, you did live here for a long time, honey, so I figured it out as I was reading. Although, I have to admit, it took me a few books to catch on. I also recognized your writing from the collection of short stories you wrote and asked me to read over when you took that literature class in college."

"I forgot about that," I murmured.

"Why didn't you just tell me?"

"I was afraid you'd feel like you had to tell Dad, and he'd tell the boys," I admitted. "You didn't, did you?"

"God no." She scoffed. "Your dad would have a stroke if he read what you wrote. Your brothers may even be worse." She took a sip of her wine before continuing. "But I do think we have to tell them. Especially now since I read the note, and I think your stalker might be a fan of yours."

I chewed on the corner of my lip. "I know. I thought the same."

"Have you told Tyler?"

"Not yet," I admitted. "It's just, sometimes there's a stigma with writing romance and erotica. I love writing what I write, but unfortunately, those genres aren't always considered serious writing. I've seen other authors looked down on for writing them, and I guess"—I paused, trying to find the right words—"I think the boys will do that too."

"Grace, your brothers love you and will support you. They will never understand why you write the books you write, but who cares. As long as you're happy, that's all that matters."

"You're right," I conceded.

She patted my hand. "I know, honey."

I saw the laughter in her eyes before she let it escape, but when she did, I laughed along with her.

"Did you like them?" I asked, nervously.

She smiled. "Honey, I can honestly say they're the best books I've read in a long time. And," she said with a wink, "your father appreciates your writing too. He just doesn't know it."

My eyes widened, and we shared a laugh, but that was where it stopped for me. My parents were not afraid to show their love for each other with kissing and hand-holding, hugging all the time, but anything beyond that, I didn't want to hear about.

My mom knew my secret, and she'd known for a while, just letting me have it as my own. Allowing me the time to get settled into who I wanted to be. That was a gift in a family like mine where everything was out in the open, and everything was shared, whether it was in grief or excitement, and we managed it together, as a family. I loved that, but I never had the opportunity to have something all mine.

My mom gave me that opportunity for a little while at least.

My time was up, though, and I needed to come clean, if for no other reason than to eliminate the worry I saw lingering in my mom's eyes.

Chapter Thirty-six

Tyler

The party was over, and I was relieved, although I had to admit I'd had a good time. Grace's family was warmer toward me, especially Jake and Ben, but even the twins Cam and Chris seemed better. Luke still wasn't sure about me and neither were Jax or Brody, but it was better than it had been. Grace's dad I couldn't read at all, but her mom was amazing and reminded me so much of my own mom that sometimes it hurt to be near her.

I'd spent a lot of the evening talking to Chase again and even agreed to take Seth out to meet his sister. I asked Seth if he wanted horseback riding lessons, and his eyes lit up, so I took that as a yes and signed him up. Before the night was over, Andy was signed up too, so it looked like Luke and I would have to get to know each other whether we were ready to or not.

When Kate extended an invite to Seth to spend the night at their house, I could see he wanted that, so I agreed, worried, though, about how Sophie would do without him. I didn't worry for long because Kate also invited her, Lexi, Mia, and Bray for a cousins' sleepover at their house. I'd walked the kids upstairs to pack and asked them separately if they wanted to go. They both said yes and seemed excited, but I still pulled Luke aside and explained they didn't always do well through the night. He promised to call if they needed me, which I appreciated.

"Tired?" Grace came out onto the front porch where I stood and had been standing since Luke pulled away with Seth and Sophie in tow.

"A little."

"Worried?" She guessed right the second time.

I took another sip from my beer, dropping the bottle to my fingertips and letting it dangle by my side. "They don't sleep well."

She laid her hand on my back. "I think they'll be pretty worn out, and I heard talk of a fort meaning they won't be alone." She rubbed her hand soothingly along the muscles of my shoulders. "Luke will call if they need you, I promise."

I only nodded. I had no idea if he was a man of his word, but I guessed from watching this family that he was. We stood quietly, side by side, her hand resting on my waist, her head laying against my bicep, and let the warm air blow across our skin. It was comfortable, and I always loved the quiet, but right now and more often lately when I'm around Grace, I wanted to talk.

"It eats away at me that I turned my back on them." I admitted what I never thought I'd say out loud.

She pressed tighter into my arm. "The kids?"

"All of them," I admitted. "I had so much resentment, so much anger and for what. What did that bring me, except loneliness?"

She propped her chin against the side of my arm and looked up. "You being here for them now is what matters the most."

"But I almost wasn't." I stared into the darkness. "If you hadn't been there, hadn't gotten in my face, I would've sent them to live with Tara's family. That would've destroyed them. Look at what that family has done to Natalie." I ran my hand through my hair, remembering her face when we yelled surprise. "Christ, Grace, she'd never even had a birthday party."

She sighed. "I know. It was so sad to watch, but think about what we gave her tonight. We gave her family, we gave her a celebration, and she left here happy and with more invitations to things with my family than she'll ever be able to attend."

"You did that. Not me." I took another sip, longer this time from the bottle before I set it along the wide plank of the white wooden railing. "I wouldn't have thought of that."

She moved around to stand in front of me and pushed me back until I sat on the oversized chair behind me. I lifted my hands to her hips when she settled herself on my lap, legs on either side of mine, her face close to my own. "I want you to hear me, really hear me right now, Ty. Okay?"

I only had time to nod before she continued. "You have stepped up and done more than anyone expected. On one of the worst days of your life, I watched you welcome Natalie into your little family at the church. You could've sent her away and never let her see the kids, but you didn't." I started to protest, but she held her finger against my lips to silence me. "You gave her the family back that she thought she lost. And you gave the kids back a little piece of their mom by keeping her sister in their lives." She dropped her finger, her expression one of understanding.

"I don't know how to be a father, Grace, and that's what they need, a father," I admitted quietly.

Her eyes flicked back and forth between mine. "Don't you see, Ty, that's exactly what you've been doing." When I didn't answer, she dropped her head and sighed. "I can see you're going to need examples."

My lips tipped up in a small grin that she leaned in and kissed before she continued. "You've displayed things all through your house that belonged to Tara and your dad just to make the kids comfortable and make it feel like home for them. You even brought some of the furniture, including the couch and dining room table and chairs. You arranged for them to switch schools, stood up to the bullies for Seth just by taking him off the bus, and by the look on his face, no adult has ever done that before. You took Sophie to the store so she could get her special strawberry shampoo, and you made sure it was the brand Tara always bought for her." She ran her thumb across my bottom lip, her eyes filling with moisture. "And most importantly, Ty, at night when I know you need some time to yourself, when you crave the quiet, you let two little kids climb into your bed so they can sleep against you and feel safe." She ran her fingertip along my cheek until she could wrap her entire hand around the back of my neck. "Should I continue? Because I can."

I swallowed hard and shook my head. Words were failing me, but she knew that, and she accepted that. Leaning in, she pressed her soft lips to mine. "You're a good man, Tyler Morgan."

She pulled back when I tightened my hands on her waist and lifted her hands to lay flat against my chest. She seemed to hesitate but then took a deep breath and exhaled. "I want to tell you something."

"You can tell me anything."

She smiled softly. "I believe that, Ty." I waited patiently, giving her the time I knew she needed, but she didn't make me wait long before spoke. "I write books."

She said it so quietly, I thought I missed it. "You write books?" She nodded, but her face was aimed at her lap, so I put my finger under her chin and lifted it so I could see her beautiful eyes. "Why do you seem afraid to tell me?"

She swallowed hard and straightened her shoulders. "It's hard because I've never really told anyone. It's like any secret, I think, the longer you hold onto it, the harder it is to confess, you know."

"But it's not a bad thing to be a writer, Grace. It's actually pretty amazing."

She beamed at the compliment. "I know, and I'm so proud of it, but…"

I raised an eyebrow. "But?"

"I write erotica, Ty," she said quickly like she needed to or she would chicken out.

"I'm not sure I know what that means," I admitted. "I'm not much of a reader." I shrugged my shoulders. "Obviously." When I grinned, her smile widened.

"Erotica is a kind of writing that is meant to be really provocative and sexy. If written well, it should make you feel, well, a lot of things, but especially sexual things." I waited patiently for her to continue. "The stories are romance, but they tend to be more erotic than a traditional love story."

I considered that and knew I needed to get my hands on those books. "Can I read them?"

Her eyes widened in surprise. "I'm not sure you'll like them."

"Grace," I said, pulling her closer and shifting my body so she could slide down putting her chest almost right against mine. "There hasn't been anything yet that you've done that I haven't loved. I doubt this will be any different." I ran my fingers through the ends of her hair like she always does and immediately knew why it was addictive to her. I could do this all night. "Why don't you want to tell your family?"

"Well, my mom already knows. She figured it out, and Charlie knows, of course, but I think if you actually read one, you'll understand why I've hesitated to tell my dad and brothers. Although, I have been thinking it's time to tell them."

"Why tell them now?"

She frowned. "Because I'm worried I may have a crazy stalker fan."

I nodded, remembering the words in that letter. "Can I read one now?"

She looked surprised. "Now? I thought you were tired."

"I am," I admitted. "But I'm curious."

She hesitated but only for a moment. "Okay." She gestured toward the door. "I have them on my Kindle."

I let her get up and followed her inside, locking the door behind me. She turned from her purse on the counter when she heard the lock. "Am I staying?"

"Are you really asking me that shit?"

She laughed and pulled out her Kindle, walking toward me, and only then did I notice how tired she looked. She had to be. We hadn't slept much last night because it was late when we got home, and today, she put together a party.

"Here you go." She handed it to me. "They're in my library under Grace Monroe."

"Monroe?"

"My grandmother's maiden name."

"Why don't you go up to bed? You look really tired," I suggested.

"I am tired. Plus, I don't want to watch you read," she admitted bashfully. "It'll make me nervous. But do you promise to give me your honest opinion tomorrow?"

I pulled her to me and kissed her slowly, taking my time with her mouth, enjoying her small sigh when she leaned against me, but I pulled back. "Go."

She smiled softly. "Night, Ty."

I watched her move up the stairs before I finished locking up the house and settling down on the chair in the living room. I knew I would only fall asleep if I tried to read in bed, so this was better. Not to mention, the distraction of Grace would be too much to resist if I went up there.

So I stayed downstairs and read.

Until I couldn't read it anymore.

Chapter Thirty-seven

Grace

I shifted my legs, arousal deep in my belly making me restless while my panties were pulled from my body. In my dream, I moaned while Ty worked his way down my body, his hands everywhere, his mouth wet and warm while it skimmed over my hot skin. I shoved my fingers in his hair, and lifted my hips when his tongue licked along my slit. The pressure in my belly became almost unbearable when his tongue flicked over my clit repeatedly. I was hot and torn between needing to wake up and wanting to stay in the dream so I could feel my body burst apart because that was exactly what it felt like it was going to do. My breath was coming in short gasps when his finger pushed into my already soaked pussy, and he quickly added a second finger before I'd even adjusted to the first. I was in agony. I was so close to orgasm, but I loved every minute of it. I wanted his skin against mine, needed to feel his body on top of my own, but right now, more than anything, I needed to come. I forced his head tighter against my core, urging him on, my skin on fire, sweat beading on my forehead while my orgasm built.

And then it hit.

My eyes flew open when my body bucked hard enough to force me into reality, and only then did I realize my reality and my dream were one and the same. Ty rose over me, his eyes flashing, and his skin slick with sweat. He pulled the tank top from my body and I barely had time to register what was happening before he spread my legs, grabbing behind my knees to push them against my chest, and slammed into me. My back rose again when another orgasm started to build. I didn't think I could take another one because I was still tingling from the last one, but the energy and force of his thrusts began building something in me that I couldn't describe. His thumb found my clit, and he rubbed fast, his wide chest pinning my thighs against my own chest, his head bent low over mine, putting us face to face.

"Come for me, Grace." He grunted. "One more, baby. I need to feel it when I'm inside you. Need to feel you tighten around me."

His thrusts changed while he was talking. They were harder and deeper, but it wasn't until he shifted a little and angled his hips did I feel it coming again and stronger than the last time. I would never have thought that possible. My orgasm rose quickly, and I wrapped my arms and legs around his strong body when he slid one arm under me and jerked me into his chest. He was practically holding my body to his with only his arm, and I let my head fall back to ride the climax scorching through my body. I felt his body tense, and he thrust hard a few more times before he put his mouth to my shoulder and groaned.

His body collapsed in complete exhaustion, but he shifted enough that his weight was off to my side. We both lay quietly; the only sound was our heavy breathing while our bodies calmed. I'd always guessed sex could feel like that, always hoped, but it never had for me before. I had no idea if it had for him.

"I like your books."

His growly voice came from beside my ear, and I turned my

head sharply, settling in tight against him when I saw the expression on his face.

"You really liked them?" I asked hesitantly.

"Baby." He lifted his arm and wrapped it around my stomach, pulling me in tight against his side. "I nearly fucked you through this mattress, I was so wound up. You tell me if I really liked what I read." I smiled and rolled, pressing my front to his side.

He shifted his body so he was facing me and lifted a finger, running it along my jaw until he reached my hair where he wrapped a few strands around it. "You're really talented."

I grinned. "So are you."

I cuddled closer when he laughed, loving the sound of it. Making Tyler laugh used to be a feat, but lately, it was happening more and more. "I mean it. Your story was incredible, and I only made it about halfway through before I needed to find you."

"Really?" I asked, hopefully, only now realizing how much I'd been anticipating his reaction and how much I wanted him to like it.

"Grace, I don't read, never really cared to, but I was turning pages and completely absorbed in your story." He leaned his forehead against mine. "I'm so lucky just to know someone like you, but the fact that you let me touch you and hold you blows my mind."

I ran my fingertip along his full bottom lip. "I feel the same way about you. My big, bad football player."

"Retired football player," he reminded me.

I dropped my hand to his chest, letting the short hair drift through my fingertips, appreciating the masculine feel of him, his strength, the sheer power he keeps a tight leash on, a leash I just felt a little slack in. I wonder what would happen if he took the leash off just once, just so I could feel all that power. "I'm happy you're retired, Ty."

He raised an eyebrow. "Why?"

"Because I get you all to myself." I pressed my lips against his neck. "And I don't have to worry about you getting hurt all the time." I let my tongue flick out and run up the side of his neck. "Or all those beautiful cheerleaders ogling you."

He rolled onto his back, dragging me with him, making me squeal. When he situated me on top of him, he looked deep into my eyes. "I have never met a woman more beautiful than you are, Grace. You'll never have a thing to worry about."

I leaned down and pressed my lips to his, only pulling back enough to mutter, "That's good, Ty, because I'd hate to have to kick her ass."

He snorted, and my head shot up, eyes narrowed, watching him laugh. "Why are you laughing? Don't you think I can do it?"

"I think you can do whatever you put your mind to," he said, but it sounded awfully patronizing.

"You know I slapped Ben's ex-girlfriend once." I bragged.

He got a handle on his laughter, but that damn grin still flirted around his mouth. "Why?"

"She cheated on him." I put my palms on his chest and pushed up. "Charlie and I threatened her."

His eyes widened, and he nodded. "Well, now, Charlie I could see kicking ass."

"Hey!" I slapped my palm against his chest. "Why not me?"

He ran his hand up my naked back until he could tangle it in my hair and pulled me gently back down. I resisted but only until he spoke. "Because, baby, that's not who you are. You're sweet, so fucking sweet, and nice to everyone, even those who don't deserve it, like me. I don't think there's one person in this world who you wouldn't believe deserves a second chance. Even Ben's bitch of ex-girlfriend."

I exhaled the breath I hadn't even realized I'd been holding. "Nice save, Morgan."

He ran his lips softly along mine. "It's all true."

I shifted so my legs fell to either side of his hips and pulled back some. He held me tighter. "Where are you going?"

"I was going to grab my tank top and panties."

"Not yet."

I pushed against his arm banded around my waist and narrowed my eyes. "Ty."

His lips twitched, and I jerked harder against his arm. I angled my head slightly when I saw a mischievous spark in his eye, and then I felt a slap. My eyes widened, and I jumped, but his arm held tight.

"Ty," I warned.

A cool breeze floated across my butt right before his hand came down again, slapping the other side. I felt a flutter along my clit that made my breath catch a second before his hand came down again, harder than before. But this time, I let the moan escape, a little embarrassed by how turned on I was from him slapping my ass, but then I shifted and slid up his body, fitting his cock right against my slit, rocking on it when I felt how hard he was.

"Again," I whispered.

His eyes flashed right before his hand came down hard on the opposite cheek. I moaned and dropped my forehead to his, my breath catching as I rubbed my body over his slowly, his cock hitting my clit with every forward rock. He moved his hands to cover both of my butt cheeks and squeezed, pushing me down harder against his hot length. His groan sounded tortured when he flipped me onto my back, slid between my thighs, and in one long thrust, he was deep inside me. His body felt hard and heavy above me, his back hot to the touch when I ran my hands down it, grabbed his butt, and pulled him closer to me, forcing him even deeper inside my body.

His lips came down to lay against mine when he whispered the words that were a direct link to my heart. "I'm never letting you go, Grace. I'm never letting you go."

I smiled and pulled him tighter against me, wrapped my legs around his waist and let the sensations overwhelm me while I lifted my lips to his ear. "I'm considering that a promise."

Chapter Thirty-eight

Tyler

"She's great with kids." I gestured toward Chase's sister, Callie.

Chase leaned further into the wooden fence where we both stood watching Seth during his first riding lesson. "She is." He angled his head to look my way. "How are things?"

"Getting better," I answered, truthfully.

It had been two weeks since we had the party for Natalie. Grace and I had finally had an entire night to ourselves. The kids made it through that sleepover really well with Sophie only calling once the next morning because she wanted to make sure I was okay all alone.

I told her I wasn't lonely, and I'd meant it. Grace and I spent the morning trading off between fucking like bunnies and talking, something I'd never done with a woman in my life. Since then, though we haven't had another night all to ourselves.

Convincing Grace to stay with me until her brothers found out who was fucking with her, hadn't really taken much effort. She said it was because my place was where she really wanted to be, but I also knew she was afraid of whatever the lunatic might do next. If I was being honest, the idea of letting her out of my sight was unbearable. When I told her that, she'd agreed almost immediately. I told the kids she needed to stay with us for a little while, and they didn't ask questions, but Grace decided she'd sleep in the guest room. The kids weren't completely out of my bed yet, and we needed to give them the time they needed. I loved that she thought of their needs and not only understood, but insisted that I put them first.

Brody installed a high-tech alarm on her apartment that he promised no one was getting past. He also set it up so it would trigger an alarm on his phone, Luke's phone, and the police station if she pushed the emergency button on the panel or if it wasn't turned off within the one minute timeframe. It all sounded good, and he assured her, and me, that once she was locked in at night, she would be fine until morning. But I didn't trust it, and I knew she didn't either. She would go to her apartment to grab clothes after work sometimes and pick up her mail, but she hadn't spent any real time there in two weeks.

I was fucking ecstatic knowing we were putting real distance between the woman I love and a psycho.

I figured out I loved her pretty quickly. I think part of me loved Grace the day I met her over a year ago, but after spending time with her, it was clear that if she'd have me, I'd never let her go. We hadn't said the words, hadn't even talked about it because this stalker was like a dark cloud of fear hanging over us, and until that was settled, I doubt we'd take our relationship any further.

"Nothing new on the stalker?" Chase's words interrupted my thoughts, but strangely, his thoughts were very near to my own.

I shook my head. "Not yet. He must be laying low for a while or something."

"I thought you would've talked her into living with you permanently by now. I even bet Jake you would have moved all her shit to your place," he teased.

I grinned. "I'm trying to figure out how to do it without pissing her off."

We laughed, but the sound of shale kicking up shifted our attention from the conversation toward the road. I turned my head and watched Luke's SUV pull down the driveway and park next to mine. I knew he was coming. Chase told me after he explained the situation to his sister, she had arranged this so the boys' lessons would overlap but also give her some one-on-one time with each of them.

"Fuck," I whispered when I saw not only Luke and Andy emerge from the vehicle, but also Jack.

"Still not going well?" Chase surmised.

I exhaled heavily. "I don't think I have the words he needs to hear to put him at ease that I'm with Grace."

They started toward us when Chase spoke. "I'll let you in on a little secret, Ty. Jack Dimarco is not about the words. He's about the actions. I imagine if you treat her like she's your whole world, you'll be just fine."

"She is," I admitted easily.

"I wouldn't be surprised if he already knows that."

Chase stepped forward just as they got to us, and we all exchanged hellos before he looked down at Andy. "You ready to ride?"

Andy's smile grew. "I can't wait."

He gestured toward Callie. "Then let's go."

"Thanks, man," Luke said.

I turned back to watch Chase usher Andy through the gate where he waved excitedly at Seth. Callie guided the horse back to where her brother and Andy now stood, and I assumed they were making introductions.

"Gracie didn't come?"

I swallowed hard when I heard Jack's voice, but answered. "No, she stayed with Sophie. We think this should just be Seth's thing for now, and Sophie would…"

I trailed off, not sure of the right words until Jack spoke again. "She'd take over."

I grinned at Jack who now stood beside me at the fence, his heavy boot planted on the lower board of the fence, his forearms stretched across the top, hands clasped together. "Yeah."

"She's good for him, though. I have a feeling without her, he'd stay in the shadows."

I swallowed hard, remembering growing up in the shadows. I never wanted that for Seth. "He would." I gestured toward Andy. "Andy's helping a lot too."

"Andy's a good boy," Jack shared when he saw Andy get up on the horse for the first time. "He was a little shy when we first met him, but nothing like your boy."

That took me off guard. "I'm not his father."

Jack exhaled heavily. "It's a shame if you really believe that."

My head jerked his way, but he was still looking at the boys, both on horses now and trotting slowly in a small circle. "I'm his brother, that's all."

Jack nodded his head. "You are that, but it seems to me that a father would worry about school and bullies, and that a father would do everything he could to make that boy's life a little easier than his own had been."

I faced the boys again. "You sound like Grace."

"Gracie's a smart girl."

I grinned, thinking of her this morning, braiding Sophie's hair and planning a shopping trip for just the two of them, she said, which made Sophie squeal loud enough that I'd bet dogs were barking in the next neighborhood over.

"You don't have to worry about forgetting she's smart. She'll remind you."

My head turned to the left in surprise when I heard Luke's voice because the last time I looked, he was talking to Chase. Now he was standing on my other side and grinning. "She lets us know all the time."

I chuckled. "She's definitely not shy."

"She still sleeping at your place?" Luke asked.

I kept my eyes on him when I answered, unsure how Jack felt about it. "Yeah."

"Good," Jack said, and my head snapped in his direction. His eyes were on the boys, though. "I don't like the idea of her in that apartment. Something doesn't feel right there even with the alarm Brody put in."

"I know," I agreed with him, having felt the same way.

"Coming to dinner?"

Today was Sunday. I hadn't been to dinner since that one time with Dex, but I had a feeling that was about to change.

"Kind of taking a long time to answer, man," Luke goaded, and I heard Jack chuckle beside me. "You don't wanna come, don't come."

"It's not that." I let my gaze settle back on Seth. "It's just, well, your family can be a little overwhelming."

"A little is an understatement," Luke joked, and I snorted out a laugh.

"For Seth." Jack guessed correctly.

"Yeah, but I don't want that for him." Getting lost in my own memories of being shy and awkward, especially as a boy, and only being accepted when my football skills became invaluable made me talk in way I hadn't before. "I want more for him. I don't want him to stand in the middle of a crowd and still be alone. And I sure as hell don't want him to believe if he loses the only thing he's good at, he'll end up back in the fucking shadows."

"Then show him there's more," Jack said, slapping the back of my shoulder. "For both of you."

Thankfully, the lesson had just wrapped up, and Chase was heading our way, the boys walking side by side, theirs heads together and talking while Chase slung his arm across Callie's shoulders and pulled her along beside him.

"Dad, did you see me?" Andy called out excitedly.

"I saw, kiddo." He grinned down at him and Seth when they made it to us.

Seth rolled his lips together and moved quietly to stand beside me. I squatted down beside him. "Did you like it?"

He nodded his head quickly. "I really liked it."

His voice was quiet, but I could hear the excitement, so I ruffled his hair and stood back up to face Callie. "Callie, can we make this a weekly lesson."

"Umm…sure." She answered, blushing furiously, her eyes flicking to me, but then quickly away.

"What day would you like him?"

"And me too?" Andy said from beside Luke. "I can come too, right, Dad?"

Luke smiled down at Andy before bringing his attention back to Callie. "Andy too, if you can."

"That'd be great," she said quietly but lifted her head and glanced back and forth between me and Luke. "Would Saturdays at three be okay?"

"Yeah," I answered, and Luke agreed.

Chase leaned down and spoke quietly to her, but I was the only one standing close enough to hear him. "You did good, Callie."

She nodded and squatted down in front of the boys. She lifted her hand and gave them each a high five. "You guys were awesome. I can't wait to see you next Saturday."

Her voice was still quiet, but she spoke to both of them directly before she stood and waved good-bye, almost sprinting to the barn.

I raised my eyebrows at Chase, and he put his hands on his hips. "Just like I told you, great with kids, but adults…"

He didn't need to say more because we'd all just witnessed it. I felt a punch to the side of my arm and looked over to see Luke grinning at me. "She might actually be worse than you at conversation."

I dropped my head and laughed, enjoying the sound of Seth laughing beside me. I tapped him playfully in the arm. "What are you laughing at?" His eyes widened, but I kept laughing so he'd know I was teasing him. "Are you laughing at me?"

"No." He shook his head, but he was smiling. "I promise."

"I think you are." I bent over and grabbed him around the waist, then slung him over my shoulder and started toward the SUV.

"Andy, help me!" he called out, laughing so hard he snorted, and I felt something swell in my chest at the sound.

I paused and glanced behind me when I heard Andy jumping up and down behind us, trying to reach Seth's hand. "I can't reach you! He's like a giant or something."

I turned sharply. "Are you making fun of me?"

"No." Andy giggled and stumbled back a few steps. "I'm not. I swear."

I acted like I was thinking about it, but instead, I lunged, taking him completely off guard when I bent down and slung him over my other shoulder. I chuckled when they both squealed.

"It's a good thing you're both skinny little shits," Luke teased as he walked toward me, chuckling.

"Pappy!" Andy yelled from over my shoulder. "Can we go for ice cream?"

Jack started toward us, but when he called out his answer to Andy, his eyes stayed on me. "We can't. Grandma probably has dinner ready, and we're all heading there."

"That's right, it's Sunday." Andy bounced on my shoulder excitedly. "Seth, you're coming too, right?"

"Of course, he is, Andy." Jack smirked when he walked around us. "See you at the house, boys."

Luke whistled and grabbed Andy off my shoulder, throwing him over his own. "Guess I'll see you at the house."

I gestured in Jack's direction. "He do this to your women?"

Luke shook his head. "Nah, but he liked them."

I nodded but grinned when Luke punched me in the shoulder and stopped to talk to Chase for a minute. I heard my phone ringing in my pocket, so I put Seth down and pulled it out, smiling a whole lot bigger when I saw Grace's name.

"Hey, baby."

"Ty."

My back snapped straight. "What's wrong?"

"Ty, someone broke into my apartment."

I started toward the SUV, but Luke's hand on my chest stopped me. "What happened?"

I ignored Luke and spoke again to Grace. "Are you in your apartment now?"

"No." Her voice trembled when she answered. "No, we just left, but I'm in the parking lot."

I pulled the phone from my mouth. "She's in the parking lot of her building. Someone broke in to her apartment."

"Tell her to stay put," he said, his phone already out and up to his ear.

I put my phone back to my mouth. "Okay, Grace, hold on. Lock your doors and don't open them until we get there. Luke's with me, and we're on our way."

I heard Luke talking to someone while he moved quickly to his vehicle, and I ushered Seth into ours.

"Will you stay on the phone with me?" she asked.

"I had no plans to hang up, baby." I threw it in reverse and turned, spinning my tires and peeling out of Chase's driveway, but I didn't give a shit.

The fear in her voice was the only thing I cared about.

Chapter Thirty-nine

Grace

I breathed a sigh of relief when I saw Ty's SUV turn sharply into the parking lot, straight toward me, Luke's not but a car length behind. We'd just hung up when he said he would be pulling in, and I unlocked my door and threw it open, doing the same for Sophie who was sitting in the back playing on her tablet. Thank goodness she was only five and didn't seem to understand what we just saw in my apartment.

Ty's tires squealed when he slid into the spot only one down from mine and jumped out. I stood still, not wanting to leave Sophie who was still just playing, but really needing Ty. He was in front of me within seconds and had me pulled tight against his chest. I hung on, absorbing his strength and warmth while it calmed the trembling I'd had since I ran back down to the car.

I felt others behind me, but I stayed buried against his chest until Ty spoke. "Grace, baby, we need you to talk to us."

Sirens blared behind me when I lifted my head. "Okay."

He put his hands on either side of my face and leaned down. "You okay?"

I touched my lips to his. "I am now."

His eyes softened, and he turned me to face my brother. I saw my dad and moved right into his arms that were just as comforting to me as Ty's. "Gracie girl, what happened?"

Dad's voice was low, and I pulled back to see the worry sketched throughout his expression. I turned again and shuffled to the side to press my back against Ty's chest, his arms banded tightly around my waist. "Sophie and I—" My heart beat harder when I looked over Luke's shoulder. "Where are the kids?"

"They're in my vehicle together. They're fine," Luke answered calmly, but his body was tense, and his hard eyes were focused entirely on me. "Tell me what happened. I have officers ready to go in, but I need some information from you."

I relaxed against Ty's chest again and nodded. "Sophie and I stopped by for the mail and some clothes, like I usually do after work, but I didn't have time Friday. Well, I didn't make time." I leaned my head back so I could see Ty. "I'm sorry, I shouldn't have had Sophie with me, it's just been so quiet lately, so I didn't think much of it, plus with the alarm…"

He squeezed his arm around my waist a little tighter. "Don't apologize, Grace. I know you'd never put Sophie in danger." He gestured with his chin toward Luke. "Just tell Luke what happened."

I exhaled heavily and faced my brother. "Okay, right. Anyway, we grabbed the mail and walked up to my apartment. When I unlocked the door, the alarm wasn't beeping, and at first, I wasn't worried because everything seemed fine. I threw the mail on the counter and headed for my bedroom."

"Tell me what your bedroom looked like," Luke encouraged.

I swallowed hard. "There were things everywhere and all my clothes were cut up. All of them, Luke," I stressed and shook my head in confusion. "Why would he cut up my clothes?"

"Keep going."

"The bathroom was the same with everything torn out, and

something was written on the mirror, but I honestly didn't read it. I just grabbed Sophie and ran. I came down here, locked us in the car, and called Ty." I looked over my shoulder again at Ty. "Luckily, she was behind me, so I don't think she saw much, but I know she felt something was wrong."

"You stay down here with Ty, and I'm leaving an officer while I go up with the others, okay?" I nodded and stepped out of Ty's arms toward Luke.

He put his hand around the back of my neck and pulled me tight to his chest.

"Thanks, Luke," I said.

I heard his low voice against the top of my head. "We're going to put an end to this."

I stepped back when Dad called out Luke's name. "Give me your keys. I'll take the kids home with me. Ty and Gracie can bring you to the house after you're done."

Luke tossed his keys to him, which he caught easily, and looked over my head at Ty. "I'll be down as soon as I can."

I felt Ty nod, but I was already moving away from him and into my dad's arms for another hug. He wrapped his arms around me and squeezed tightly before pushing me back a little so he could look into my eyes. "Who are you staying with?"

I knew what he meant, but honestly, since this happened, I didn't want to stay with anyone. What if this person came to their house? I was putting everyone in danger. Dad shook his head. "I know what you're thinking darlin', but Brody and Luke will make sure wherever you are, everyone is safe."

"I'll think about it," I agreed.

"Okay, I'm gonna get these kiddos home and wait for you guys there."

"Thanks, Dad."

He wrapped his hand around the back of my neck and pulled me close, laying a kiss on my forehead. "You need to be safe, Gracie."

"Or you won't sleep?" I guessed correctly.

"Haven't slept well in a long time," he admitted. "But the past two weeks, knowing where you've been, I've done better."

I smiled softly. He kissed me again and pulled back, looking at Ty over my head. "Take care of my girl."

I looked up in time to see Ty nod, but a silent conversation seemed to go on between my dad and him. What Ty didn't realize was my dad had just given him the highest compliment he could. His trust.

That didn't come easily, but when it was earned, it was something valuable.

Dad moved away toward Luke's SUV, and I turned back to Ty. His face was filled with concern, but it had been since he arrived. I didn't expect that to go away anytime soon.

He laid his palms against either side of my neck and dropped his forehead to mine. "You scared me."

I gestured toward the apartment building. "That scared me."

He shifted so he could look into my eyes. "You're staying with me."

"I don't know," I teased. "You're pretty bossy."

His eyes narrowed, but his lips twitched ever so slightly at the corners. "Don't piss me off, Grace." His grin grew when I rolled my lips together, trying to hold back my smile. He laid his lips against mine and kissed me softly, but it only lasted a few seconds. "Besides, you like it when I'm bossy."

I smiled that time and laid my cheek against his chest. Inappropriate as it seemed, considering I was standing outside my apartment while the cops were inside and my clothes had all been shredded, I thought about Ty being bossy, and my body warmed. Who knew I would like his dominance in bed? Not me, that was for sure, but I did. I liked that he took charge, and I loved that he wasn't afraid to get a little aggressive—not in a scary way, but in a dominant way.

I snuggled in tighter and watched as people went in and out of the building, their curious eyes looking at the police cars and at Ty and me holding onto to each other. I couldn't blame them; I'd be curious too.

"You're telling them today." His low voice sounded from above me.

I nodded against his chest. "I know."

"They'll all be there?"

I sighed long and loud. "After this, they'll definitely all be there."

We stood together quietly for the next few minutes, both lost in our thoughts until we saw Luke exit the building and head straight toward us. I pulled away from Ty's chest, but he kept his arm around me.

"Well...?" Ty asked as soon as Luke reached us.

"Officers are gathering the evidence." He exhaled loudly. "There were no signs of forced entry, the alarm is fine as far as I can tell but isn't set." He looked directly at me. "Do you remember setting it the last time you were here?"

I thought back, but I was positive I'd set it. "Yeah, I know I did."

He rubbed his hand along the back of his neck before he reached behind him and pulled something out of his back pocket. He held it out to me. "I went through your stack of mail and found another letter."

I jerked back in surprise because I hadn't even noticed a letter, but I hadn't exactly taken the time to go through the stack. I took it from his hands. "It's opened." He nodded. "Did you read it?"

His jaw hardened, and his eyes shot to Ty behind me before he answered. "I did. I'll need it back. It's evidence."

"Do I want to read it?"

"You need to."

"Okay." I unfolded the letter and cringed when I saw the same professionally typed note as before.

My Grace,
This was your only warning.
I don't share.
You can't keep me out.
Your love.

I felt a chill run down my spine at the abruptness of the letter. I read over the words again before I looked back up at Luke. "I don't understand."

"My guess." Luke put his hands on his hips. "He's pissed about Ty."

"What does you can't keep me out mean?"

"The alarm Brody installed," Ty concluded.

Luke nodded. "That would be my guess. There was no stamp on the envelope again, telling me he was in your apartment, then came down and slipped the letter in your mailbox."

"What was on the mirror?" Ty asked.

Luke's expression hardened further. "He wrote Time's Up."

"Boss," a voice called across the parking lot, and Luke looked back. "Done."

Luke lifted his chin at the officer and faced us again. "I'm going in to make sure everything's done correctly, and nothing was missed. Shouldn't take long and we can head out."

Handing him the letter, I leaned back into Tyler and waited while Luke jogged toward the building.

I looked around when the sensation of being watched surrounded me, but I didn't see anyone.

I could feel him, though.

Chapter Forty

Grace

We walked through the front door of my parents' house, and from the noise, I knew everyone was here today. I sighed when I felt Ty's hand wrap around my own. We made our way down the short hallway to the back of the house where everyone was standing around the dining room table.

Kasey was the first to see us.

"Oh my god, Grace." She rushed toward me and pulled me in for a hug. "Are you okay?"

"I'm fine," I answered quietly, and then to the room at large, I repeated it a little louder. "I promise, I'm fine."

My mom's arms wrapped around me after Kasey moved away, and she hugged me tightly. "I think it's time."

"I'm telling them now," I whispered.

She shifted back, but kept her hands on my shoulders. "Good."

"Find anything useful?"

Mom and I both turned to face Cam when we heard his voice, but his stare was locked on Luke. Luke frowned and shook his head. "Need to wait and see if we got any prints. Nothing else useful."

"Why the fuck didn't you call me to check the alarm?"

"Brody," Mom snapped, but looking around, I didn't see any kids, so her warning, probably done out of habit, wasn't going to stop the language today.

"It's a crime scene, brother, you know that," Luke answered calmly.

"I would've been in and out before the cops, brother, and you know that." Brody lowered his voice at the end of the sentence, and I knew shit was going to hit the fan. Brody, Jax, and Luke grew up the closest in age and have remained very close, usually never in disagreement, but there were always exceptions.

"Maybe if we'd have been involved from the beginning, it wouldn't have gotten this far." Jax stepped forward.

"You saying I'm not doing my job?" Luke's eyes flashed, and I looked at Ty, knowing I needed to interrupt before this got any more out of hand. By the look on his face, he agreed.

I stepped forward. "Guys."

"I'm saying, where your hands are tied, mine are not," Jax responded. "And when did we start keeping shit from each other in this family?"

I stepped forward, repeating louder, "Guys!"

"About the time you guys starting interfering in official police business," Luke said.

"You didn't seem to mind us interfering when you needed us to help Maggie," Jax reminded Luke, and I saw his jaw clench.

"I couldn't help her, and you know that." Luke growled.

I put my hand on Luke's shoulder, knowing he still held a lot of guilt over that case. Maggie was young, in her twenties, and stuck in an abusive relationship. Luke's job with the department is investigating special cases, almost always involving women and children, but Maggie continually refused his help. He did what he could, pissed off the wrong people trying to help her, and almost got himself and his fiancée killed before Maggie essentially saved him. She basically became an informant on the motorcycle club her boyfriend was a part of, saving Luke but putting herself in very real danger. From what I heard, Jax stepped in with another motorcycle club who are very much respected, and pulled Maggie out before she got hurt. Luke's hands had been tied, but Jax's weren't, and he didn't hesitate when Luke needed him.

I stepped forward and stood in front of Luke, happy the dining table was separating Jax and Luke. "Listen…"

"And we'd do it again, but you have to let us know what the fuck is going on." Jax leaned forward. "Especially when it involves our goddamn sister."

"When the department couldn't do any more, and my hands were fucking tied, I would've." Luke raised his voice, and my eyes widened. Luke, very much like my dad, was the voice of reason in our family and always stayed calm when dealing with the others. I guess everyone had their limit on how much they'd take.

"Jax, you need to get the fuck over it. Luke did what he thought was best, and I agreed with him," Cam interjected.

"Of course, you agreed," Brody stated. "You work for the same damn department."

I waved my arms in the air. This was getting even more out of hand if everyone was going to start jumping in. "Guys, listen. I have—"

I dropped my head when Chris's voice interrupted me. "All we're saying is together we may have shut this shit down before it got to the point where her apartment was trashed. What if she'd have been there, man?"

Cam tensed beside his twin, and I heard Mom sigh deeply behind me. "Allowing Brody in to do the alarm was the most we could involve a private security company, you guys know that. We have fucking protocol we have to follow. We can't work underground like you guys do. We actually have people we answer to."

"We have people we answer to, too, Cam. They're our clients who come to us because the department can't keep them safe."

"Get off your fucking high horse, Jax," Cam said. "The

department was protecting this city long before you opened the doors to your company, and it will long after you close the doors."

"Okay, guys!" I raised my voice to be heard above them. "If you'd just listen to me—"

Jax's eyebrows raised. "My fucking high horse, Cam? Is that—"

"Enough!" A really loud voice echoed behind me, and I jerked my head around to stare at Ty. "Grace has been trying to talk, but you fuckers keep interrupting her. Now shut the hell up and listen to her."

I took in my Mom's wide eyes and her rolled lips, obviously trying very hard to hide a smile. Ty never looked down at me, just stared at my brothers over the top of my head. They looked pissed, but more than that, they looked shocked. I was going to take advantage of the shock before the pissed really settled in because nobody and I mean nobody talked to my brothers that way unless it was my brothers to each other.

I moved to stand in front of Ty and glanced up. "Thank you, Ty."

He nodded down at me, but his eyes quickly flicked back to the room as a whole, so I turned my attention back to my brothers. "I write books," I announced.

Wow, I actually felt lightheaded saying it out loud. I'd kept it from them for so long, it felt like I was dreaming right now.

Luke shook his head, almost as if he was trying to clear away the confusion. "What?"

I took a deep breath and exhaled. "Yep, I write books, and I've been keeping it a secret for about two years." I looked over at Jax and Brody. "So if you want to be mad at someone for keeping secrets, be mad at me."

"Grace." Brody rubbed the back of his neck. "What does that have to do with this?"

When Ty's hand came to rest on my shoulder, I felt a wave of calmness. I wasn't alone. He literally and figuratively had my back right now. "I think the person who's doing all this crazy stuff has read my books."

"Why would you think that?" Cam asked.

I chewed on my bottom lip for a second before answering. "Because of the letter he sent."

"The first letter." Luke guessed.

I nodded. "Yeah, the things he said in the first letter, like when he hinted that he knows what I like, makes me think he's read the books."

Jake, who had been quietly standing beside Ben up until now, spoke up. "I'm so fucking confused. Is anyone else?"

There were a lot of murmurs of agreement, and all eyes were on me, so it was now or never. "I write erotica."

You could've heard a pin drop in the dining room. I'd honestly never heard it that quiet in my whole life. I looked over my brothers' faces all staring back at me, but not one of them had a thing to say. I guess I didn't need Ty to shut them up. I just needed to tell them I write erotic novels.

"Can we read them?" I looked across the table at Sydney and Lucy who were standing next to each other and grinning.

I smiled. "Yeah, you can read them."

"I'm excited." Lanie squealed. "I love to read. Grace, you should've told me. I devour erotica novels. My friend Paige loves them too."

Jake's head turned sharply to stare at Lanie, but when Gia, who was always quiet, spoke up, all eyes shot to her in surprise. "I'd love to read them too, Grace, and if you need any great story ideas, we can chat. I spent a lot of time on porn sets and at some pretty crazy parties, remember?"

"Gia," Brody said. "What the hell? You can't read her books."

Gia threw her hands on her hips. "Why not?"

"Because I don't want to know what's in them." He ran his hand through his hair. "Jesus, my little sister writes trashy books, and you want to read them."

"Erotica is not trashy, Brody, and you should be thanking some erotica authors out there because they've made you very happy."

Brody looked confused for only a moment before his eyes flashed, but Ben spoke up before he could. "What's erotica? Like porn?"

Lucy giggled. "I'll tell you later."

"No, you won't." Chris scowled down at his girlfriend, Lucy, before he looked at Ben. "It's that *Fifty Shades* shit."

"It's not all like that," Kasey interrupted, earning her an eyebrow raise from Jax.

"Do you read this stuff too?" Luke looked over at his fiancée, Kate, and she shrugged. "I used to read it all the time, but then I had Andy and was working so much, I just never had time." She beamed at me. "But I would love to read yours, Grace."

"I think we all need to sit down."

Our heads all snapped to the head of the table where my father stood and had been standing since the conversation started, but he hadn't said a word. If I'd been nervous about my brothers' reaction, I was terrified of my father's.

Everyone was mumbling to each other while they found their seats, and I tried really hard to hold in my laughter when I caught my brothers looking at their significant others differently. Brody was still scowling at Gia, but she was ignoring him. She'd gotten good at that and she had to since he could be really moody. Jake was staring at Lanie, but I knew my brother, and Lanie was going to be sharing the erotica books she'd already read with him. Jax and Luke looked confused, and I felt a little bad for them. Neither of them had ever been the type of person to get lost in a book. I didn't think they could sit still long enough to read it, so I knew they couldn't understand Kasey's and Kate's interest. Sydney's and Lucy's interest didn't surprise me, and from the looks on the twins faces, it didn't surprise them either.

Chapter Forty-one

Tyler

I wasn't sure what came over me when I yelled at Grace's brothers except that she needed someone to have her back, and I decided it was going to be me. Actually, I didn't remember deciding that. I just knew it was what I wanted to do. I had never in my life raised my voice like that, knowing all the attention would shift toward me, but surprisingly, with Grace in the room, it didn't feel so impossible. I knew she was nervous to share her writing, but I couldn't figure out why. This family was so different from any I'd ever known, and she had to know they wouldn't give a shit as long as she was happy.

I grabbed her hand under the table and set it on my leg, holding it tightly while she faced the table. I thought her dad would speak first, but it was actually Kate who spoke up. "Grace, what name do you write under, so I can look up the books when I get home?"

"Grace Monroe."

"After Grandma." She nodded at Ben, and he smiled. "That's cool."

"Okay, boys, so what's the plan?" Jack's voice interrupted any further conversation.

"Well"—Luke leaned forward and put his elbows on the table—"him reading your books doesn't necessarily narrow down the list of possibilities. Yes, it could be a man who bought the books, but it could also be a man who has a wife or daughter who bought the books."

"Is there a way to tell who bought them locally?" Jax directed his question to Grace.

"If there is, I don't know how, but I can give you guys all my online information and see if you can figure anything out from that."

"I can hand it off to Kyle." Brody looked at Luke. "Unless that'll fuck with your case."

I squeezed Grace's hand when she lowered her head and grinned. They were making amends. I knew that had to make her happy.

Luke gave Brody a chin lift. "It won't."

Brody's eyes shifted to Grace. "Did you have trouble with the alarm? Is that why it wasn't set?"

"I did set it," she insisted.

"Grace." He frowned. "I know you think you did, but there is no way to bypass that alarm without an alert going to either me or Luke. And we didn't get anything."

"Do you think someone could've guessed the code?" Jake asked.

"No," Brody stated. "We did a series of numbers and letters, completely random."

Jake looked at Grace. "How do you remember it?"

"I keep it in my phone, but my phone's locked and the only person with the code besides me is Ty."

She pointed over at me, and all eyes shifted, focusing on me. I raised my eyebrows. "Don't even go there again. We are way past that shit, aren't we?"

Jack snorted, and I saw her brothers grin—well, most of them anyway. Her dad spoke before the boys could. "I was there when he got the call from Grace. There's no way he's had anything to do with this."

Luke surprised me when he agreed. "Dad's right. I was there too."

"Where the hell were all of you?" Cam asked.

"It was just me, Ty, and Dad." Luke explained. "We took the boys horseback riding at Chase's farm. His sister gives lessons."

"Do you ever leave your phone laying around anywhere?" Jax re-directed the conversation.

"No." Grace shook her head. "It's always in my purse."

"No one's going to find it in there," I mumbled.

Grace pulled her hand from mine and sent me a glare which had her brothers laughing until Ben spoke up. "He's not wrong, Grace. That thing's a pit."

"I know." She rolled her eyes. "I need to clean it out."

"You've been saying that for a year, Grace," Anna said, and Grace smiled.

"So, we're back where we started," Cam surmised.

"There's just no way to get past that damn alarm if you set it." Brody looked thoughtful. "Are you sure no one but me, you and Luke have the code?"

She looked thoughtful. "No, no one. Except…"

"Except who?" Brody leaned forward.

She looked between her brothers. "Well, the landlord has it, but it's in the lease that if a tenant has an alarm, he needs the code in case there's a problem, like a gas leak or something."

Luke narrowed his eyes. "What's his name?"

Grace scoffed. "You can't be serious, Luke. My landlord's like sixty years old and ridiculously sweet. He wouldn't even know what erotica is, let alone where to find it."

"You never know what people do behind closed doors," Jax said. "Does he know you write books?"

She looked thoughtful. "No, he couldn't. I honestly didn't tell anyone except Charlie. Well, Ty and Mom know, but we can rule them out."

Jack's eyes flicked over to Anna, and I think she squirmed in her seat a little before she met his stare. "We'll talk about it later."

"We don't have to. I already knew," he admitted.

Anna jerked her head in his direction. "How did you know?"

"Darlin', I laid beside you in bed while you read. Did you think I wouldn't see the name Grace Monroe? Not to mention, she was able to buy a new car and move to a nicer apartment building. I just connected the dots."

"Wanna come work for me?" Jax smirked at his dad, but you could tell he was impressed.

"You didn't read them, did you?" Grace asked, panic in her voice.

His eyes softened. "No, darlin'. That's not for me to read, but I am proud of you. We all are. That's quite an accomplishment." He leaned forward, his eyes focused solely on Grace, his expression serious. "But next time, have a little faith in me, in your brothers. We'll always support you, no matter what you decide. Just remember that."

She nodded, and I felt the relief run through her at his words. I was learning Grace did not like her family upset with her, and if she thought they would be about this, it made sense why she wasn't telling them.

"So, we have somewhere to start," Luke said. "I'll question the landlord tomorrow."

"If you think the stalker and the guy who drugged me are the same person, then you can forget my landlord because it wasn't him in the club that night."

Luke considered that. "Still worth having the conversation."

"And I'll have Kyle scour through Grace's book accounts," Brody added.

"Anything else you wanna tell us?" Chris directed his question to Grace.

"I'm moving in with Ty," she said hesitantly.

"We already knew that shit." Jax waved his hand in the air. "We can't curtail all your bad decisions, Grace."

My eyes snapped to him, but he grinned, and that was when I noticed they all were grinning in my direction. They were teasing me. And I had to admit after all the shit they were causing because of me, it felt nice to be accepted.

For me and for Grace.

Chapter Forty-two

Tyler

"I think my brothers are getting restless that it's been over a month, and there hasn't been one lead."

"I know they are."

"I knew my landlord wasn't involved, but I was hoping Luke would've found prints on the letters or from something in my apartment."

"Me too, baby." I answered while I watched her set plates out on the dining room table. "Grace, we're only having pizza, you don't have to put all that out."

She shrugged. "I know, but Natalie's coming and when she was here on Monday, she didn't seem herself, so I thought I'd make it like a dinner at my mom's where she gets to sit with the family and chat. I know she doesn't have that at home, and she's rarely here at dinner for us to do this."

I moved behind her and kissed her neck, wrapping my arms around her tightly when she moaned. "That's sweet, baby, but I don't think it's necessary."

The doorbell rang just then, and Sophie yelled from where she was watching TV in the living room. "Can I get it?"

I kissed Grace's neck one last time before moving toward the door, calling out when Sophie raced past me. "Wait for me."

I pulled open the door, and it was the pizza man. Sophie would've been happier with Natalie, but she was pretty satisfied her pizza was here. I handed her the boxes to take to the kitchen and paid the kid who shifted on his feet nervously.

When he didn't walk away, I lifted my eyebrows and waited. "Umm, dude there's a chick walking down the road toward your house and she looks kind of messed up. Just thought you'd want to know."

He turned and walked off the porch back to his little red car, jumped in, and threw it in reverse. Should I believe him? He smelled like pot, so maybe not, but if Natalie was walking, I needed to check on her. I motioned for Grace, who walked straight to me, and I told her what the kid said.

"Go check," she encouraged. "I'll wait right here, but take your phone just in case."

I kissed her quickly before jogging out to my vehicle. I pulled the keys from my pocket and hopped in, started it up, and threw it in drive. I was only about a quarter of a mile down the road when I saw a short brunette walking. I drove a little past, and she didn't look up from her feet so I did a U-turn and headed back, putting the passenger door on her side of the road.

I slowed when I was near her and put the window down. "Natalie."

Her head snapped up, and when my eyes landed on her, I growled. "Natalie, get in."

She waited for me to stop before she climbed into the passenger seat and turned her head to stare out the window. I drove the short distance to the house and pulled in the driveway, threw the SUV in park, and shut off the engine, all before I turned to face her.

"What happened?"

"It's no big deal," she whispered.

"Natalie, don't tell me it's no big deal. You have a black eye and a bloody lip, plus I can tell by the way you're walking that you're favoring your side."

"I just did what I had to do for Seth and Sophie." I looked past her injuries when her eyes met mine to the steely resolve in her expression.

"What do you mean?"

"I recorded her."

I slanted my head to the side but didn't have to ask. She just continued. "My mom. She was trying to find a way to get custody of Seth and Sophie, talking to a lawyer and everything to fight the will, but all she wanted was their inheritance. She doesn't care about them, and I don't want them growing up there." She looked down at her folded hands in her lap. "They love it with you, and they're doing so well here. It wouldn't be fair if she got them."

"What did you record?"

She swallowed hard. "I recorded her and her boyfriend discussing the plan, including the plan for their inheritance. It was really bad. The things she said about the kids, the money, her plans for the money; she was even going to try to extort more money from you because she knew you'd fight to get them back." Her face filled with disgust when she lifted her head. "She was going to try to sell them to you after she had control of their inheritance. It was so messed up." She took a deep breath, exhaling slowly while she faced the house. "I made a bunch of copies, gave one to the police department, one to Tara's attorney, who I guess was your dad's too, and even one to my mom's attorney."

"Then what?"

"She found out before I could leave tonight. Her attorney called her right away. I didn't know he's sleeping with my sister, and that's how they could afford him, so he called and told her about the recording. She cornered me, and I confessed."

"She hit you?"

She snorted. "She hits me all the time, Ty, so this was nothing new. She hit us all. I was only staying there to finish high school, but I left and obviously am not going back."

"You'll stay with me."

She smiled. "That's sweet, but don't worry about me. I'll figure it out. I just wanted to come see the kids because I probably won't be able to for a little bit, while I figure out what I'm going to do."

"You'll stay with us," I repeated.

"You have a pretty full house, Ty. You don't need more houseguests," she argued.

"You're not a houseguest, Natalie, you're family and you're staying with us."

I wasn't ready for her to cry, but when she did, I reached out and laid my hand on her shoulder, not knowing how else to comfort her. She sniffled while we sat together in the otherwise quiet vehicle. "You know, Tara talked about you a lot."

My head jerked back. I hadn't expected that. "She did?"

Natalie nodded and sniffed again, her eyes pointed forward. "She always felt so bad for coming into your life because she felt like she caused a rift between you and your dad. She used to tell me that you got a raw deal when your mom died so young, and she hated that for you."

She wiped under her eyes with her fingertips. "But she really wanted you to know Seth and Sophie, so I'll bet wherever she is right now, she's so happy they're with you." She smiled and turned to face me. "And your dad, I don't know if you know it, but he bragged about you all the time. Ty this, and Ty that." She lowered her voice to mimic my dad's, and I grinned at her rendition. "Ty was a second-round draft pick, Ty was an MVP in college, Ty's the best center the league ever saw." She shook her head, her expression turning serious.

"Tara told me he was so scared when you got hurt, but that he bragged to anyone who would listen how well you handled it, how hard you worked. She said he told her he wouldn't have had the strength you did to keep fighting your way back, and that he secretly hoped you never played again. That you had time to find yourself, find someone to love and have your own family." She reached over and laid her hand over mine.

"He told Tara he spent too many years on the road and never valued family like he should've, but he wanted you to have more." Her eyes watered. "God, I bet he's watching you and just bursting with pride right now."

"I wasn't a great son to him, not the last two years of his life especially." I admitted.

"That's not the way he saw it. I honestly thought you walked on water the way he talked about you," she shared.

I dropped my head. I needed to process what she told me, and I couldn't do that right now. Plus I knew I wanted to process it with Grace, so I lifted my head and pointed at the house. "We should go in. Grace is probably pacing inside wondering what's wrong that we're sitting out here."

She reached for her door handle, but when I put my hand on her arm, she turned back. "Thank you."

She laid her hand on top of mine and squeezed before she shoved her door open and jumped down from the seat, heading toward the house.

I wasn't surprised when I walked in, and Grace was already helping her clean her cuts. I looked around the room at my small, unexpected family and remembered something my mom used to do even though it was only the two of us most often, and realized I wanted to do that. I needed to explain a lot of things to the kids, and I wanted Natalie and Grace to be there too.

"I'm calling a family meeting," I announced and almost laughed when they all looked at each other like I'd lost my mind, but I continued. "Things have been changing here and are going to change a little more, so I think we should talk about it."

Grace's eyes softened, but she just sat down in her seat and waited, encouraging me to continue with her silent support.

Sophie wrinkled her nose. "What's a family meeting?"

"It's a chance for us to talk about what's been going on."

"Oh, okay." Sophie smiled wide. "Grace let me pick out new nail polish at the store. It's pink and sparkly."

I chuckled, along with Natalie and Grace. "That wasn't exactly what I meant, Sophie."

She looked confused so I continued. "I wanted to let everyone know that Natalie is moving in with us."

Sophie sat up straight and squealed. "Yay, Aunt Natalie and Grace are gonna live here?"

My eyes found Grace who looked a little surprised, but I knew she trusted me to explain later when she smiled softly. "And Dex is moving in after Christmas."

"Oh shoot, I forgot about that, Ty. I can find somewhere else to go." Natalie offered.

"We have plenty of room. This is a big house, and it has lots of rooms, but most of them need paint and new carpet, so I was thinking we should start doing some remodeling."

Grace's eyes widened in surprise, but she still stayed silent while Sophie spoke up. "Can we paint my room yellow like Grace's car?"

Grace giggled and nodded at Sophie. "I think that would be a great color." She looked at Seth. "What about you, Seth?"

"I like blue," he said quietly, but while looking at Grace and then me, so that was progress.

"What are you gonna pick, Aunt Natalie?" Sophie asked excitedly.

"Hmm…" Natalie put her finger to her lip like she was thinking. "I like purple."

"I like purple too." Sophie announced. "That was Mommy's favorite color."

I watched her smiling and laughing, even when talking about Tara, and hoped it would continue that way for her. I hoped she wouldn't carry the pain of their loss, but happiness in their memory.

"What about you Grace?" Seth asked quietly.

Grace bit her lip like she was thinking. "Well, I like…"

"Grace and I will be sharing my room." I announced, and all heads swung toward me.

"You mean like Mommy and Daddy?" I nodded, and Sophie looked like she was considering something. "You should still let her pick the color, Tyler. Girls like that."

I chuckled. "That's a good idea, Sophie."

She sat back, pretty pleased with herself, and I announced we'd start this weekend with the kids' rooms and go from there. When we were all done talking, Sophie declared she loved family meetings before she skipped up the stairs, pulling Natalie to her room, which Sophie declared would be right next to hers. Grace stood and went to the kitchen, leaving just Seth and me behind.

I looked his way, but he stayed seated, more quiet than usual, which was saying something. "You good, kid?"

His head popped up and he bit his lip before he spoke. "Is Grace your girlfriend?"

I considered that. We hadn't officially called our relationship anything, but she was, and if I had my way, she'd be more than that. "Yeah."

He twisted his fingers in his lap, and I narrowed my eyes, wondering what was going on with him, but I waited, knowing with Seth patience would pay off. "Do you love her?"

My eyebrows shot up, and I peeked into the kitchen, but I saw she was talking on her phone, probably to Charlie, so I faced Seth again who was watching me closely. "I do love her." I leaned in closer to him, and whispered, "But I haven't told her yet. Don't want to scare her off."

Seth cocked his head to the side. "I think girls like that mushy stuff."

I grinned. "How do you know what girls like?" He remained silent, so I continued. "Do you think I should tell her?"

He nodded his head. "I think she'll stay then."

My eyebrows pulled down. "You afraid she's gonna leave?"

He shrugged, and I waited patiently. "I just like it the way it is now. It's like we're a family or something."

I closed my eyes briefly, realization hitting me before I opened them again and met his stare. "I like it too."

He smiled and moved from his seat, heading toward the stairs. He was almost at the top when I felt Grace come to stand beside me. I pushed my chair back, and she sat on my lap, putting her face almost level with my own.

"He okay?" she asked softly.

I nodded and took a chance. "He said he likes our little family."

She smiled and touched her lips to mine. "I do too."

"He asked if we can keep you."

She laughed. "You just try to get rid of me." I laid my hands on her hips and squeezed, making her wiggle around on my lap. "You sure it's a good idea for me to be in your bed?"

"Yeah, they don't come in as much anymore. Plus, I need you to sleep beside me Grace. This running back and forth between beds at night was okay for a while, but I want you next to me all night."

"I want that too," she admitted, pressing one more kiss to my lips before climbing off my lap and grabbing another dirty plate from the table.

I stood and pushed my chair in, watching her walk back toward the kitchen. "Oh, by the way, Seth thinks it'll make you happy if I tell you I love you."

She stumbled, and I grinned, turning my back and heading for the stairs when she called out. "Ty, wait, what did you just say?"

Chapter Forty-three

Grace

I hesitated. Did I hear him right, or was I only hoping I'd heard that? I followed him up the stairs and down the hallway toward his bedroom, well, our bedroom, I guess.

I'd barely crossed the threshold when he turned to face me. "I thought we could go for paint tomorrow. What do you think?"

"What do I think?" I stood in awe with a dirty plate still in my hand.

"Grace, the plates go in the sink." His eyebrows lifted. "You're in the wrong room."

"What did you say?"

"I said the plates go in the sink," he repeated.

"Downstairs."

"Yeah, downstairs." he agreed.

"No," I said, frustrated. "I know where the plates go."

"Then I don't know what you're asking, baby," he said seriously, but I saw his lips twitch.

I narrowed my eyes, put the plate on the dresser beside me, and threw my hands on my hips. "Tyler…what's your middle name?"

"Francis."

I wrinkled my nose. "Francis?"

His eyebrows shot up. "You making fun of my name?"

"No, I just…" I trailed off, not knowing how to say I thought he'd have a really cool middle name, something to match his first name. "Francis? It just doesn't fit you."

"It was my dad's middle name," he explained. "Why, what's yours?"

"Elizabeth, same as my mom." I shook my head; we were getting off track. "Anyway, what did you say downstairs?"

"I actually said a lot downstairs." He seemed almost proud of himself, and he should be. I was proud of him. That he made a decision and talked about it openly was a big deal for him. What seemed like an easy thing for most, I knew was actually difficult and foreign to him.

I took a deep breath and exhaled loudly. I knew he was messing with me, but I needed to hear him say it again, so I knew my mind wasn't playing tricks on me. "Ty…"

"He said he loves you," a quiet voice said behind me, and I spun around to face Seth.

I flicked my attention back and forth between the two of them, who were grinning at each other, before landing on Seth. "He told you that?"

He nodded, so I squatted down. "Could you give him a message for me?" Seth nodded again, a full smile gracing his lips. "Tell him I love him too."

Seth giggled and looked toward Ty who held out his fist, and when Seth lifted his little fist to bump against his brother's, I sighed quietly. He'd come so far in such a short amount of time; they both had. Maybe all this time, they just needed each other. Needed someone to make them feel normal and like less of an outcast, someone who understood them.

"I got it from here, kid." Seth laughed and started to back out of the room when Ty called out to him. "Thanks for the good advice."

Seth blushed and ducked his head, but he did it with a smile. When Ty faced me again, his expression was all-knowing. "You love me?"

I lifted an eyebrow. "You love me?"

He shrugged, feigning disinterest, but I saw the light in his eyes. The same light I'd been seeing more and more lately. I moved closer until I was standing right in front of him. "Because if Seth is wrong, I can just…"

I squealed when he grabbed me and picked me up, his lips pressing down to mine, a grin still lingering on them. "Seth's not wrong."

I let him deepen the kiss before I broke away and slid back down his body. I laid my hands against his chest and confessed something that had been nagging at me. "Do you think we're moving too fast?"

He ran his finger along my cheek, resting his palm against the side of my neck. "Grace, over the past two years, I've learned a lot of lessons, but most importantly, life is unpredictable. I'm not going to take one more minute for granted. And I'm definitely not going to waste any more time on what-ifs or maybes."

"You're right." I pushed up on my toes and kissed him softly before dropping back down to my feet. I spun around taking in the room with its sterile white walls, just like every other room in the house and smiled to myself. "Pink would look great in here."

"I'm not sleeping in a pink bedroom." I turned just in time to see him grin mischievously. "But we could paint Dex's room pink."

I laughed and slapped his chest. "You wouldn't."

He laughed with me. "Fuck, yeah, I would." I dropped my head, only looking back up when he spoke and his voice had lost its playfulness. "You okay with everyone being here for a while?"

"I'm fine with it, but it's not really my decision."

He frowned. "Why isn't it your decision?"

"It's your house, Ty," I reminded him.

"It's our house." He fumbled, and I saw a tiny glimpse of the old Ty in front of me. "Unless that's not what you want."

"Ty, I know you're not great at verbalizing your thoughts, but you need to tell me what you want without assuming I already know."

I waited while his eyes scanned my face. "I want you here with me. Always."

I laid my hands against his chest. "Okay, but you need to promise me if that ever changes for you, you'll talk to me about it."

He shook his head. "It won't."

I sighed. "Ty."

"Okay, I promise I'll talk about it, but I can promise you, I won't change my mind." He ran his fingers through my hair. "So are you okay with them staying here?"

"Yeah, of course." I paused, not wanting to overstep but was very curious. "Can I ask what happened with Natalie?"

"She went to bat for the kids with her mom." He looked impressed and a little surprised.

I nodded. "She told me that. She also said she's considering pressing charges for assault. Just one more strike against her mom so she leaves you guys alone. But I mean what happened in the driveway? You were out there for a long time."

I nodded. "She told me stuff Tara had told her. Stuff about my dad."

"Like what?" I held my breath, hoping it was good, hoping he wouldn't have more guilt to carry than he already was.

"She said he was proud of me, bragged all the time about what I was doing, how I recovered from my injury, stuff like that."

Relief washed over me, and I wrapped my arms around his chest. "I'm glad she told you that."

"Me too." His head jerked up, and he frowned. "Was that the doorbell?"

We waited until we heard it again. "Guess so."

I grabbed the plate and followed Ty down the stairs, but headed for the kitchen to set it in the sink while he went to the door. I moved out of the kitchen toward the door when I heard Luke's voice.

"Luke?"

Andy came barreling through the door, his eyes searching the room before they fell on me. "Hi, Aunt Grace. Is Seth home?"

I smiled and pointed at the stairs. "Sure is, kiddo. He's up in his room."

"Okay," Andy yelled, heading to the stairs but then he turned and called out to Luke. "Don't ask without us, Dad."

"I won't," Luke promised.

"Oh no." I walked the rest of the way to stand beside Ty who had closed the door when Luke came in, but hadn't moved much since. "What have you done?"

He put his hands up in surrender. "Nothing. It's all Andy and Seth. Well, Kasey too."

I narrowed my eyes when two little boys came running back down the stairs, stopping only when they made it to Luke and Ty. "Okay, Dad, we're ready."

Luke smiled down at Andy before facing Ty directly. "Kasey called me and asked if I knew anyone who would be interested in a coaching position with the school district. She thought I may know someone because I coached Andy's baseball team this past summer. I told her I did."

"They want you to coach football," Andy blurted out.

My eyes widened because I doubted Ty had ever considered coaching as a profession, but I waited patiently, along with everyone else to hear his response.

He lifted his hand to run across his beard before he dropped it again. "Coaching?"

Luke looked at me, and I shrugged unsure of what he was thinking. Ty put his hands on his hips and looked down at Seth. "You two knew about this?"

Seth shifted on his feet. "Andy told me his aunt Kasey was going to ask you."

Ty considered Seth for another moment before he nodded. "I'll only agree to coach if you play."

Seth's eyes widened, and a huge smile stretched across his face. Ty waited patiently, though, because he wanted the words from Seth, something we'd both been trying to do more. His patience, once again, paid off. "Okay."

Ty nodded, but then he frowned, like something had just occurred to him. "I'll coach, but isn't it late in the season to start?"

"Yeah," Luke explained. "Right now, it would be working on skills with the elementary and middle school kids. The high school team didn't win any games, so their season is already over. They'll need skill training, but time in the weight room too, Kasey said."

Ty jerked back. "High school?"

"I didn't mention that? It's elementary, middle school, and high school." Luke smirked. "It's a small town so they only hire one coach." He slapped Tyler on the back of his shoulder. "I'll tell Kasey you accept. Oh, and one more thing. Jax, Ben, and the twins all played high school ball, so they said they'd be happy to help out, like as an assistant when you need one."

"What, no Jake?" Ty asked sarcastically.

"Nah, Jake coaches baseball with me."

"What's Brody going to do?" I asked.

Luke snorted. "Probably be a dance teacher if Gia keeps popping out girls."

Luke and I shared a laugh imagining Brody doing anything girly. Luke was right though, with two girls already, it seemed Brody was going to have a lot of little women to keep up with.

"When do I start?" Tyler asked.

Luke shoved his hands in his front pockets. "The coach who's leaving said he'll show you how things work, but then he's moving, and he wants to be gone by Thanksgiving."

"That's in two weeks," Ty pointed out.

"Guess you better give Kasey a call and figure shit out then."

He grinned and jerked his head to the door. "Let's go, Andy, we've got to pick up your mom."

We said our good-byes and watched them walk through the door before Tyler closed it and faced us. Seth stepped forward and smiled, seconds before he threw his arms around Ty. He pulled back quickly, but the smile never left his face. "Thanks, Tyler."

He took off like a shot up the stairs, and Ty stood still, watching him go. I moved to stand in front of him and wrapped my arms around his waist. "You just made his day, maybe his whole year."

Ty dropped his eyes to mine. "He looked really happy when I agreed."

I melted at the look of happiness on his face. "Yeah, he did." I ran my hands up his chest to wrap around his neck and lowered my voice. "Should I call you Coach now?"

He dropped his forehead to mine, his voice growly. "Maybe when I'm fucking you."

My stomach tightened, and I knew just from his growly voice alone that I was wet, not to mention what his words were doing to me. "So Charlie was right. You do have some kinky fantasies."

He pushed his lips against mine and grinned, pulling back only enough to speak. "Yeah, well, don't tell Charlie, or I'll have to deal with Dex's dumbass comments."

I giggled and pulled him closer so I could deepen the kiss.

That would definitely be our little secret.

Chapter Forty-four

Tyler

"Hey, is everyone ready?"

Grace's voice sounded while she was coming down the stairs, right before I heard Sophie call her name and her feet heading back up the stairs. I waited for the pang of anxiety that usually followed a statement like that, but it never came. I realized over the past couple of months, time spent with Grace's family had stopped being overwhelming and became something I almost looked forward to.

Being around Jake and Ben reminded me of being with the few friends I had in college, including Dex. Luke and Jax had both come around, especially with Jax volunteering to coach with me, and Luke at riding lessons on Saturdays. Cam and Chris seemed pre-occupied with something, even Grace had pointed that out, so they hadn't given us too much trouble with our new living situation or relationship. That only left Brody, who was also the only brother who hadn't seemed to change his opinion, but he was also the one brother I hadn't spent much time with.

I'd take six out of seven. I wouldn't actually care, but I knew how much it meant to Grace for us to be friends, so I'd been making a real effort and so had they.

I stretched out my arms and put my hands behind my head while I watched three girls scramble down the stairs. Seth's head jerked up when he heard their voices from where he'd been sitting beside me watching pre-game shows, but only for a moment until his attention was once again on the television. It wasn't even a year ago that I wouldn't have turned on the television, never would've considered watching the game, but lately, I didn't miss playing football as much as I had, and I was really starting to like coaching the kids. Granted, I'd only been doing it for two weeks, but I'd met with every age group a few times, and I liked watching the different stages of ability and knowledge. It was a good fit for me, and something I would never have considered had it not been for Kasey.

When the girls finally made it to the bottom, my eyes found Grace, who looked fucking incredible in her jeans and dark sweater. Hell, Grace looked good in everything, and I actually know that now, sharing a bedroom with her and having seen her in all sorts of shit.

"Do you like my dress?"

My eyes shifted from Grace to Sophie when her little voice rang out, and I looked at her all dressed up with her hair in a French braid. "I love it."

She beamed and bounced on her toes, always ready to get going and not anything like her brother who was satisfied to sit quietly.

"Are you sure it's okay if I come?" Natalie asked, hesitation clear in her voice.

"My mom called me this morning to make sure you're coming, so yes, I'm definitely sure."

Natalie looked my way, and I nodded my agreement. I knew she was still feeling a little out of place, but Grace was determined to shake that out of her, and I completely agreed. Natalie needed family in her life, and the Dimarcos were determined to give it to her, just like they'd been determined to give it to me, Seth, and Sophie.

I'd decided a while ago to take it, at first for Grace, then for the kids, and now for myself.

I stood from the couch and gestured toward the door. "Let's go."

Everyone grabbed their stuff and headed out to my SUV, piling in for the short drive to Jack and Anna's house.

It was Thanksgiving Day, and I was very curious to see how they fit all their kids, wives, girlfriends, and grandkids into their house. Granted, their house was big, about the same as mine and similar in style, being they were both farmhouses at one time, but still even a big house would fill up quickly when all the Dimarcos were there.

We pulled onto the side of the street to park, and I took in all the cars, trucks, and SUVs already parked there. I felt Grace's soft hand on mine and heard her even softer words telling me we'd be fine before we got out.

I'd been right. The inside of the house was nothing but loud voices and what appeared to be chaos, but when I watched closer, it seemed everyone was doing something to help get food on the table while maneuvering the kids where they needed to be. Grace would say it was organized chaos, and I'd agree that was the perfect description.

I'd barely moved out of the way before Andy zipped by me and grabbed Seth's hand while being chased by Andy's golden retriever, Cookie. I peeked into the living room and saw one of Jake and Lanie's dogs Beasely sleeping on the couch with Bray running a small truck over his back.

I'd met Andy's dog, Cookie, when I picked up Seth from Luke's house one afternoon after school and realized quickly the dog was fucking crazy. Like might need medication crazy, but he sure as hell was fun to watch with the boys.

Lanie and Jake, who live next door to Luke, have two dogs who had been out in the yard with Jake that same afternoon, but weren't nearly as insane as Cookie. Beasley's a giant St. Bernard who barely lifted his head when he saw me before he dropped it and went back to snoring while a little dog, who couldn't be more than five or six pounds, ran circles around the sleeping giant.

"Bray, let's go." Jake appeared at the mouth of the hallway holding their little dog. Bray scurried around the corner, and Jake bent down, handing him the dog he was holding. "Here, put Bob in the living room."

"His name's Bobby," he said, giggling and running back into the living room.

"Let's go." Jake gestured for us to follow him. "I'm starving, and Mom made us wait for you."

Since we were the last to arrive, which I'd learned would always be the case when Grace was going, we followed Jake into the dining room to find seats. The table had to be groaning under the weight of the food although the table itself was massive. They had a smaller table set up for the kids to sit together, which opened up some room at the big table, but not much. Natalie offered to sit with the kids, but Anna waved her over to the table where she had a seat for her beside Grace.

Conversations moved quickly around the table, and for the most part, I stayed quiet. I had no idea who was talking to who and didn't participate until Grace tapped me or someone said my name.

"Tyler." I looked across the room toward the kids' table when I heard Sophie's voice. "Can we get a dog?"

I shook my head. "No, we're getting a Dex pretty soon. He'll be enough to clean up after."

I was surprised when laughter filled the room, and Jake announced he was going to tell him I'd said that, but I guess it had been funny. I was a little serious, though. They'd never lived with him; I had, and he had not been neat. Far from it, actually.

Grace leaned against my arm when Kasey called my name. "How do you like the coaching job so far?"

I looked at Kasey who was seated a little ways down the table. "I like it. Thanks again."

She flicked her wrist in the air like it was no big deal. "I just happen to know some people on the hiring committee and put your name in. Your reputation and experience in football got you the job."

"You mean it wasn't his sparkling personality?" Jake teased.

"Or his conversational skills?" Ben piled on. "That's strange."

I grinned. "You heard her. It's because I was the best player in the league."

There were a lot of hoots around the table and a lot of comments about my ego, which I knew there would be, but I only took another bite of food and let them go. It didn't take much to get these guys wound up.

"Those are some big words, man," Jax said.

"Anyone can play football professionally when you have coaches, trainers, and therapists all at your fingertips," Cam stated.

"That's true." Luke added, sitting forward in his seat. "Now, backyard ball is a whole different kind of game."

Grace looked across the table where Charlie sat and rolled her eyes. "Oh please, it's a whole different game because you make up ridiculous rules and cheat."

Brody looked offended. "We don't cheat."

Charlie snorted, and I heard Jack chuckle, surprised he hadn't jumped in yet. "Yes, you do."

"Charlie," Ben said, his voice exaggerated. "I can't believe you would say that."

"It's true." She laughed. "If you guys actually played by the real rules, none of you would be any good."

"Oh, that's it." Ben stood. "I say game on."

"Me too." Jake stood. "And since Charlie knows so much, I think she should play too."

Charlie beamed, and I dropped my head to hide the grin. Something told me she knew just how much to poke to get what she wanted.

Jax stood. "I'm in."

Cam and Chris stood. "We're in."

Grace stood next. "I'm in."

The other girls all followed, and before I knew it, Kasey, Natalie, and I were the only ones besides Jack and Anna who were still seated.

Natalie blushed. "I don't know how to play football."

"Oh, it's easy." Kasey waved her hand in the air. "They can teach you. Besides, you have to play." She pointed at her very pregnant belly. "I obviously can't."

"Okay, I guess," Natalie said.

I was a little annoyed Kasey said it was easy. Fuck, I spent my whole damn life getting the shit kicked out of me, and it wasn't easy. But then I considered backyard ball and realized no one out there was looking to annihilate me, so maybe it would be easy.

At least I hoped no one was.

I wasn't surprised when Ben faced me directly. "Ready to put your money where your mouth is?"

I stood slowly and looked around the table at all the people standing and only wondered one thing. "How're we making the teams?"

A lot of hoots meant a lot of noise, but Jax hollered over it. "Dad, you gonna ref?"

"Right behind you," he announced.

We all made our way outside, kids too who became the cheering section, along with Anna who was taking care of Brody's youngest daughter, Kennedy. Their yard was big, definitely big enough to have a decent-sized field. The teams were made up by Jack picking two team captains, who happened to be the two oldest in the family, Jax and Luke. When someone pulled out a quarter to flip and see who picks first and Jack came out of the small shed in the back of the yard with a cans of spray paint, I realized this was not the first time they'd done this.

I watched Jack spray lines to create end zones and sidelines, clearly marking what was out of bounds until Anna stepped up beside me. "They used to do this all the time growing up." I turned to face her. "Jack was always the ref, and they always picked teams, although this will be the first year the girls are playing."

"Grace didn't play?" I asked, curiously.

She smiled softly. "No, she was more like your Sophie when she was younger. She wouldn't have wanted to get her dress dirty."

I chuckled when she continued. "Now she'd kick their asses even if she was wearing a dress."

Anna leaned in close to my arm and lowered her voice. "Okay, since you're new here and don't know the ropes just yet, I'm going to give you a little bit of information." I nodded, shocked when she started talking again. "Jax has a bad knee from a fight he was in his senior year. He was kicked hard and has always favored it a little." She rolled her eyes. "The fight was over a girl. I'm glad he's smartened up since then." She gestured toward Ben. "Ben hates dirt in his mouth, always has, won't be able to play until he cleans his mouth out."

My eyes widened. "Are you telling me to push his face into the dirt?"

She looked me in the eye. "Do you want to win?"

I felt the grin slowly spread across my face when her eyes twinkled. "Hell, yeah."

"Okay, then, listen up. Jake can't stand Lanie's attention on another man, even his brothers, so whichever team picks Jake, make sure the opposite gets Lanie. It'll throw him off the whole game." I laughed to myself because this information was useful, but at the same time, it felt so wrong coming from their mom.

"Chris had a groin injury in high school so if he has the ball, aim low. He drops it every time to protect himself." She cringed. "But don't hit him there, I want more grandkids." I rolled my lips together to keep from laughing too loud.

"Cam is a dirty player, especially if he's losing, so watch for eye pokes, horse-collaring, stuff like that. He's also not opposed to tripping. He'll do whatever it takes." She pursed her lips. "You may want him on your team actually. Trust me, he knows the stuff I'm telling you about his brothers, and he'll use it against them just to win. That leaves Brody and Luke." My eyes followed hers across the yard and saw Jack was almost finished.

"Brody's a tough one. Not much distracts him except Gia and his girls, so find a way to get Gia the ball, and it'll fluster him." I followed her gaze, not surprised when it landed on Luke. "Leave Luke alone, he was shot last year, he's been through enough." She lifted her finger and pointed at me. "But don't tell him or the boys I said that, or said any of this."

"My lips are sealed," I promised.

"One more thing." She paused before continuing. "My boys are stubborn, and they play hard to win. But they're also cheaters." I snickered, and she shook her head smiling. "I love them, but they are very competitive, especially with each other and now you too, so whoever's losing, watch that team's players because I promise you, they'll be trying to cheat."

I nodded, and she gestured toward them all making their way back to form a group. "Go."

"Thanks, Anna."

She smiled sweetly, and if I hadn't just listened to her telling me all that shit, I would never have believed Anna was capable of it. I moved quickly toward the group and just as I think Anna predicted, after Luke won the toss, he picked me first.

After Jax picked Brody, Luke was looking over the group when I leaned in. "How about Cam."

He didn't look my way but nodded and called for Cam. I chanced a look over at Anna who smiled in approval. Luke and Jax continued to pick, and by the time they were done, I thought we had a winning team. Ours consisted of Luke, Cam, Jake, Charlie, Grace, Sydney, Lucy, and me. While Jax's team had Jax, Brody, Chris, Ben, Gia, Natalie, Kate, and Lanie.

Jack blew a whistle to start the game after we all discussed strategy, and then it was game on. Our team had the ball first, and Luke was all-time quarterback, which was a pretty safe spot for him. The game was pretty calm. Everyone seemed aware of the rules and were following them. For a while, I thought maybe Anna had exaggerated, and it wasn't until Jake ran in our first touchdown that I realized she hadn't exaggerated at all.

Apparently Jax's team hadn't taken it lightly that we had points on the board first, and Jax also seemed to have the same information as Anna about Jake and Lanie because he made sure he got the ball to her a lot, which meant everyone headed for her. To say Jake was pissed was an understatement.

After they scored, he called out. "Are you ever going to give the ball to someone else?"

"She's our receiver, Jake, and she's a good, so no, I'm not."

Jake glared at Jax while he jogged past him and I glanced over at Anna who rolled her eyes while shaking her head.

"Wanie!" I looked up toward the house and saw Braydon waving at Lanie. "You won, Wanie!"

She waved back and smiled before jogging over to Jax and the huddle her team was forming.

We were up again, and Luke threw a pass to Sydney. I watched in amazement as Cam blocked for her the entire way down the field. He tripped Chris when he tried to grab the ball out of her arms and actually grabbed the back of Brody's shirt at the collar and pulled him down. He landed hard on the ground, but Cam only jumped over him and kept running beside Sydney while she made her way down the field. When Cam seemed distracted by Natalie who kept running this weird zigzag pattern around Sydney, Ben spun out of the back and came up on her other side. He was almost there when Charlie ran across the field and literally jumped on his back.

He tripped and fell face first on the ground with Charlie sitting on his back, holding his face in the dirt and yelling at Sydney. "Go, go, go!"

I just hung back with Luke who had his hands on his hips and was shaking his head as he watched the show. He threw his elbow into my side and gestured with his chin down the field. "Watch this."

I watched while Brody, who apparently was pissed about the horse-collar, tackled Cam from behind, even throwing a punch into his side while he was standing up. Sydney made it in for the touchdown, but fuck if I know how, and our team celebrated a second touchdown.

Charlie celebrated by getting off Ben, who was spitting dirt from his mouth, even using his shirt to wipe out his mouth, and danced away.

"You're going to pay for that, Charles."

She only continued to dance toward me, lifting her hand for a high five when she was close enough. I slapped her hand and grinned, not surprised that she not only knew Ben's weakness, but wasn't afraid to use it against him.

I heard a lot of laughing and cheers from behind me and looked back to see the kids lined up on chairs, all drinking from juice boxes. My eyes landed on Sophie, who was holding her juice box with one hand and waving at me with the other, her legs swinging as they dangled from the chair. I lifted my hand and waved back, making sure to find Seth and give him a chin lift.

"We waving, or are we playing?"

I raised an eyebrow in Jake's direction after he spoke and threw his hands on his hips. Deciding it was my turn to play, I looked over his shoulder and frowned. "Who is Lanie talking to?"

His head jerked around so fast, I wouldn't be surprised if he was dizzy, and he kept looking only turning his head back when he heard laughter from our group. He glared at me, but his lips were smiling. "Fucker."

Charlie clapped her hands before putting them on her knees and staring at me and Jake. "Come on, ladies, are we playing or what?"

We laughed harder, and Jack who was standing in the middle of the field, threw her a wink and blew the whistle.

Jax's team lined up, but this time when Jax dropped back, he didn't throw it. Instead, he handed it off to Gia who took off down the field. I was being blocked Brody who turned his head and looked at Gia just as a baby cried. Gia glanced up toward Anna and then just stopped running. It surprised everyone so much, no one really did anything but watch as she handed the ball to Kate.

"I'll be back," she called out.

"Gia, what the hell? You can't leave during the game," Brody yelled after her.

I ran around Brody, curious if we were just going to overlook the illegal handoff or what, but it became clear pretty quickly that we were. I wasn't sure why Jack had a whistle other than to blow it for a touchdown or to start a new play. Otherwise, he just watched the game and grinned.

"Kennedy's crying," Gia yelled over her shoulder. "I gave the ball to Kate, but I'll be back."

"You can't just give the ball to someone, Gia!" he called after her.

I ran down the field just as Grace tackled Kate, and they both rolled to their backs, laughing. It was so different than when the guys tackled each other. There were no extra punches or jabs, just laughing and helping each other up, although glancing over at Charlie, I didn't think she'd be helping any one up. That thought made me smile.

Jack blew the whistle, and we all lined up again. I ran and blocked, but I hadn't tackled anyone yet and didn't plan to. Grace's brothers were big, but I knew my strength and from years of playing, I knew the damage I could cause, so I held back. I was still having a fucking good time, I realized, just watching the damn game.

After a few more plays, with Brody still completely distracted by whatever Gia was doing, Jax's team didn't score and had to turn the ball over to us. "Christ, Brody, get your head out of your ass and line the fuck up. We're losing."

Brody glanced over at Jax and scowled, but it was obvious he was still distracted. We waited for Gia to return so Brody could focus and ran our next play, this time handing the ball off to Lucy. I saw Ben coming across the field out of the corner of my eye and moved quickly to block him, but because Jake was too busy watching Cam block Lanie, Lucy still got knocked out of bounds by Kate.

The next play Luke threw the ball to Grace, and I was pretty fucking proud of her when she bobbled it but held on and made the catch. She started to run, and Cam was blocking for her in the same dirty fashion he'd been doing the whole game.

I was so fucking happy he was on our team.

While Grace was running, I realized she wasn't the fastest runner. As a matter of fact, she was really slow, and Brody and Chris were bearing down on her, so I took off, thinking I could block for her, but as I got closer, I knew she wasn't going to outrun Kate and Ben too. I made a split-second decision, considering no one else was following the rules, and picked her up, threw her over my shoulder, and ran the ball the rest of the way for a touchdown. On the way, I heard Brody at my back, and he tried to pull me down, but from the sounds of it, Grace was slapping him. Ben was finally the one who got me off my feet, but it was in the end zone, and I'd already scored. I pulled Grace around to my front and landed on my back, her flat on top of me.

And I was laughing. I was laughing so fucking hard, my sides hurt.

When I stopped and heard her brothers arguing, I laughed again and threw my arm over my eyes. She leaned in and pressed a sweet kiss to my lips. "I love to see you laugh."

I uncovered my eyes and sat up, but she slapped me in the shoulder in exasperation. "But I'm kind of pissed. I was going to make it to the end zone myself."

"Baby." I snorted. "No, you weren't."

I laughed harder when Jake stood beside us and looked down.

"Grace, you are the slowest fucking runner I've ever seen. I think Bray could've beaten you, and he's only two."

"He's almost three," she said as if that made any difference at all and crossed her arms over her chest. "I'm not that slow."

"You're just lucky Ty dragged your ass in." His eyes lit up. "I think I'm going to start calling you turtle."

"You'd better not, Jake," Grace warned, her eyes flashing, but he was already yelling out to the others.

"Hey guys, what's a famous turtle name?"

"Why would you want to know that?" Jax asked.

"Because I want to give Grace a nickname."

Her brothers all laughed together, and I saw her lips twitch. I leaned in and laid my forehead against hers. "I'm sorry, baby. I won't call you turtle, I promise."

"I know you won't," she whispered. "That's the only reason I'm not pissed off right now."

"Do you want me to kick Jake's ass?" I asked, making her laugh. "Because I can."

"No, just knowing you would is enough for me."

"Hey Pike, brother, you missed it," Cam called out loudly, and I looked up to see everyone facing the back of the house. A whole new group of people had arrived, including the men from Jax and Brody's company and the motorcycle club I'd heard they're friends with.

Grace groaned and shoved her head in my neck. "What great timing."

I snickered, and we stood together. She took my hand and led me the short distance to where everyone was standing and talking. After some teasing for Grace, the guys decided to have a real game, with the actual rules in place, and the girls agreed to sit this one out.

Before it even began, they all looked at me, and Luke spoke up. "This time, Ty, you play. Play the way you can, the way you fucking need to."

307

They understood what I needed, what I missed, but I still couldn't play to my full ability, not until I saw what I was up against, and once I did, I gave them everything I had. It was a game filled with hard men, who had all trained or worked with their bodies in some way over the years. I faced off with SEALs and cops, specially trained to eliminate a threat, men in a motorcycle club who took on countless gangs and clubs to protect the streets, men who used their body every day as a vessel of power to build and maintain the city. Men whose strength wasn't constructed in a gym, but from brutal work and long hours.

These were the strongest men I ever faced.

And I loved every hard-fought moment of it.

After we finished the game, covered in dirt, sweat, and blood, and long after we shared a beer and some laughs, it struck me that the game wasn't what I missed. I love playing football and always would, but I never craved playing it on a professional level. What I craved was the feeling that I belonged, that I had a team, a family.

But I didn't need football for that anymore.

I'd found a new family.

And I finally fucking belonged.

Chapter Forty-five

Grace

I couldn't believe Ty agreed to come to Hanks.

I'd been ready to just go home, but then the boys all suggested going to Hanks, and Cam called Henry to see if they were even opening that night because of the holiday. Once he said they were, it seemed almost everyone wanted to go. Natalie immediately offered to babysit, which I thanked her for, and in the end, she had Mia and Andy too. Seth and Sophie could not have been more excited. Gia and Brody were going home because Kennedy was still so young, but they took Savannah with them, so Pike and Bella could go out to.

At the end of it all, we had a huge group going and found out Henry had a band booked, a tradition he was hoping would catch on for the locals as a place to go after everyone had time with their families. I also knew he was catering to people who didn't have family to spend the day with, giving them something to look forward to. He didn't have family until recently, and I'd often thought that must've been so hard and so lonely for him at times.

I ordered a glass of wine from Logan and headed back over to one of the tables where my family and friends were congregated. I noticed Charlie was texting, and Ben was glancing her way every few minutes. I hadn't had much time to talk with my brother, but I would now that things seemed to be slowing down, and I'd finally confront him with the Charlie stuff. He was losing her, and if he wanted to stop that, he needed to make his move because Dex was moving to New Hope, and he most certainly had his sights set on my best friend.

I scooted around to stand in front of Ty and leaned back against his chest, sighing when he put his arms around me.

Lanie moved around the table until she stood beside me. "I finished the fourth book, Grace, and it was fantastic."

"Already?" I was surprised she was moving through them so quickly. After all, she had a full-time job, an almost three-year-old, and my brother, Jake, who's a handful all on his own.

She nodded her head excitedly. "Yeah, and let me tell you, your brother is very appreciative." I giggled but didn't want to hear anything about their sex life. Unfortunately, she continued. "He even makes me read him parts but pretends you didn't write them."

I laughed when her eyes widened.

"Oh, god, you probably don't want to hear this, do you?" She put her hand to her forehead. "I mean, it's your brother. I wouldn't want to hear kinky shit about my brother if I had one." She picked up her glass and gestured toward Kate. "I'll just go share notes with Kate. I think she's on the second one." She leaned in and gave me a side hug. "Keep writing please."

I felt Ty's short beard scratch my cheek when he leaned down and put his mouth next to my ear. "Seems your fan base is growing."

I angled my head and kissed him softly. "Thanks for being with me while I told them. It was easier than I thought it would be." I turned to face him a little more. "Brody pulled me aside before we left and apologized for saying they were trashy. He said Gia read him some innocent parts, and he thought they were great."

"Good." Ty exhaled slowly. "Because if he didn't apologize, I was going to kick his ass."

My lips tipped up. "You know, you've threatened both Jake and Brody on my behalf. You better be careful. You're starting to sound like them."

I shrugged. "That's not such a bad thing."

I smiled against his lips and sighed. "I think I'm going to run to the bathroom before the band starts."

"Okay, baby." He ran his hand down over my butt cheek and squeezed.

I slapped him in the chest but still moved away, pushing through the growing crowd toward the bathrooms. I heard a little ruckus over by the door and knew, even though Pike was technically off tonight, he'd go over there and help Dylan with whoever was causing problems. I pushed the rest of the way through until I got to the bathroom and went in. I finished quickly only to hear the argument I'd heard on the way in had gotten louder. I stopped, just as I moved out of the hallway facing the room and saw a crowd of people near the doorway, including some of my brothers.

A prickle ran across the back of my neck just before a hard body pressed in tight to my back. I swallowed hard when his arm came up around the front of my neck, and his hot breath floated over my ear. "My Grace."

I trembled but pulled hard against his hand until I felt something cold press against my side. "I gave you time, Grace. Now, your time's up." He pushed it harder into my side. "If you scream or in any way try to get the attention of anyone, I'll kill the man you're living with. I've been watching, and I know who he is. I also know the other men you're always with, and I will take each and every one of them out before they even know who's shooting."

"How did you know I'd be here?" I whispered.

"We'll catch up later." He started moving backward and dropped the hand around my neck to my waist. "Right now, we'll need to go while Dylan is handling things out front."

"Dylan? You mean Dylan who does security here?"

He tightened his hand on my waist until I knew it would bruise. "Let's go and smile at anyone who looks our way." He ran his lips along my neck, and I fought back the bile rising in my throat. "That shouldn't be too hard since we're in love."

I shuffled my feet, moving as slowly as I could, trying to think of a way out of this. If I screamed, would he shoot? Did I really want to take the chance? No, I couldn't do that. My brothers were here, hell, most of my family was here. Ty was here. I swallowed hard, my eyes glancing around the bar quickly until they landed on Logan who'd just turned to face me. He narrowed his eyes and opened his mouth, and I knew he was going to call out, so I only widened my eyes and mouthed, "No," to him, hoping he would understand I couldn't even shake my head at him.

We were close to the hallway leading to the office and back exit, and I had no plan. I couldn't even get to my Taser because I'd left my purse at home. I saw Logan lean over the bar and call out to someone close, but he couldn't get anyone's attention over the noise of the band starting and whatever was going on at the door.

I saw him swear and come to the end of the bar, his eyes on me. I mouthed, "No," again, but this time he didn't listen. "Grace!" he called out.

I felt the gun leave my side, and I screamed. "Logan, no."

I wasn't fast enough because I saw him drop to the ground behind the bar and the guy holding me swung the gun in the direction of the front door. "No," I begged. "Please, I'll go with you. Let's just go."

I knew the minute my brothers saw me and pushed back against my attacker. "Come on, just go. Please, I'll go with you," I cried.

But it was too late.

He began shooting, and I closed my eyes, terrified to see anyone I love falling like Logan had. I heard Cam's voice yell over the crowd and my eyes flew open.

"Police, drop your weapon!" But the man behind me only snorted and fired at Cam.

"No," I screamed again when Cam fell to the ground. I saw Jax moving quickly through the crowd toward me, and I focused on him. I knew his eyes were trying to tell me something, but I didn't understand. He glanced quickly to his left and back to me, but my attacker must've seen what I'd seen because he immediately shifted us and aimed the gun in that direction. My eyes landed on Chris, only a second before I felt the shot go past my hip, and Jax whistle while pointing to the right. The attacker swung quickly, his hold on me faltering just enough that I could wiggle so I picked up my foot and slammed it down as hard as I could on his.

"Fuck," he roared, and the gun went off, glass breaking behind the bar, shards flying through the air, sending people screaming and running out the front door.

And then everything seemed to happen at once. I heard sirens in the distance, but my mind was fuzzy. Jax dragged me away from the shooter at the exact moment Tyler come from his right side, grabbed his wrist, and twisted it. I could almost hear the bones crunching seconds before the gun fell, and Tyler lifted him with only one hand by the throat and threw him against the wall. He pulled back his fist and hit him over and over again, like he was a machine. Jax shoved me behind him and moved forward at the same time Chris did, but it was no use. Pike was already there and talking to Ty, and he wasn't stopping. It was almost as if he couldn't hear him.

Tyler let go of his neck, and he slid to the floor, unconscious and bleeding. He kicked him hard in the side with his boot over and over again until Jax, Chris, and Pike were able to finally pull him back. I stood against the wall, shock overwhelming me, unable to control my crying. Charlie rushed to my side and put her arms around me, but I couldn't look away from Ty or the man lying on the floor. The police exploded through the front doors, paramedics rushing for Logan who still lay behind the bar. I scanned the room frantically until I found Cam standing beside Luke. He looked okay. He wasn't bleeding, and he was talking, so I exhaled shakily.

I felt the heat of his stare before I even turned my head, but when I did, I had to lean against Charlie. The pain on Ty's face was indescribable, and the fear still lingering in his eyes would haunt me for a long time. He lowered his head to look at the floor when two officers arrived and pulled his hands behind his back. He didn't struggle. He held still while they cuffed him and let them push him through the crowd and out the door.

He never looked back.

I jerked forward, shaking my head. "Where are they taking him?"

Charlie squeezed me tighter. "I don't know."

I searched the room until my eyes landed on Luke, and I called his name. He came directly to me, followed by another paramedic. Charlie dropped her arms when Luke pulled me forward and wrapped his arms tightly around me. "Are you okay?"

I nodded and pulled back so I could look at his face. "Where are they taking Ty?"

Luke put his hand around the back of my neck and squeezed. "It's standard procedure. Don't worry, he'll be out as soon as Cam and I get there. I needed him to give his statement, but he won't be charged with anything."

I felt my body relax some. "Can I go see him?"

"I need you to let the paramedic check you out, and then I'll go get him and bring him to the house. Okay?" I nodded, and he continued. "One of the boys will take you home as soon as you're cleared."

I spoke with the paramedic for a few minutes, and when it was determined that I wasn't injured at all, he released me. Charlie and I rode quietly in Jax's SUV back to Ty's house where we waited for hours until Luke finally showed up.

Alone.

They'd released Ty, and he left.

314

He just left.

And he hadn't come home.

I woke the next morning on the couch with Charlie still sleeping on the chair close to me and the sun shining through the front window. I jumped up and turned to face the kitchen where Luke and Jax stood, drinking coffee, and by the look on their faces, I didn't have to ask to know the answer to my question.

He never came home.

I grabbed my phone from the coffee table and made a call.

Chapter Forty-six

Tyler

"Thought I'd find you here."

I didn't look up. I knew that voice. He sat down beside me on the grass and leaned back against the headstone currently propping me up.

He gestured toward the bottle of whiskey in my hand. "Little cliché, don't you think?"

I snorted and lifted the bottle, not even feeling a little bad about the quarter of the bottle already swimming in my stomach. "I'm the picture of cliché, Jack."

"How do you figure?"

I huffed. "I'm a mess."

"Right this minute, I'd have to agree."

I dropped my head. When did this man's opinion of me become so fucking important? I ran my hand across my forehead and down over the stubble on my cheek. Thoughts of Grace running her hand over my cheek and smiling while curled up against my chest, bombarded my mind.

"You hurt my girl."

Another direct hit. I pulled my legs up and dropped my head even lower between my knees.

"I've stepped back. Watched you with her. I liked what I saw. Thought you were good for her. Thought you'd protect her with your own life. Never in a million years did I think you'd hurt her."

I took a deep breath and exhaled heavily before lifting my head. "I'm giving her up, Jack, so I'll never hurt her again."

He stretched his legs out in front of him and crossed his feet at the ankles. He folded his hands together and propped them on his stomach, looking up at the clear blue sky. I had no idea what time I'd actually arrived here, but it had been dark and now the sun was shining and warming my skin. I hadn't even realized I was cold.

Jack looked out into the distance and smiled. "You know when Gracie was small, she used to give her brothers shit all the time for getting into fights." He chuckled, probably unaware that just saying her name was causing me pain. Or maybe that was his intention. "She'd stand in the yard or kitchen, wherever the hell they were when she found out they'd fought, throw her little hands on her hips just like her mom, and glare at them. She hated fighting. She didn't understand it, and as much as her mom and I explained that sometimes that's how boys communicate, she would not accept it." He paused and sighed. "Until something awful happened."

"What happened?"

"Someone hurt her brother." He shook his head side to side. "In Gracie's world, her brothers were strong and fearless, no one ever hurt them, but he was hurt and hurt in a way no one could put a Band-Aid on and fix." He swallowed hard. "I came home from work one night and found her pacing in her room. She told me she wanted to hurt her, to physically hurt her, that she was so angry with her for hurting Ben."

"What did you say?" I asked, curiosity getting the better of me.

He lifted his shoulder before dropping it back down. "I reminded her she's a peaceful soul, that she wouldn't be able to live with the guilt she'd feel if she hurt someone else." He sighed heavily. "I'll never forget her words, Tyler, never forget the look on her face when she said she couldn't let it stand. She couldn't sit back and let someone she loved feel that much pain and just look the other way, that it wasn't right, that someone needed to defend him because she knew at the moment in his life, he couldn't defend himself." He looked over at me. "It's actually when she started talking about law school, wanting to defend people who weren't strong enough to do it themselves."

I laid the bottle on the ground beside me, the thought of one more shot making me sick. "Are you upset she didn't go to law school?"

He waved his hand in the air. "Nah. My Gracie was made to bring dreams to people, to share her love of, well, love."

"She does that," I admitted. "She makes you feel like no matter what you've done or who you are, you're still someone worth knowing."

"She's like her mom that way." He grinned. "I was a mess when I met Anna, but she looked past my shitty clothes and bad decisions and saw something in me that I was having a hard time seeing in myself. The day I met Anna, my entire life changed."

I was quiet for a moment as I thought about that. My life completely changed when I met Grace. Fuck, I hadn't even been drunk since I met her, until today, that was, and now look at me, sitting in a graveyard, leaning against my mom's stone, feeling sorry for myself. My mom would hate who I was at this very moment.

"She makes me want to talk." I looked up at the blue sky. "She makes it all seem so easy."

"That's her way."

"My mom was like that," I said quietly.

He lifted his hand and rested it on my shoulder, squeezing. "Tell me about her."

I smiled genuinely. "She was great. She was funny, but only with me and my dad; otherwise, she was shy. It was always just me and her. Dad was off playing ball and hanging with his buddies, but she was always there." I paused and let the grief settle in. "Until she wasn't."

"Your mom wouldn't want this for you, Ty." He gestured to the bottle by my leg. "She wouldn't want you to stop living because she did or because your dad did."

"I deserve this, Jack." I ripped my hand through my hair in frustration. "I scared her. You should've seen her face. She was afraid of me. Christ, all I wanted to do was protect her, but when he had his hands on her, I lost it, and I couldn't stop. It was the only time in my life I felt like I could've killed someone with my bare hands."

"You did stop."

I scoffed. "Jax stopped me by pulling me off him, and when I looked over at Grace, she looked terrified. I couldn't even look at her. I didn't want to see her disappointment, so I didn't look at her while they handcuffed me." I turned my body and faced him. "Why are you here, Jack? Why would you want someone capable of that anywhere near your daughter?"

He lifted his hand and laid it on my shoulder, his expression serious. "You protected her and helped save her life. That's what matters. I've known for a while now that you'd protect her, but you showed me last night that you'd lay down your life for her if you had to." He wrapped his hand around the back of my neck and pulled my head toward him. "There isn't a doubt in my mind that you're the man for Gracie, and I couldn't have picked a better one myself. You and I are a lot more alike than you realize because I would've choked the life out of that bastard if I'd beaten you there."

"She was afraid of me," I whispered, remembering the tears in her wide eyes.

He shook his head. "She wasn't afraid of you, Tyler. She was afraid for you, afraid for her brothers, and from what my boys tell me, probably in shock." His eyes met mine, his serious. "She called me this morning, crying, because you didn't come home and asked me if I had any ideas where you might be because she didn't want you to be alone. She needs you, Tyler. Right now, you're letting her down, and I can't let that stand, so you need to get your giant ass up and let me take you home to my daughter."

He squeezed my neck one last time and stood. "Goddamn, I'm getting too old to be sitting on the ground. Next time you need to talk, son, do me a favor and find a more comfortable spot."

"Son," I mumbled and stood.

His eyes softened. "Ty, this whole family has accepted you as one of our own; you, Seth, and Sophie. You've been so busy trying to show us who you aren't that you didn't realize all you needed to do was show us you love Gracie."

"I do love Grace," I admitted quietly.

"I wouldn't be here right now if I didn't believe that."

I bent down to pick up the whiskey bottle. Straightening, I stared at the gravestone for a moment and closed my eyes, exhaling loudly. "Love you, Mom."

Jack walked slowly beside me, his gait strong and steady, a description that fit the man perfectly. We got to his truck, and I climbed in, thankful there was room to put my seat back and stretch my legs a little in front of me.

We were on the road heading to my house when the courage struck, whether from the alcohol or our conversation, I wasn't sure, but I knew enough to just go with it. "I'd like to marry her."

He flicked on his turn signal. "You asking my permission?"

I cleared my throat. "Yes, sir."

He chuckled. "You really think right now is the best time to ask?"

I grinned out the side window. "Figure if you say yes at my worst, then you're bound to be okay with it."

"I figure you're right, Tyler," Jack agreed.

"Is that a yes?"

"A little while ago, Anna told me Gracie moved away to find herself. As far as I can tell, since she met you, she's done that. You keep my daughter smiling and coming to Sunday dinners, spending time with her family again, and you have my permission."

I smiled. "Deal."

Chapter Forty-seven

Grace

Pacing in front of the window overlooking the road, I kept glancing outside to see if they were pulling up. Dad had texted me over an hour ago that he found him and would bring him home, but they still hadn't arrived, and the longer it took, the longer I worried he didn't want to come back.

I just didn't understand why.

I jumped when I recognized my dad's truck coming up the road toward the house and moved to the front door. I yanked it open, never considering I should wait for him to come in. I needed to see him, needed to know he was all right. I knew he wasn't physically hurt, but last night, when he dropped his head and stared at the ground, something he hadn't done for a while now, I knew he was hurting in another way and for him, probably the worst way.

I stood on the big front porch and waited while he lifted himself out of Dad's truck and leaned back in to say something before he closed the door. Dad winked and smiled at me before he backed the truck out of the driveway, but his smile wasn't genuine.

I knew he was scared about what happened last night, I was too, but I had something more important to focus on just now.

Ty slowly made his way up the driveway, stopping at the bottom of the few steps leading onto the porch. He set down the bottle hanging from his hand on the top step and finally raised his eyes to mine.

I let out a sob I didn't know I'd been holding and jumped from the porch into his arms. I wrapped my body around his when his big arms enfolded me in a hug, and he buried his face in my neck.

"Are you okay?" I asked quietly.

He pulled back enough to see my face. "I'm sorry, Grace." I shook my head, but he continued. "I'm sorry I scared you last night, and I'm sorry I didn't come home and talk to you about it."

I put my hands on either side of his face. "You didn't scare me last night, Ty. I was scared, but not because of anything you did."

"I would've killed him," he admitted. "If your brother hadn't stopped me, I think I would've killed him."

I nodded, but I wanted to take some of the pain out of his eyes. "Well, in that case, I don't think we should ever go out without any of my brothers," I teased softly. "And I'll do everything in my power to discourage the stalkers." His lips twitched, and I continued, more seriously now. "Next time, just talk to me, Ty. Please."

"I will."

I gestured toward the door with my head. "Let's go take a shower. I still feel gross from last night."

"Why didn't you shower already?"

I grinned. "I was waiting for you."

He dropped his mouth to mine and kissed me, deepening it only enough to make me moan and wiggle closer before he pulled back. "Are the kids sleeping?"

"Yeah, they were up late with Natalie. She left a note that they would probably all sleep in."

He groaned. "I shouldn't have let you alone last night, Grace. I'll get better at this shit."

I slid down his body. "Come on, let's shower."

"Why aren't you making this harder on me, Grace? I deserve it. What I did was shitty, and you're just letting me off the hook."

I laid my hands on his chest. "I just figure you've probably beaten yourself up enough already." I put on my most serious expression. "Now, if you do it again…"

"Never," He promised.

We snuck in the house and tiptoed up the stairs to our bedroom, closing the door before we headed into the bathroom and closed that door. We undressed slowly, unable to stop touching each other, maybe as a reminder that we're both still alive. Ty leaned in and turned on the water, holding me close to him while the water heated. When the bathroom began to steam, we both stepped inside.

He grabbed the body wash and poured some into his hand, before running it along my arms and over my back. I stepped in close, molding my body to his and running my hand down over his hard chest and muscled abs until my fingers found his hard cock. He groaned long and loud when I wrapped my hand around him and squeezed gently.

I pushed up onto my toes and kissed along his jaw. "Shh, we don't want to wake anyone up."

He swallowed hard, running his soapy hands over my breasts and down until he could cup me. He slid his thick finger through my sensitive slit. I moaned softly, rubbing my hand slowly along his long, hard length, smiling to myself when he backed me up against the cold tiles of the shower wall. He dropped his head and ran his lips along my neck, sucking on the sensitive skin while he made his way to mine. Our lips crashed together, mouths opening without any teasing, fear of what we almost lost driving our hunger.

He broke the kiss and moved his head lower, running his tongue along my neck on his way to my breasts. I let out a long sigh when his lips wrapped around my nipple, and he sucked hard. I shoved my hand into his hair, my hand on his cock tightening and rubbing his length faster. He pulled back quickly, forcing me to drop my hand before he turned me to face the wall. His lips skimmed over my back and shoulders while his hands slid down my sides, moving across my hips to lay against my butt. He rolled his hands, massaging my butt, his thumbs fitting themselves just inside the crack to run down to my pussy. I moaned again, louder this time as his thumbs moved, arching my back, and pushing my butt out toward him.

He put his foot between mine and gently kicked the insides of my feet, forcing my legs apart. "Spread your legs, baby."

I did what he said and rested my forehead against the tiled wall, but all I felt were his hands on my waist. I lifted my head. "Ty?"

"Shh, Grace." He squeezed my butt again. "I'm enjoying the view."

I waited, the anticipation making this moment impossibly hotter, moaning when I felt him finally line up his cock and push slowly inside me. I dropped my head back down, forehead against the wall, and put my hands flat to the wall on either side. My body moved with each of his slow thrusts, his hands reaching around to grab my breasts and play with my nipples. I arched my back farther, heat building low in my stomach, but it wasn't enough. I was just about to drop my hand to find my clit, when he slid one of his hands down my body and his finger landed on my clit, rolling it slowly. I jerked and moaned loudly, but I still needed more, so I pushed my butt back, forcing him to speed up.

He dropped his one hand from my breast and grabbed my waist. "Faster, baby?"

"Please," I whispered.

My head dropped back when his thrusts became more powerful, more intense. I pushed my hips back, forcing him deeper.

"Fuck." He groaned, his thrusts increasing in speed, his finger rolling my clit harder and harder, until I was panting with need.

He pushed me flat against the wall, my cheek turned, lying across the tiles, and pushed his body in deeper, deeper than before, forcing me onto my tiptoes. That was all it took, and my orgasm crashed through me. White spots invaded my vision, but I still felt him pounding into me from behind until he pushed in one last time and roared my name into the side of my neck.

"Wow," I whispered after I caught my breath. I could feel his chuckle rumble across my back.

He slowly put me down, and we silently finished our shower, dressing together in his bedroom, a bedroom now free of kids. About a week ago, we realized they'd slept without waking up, and it just continued that way. It was good thing for all of us because it meant we were all in a place where we felt happy and safe.

I followed him downstairs, his hand holding mine tightly while we made our way to the kitchen. I started to make us coffee when I heard his voice. "I need to go put the horses out."

"Okay," I said softly, pulling one cup from the Keurig machine to replace it with another and added another pod.

"I think I'll wait for Seth."

I smiled and handed him his cup. "I think he'll like that."

We both startled when there was a soft knock on the door. I shrugged when he looked at me but followed him through the living room, stepping aside when he pulled it open. I wasn't exactly surprised when I saw a couple of my brothers on the porch. Ty waved them in and closed the door behind them.

I held up my mug. "Coffee?"

Jax shook his head. "Nah, I'm good."

Luke and Pike both shook their heads too before Luke spoke up. "Is now a good time to talk?"

Ty and I both nodded, and we all made our way to the kitchen. I sat beside Jax on the stools in front of the island while the other three men stood across from us.

I took a sip of my coffee. "Is there news on Logan?" My stomach dropped, remembering last night, but there hadn't been any updates when I told Jax and Luke to leave earlier, and I needed to know.

"He's going to be fine. It was a clean shot through the shoulder. They bandaged him up, and the last I heard, he's waiting for his discharge papers." I breathed a sigh of relief.

"Was anyone else hurt?" Ty asked quietly.

"Couple of people were grazed by stray bullets, but nothing requiring much medical care and a few with deep cuts from the glass that shattered and flew. They all received stitches and were sent home." Luke said, relief clear in his expression.

"Do you know anything about this fucker?" Ty asked anger still clear in his voice.

"That's why we're here." Luke said and crossed his arms over his chest. "His name is Sam Owens. He's twenty years old and just moved here two years ago to live with his brother after he was released from juvie."

"Juvie?" I asked. "You mean like a juvenile detention home?"

"Exactly," Luke confirmed. "He's spent years in and out of them, but always found trouble and landed himself in one again. Once he aged out at eighteen, he had nowhere to go."

"Who's his brother?" Ty asked.

Pike rubbed his hand along the back of his neck and sighed. "Dylan, one of my security guys."

"Oh, that's right. He said Dylan's name," I remembered.

Pike narrowed his eyes. "What did he say?"

"Not a lot, but he said we needed to leave while Dylan was handling things at the door."

"Sounds right," Pike concurred. "Apparently, Dylan offered for his brother to move here, found him a job, and was trying to give him a fresh start, hoping he'd keep himself out of trouble. And it worked for a little while until he saw you, Grace."

"Where did he see me?" I asked.

"He works in maintenance at your apartment building." Luke dropped his hands and put them on his hips. "That's how he was able to get into your apartment. He had the code for the alarm, given to him by the landlord who needed him to do the repairs he was obviously getting too old to do himself. He also went in during the day while you were working and dug around on your computer."

"How did he know your password?" Ty asked, but then exhaled in frustration. "Is it your birthday?"

"Yeah," I admitted solemnly.

Luke nodded. "He would've had your birthdate from the landlord's files. That's how he found out about your books, but he never bought them. He just read parts on your computer. He also had keys for the mailboxes, which is how you got the letters with no postage or return address."

I knew my jaw was hanging open in disbelief, but I couldn't believe he'd done all that, and then a shiver ran through me at the thought of him in my place, going through my things while I wasn't there.

"He was smart enough to stop following you after we all started nosing around and instead followed Charlie knowing where she went, you usually went."

"That's how he knew where to find me," I surmised. "How do you know all this?"

"He told me." Luke ran his hand around the back of his neck. "He was pretty proud of himself too, bragging about how he knew to cover his tracks and how he fooled all of us. He admitted to using a fake ID to get into the club in the city after he followed you when you got into the Uber. Apparently, you and Charlie are creatures of habit and go out every week on either Friday or Saturday. He'd wait for you to leave those nights and follow you."

"How did I not notice that?" I remembered all those lectures from my brothers to be vigilant and always check my surroundings, but I guess I wasn't as observant as I thought. "Now what?"

"He's in jail. He confessed, but he'll still have a trial or maybe arrange a plea bargain. Either way, he's not getting out anytime soon."

I breathed a sigh of relief until Ty spoke. "And when he does?"

"We'll take care of it then, but he won't make a move without me being notified. I've already made that clear." Luke's voice dropped. "You don't fuck with a cop or a cop's family. The boys will protect her."

Ty faced Pike. "What about Dylan?"

Pike took a deep breath and exhaled slowly. "I'm keeping Dylan on." Ty opened his mouth to speak, but Pike held up his hand. "Let me finish before you chew me out." Ty nodded, and Pike went on. "Sam said that Dylan didn't know what he was up to. He actually bragged that he'd fooled him too, laughed while he explained how Dylan got him a job and left him in the bar the nights he covered the door even though he was underage because he felt sorry for him. If I hadn't heard that or seen Dylan's face after the shooting, I probably wouldn't have given him a second chance, but I think he was taken advantage of and never saw it because it was coming from his own brother." Pike put his hands on his hips. "He's on probation with the company and won't be on the door for a while, but I'm trusting my instincts, and my instincts are telling me Dylan deserves this chance."

"I agree," I said, not surprised when Ty's head popped up and he glared at me.

"He wouldn't have been in that fucking place if his brother hadn't helped him," Ty said, angrily. "And all the shit at the door was the reason the guy was able to get his hands on you without anyone really noticing."

"What was going on at the door?" I asked.

"Sam told Dylan he saw two guys doing lines of coke in the men's room, and he pointed them out. Dylan stopped them before they could leave. They were belligerent because they were drunk, and it led to them making a scene. I don't think Sam knew the guys, but he just got lucky they were assholes and detained security at the door for a while."

"Were they doing drugs?" I asked.

Luke shook his head. "No."

"Dylan feels like shit, wants to talk to you, but that's up to you, Grace," Pike said cautiously.

"No." Ty exhaled loudly. "Absolutely not, Grace."

"Ty," I said softly. "Everyone deserves the benefit of the doubt. You know that better than anyone." I reached over and grabbed his hand in my own. "Come with me to see him and judge for yourself after we talk to him. I'll make sure Pike and Luke are there too."

"Grace." He ran his hand along the side of his cheek where his beard was starting to grow in heavier. I'd have to let him know I liked it, especially after this morning in the shower.

"I'm not letting him pay for the crimes of another person. I just can't do that. I couldn't live with myself." I said honestly.

"I know." He sighed and looked at Pike. "Set it up."

I squeezed his hand and looked at Jax. He hadn't said a word since we sat down. "Do you have information too?"

He shook his head. "Nah. I just didn't want to feel left out."

I laughed, only stopping when he spoke again. "Just needed to make sure everything worked out for you the way it should."

I leaned my head against his shoulder and felt him kiss the top of my head.

"We're gonna get going." Pike said. "I'll call you with a time to meet at Hanks after everything's been cleaned up." I nodded and thanked him.

We followed them to the door, and I agreed to call Luke and Jax when their kids were awake and ready to go home. We had only just said our good-byes and closed the door when I heard movement upstairs. "Sounds like they're getting up."

"I'm glad they weren't up when everything was happening this morning," he admitted.

"Me too." I frowned and faced the door when the doorbell rang.

"Who the fuck is here now?"

"Umm." I hesitated, but only for a moment. "My family might be over a lot today."

The tension in his face eased, and he kissed my forehead before backing away toward the door. "Why don't you just invite them here? We'll get it over with all at once."

"You sure?" I asked.

"Yeah, baby, I'm sure."

I grabbed my phone off the table and turned to see he'd let Brody in. I dropped my phone to my side when Brody came straight to me and wrapped his arms around me tightly. He held on for a long minute, speaking no words, but he didn't need to. He, very much like Tyler, was a man of few words, but his actions spoke for him.

He pulled back, slung his arm around my shoulders, and faced Tyler. They stared at one another for a moment until Brody held out his hand to shake, which Tyler accepted. "I heard what you did last night for Grace, for my brothers. I'd have done the same thing if I'd been there, except I would've probably killed the fucker. I admire your restraint."

"I would've killed him, but your brothers pulled me off," he admitted.

"They weren't moving you if you weren't willing to be moved," Brody pointed out, and I rolled my lips together to hide my smile. "I played ball with you, man. You're a tank."

Ty grinned, but I knew Brody's words meant a lot. I smiled up at Brody. "We're having a little get-together this afternoon, can you guys come?"

He looked down at me, his expression more relaxed than I'd seen it in weeks. "We'll be here. Just let us know what time."

"Apparently, any-fucking-time," Ty said sarcastically, but a smile still played around his lips.

Brody chuckled and moved away from me, punching Ty in the shoulder on his way to the door. "Get used to it, brother, you're a part of the family now. You get one, you get us all," he called out over his shoulder right before he closed the door behind him.

Ty stared at the closed door. "He might be my favorite of your brothers."

I giggled beside him. "Why, because he's the most like you?"

"Maybe." He grinned at me. "He called me brother. What does that mean?"

I faced him and looped my arms around his neck. "That means you've won them over."

"Hmm." He said like he was considering something. "And all it took was me kicking someone's ass."

"I think you won them over when you carried me into the end zone so I could get my first touchdown." I put my hands on the sides of his neck when his grin grew and waited for him to drop his head, which he did almost immediately. He rubbed his lips against mine, kissing me slowly, like we had all the time in the world, and I knew nothing could ruin such a perfect moment.

"Eww, gross. Not again."

Ty pulled away and dropped his forehead to mine, his body shaking with laughter.

Nothing could ruin the moment, but that definitely made it one we would never forget.

Epilogue

Grace

"It's the perfect day."

"It really is," Mom agreed.

"I mean, blue skies and beautiful temperatures, especially for April. Everything is so perfect as if it was planned specifically for them."

"They deserve this," Mom said wistfully. "They've been through a lot."

I reached over and squeezed her hand before putting my hands back in my lap. Luke being shot had scared her, scared all of us, but I don't think any of us, not even Mom, had considered life without him until that day when we were forced to. It changed us individually and as a family, but it also strengthened us.

I leaned my shoulder against Tyler's and grabbed his hand. He smiled and sat back, stretching his long legs out in front of him. Seth sat beside him, his legs swinging, looking bored, but his best friend hadn't been able to sit with him today, and I'd bet that was causing a little anxiety for him. He'd been better but would always be a little shy and reserved just like his big brother and that was okay. It's who they are and to me, there couldn't be a better version of either of them. I peeked across the aisle and saw Sophie tucked in tight between Mia and Lexi, talking up a storm, and I wondered what three little girls could possibly have to talk about, but with Sophie, you never could guess.

I smiled at Dex and Charlie who sat on the other side of Seth when I noticed their attention on me. Dex moved in at the beginning of February, and to say it's been interesting living with Dex and Ty would be an understatement. They've been anything but boring when together and keep me, Natalie, and the kids laughing all the time. Dex and Charlie had unofficially been seeing each other, unofficially because neither of them would admit they were dating. I could hear Ben talking to Natalie in hushed tones in the row of seats behind me and felt a sadness for my brother. Over the past few months, I'd tried several times to bring up Charlie, but each time, he changed the subject, making it all too clear that he had no plans to talk about her. Definitely not with me, but I was guessing not with anyone.

I jolted when the music started to play and quickly turned, not wanting to miss a moment of this. I watched Lanie walk down the aisle first, not at all surprised Kate had picked her as her maid of honor. They'd become close living next door to each other, but they also just hit it off. I often wondered if it was because they both had some difficulties in their past, but whatever the reason, I was happy they had each other. Just like Jax's wedding and Brody's, Luke and Kate decided to only have one person stand up for them. The wedding would be ridiculous if we all were up there, and besides, we all know what we mean to each other. We didn't have to stand in front to show it.

Lanie was down the aisle and moving up to stand by the priest when I smiled at Luke standing proudly beside his best man, who was Andy. He couldn't have chosen a better best man, and my brothers all agreed. Andy was the obvious choice, and from the look on his face, he was taking his position very seriously. Besides,

I knew Luke and he could've never chosen between our brothers; they all meant too much to him and all for different reasons.

"Mom!" Braydon waved at Lanie, and her head jerked back before she just stared at him. I heard my mom sigh and then sniffle beside me, but I think I was in shock, maybe we all were. Bray has called her Wanie since she came into Jake and his lives, and we all assumed one day, when he could say the "L" sound, he would call her Lanie, but it looked like Bray had other plans.

He stood on Jake's legs, like maybe she hadn't seen him or heard him and yelled again. "Hi, Mom!"

She lifted her hand, waving back at him, and I watched her try to hold herself together, but she couldn't. She had big tears running down her cheeks, her face alight with happiness. I heard Jake whisper, "Baby" behind us and closed my eyes at the tenderness in his voice.

"Why is Mom cwying?" Bray asked loudly.

"She's happy," Jake said simply.

"Oh," Bray said, and I reached back my hand, smiling when I felt Jake grab mine with his own and squeeze tightly before dropping it.

"Why are gwirls weird?" he asked, causing a lot of low chuckles to pass through the rows of chairs.

"That's a conversation for another day, buddy," Jake answered.

I heard a small slap and then, "Ouch. Dammit Lucy, that hurt."

"The correct answer is they're not," Lucy whispered.

I giggled and felt Ty squeeze my hand, his body shaking with silent laughter. When the music changed, we all immediately stood and turned, waiting to see Kate. She appeared, my dad proudly at her side and started down the aisle dressed in an all lace wedding gown. She didn't have a veil, but she didn't need one, the dress was fitted perfectly to her and yards of lace trailed behind her when she passed us. I wiped a tear from my eye and settled back in my seat, listening to my brother recite the most beautiful vows I'd ever heard to his soul mate.

Andy did his job well and walked Lanie down the aisle, just as he'd practiced, after the priest pronounced Luke and Kate husband and wife. According to Mom, he'd been practicing every day for a week, even going to Lanie's and making her practice with him. She did and she did it patiently because that was Lanie, always sweet, always patient, and always forgiving. She and Jake are engaged, as are Lucy and Chris who'd announced their engagement on Christmas Day. It wasn't a big surprise. We all knew it was coming, but we just didn't know when.

Sydney and Cam were married on New Year's Eve. The church was still decorated for Christmas and with all the lights and violins playing, it seemed like a fairy tale. They'd told us on that Friday after Thanksgiving that they were getting married, and when they gave the date, I heard my mom sigh. She'd been planning weddings for two years on the fly and it seemed like this one wouldn't be any different. But no matter how little time they had to plan, it was perfect, and Sydney looked like a princess. She wore a beautiful ballgown decorated in tulle and rhinestones, and walked to her prince dressed in a tuxedo. It was, by far, the fanciest wedding anyone in my family had, but it was also small and intimate. They filled the church with everyone they loved and had their first dance together under the stars while we watched.

I stood and watched Luke and Kate, arms around each other, walk down the aisle next, their heads close together, their faces lit by their smiles. I turned to face Mom when I heard a baby and wondered how she was suddenly holding Jax and Kasey's newest addition. Ronan was born early, having decided he was coming into the world almost six weeks before he was due, but he was strong and healthy. Currently three months old, he was right on target for where he should be. I bent over and kissed his chubby cheek, smiling down at him when he reached his arm up for me.

Ty's hand wrapped around mine, and I turned, following him onto the patio where everyone was congregating. This was my parents' third backyard wedding, and they'd definitely become pros at having it all set up. I listened to the toast given by Brody and then Jax who'd grown up closest to Luke and had some funny stories to share, stories I wasn't sure my parents knew until that very moment. It seemed Luke wasn't always quite as innocent as he appeared, and it brought a lot of laughter to an already incredible day.

The mood of the party continued while I chatted with people I hadn't seen in a while and introduced them to Tyler, Sophie, and Seth. A lot of my family had met them at Christmas or at Cam's wedding, but many from out of town hadn't. After a little while, I wandered over to grab a glass of wine, leaving Tyler and Dex talking to Chase and Kyle. I wasn't surprised Dex and Kyle had hit it off after Ty told me how much Dex loved messing with technology and gaming. It seemed they had a lot in common, and the last I heard, they were working on developing a game of some kind.

I leaned back on the bar and smiled at Bear when he came over and ordered a beer from the bartender. Bear was a friend of Pike's originally, but after he helped Luke through the ordeal with Maggie, they became close. It was odd for a cop to be friends with the president of a motorcycle club, but my family never seemed to do things like everyone else, so it was fitting.

He moved to stand beside me after he had a beer in his hand and lifted his chin in my direction. "Grace."

"Hey, Bear." I looked around before letting my eyes find his again. "No date tonight?"

He snickered. "I don't date, sweetheart. You know that." He leaned in close and whispered, "Unless you're offering."

I took a sip of wine with a smile still on my lips. "I'm not sure Ty's all that good at sharing."

He snorted out a laugh. "I don't even have to know Ty well to know he's not good at sharing." He tapped his bottle against the side of my glass. "Happy for you." My gaze dropped, the smile lingering when he continued. "I know your brothers are too."

"Thanks, Bear," I answered sweetly. "I don't know why people are so scared of you. You're just a big teddy bear."

His shoulders shook with his laughter. "Never been called that before."

I was just about to tease him a little more because talking to Bear was fun when a woman came up to him, her eyes wide. He glanced her way and then back at me. "Grace, this is my sister Becs."

"Hi, Becs." I said, but noticed she looked pale and nervous.

He pushed off the bar where he'd been leaning, his eyes narrowing. "What's wrong?"

"It's Maggie," she said, her voice trembling.

He set his beer on the bar. "What about Maggie?"

"I know you're going to be mad, but I brought her." His eyes flared with anger. "I know it was stupid, but she begged me, and I felt so bad for her. She's always stuck inside, and I think…" She hesitated. "Well, I just think she needed to see Luke get married."

"Where is she?" he asked, his voice dark.

"That's just it." She shook her head. "I don't know. She had me drop her about a mile from here and said she was going to walk and watch from the side of the house because she didn't want anyone to see her."

I felt Ty come up to stand beside me then and wrap his arm around my waist. I looked up and met his worried eyes. It was obvious he'd heard most of what Becs was saying, and he knew the story of Maggie, knew they were hiding her to keep her safe, and he knew, just like I did, that she should never have been out today.

"Fuck." Bear swore. "Becs, you know how dangerous it is to have her out in plain sight. Jesus, no one has heard from Snake. He's gone quiet, but he's not going to stop looking for her."

His head popped up, and I saw him signal Pike over, who happened to be talking to Cam. They moved quickly across the lawn to stand with us. Bear exhaled loudly before repeating what Becs had just told us.

"Shit." Cam looked around the yard before his eyes landed on Becs. "We don't want to overreact. Where were you supposed to meet and when?"

"The same place as I dropped her, and she was going to leave as soon as the ceremony ended. I left right after, but I waited there for a long time, and she didn't show."

Cam pulled his phone from his pocket. "I'm going to have the area searched."

Bear jerked up his chin. "Good. I'll send my boys to scope out their clubhouse and see if there's any activity."

"We telling Luke?" Pike voiced the question on everyone's mind.

Cam took a deep breath and exhaled, glancing over at Luke who had his arm around Kate and was talking to Brody, whose hand was resting on Gia's pregnant belly. "I think we're gonna have to."

When he caught Brody's eye, and his head turned our way, Luke's followed. His back snapped straight, I could only assume because of the look on our faces, and he leaned down, whispering something in Kate's ear before he fell into step beside Brody and headed our way.

I listened, wrapped up in Ty while they repeated the story, and Luke's expression darkened with each word. I watched while men from all different aspects of life pulled together and arranged the search for this one woman, a woman who had put her life in danger, not only to save Luke, but to stop a club full of men who were selling women and drugs for profit.

In my mind, she was a one-woman crusader, a champion for women everywhere, a reminder that, strong or weak, we still held an enormous amount of power in our knowledge alone.

All she had to contribute was information, and she saved more people than she probably realized.

But she was missing.

And from the look on these men's faces, they would stop at nothing to find her.

Enjoy a peek into Maggie's story, the first in a new series!

OUT OF TIME
THE SINNERS MC, BOOK 1

JENNIFER HANKS

Chapter One

Maggie

The shrill sound of sirens screamed through the night air, waking me from what could have only been a black out. I lifted my head before immediately letting it drop back to the cold floor below me, the pain searing through my head and neck was overwhelming. My eyes wouldn't open, I knew that without trying. I'd actually felt them swelling shut with each blow.

Pounding on the door not far from where I lay caused panic to move through me. I tried to move my body back, forcing myself into a small ball, wanting to hide, hoping he wouldn't see me if he'd come back and was the one pounding on the door. The pounding became louder, but I didn't call out, needing for my own peace of mind to stay silent, to protect myself with my silence. Car doors slammed and my body twitched with each new noise, bracing for what may be coming, hoping to black out if he was back, to avoid any more pain.

"Maggie!"

My name was yelled through the closed door and I vaguely recognized the voice, relieved when it didn't send a chill down my spine.

Like when he would scream it.

"Maggie, honey, if you're near the door, move back!"

I had no idea if I was near the door, I couldn't remember where we were when I took the last blow, before I felt the darkness overtake me.

My body reacted to a loud crashing and I winced from the pain, but I didn't move, I couldn't have if I'd tried.

"Check the bedrooms!"

I heard shouted, but it was only a moment more until I heard his voice and it was much closer. "I found her."

A hand touched my face. "Maggie, honey, it's me Luke. You're safe now. The ambulance is only a minute out."

I winced again when he pushed my hair out of my eyes, even though I could tell he did it gently. "Can you talk to me?"

I swallowed hard, but opened my mouth to acknowledge him even though I felt the darkness starting to pull me under again. "Luke." I whispered.

He gently pulled my hand into his. "Yeah sweetheart, it's me. Do you know where Snake is?"

Luke's voice sounded distant and I welcomed the darkness clouding my mind until he called my name. "Maggie, stay with me."

But I didn't want to, I wanted the darkness, I wanted the peace it would bring me. My last thought before succumbing to the comforting silence, was maybe he finally did it.

Maybe he finally killed me.

Chapter Two

Maggie

'Never trust them, baby, never trust anyone.'

I listened to the sound of machines beeping every few seconds, recognizing I was in the hospital and somehow still alive, but lost in my memories while my mom's words circled my mind with the last vision of her I still had. It brought me peace, but then again, she'd always had a way about her. She was calm and simple in a world filled with violence and anger. At least that was the world I'd grown up in. But as bad as it was, I had my mom and I loved her more than anything. I would've walked through fire to be with my mom, would've moved anywhere she wanted to go and I did, until I couldn't anymore.

Until the day I had to call an ambulance. The day I had to hold her hand during what felt like the longest trip we'd ever taken. The day I had to kiss her good-bye when the cancer eating away at her finally took her life.

And in less than a week after I'd lost her, I'd run away.

I was fifteen.

I was homeless. I was hungry to the point of pain. I had no

prospects, no idea how to survive alone, but it was still better than staying with my mom's brother who was the only family I had left. Or the only family I knew about. He said he'd take me in, but I knew by the way he looked at me, that I'd have to pay for my place in his home and not in a way I would ever pay voluntarily.

I spent two years begging for money and food, moving from shelters to squatting in abandoned homes, and stealing. I kept my head down so my age wouldn't be discovered and I made sure I was never in a position to be picked up by the police for fear they'd move me to a boarding home or worse, back to my uncle's.

I thought fate was finally shining down on me when I met Snake. He found me, hiding behind a dumpster in the alley behind a popular restaurant, waiting in the black of night for the trash to be thrown out. I was mesmerized by him. He was big and strong, but sweet to me. He offered me food and shelter and I was so damn tired. Tired of running, tired of hiding, tired of being alone.

Always alone. I couldn't even remember the last conversation I'd had with a person.

He found me eighteen days before my eighteenth birthday and I considered that a sign, so I followed him back to what he called a clubhouse and I never left.

He never let me.

He said over and over again that he'd never let me go and what once felt like my only chance at freedom quickly became my prison. I still thought it was better than the alternative. By age eighteen, I wouldn't have to go back to my uncle, but I had no job, I hadn't even graduated high school. And he kept me locked away in that damn clubhouse or in our shitty apartment, like I was a dirty secret or worse, his property. He owned me and he knew it.

I had no-where else to go.

The beatings started shortly after I moved in with Snake. A slap in the face, a punch to the ribs became a weekly occurrence if he was drinking or upset about something. I came to learn the sounds he would make if he was agitated late at night when he was coming home and I'd try to hide, feign sleep, whatever I could to become inconspicuous, or hopefully invisible to him. It never worked. I would take a beating, usually accompanied with sex if he was drunk and then he'd collapse beside me, while I would lay awake and know in my soul that if my mom could see me, she'd be disappointed.

She taught me to be resilient in an unforgiving world, but she didn't live long enough to teach me to be strong enough to break free from my own prison.

I'd often heard growing up, that people, mainly women, would find themselves trapped in situations, under the control of another, but I never believed they couldn't find a way out if they were strong enough, if they tried hard enough, until I was living in the same situation. Over the years with Snake, he slowly tore down the little bit of confidence I had until I believed I was nothing with or without him. He told me repeatedly no one would want me, that I was trash he found amongst the trash and I would always be trash. I believed him. After all, he was the only person I ever talked to.

Until I met Luke Dimarco.

The first time Snake beat me badly enough that I had to go to the hospital to have my broken wrist set, was also the first time I met a man with kind eyes. He held my hand and offered me escape from the prison I was living in, but I'd been afraid. The world was too big, too scary to me now. I was alone and as bad as Snake was, he was also all I had in this world.

So, I stayed.

I stayed and endured more beatings than I ever imagined my body could handle. He stripped me of any beauty I ever thought I had, stripped me of any confidence I may have possessed at one time and sadly he took away my belief in resilience.

He taught me I was worthless.

And he taught me well.

I denied Luke every time he'd come to see me in the hospital over the years, but truth be told, I came to anticipate his visits, to hear his voice, talk to someone who was listening. I told him about Snake, about the club, the little that I knew and he tried, he really did, but I declined his offer of help every time. Sadly, the beatings became more tolerable because I knew, in that hospital, I would talk to someone who actually gave a damn if I lived or died.

I'd come to accept this was my life, Snake was my world, and the only world I had would eventually end my life. Snake would kill me, I knew that without a doubt, his hate for me was intense, I just never understood why.

Then one day, on a rare occurrence when I left our apartment to go to the store, I saw Luke and a beautiful woman holding the hand of a little boy. I watched them, without them knowing, enthralled by their small family, the love so obvious between all of them. It was odd seeing Luke outside of the hospital and a large part of me was sad that I couldn't walk up to him and talk, but I knew I wouldn't be welcome. I also knew, for me, it would be torture. I'd developed a crush on him over the last few years and always thought of him as mine, at least for small chunks of time. It was what pushed me through, but seeing him, so happy with her, I realized I was exactly what Snake said.

Trash.

And I always would be.

I'd snuck out that day, thankful Luke had never seen me and squashed any little girl dreams I'd had about Luke Dimarco. It wasn't long after that day on a night when Snake thought I was sleeping that I heard him talking with some other members of the club and laughing about a fire they'd set at Luke's girlfriends house. I lay there that night, listening to him, knowing my school girl dreams of Luke or someone like him rescuing me from my prison were just that, school girl dreams. I made a decision, as I lay there, a decision that would change my life.

And that of everyone around me.

The very next day, I went out while Snake was at the clubhouse for a meeting, or 'church' as they call it in the motorcycle club. I'd asked for permission to go to the store, not surprised he was in a good mood when he woke because he'd caused sadness to the man he'd come to hate. Luke had arrested Snake often over the years for assault, always trying to convince me to press charges, but I never did, I never would and Snake knew that, but it didn't squash his hate for the man he felt was trying to tell him what he could and couldn't do with his property. Snake was untouchable, at least that's what he thought, and every time I didn't press charges, I proved him right. Fear is a strong emotion and being alone and afraid can drive us to do things, accept things that we wouldn't normally. Accept things we would never want for anyone else.

I couldn't drive, I'd never been taught, so over the years when I was allowed to leave, I would walk, but I knew that day I couldn't walk as far as I needed to go and be back in the time Snake expected. I had money stashed in a bag of flour in the cabinet, money that Luke had given me every time he'd seen me in the hospital, money he assumed I used to get a cab home since Snake would never come to see me or pick me up. No matter how long I was there. But I didn't use it for that. I saved it, knowing one day I would need it, I just never knew what I thought I'd need it for.

That day, I rode the bus to the edge of town, walked the last mile to the clubhouse I only knew about because I'd heard its name and location thousands of times over the years when no one knew I was around. Those were the times in my life I was happy to be shy and quiet. I was unnoticeable.

I'd walked straight up to the doors of that clubhouse, knowing there was a chance it would be empty because of the time of day, but also knowing I wouldn't have many other opportunities to do what I needed to do. I'd also realized if the men of that club wanted to, they could call Snake to come get me and that day would most likely be the last day of my life.

I'd been willing to take that chance.

About the Author

Jennifer Hanks is the author of The Dimarco Series as well as The Elite Securities Series. Her stories are contemporary romance and romantic suspense, all with the underlying message of the power and strength in love. She's also a sucker for a Happily-Ever-After. Her love of reading and books in general started at a very young age and has steadily grown into a love of writing as well. She admits to being addicted to all things romance and has no plans of quitting her habit. Jennifer lives in Pennsylvania with her two children. When she's not reading or writing, she can be found with her kids at their various activities. Her house is frequently filled with any combination of her children's friends, nieces, nephews and a variety of pets.

JENNIFER CAN BE FOUND ONLINE AT:

http://jenniferhanks.com
authorjenniferhanks@gmail.com
www.goodreads.com/author/show/15089051.Jennifer_Hanks
www.instagram.com/authorjenniferhanks/
www.facebook.com/Jennifer-Hanks-947981351951214
www.twitter.com/authorjhanks

Made in the USA
Middletown, DE
26 June 2019